Aston Cokain

The Dramatic Works of Sir Aston Cokain

With Prefatory Memoir, Introductions, and Notes

Aston Cokain

The Dramatic Works of Sir Aston Cokain
With Prefatory Memoir, Introductions, and Notes

ISBN/EAN: 9783744711838

Printed in Europe, USA, Canada, Australia, Japan

Cover: Foto ©Andreas Hilbeck / pixelio.de

More available books at **www.hansebooks.com**

THE DRAMATIC

WORKS OF SIR ASTON COKAIN.

WITH PREFATORY MEMOIR, INTRODUCTIONS, AND NOTES.

MDCCCLXXIV.

EDINBURGH: WILLIAM PATERSON.
LONDON: H. SOTHERAN & CO.

TO

JAMES O. HALLIWELL PHILLIPPS, Esq.,

F.A.S., F.R.S.,

TO WHOM THE LOVERS OF

ANCIENT DRAMATIC AND POETIC LITERATURE

ARE SO DEEPLY INDEBTED,

THIS VOLUME

IS GRATEFULLY INSCRIBED BY

THE EDITORS.

CONTENTS.

PREFATORY MEMOIR.

LANGBAINE, in giving an account of Sir Aston Cokain, says that he was "a gentleman who, in the reign of King Charles the Second, lived at his seat at Ashbourne, a market-town in Derbyshire, situate between the river Dove and Compton. He was of an ancient family, as Mr. Cambden observes in the entrance of his description of Derbyshire; nay, further, Sir John Cokain of Rushton, our author's kinsman, and cousin-german to the Lord O'Brien Cokain, Viscount Cullen, in Ireland, had an ancient evidence to prove that Sir —— Cokain, their predecessor, was anciently allied to King William the Conqueror, and in those days lived at Hemmingham Castle, in Essex.* But whether our author fetcht his pedigree from so ancient a stock or no, certain it is that he was well descended, and had a liberal education bestowed on him, being in his youth bred in Trinity College, Cambridge, and when he was about four-and-twenty years of age he was sent to make a journey through France and Italy, which he completed in a twelve-month's space, anno 1632, an account of which he has writ to his son.† He was very much addicted to books and the study of poetry, spending much of his time in the Muses' company. Amongst his other poetical productions he has written three plays and a masque, which are in print."

Whether the family of Cokain, as Sir Aston seems to have believed, was directly descended from William the Conqueror, may be a matter of doubt, but in *Lodge's Peerage*, by Archdall,—Lond. 1789, 8vo,

---

* *See* Cokain's Epigrams, l. 2, Ep. vii.
† *See* his Poems, p. 93.

voL iv., *Art.* "Cockaine, Viscount Cullen,"—it is stated that "the family of Cokyn, Cokeyn, Cockaine, for many ages was seated at Ashbourne, in the county of Derby; whereof was John Cockeyn, the father of Andreas, whose son William, by Sarah, his wife, had a son of his own name, who, taking to wife Alice, daughter of Hugh de Dalbury, left two sons,—Roger, living in 1284, and John, living in 1276, who married Matildis (Maud), daughter of Robert Olderney, and had a son Andrew, who died without issue in 1284 (12 Edward I.), and a daughter Margery."

More than one of the Cokains received the honour of knighthood from those Kings under whose banners they served, but it is doubted whether there was ever a baronet in their family. The claim of our poet to his title has therefore been disputed.

The great-grandfather of Sir Aston Cokain was Sir Thomas, who succeeded in 1544, and accompanied Edward, Earl of Hertford, in his expedition to Scotland by sea, with a large fleet and well provided army, and was knighted by the Earl at the taking of Leith and Edinburgh. After the plundering and burning of these places, he attended him by land into England. He was the author of a treatise, printed in 4to, and embellished with woodcuts (pp. 32), now of extreme rarity. It is titled :—

"A Short Treatise of Hunting : Compyled for the delight of noblemen and gentlemen, by Sir Thomas Cockaine, Knight. Imprinted at London by Thomas Orwin, for Thomas Woodcocke, dwelling in Paule's Churchyard, at the signe of the Black Beare. 1591." 4to.

The dedication is thus addressed :

"To the Right Honourable and my singular good lord the Earle of Shrewsburie, Sir Thomas Cockaine, knight, wisheth increase of all honourable vertues.

"Having (Right Honourable), at the instance of divers my especiall good friends, penned this short pamphlet of my owne experience in hunting, and entring into consideration how greatly I am bounden to the nobilitie of this land, reason challenged a speciall affection in me to preferre the patronage thereof to your honorable lordship before any other, as well in respect I had the original of my said experience under your most noble grandfather (whose servant I was in my younger years, and brought up in his house); as also in regard that I have received many extraordinary favors, both from your said most noble grandfather, from my honourable good lord your father, and lastly and most especially from yourself (my good lord), who, knowing me a professed hunter, and not a scholler, I make no doubt but your lordshippe wil affoord my plainnes herein your favourable liking. And so (my good lord) wishing you as honorable successe in all your vertuous actions as your lordshippe can desire or imagine, I humblie take my leave of your good lordship.

"From my house neere Ashbourne, this last of December 1590.

"Your honourable lordship's many waies so bounden,

"THOMAS COCKAIN."

In his address "to the gentlemen readers," Sir Thomas incidentally mentions "my owne long experience in hunting for these fiftie-two yeares now last past."

Edward Cokain, born in 1554, was sheriff of the county of Derby, 42 Elizabeth; married Jane, daughter of Nicholas Ashby, Esq.; died in 1606, and left Thomas his heir; who, by Anne, daughter of Sir John Stanhope of Elvaston (ancestor to Charles, Earl of Harrington) was father of Sir Aston Cokain, born 28th December 1608.

Sir Aston married Anne, daughter of Sir Gilbert Kniveton of Mircaston, in Derbyshire, Baronet, and, as Lodge goes on to say, "being a Romanist, suffered much for his religion and the king's cause in the civil wars, and then pretended to be a baronet, created after the king had by violence been compelled to leave the Parliament, about 10th January 1641; yet not so deemed by the officers of arms, because no patent was either enrolled or mentioned in the docquet books belonging to the clerk of the Crown in Chancery to justify it. He was esteemed by many an ingenious gentleman, a good poet, and a great lover of learning; yet by others a perfect boon fellow, by which means he wasted all his estate, having sold his lordship of Pooley to Humfrey Jennings, Esq., reserving an

annuity for life, several years before his death, which
happened at Derby in February 1683, and the 13th of
that month he was buried in the chancel of Polesworth
church."

Sir Aston has evidently been anxious to show how
extensively he was connected with the nobility and
gentry of his time, for in the collected edition of his
poetical works, titled "A chain of golden poems,
embellished with wit, mirth, and eloquence," appear
verses addressed to the following :—

"To the Right Honourable Philip, Earl of Chesterfield, Baron
of Shelford, etc., my uncle."   Two epigrams.

Of six "Funeral Elegies," the second, fourth, and fifth
are in honour of deceased female relatives, thus :—

"On my dear sister, Mrs. Isabella Cokaine, who died at Ashbourne about the 18th year of her age, and lyes there buried.

"On the death of my dear cousin-germane, Mrs. Olive
Cotton, who deceased at Berisford the 38th year of her age,
and lyes buried at Bently, by Ashbourne, etc.

"A funeral elegie on my dear cousin, Mistress Elizabeth
Reppington, who deceased at Ammington about the 18th year
of her age, and lyes buried at Tamworth."

Next come poetical "Letters to divers Persons,"
as follows :—

"1. To the Right Honourable John, Lord Mohun, Baron of
Okehampton, my uncle-in-law.

"2. To my friend and kinsman Mr. George Gifford, who
called his mistress 'the green bird of France.'

"7. To my cousin, Mr. Charles Cotton.

"8. To my son, Mr. Thomas Cokaine."

Among "Encomiastick" verses on several books is
one :

"To my most honoured cousin, Mr. Charles Cotton the
younger, upon his excellent poem."

Commendatory verses by Thomas Bancroft preface
these poems. They are addressed "To his noble
friend Sir Aston Cokain, on his poetical composures."
In Cokain's poetical "Letters to divers Persons," he
has one "To my very good friend Mr. Thomas Bancroft, on his works;" and another, among his "Encomiastick Verses," "To my learned friend Mr. Thomas

Bancroft, upon his *Book of Satyrs;"* and a third, " To my learned friend Mr. Thomas Bancroft, on his poem entituled the *Heroick Lover.*"

Above all, he appears to have been more than usually delighted at his near relationship to Viscount Cullen, which arose in this way :

William, younger son of Sir John Cockaine and Isabel Shirley, progenitor to the Lord Viscount Cullen. He was the father of Thomas Cockaine, Esq., the father of Roger of Baddesley, in the county of Warwick, the father of William Cockaine of London, citizen and skinner, and also merchant-adventurer in the Muscovy, Spanish, Portugal, and Eastland Companies, of which last he was governor. He married twice, but by the first wife, Elizabeth, daughter of Roger Medcalfe of Wensgale, had only issue, and deceasing in 1599, was buried in the church of St. Peter-le-Poor, London, under a handsome monument, at the east end of the chancel, with this memorial :—

" Here lieth the body of the worshipful Mr. William Cockaine the elder, citizen and skinner of London, who departed this life the 18th day of November 1599. Also here lieth the body of Elizabeth Metcalfe, his first wife, by whom he had 7 sons and 4 daughters ; all which daughters departed this life before any of them accomplished the age of ten years. The 7 sons lived, and the youngest of them (at his death) was fully 28 years of age. Which said Elizabeth departed this life the 5th day of April 1589. Here also lieth the body of Catherine Wonton, his second wife, who died the 19th of September 1596, by whom he had no issue."

The house of Sir William Cockaine was in Broad Street, and was burnt down not long after he had given an entertainment to King James :—

" Wednesday, the 12th of November 1623, the house of Sir William Cockayn, Knight, alderman of London, in Broadstreete, in the evening one of his warehouses began to take fire, by negligence, as was suspected, of laying up wett flaxe in the place, which fired itselfe, and ceased not till two of the clock the next morning ; in which space it burnt his whole house and three of his neighbours' houses, to the great damage and danger of many neere inhabitants, and to the great fright and terrour of the whole citie, chiefly the east part of the citie. Sir Hugh Middleton, Knight Baronet, upon the first knowledge thereof, caused all the sluices of the water-cesterne in the field to be left open, whereby there was plenty of water to quench the fire. This water (of the New River) hath done many like benefits in sundry like former distresses."—*Howe's Chronicle.*

Sir William Cockaine, who succeeded his father, was also a citizen and skinner of London, and in 1609 sheriff of that city; elected soon after an alderman. And in 1612, King James having the plantation of Ulster much at heart, granted a considerable tract of land in that province to the city of London, who sent over about 300 artificers to begin and forward the plantation thereof, and appointed Mr. Cockaine their first director and governor, who had lands assigned him there, and under whose directions the city of Londonderry was established. On 8th June 1616 the King honoured him with his presence at dinner at his house in London, when he was pleased to make him a knight; with whom he was in such esteem, that he was often heard by him in Parliament and at the Council table, and consulted with him on more private affairs; and so well satisfied was the King with his comprehension of business, his manner of expressing his intentions, digesting and uttering his purposes, that he used to say of him he never heard any man of his breeding handle business more rationally, more pertinently, more elegantly, more persuasively. In 1619 he served the office of Lord Mayor of London, and that year purchased the manor of Elmsthorpe, in the county of Leicester, from Sir John Harrington; but in 1626, after two days' sickness, he departed this life, and in a most exemplary manner, and was buried 12th December in the cathedral church of St. Paul, when a sermon was preached by Dr. John Donne, dean of that church, in which his character may be seen at large; and in the south aisle a monument was set up in memory of so good a magistrate and worthy a citizen, with the following inscription :—

"M.S.

"Gulielmus Cockainus, Eques Auratus, Civis, et Senator Londinensis, septemque abhinc Annis Urbis præfectus Antiquâ

Cockainorum Derbiensium Familiâ oriundus. Qui Bono publico vixit, et Damno publico decessit, et Gaudio Publico Regem Jacobum, ad Decorem hujus Domus Dei, senescentis jam et corrugatæ, restituendum, solenniter huc venientem consulatu suo, magnifice excepit, id circo in Templo Publico, ad Æternam Rei Memoriam.

Hic situs est.

At vero et Famæ celebritas, quæ viget in ore Hominum, et Gloria Beatitudinis, quam migrando adeptus est, et Splendor Sobolis, quam numerosam genuit atque nobilem reliquit, junctim efficiunt omnia, ne dicatur.

Hic situs est.

Una cum illo, tot homines mortui, quot in illo defunctæ sunt virtutes; simulque et Acies Ingenii et popularis Eloquii suada, et morum gravitas, et Probitas vitæ, et Candor mentis, et Animi Constantia, et prudentia singularis, et veri Senatoris Insignia.

Hic sepulta sunt.

Jam tuum est, Lector, Felicitatis ad culmen anhelare per ista vestigia Laudis et venerandi Imitatione Exempli, curare, ne unquam virtutis sic semina intereant, ut dicatur,

Hic sepulta sunt.

Obiit 20 Octob. An. Dom. 1626,

Et Ætatis suæ 66."

His wife was Mary, daughter of Richard Morris of London, Esq., by whom he had two sons,—Charles (created Viscount Cullen), William,—and six daughters.

The family continued to flourish as Irish Peers for considerably more than a century after the date of their creation as Viscounts Cullen, but became extinct in the year 1806, in the person of the half-brother of Charles, whose death is thus recorded in the magazines of the day :—

"*7th June* 1806.—At his seat at Rushton Hall, co. Northampton, in his 92d year, the Right Honourable Charles Cockayne, fifth Viscount Cullen of Ireland. He was born Sept. 21, 1710, and attained the above advanced period of life in the enjoyment of an uninterrupted state of good health, of excellent abilities, and of a very cheerful turn of mind, to which he united the inestimable virtues of true benevolence and unbounded generosity. His lordship was of ancient lineage, and paternally descended from Andreas Cockayne, lord of Ashbourne, in Derbyshire, in the reign of King Henry II., whose descendants frequently represented that county in Parliament. With others of his maternal ancestors may be named the O'Briens, Earls of Thomond, and the Lords Willoughby of Parham. Of the elder branch of the former his lordship was the representative; and by the latter he derived his descent from the illustrious houses of York, Lancaster, Arundel, and Rutland. He married, first, May 4, 1732, his first cousin, Anne, daughter of Borlase Warren, Esq. of Stapleford Hall, co. Nottingham, by whom he had three sons and six daughters—only one daughter living; secondly, Sophia, daughter of John Baxter, Esq., by whom he had William, married to Barbara, youngest daughter of Sergeant Hill, and now Viscount Cullen. This second lady survived him but five weeks, dying July 12," at the King's Arms Inn, Oxford, on her way from Bristol.

His successor enjoyed his honours for a very few years, he having died in 1810; and, as no claim has been made by any of the male descendants of the first Viscount, there is every reason to believe that the viscounty is extinct. His death is thus noticed in the *Gentleman's Magazine* for Aug. 1810 :—

"At St. Alban's, where he had been five-and-forty years under the late Dr. Cotton and his successor Dr. Pellet, aged 74, the Right Honourable Borlase Cockayne, Lord Viscount Cullen of the kingdom of Ireland. His only half-brother, William, having died without male issue 8th October last, the title is supposed to be extinct, as there are not known to be any male descendants of the earlier Peers surviving. He was to be buried with his ancestors at Rushton, in Northamptonshire."

In the supplement to the *Gentleman's Magazine*, 1801, there is a letter, signed "Matt. Rugeley," giving a brief notice of "a pleasant village" in Bedfordshire called "Cockayne Hatly;" more particularly in regard to the ancient church, which he describes as "an ancient regular structure, with a nave and side aisles, built, as is supposed, by Sir John Cockayne, as his arms are in the brackets that support the roof, and in many other parts of the church. On the north side of the nave is a raised altar-tomb, which covers the remains of Sir John Cokayne, Kt., Chief Baron of the Exchequer in the reign of King Henry IV. On the top was his effigies engraved on brass, with his arms at each corner, but now entirely gone."

The writer next notices "a very handsome monument in the south aisle, with the figures of an armed knight and his lady kneeling at an altar, with the following inscriptions," which evolve the remarkable fact of a connection of the family of Cokain with that of the Humes of Wedderburn.

Over the knight is this :—

"S. Deo O. M.
Memoriæq. et mortalibus
Exuviis C. L. V. D. PATRITII HOME,
Equitis Aurati, cui ex nobilissimâ
Familiâ HOMEA DE WEDDERBURNE,
Apud SCOTOS oriundo, Musis sanct.
ANDREANIS innutrito, Artiumque ibidem
M^{to}. dein circa annum Salutis
CIƆ.IƆ.LXXXVII.
à Rege Magisterio canum leporum
rariorum donato, Regemq. eodem munere
in ANGLIAM secuto ibique accipitrum
Regiorum."

Over the lady is this :—

"Custodiam
Adepto probeq. functo,
denato denique ætatis X'ti
Aº. CIƆ.IƆCXXI, suæ vero
XLIX. atq. in coloniâ cœlesti
nunc recensite, lectissima conjux
ELIZABETHA, Filia JOHANNIS COKAYNE,
de COKAYNE HATLEY, in com.
BEDF. Armigeri, iu conjugalis fidei
Corporisq. æternum indivulsi sponsionem
Amorisque monumentum hoc statuit."

Under the lady is :—

"In Cl. V. Dominum PATRITIUM
HOME, vulgo HUME, SCOTUM.
Quam malè convenit tibi natis,
Quam malè nomen !
Istud Humum Hominemq. sonat,
sonat illa Tenebras."

Under the knight :—

"Vita sed illustris, nec propter
HUMUM tibi neque
nudum Hominem sperarat, erat :
nunc corpore tandem,
atq. homine exuto, O quantum mutatus
ab ILLO es !

Corpus Humo Tenebrisque relinquis,
cætera vivis,
Æternum indutus Lucemq. Polumq.
Deumq."

There are other inscriptions throughout the church over the remains of several members of the family of Cokain, given in detail in Mr. Rugeley's letter, which concludes thus :—

"At the east end of the church stands the old family mansion of the Cockaynes, surrounded with a broad and deep moat, over which is a drawbridge. The entrance to the house is through an ancient porch into a large hall (that occupies the whole height of the building), with a curious timber roof, and a music gallery at one end, built in the reign of William Rufus. The ends of the house are of a more modern date. The estate continued in the family of the Cockaynes till about the year 1740, when it came to Savile Cockayne Cust, Esq., who left it to Sir John Cust, late Speaker of the House of Commons, and is now in possession of Miss Lucy Cockayne Cust."

The works of Sir Aston Cokain are these :—

1. Masque: presented at Berthie, in Derbyshire, 1639, before the then Earl of Chesterfield, on a Twelfth Night.

2. Dianea: an excellent new Romance. Written in Italian by Gio. Francisco Loredano, a noble Venetian. In foure books. Translated into English by Sir Aston Cokaine. London, printed for Humphrey Moseley, at the sign of the Prince's Arms, in St. Paul's Churchyard. 1654. 12mo.

This is dedicated "to the Right Hon. the Lady Mary Cokaine, Vice-Countess Cullen." "My best of friends, Colonell Stamford, gave me the author, and intreated me to teach him our language." To this "worthy friend" he has an epigram, p. 157 of his poems.

3. In 1658 appeared "Small Poems of Divers Sorts. Written by Sir Aston Cokain. London, printed by Will. Godbid."

To these were appended :

4. "The Obstinate Lady: a Comedy. Written by Aston Cokain."

5. "Trappolin Creduto Principe : or, Trappolin suppos'd a Prince. An Italian Trage-Comedy."

6. In 1662 these were re-issued, with the addition of "The Tragedy of Ovid, written by Sir Aston Cokain, Baronet," and a general title-page thus : "Poems. With the Obstinate Lady, and Trapolin a supposed Prince. By Sir Aston Cokain, Baronet. Whereunto is now added the Tragedy of Ovid, intended to be acted shortly. London : Printed for Phil.

Stephens, junior, at the King's Arms, over Middle Temple Gate, in Fleet Street, 1662." The *Tragedy of Ovid* appears to have also been issued separately at this time, as well as in 1669.

"Thersites, and Tyrannical Government, which may well be supposed to be none of his, though placed to him by Winstanly and Phillips. You may find it in their alphabet of anonymous plays."—*Continuation of Longbaine*, 1699.

The biographers of Sir Aston Cokain have universally, when noting the printed edition of the *Tragedy of Ovid*, added "with his bust laureated, and four lines underneath."

The portrait prefixed to the *Tragedy of Ovid* is not that of Sir Aston, but of Ovid. It is a medallion in which is the bust of Ovid, his head encircled with a laurel leaf, with the legend around, "Poetarum ingeniosissimus. Publius Ovidius Naso, eques Romanus." And underneath are these lines :—

> " The sweet-tongu'd Ovid's counterfeit behold,
>   Which noblest Romans wore in rings of gold ;
>   Or would you that, which his own pencil drew,
>   The poet in his deathless poems view."

There is, however, a portrait of Sir Aston Cockayne, without an engraver's name, a laurelled bust, with these lines :—

> " Come, reader, draw thy purse, and be a guest
>   To our Parnassus ; 'tis the Muses' feast.
>   The entertainment needs must be divine ;
>   Apollo's th' host, where Cockain's head's the sign."

The merits of his several dramatic pieces which form this volume have been individually discussed in their relative prefaces, and it will be some satisfaction to the editors to learn that their readers' opinion coincides in some measure with their own.

JAMES MAIDMENT.
W. H. LOGAN.

EDINBURGH, *20th January* 1874.

A MASQUE,

PRESENTED AT BRETHIE, IN DERBYSHIRE, ON TWELFTH NIGHT, 1639.

A

From A Chain of Poems, written by Sir Aston Cockayne.
London, printed by W. G., and are to be sold by Isaac Prid-
more at the Golden Falcon, near the New Exchange. 1658.
12mo.

THE following *Masque* was presented at Brethie, in Derbyshire, on Twelfth Night, 1639, before the Right Honourable Philip, the first Earl of Chesterfield—uncle of the author— and his Countess, "two of their sons acting in it. The diversion terminated with a ball." Langbaine observes: "This Entertainment has been omitted in all former catalogues, as, I suppose, through an oversight, it being but short, and printed in the body of the author's poems amongst others of a different nature."

Philip, first Earl of Chesterfield, was son of Sir John Stanhope, who, in the 38th of Elizabeth, was constituted Treasurer of the Chamber, and, in 24th of the same reign, was made Constable of the Castle of Colchester, both of which appointments were for life. Philip, in the 14th of James I.,—*i.e.* in 1616,— was advanced to the dignity of Baron of the realm, by the title of Lord Stanhope of Shelford ; and in the 4th of Car. I. created Earl of Chesterfield, in *Com. Derb.* He was twice married— first to Catharine, daughter of Francis, Lord Hastings, son and heir to George, Earl of Huntingdon, by whom he had eleven sons ; of which John, Charles, Edward, William, Thomas, Michael, and George died young ; Philip was slain in defence of Shelford House, his father's residence, in the time of the Civil War ; and Ferdinand had also lost his life in the King's cause some two years previously. Henry thus became heir-apparent to the earldom, but, dying during his father's lifetime, Arthur only survived, and two daughters,—Sarah, married to Sir Richard Houghton, Bart., and Elizabeth, to Edward Darcy, Esq. of Newhall, in *Com. Derb.* By his second wife, Anne, daughter of Sir John Packington of Westwood, in *Com. Wigorn.*, knight, and widow of Sir Humphrey Ferrers of Tamworth Castle, *Com. War.*, he had only one son, Alexander, who became Ambassador to the Court of Spain, and afterwards Envoy Extraordinary and Plenipotentiary to the States of Holland. This is the account given in the *Peerage of England*, 2d edition, 1710, 8vo, supposed to be written by Collins ; but in the case lately presented to the House of Lords by George Philip Stanhope, who successfully claimed the earldom, it is stated that there were two sons the issue of this marriage,— Alexander and George,—the two young gentlemen, it is to be presumed, who performed in the *Masque.* The earl died 12th Sept. 1656, and was succeeded by his grandson Philip, only son of Henry, heir-apparent.

In Sir Aston's Poems these lines, dedicated to the memory of one of his cousins just mentioned, occur :—

An Epitaph of Colonel Ferdinand Stanhope, son to the Earl of Chesterfield, who was slain about Shelford, and lies there buried.

"Here underneath this monumental stone
Lie Honour, Youth, and Beauty, all in one;
For Ferdinando Stanhope here doth rest,
Of all those Three the most unequal'd Test.
He was too handsome and too stout to be
Met face to face by any enemy;
Therefore his foe, full for his death inclin'd,
Stole basely near, and shot him through behind."

THE PROLOGUE.

To be spoken by whom the Masquers shall appoint.

To you, great lord, and you, most excellent lady,
And all this well met, welcome company,
Thus low I bow, and thank, that you will grace
Our rude solemnities with such a presence.

A MASQUE.

The LAR FAMILIARIS *of the house being proud of so much and great company, and glad of their free and noble entertainment, appears, to congratulate the hospitality of the Lord and Lady, and speaks these lines :—*

Better than I could wish !   Superlative
To all relations, not examples now !
I've known the household gods of Rome and Greece,
And all the good Penates of fam'd Troy,—
Heard what they could triumph in, of their fates ;
Tell jovial stories of the frolic Greeks,
And the great banquets of fam'd Ilium ;
Have been inform'd of Egypt's glorious feasts
To entertain the courtly Antony :
Yet was there or necessity, or pride,
Or empty prodigality in all.
Here is a course steer'd even and voluntary ;
And I rejoice as much as Ganymede,
Olympus' nectar and ambrosia keeper.
Here I grow fat, with plenty of all sorts
That either seas, or land, or air can yield ;
And here I live as well admir'd, as envied
By all the Lares of all other places :
For there's a constancy in my delights,
A blest Elysium, where I do not want
The tithe of any wish I ever thought.
The proudest Lares of the greatest princes
May boast of state, and languish in a noise,
Whilst here I live secure, and do enjoy
As much of everything but fears and dangers.
And may it last while fate attends on time,
Until the supreme deities of heaven

Think you too worthy to adorn the earth,
And mean to fix you glorious stars in heaven !
And while there's air but to receive a sound,
May your names busy it to speak your praise !
Continue ever matchless, as you are
A pair without compare, and but a pair.

A SATYR, *invited by the loudness of the music and the*
perpetual concourse of people, to inform himself to
what end all tended, comes boldly in, and meets with
the LAR FAMILIARIS.

Lar. What means this bold intrusion ?
Sat.   Friend, forbear !
Though I was born i' th' woods, and rudely bred
Among the savages, I have a mind
Aspires the knowledge of great princes' courts.
And to what end aims all this jollity
In yours as well as others' palaces ?
  Lar. Dost thou approach to censure our delights,
And nip them in the bud ?   Satyr, take heed !
We'll hunt you hence through all the woods and lawns,
And over all the brooks thine eyes have seen.
  Sat. You threaten more, perhaps, than you can do.
What art ?
  Lar.   I am this palace deity.
  Sat. I wish thou wert a servant unto Pan,
Or any god that doth frequent the fields.
  Lar. So would I not ; I'm better as I am.
  Sat. Thy ignorance bewitches thee to this :
Thou liv'st among all fears, all noise, all cares,
While I walk merry under heaven's bright eye.
We in the fields are free from any sin
Against th' almighty deities of heaven ;
We know no law but nature's, do not tremble
At princes' frowns, have neither fear nor hope,
And are content,—a state the gods exceed not.
You languish in a perpetuity
Of thoughts, as unconfin'd as are your ends;
You truly lavish all your faculties
In getting covetous wealth, which we contemn.

Your sleeps are starting, full of dreams and fears,
And ours as quiet as the barques in calms.
The youthful spring makes us our beds of flowers,
And heaven-bright summer washeth us in springs
As clear as any of your mistress' eyes.
The plenteous autumn doth enrich our banquets
With earth's most curious fruits, and they unbought.
The healthful winter doth not pain our bones,
For we are arm'd for cold and heat in nature.
We have no unkind loves in meads or fields
That scorn our tears, or slight our amorous sighs ;
Nor are we frantic with fond jealousy,
The greatest curse Jove could inflict on's Queen
For all her curious search into his life.
We in the woods esteem that beast the stateliest
That hath his head the richliest spread with horns.
The Golden Age remains with us, so fam'd
By your Athenian and Roman poets.
Thus we enjoy what all you strive to get
With all the boundless riches of your wit.
    Lar. Satyr ! when I but say th' art ignorant,
Thy flourishing boast is answered at the full.
    Sat. But I desire a larger way.
    Lar.   And take it !
Canst thou compare the rags of nakedness
Before the studied dressings of these times,
And canst thou, like a cold and stony cave
Before the perfum'd beds of palaces,
Admire the melancholy falls of waters,
Or whistling music of th' inconstant winds ;
The chirping discords of the wanton birds
Above the angel-voices of our ladies,
And th' exquisite variety of music
Order'd to thousand several instruments ;
Content to cloy thy homely appetite
With crabs, and sloes, and nuts, and rude-mix'd herbs,
Before the stately banquets of the great ?
How canst thou like beasts' inarticulate voices
Above the Heaven-given eloquence of men ?
Forsake the woods, fond Satyr, and but try

The unthought difference 'twixt them and us!
The hills are fit for beasts. Converse with men,
And thou wilt never like thy cause again.

    Sat. Thou almost dost persuade me; but then I
Shall leave mine old and honest company.

    Lar. Thy new ones shall exceed them. Here's a
      butler
Will give thee wine as rich as is thy blood;
And here's a cook will clothe thy bones with flesh
As rich as was young Jason's golden fleece.

    Sat. Well! I will live with thee.

    Lar.   And welcome, Satyr!

    Sat. Spite of the fates, and Grecia's best protector,
• I'll be Achilles, and o'ercome by Hector.*

    Lar. A resolution worthy thy Sylvanus!

    Sat. But for my last farewell unto the woods,
I'll show you a wild dance of nimble Satyrs;
For we do dance as much as they that live
In princes' courts and tissue palaces.

First Song.

You Satyrs that in woods
Have frozen up your bloods,
Advance yourselves, and show
What great Pan's men can do!
    Appear!

Here you had need beware,
And move as swift as air;
These are not sylvan swains,
But courtly lords and dames
    Sit here.

* The cook's name.

The Anti-Masque.

SATYRS *rudely but decently attired, stuck with flowers, and bay-chaplets on their heads, come in, and dance as many several antics, and in as many several shapes, as shall be necessary. Being ready to depart, two excellent youths, in rich apparel, come striving in together, to whom the* LAR *speaks.*

Lar. What do you mean, sweet boys, to interrupt
Our sports? I pray you leave your wrestling thus,
And do not strike your skins, too soft for blows.
   1 *Boy.* He would outrun me, and be kiss'd before me.
   2 *Boy.* And he leave me among these dreadful Satyrs.
   Lar. Whence come you?
   1 *Boy.* We both were left i' th' woods, and tempted by
Such things as these to live abroad with them.
   Lar. What would you have?
   1 *Boy.* I would go to my father.
   2 *Boy.* And I unto my mother.
   Lar. Who is your father?
   1 *Boy.* The ever-honour'd Earl of Chesterfield,
Worthy of all his titles by his virtues,
And full of noble thoughts,—a great maintainer
Of our great-grandfather's virtue—hospitality;
The feeder of the poor; whose gate 's so open
It doth not need the office of a porter;
Whose house is now Delphian Apollo's seat,
For he's the patron of all arts and wit!
   Lar. And who is your mother, pretty one?
   2 *Boy.* She is the Countess to that noble Lord,—
A lady worthy more than earth can give her;
Rich in those virtues make her sex admired;
A fair exceeder of the best examples
That Greek or Roman stories ere produc'd;
Goddess of Tame, of Anchor, and of Trent.

She's such an one as hath none equal to her,
And therefore you may very easily know her.
    Lar. I know them both, and honour'd in my know-
      ledge.
Sweet youth, yond' is your father; kiss his hand!
And that, fair little one, th' unequall'd lady
You asked for.   Go, and beg a kiss of her!

Here the Lord of the house gives his hand to his son, and
    the Countess kisses her son. Then the SATYR *speaks*
    to his companions.

    Sat. Fellows, since you have done, farewell! I'll
      leave you
And all the rural pastimes of the woods;
I like this noble company so well,
That I hereafter here intend to dwell.

The ANTI-MASQUERS *depart; then the* LAR FAMILIARIS
    speaks to the SÁTYR.

    Lar. Now, Satyr, I will let thee see how far
The palace-pleasures do exceed the woods.

The LAR *leads the* SATYR *to a curious bower, all deck'd*
    with the best and finest flowers of the season, and
    opens a wide entry into it, where, sitting upon
    pleasant banks, full of the sweetest herbs and deli
    catest flowers, he discovers the MASQUERS, *then*
    presently invites them forth with this song:—

Second Song.

I.

It is unfit we should be dumb,
  When beauties like to those of heaven,
To grace our mirths, are hither come,
  And help to make our measures even.
      Then let us dance, and let us sing,
      Till hills and dales with echoes ring.

II.

Now it is fit our souls should know
   No thought but what is full of pleasure ;
That we our sorrows should out-go,
   And tread them down in every measure.
      Then let us dance, and let us sing,
      Till hills and dales with echoes ring.

III.

'Tis mirth that raiseth up the mind,
   And keeps diseases from the heart ;
Sports harmless never were inclin'd
   To cherish vice, but to divert.
      Then let us dance, and let us sing,
      Till hills and dales with echoes ring.

Here the GRAND MASQUERS *come forth, the ladies dress'd
like the ancient goddesses.   Then the* LAR *speaks to
the* SATYR.

Lar. Satyr, sit ! and observe awhile alone,
For I do mean to mix with these in dance.

*Here they dance what or as many set dances as they
please, the* MASQUERS *being men and women, or
only women. When they have danced all they intended, the* LAR, *or one of the* MASQUERS, *invites the
spectator-ladies with this song to join with them :—*

Third Song.

I.

Come, ladies, rise, and let us know,
Now you have seen, what you can do.
Hark ! how the music doth invite
All you to solemnize this night ;
Then let the sounds that you do hear
Order your feet unto your ear.

O rise ! rise altogether,
   And let us meet ;
Music's divine, and well may join
   Our motions rude unto a sweet.

II.

The figures of the magic art
We'll equal in a better part ;
Judicial astrology
Cannot cast such an one as we ;
Add but your skill, as we desire,
And we'll keep time to Phœbus' lyre !
   O rise ! rise altogether,
     And let us meet ;
   Music's divine, and well may join
     Our motions rude unto a sweet.

*Here all the company dance what they please and while
they please.   When they leave, the* LAR, *or one of
the* MASQUERS, *sings this to the spectator-ladies as
they go from them :—*

Fourth Song.

Ladies, enough ! we dare not
   Tempt you to more than this.
Now may your servants spare not
   To give each of you a kiss.
If we were they, you should have them,
   To recompense your pain.
O happy they that gave them,
   And may give them again !
'Tis late—good night ; go sleep, and may
Soft slumbers crown your eyes till day !

This being sung, the MASQUERS, *the* LAR FAMILIARIS,
and the SATYR *go into the arbour, which closes on
them.*

———

THE OBSTINATE LADY:

A COMEDY.

The Obstinate Lady ; A new Comedy never formerly pub-
lished. The scene London. Written by Sir Aston Cockayn.
London, Printed by W. Godbid for Isaac Pridmore, and are
to be sold at his shop at the sign of the Falcon, beyond the New
Exchange, in the Strand. 1657. 4to.

The Obstinate Lady ; A Comedy. Written by Aston Cokain.
London, Printed by William Godbid. 1658.

THE first edition of *The Obstinate Lady* was printed in 4to in 1657, but without the knowledge or consent of the author. The year following appeared "A Chain of Poems, embellished with wit, mirth, and eloquence; together with two most excellent comedies, viz. *The Obstinate Lady* and *Trappolin suppos'd a Prince*, written by Sir Aston Cockayn. London, printed by W[illiam] G[odbid], and are to be sold by Isaac Pridmore, at the Golden Falcon, near the New Exchange. 12mo." The author, in his "Apology to the Reader," affords this information: "These poor trifles, courteous reader, had not now become so troublesome to the world, if it had been in my power to have prevented them; for at my going once out of London, I left them with a friend of mine, who dying, they were dispersed into divers hands. Mr. William Godbid got my *Obstinate Lady*, and though he found it with the last leaf torn out, wherein my conclusion to the play with the epilogue were, he procured some acquaintance of his to supply the defect at the end, and so printed it. And though that comedy be very much of it writ in number, he put it forth as if the most part of it were prose. Here you have that defect much amended, and my own conclusion and epilogue added. I was fearful my *Trappolin* and other poems should have run the like misfortune, and therefore made a diligent inquiry after them, and when I had found them out, could not get them delivered without parting with some money, and promising my honest friend, Mr. W. Godbid,—after I had afforded him some small correction,—I would bestow them on him, with my consent, for the press; for, indeed, without his assistance I should not have recovered them out of a gentleman's hands, whom I will forbear to name." Mr. W. Godbid, printer, although his "honest friend," would seem to have secured his own advantage in the transaction. However, there is not much to complain about, apart from monetary expectations, if such there were on the part of the author, inasmuch as that portion of *The Obstinate Lady* which Mr. Godbid's "acquaintance" had supplied consists of ten lines only. It is a continuation of Falorus' speech, and comes in thus, after he has said, "How you have fix'd me in a fortunate and glorious life:"—

"Madam Rosinda, I thank you. Come, my dear Lucora, let us bid our friends good night, with as short a compliment as may be, —for I'm in haste,—that so we may congratulate each other's happiness in a place more convenient.
  "*Jaq.* I'll follow you, I'll warrant you,
        Into the cellar. But stay—O!
  I had almost forgot—

B

> Thus have you seen, by patience great,
> You may o'ercome a lady obstinate."

Copies of the collected editions of Sir Aston Cockayne's works are very scarce, and command a high price in the book market. The rarity of the quarto edition of *The Obstinate Lady* forms the principal claim to its being reprinted here; while at the same time the author's clever plays of *Trappolin* and of *Ovid's Tragedy*, which follow, determined the publication of his entire dramatic works.

Of the play itself, the *Biographia Dramatica* says, but upon what authority is not stated, "it met with no great success." That it was ever performed appears questionable, for although not devoid of some merit, the incidents and some of the characters of the piece did not present sufficient novelty at the time to render it more than usually attractive. There is a close resemblance throughout to Massinger's *Very Woman*, and the "Carionil" and "Lucora" of Cockayne appear to be the reflex of the "Don John Antonio" and "Almira" of Massinger, to whom our author in his poems addresses, as his friend, some eulogistic verses on his tragi-comedy called *The Emperor of the East*, and others on his tragi-comedy called *The Maid of Honour*. These are reprinted among the several commendatory poems prefacing Gifford's edition of Massinger's plays, 4 vols. 8vo, 1805-13. The first of these was written at the instigation of Lord Mohun, Cockayne's uncle, to whom the tragi-comedy was inscribed, and who was so pleased with a perusal of Massinger's printed works, that he not only commissioned his nephew to express his satisfaction, but to present the writer "with a token of his love and intended favour." Here is an excerpt :—

> "Thou more than poet! our Mercury, that art
> Apollo's messenger, and dost impart
> His best expressions to our ears, live long!
> To purify the slighted English tongue,
> That both the nymphs of Tagus and of Po
> May not henceforth despise our language so.
> Nor could they do it if they e'er had seen
> The matchless features of the *Faerie Queene*—
> Read Jonson, Shakespeare, Beaumont, Fletcher, or
> Thy neat-lined pieces, skilful Massinger.
> Thou known, all the Castellians must confess
> *De Vega Carpio* thy foil, and bless
> His language can translate thee, and the fine
> Italian wits yield to this work of thine."

Through Sir Aston Cockayne's poems one fact was contributed to the meagre biographical history of Philip Massinger,—that he assisted Fletcher in the composition of several of his plays; and this has been confirmed by Malone, who, when an inquiry was set on foot, succeeded in finding evidence in the archives of Dulwich College. These confirmatory documents will be found in Gifford's *Life of Massinger*, prefixed to his dramatic works, vol. i. p. 49.

Attention was first called to this by Sir Aston's poem addressed to Humphrey Mosley and Mr. Humphrey Robinson, the publishers of Beaumont and Fletcher's collected works in folio, thus :—

> "In the large book of plays you late did print
> In Beaumont and in Fletcher's name, why in't
> Did you not justice ?—give to each his due ?
> For Beaumont of those many writ but few,
> And Massinger in other few ; the main
> Being sole issues of sweet Fletcher's brain.
> But how I came, you ask, so much to know ?
> Fletcher's chief bosom-friend informed me so.
> I' th' next impression therefore justice do,
> And print their old ones in one volume too ;
> For Beaumont's works and Fletcher's should come forth,
> With all the right belonging to their worth."

Again, in his letter "To my Cousin Mr. Charles Cotton," he says :

> " Had Beaumont liv'd when this edition came
> Forth, and beheld his ever-living name
> Before plays that he never writ, how he
> Had frown'd and blush'd at such impiety !
> His own renown no such addition needs,
> To have a fame sprung from another's deeds.
> And my good friend, old Philip Massinger,
> • With Fletcher wrote in some that we see here."

The incident of Cleanthe, in the *Obstinate Lady*, disguising herself and following Phyginois as a page, is borrowed from Beaumont and Fletcher's very poetical play of *Philaster, or Love-lies-a-Bleeding*. There, Euphrasia, the daughter of Dion, assumes the name of Bellario and follows Philaster, to whom she is eventually united. Tobin has made use of the same device in his excellent comedy called the *Honeymoon*.

THE PROLOGUE.

BRAVE crown of gallants, welcome! May this place
Meet expectation; you afford us grace.
We joy that such a multitude divine
Of planets in our little spheres do shine;
And that besides our horizon is stuck
With lesser lights, we do esteem 't good luck.
For the great favour, may each several scene
Affect you more than Hebe's nectar Heaven.
We can but wish 't; for if y' are come to-day
In expectation of a faultless play,
Writ by learn'd Jonson, or some able pen
Fam'd and approv'd of by the world, you then
We disappoint. Our poet had never yet
Hisses condemn, or hands commend his wit.
Troth, gentlemen, we know that now-a-days
Some come to take up wenches at our plays;
It is not our design* to please their sense,
We wish they may go discontented hence.
And many gallants hither come, we think,
To sleep, and to digest their too much drink:
We may please them, for we will not molest,
With drums or trumpets, any of their rest.
If perfum'd wantons do for eighteenpence
Expect an angel, and alone go hence,
We shall be glad with all our hearts, for we
Had rather have their room than company;
For many an honest gentleman is gone
Away for want of place, as, look ye, yon!
We guess some of you ladies hither come
To meet your servants, wh' are at dice at home;
You'll be deceiv'd, and therefore will dispraise,
And say, this is the worst of all the plays
You ever saw; but keep your censures, pray,
Until you meet them here another day.
Our poet is not confident, nor doth
Distrust his work, but labours 'twixt them both.
He hopes it will be lik'd, and well; if not,
'T can be but hiss'd at worst, and soon forgot.

* "It is not in our power."—*1st ed.*

DRAMATIS PERSONÆ.

POLIDACRE,	*An old Lord.*
PHILANDER,	*His Son.*
CARIONIL, .	*A young Lord ; the counterfeit Negro, and called Tucapelo.*
FALORUS, .	*His Friend.*
LORECE, .	*A fantastic Gallant, his Brother.*
PHYGINOIS,	*Called Draculemion.*
JAQUES, .	*An old simple Serving-man of Vandona.*

SERVANTS.   MASKERS.

ROSINDA, .	*Polidacre's Wife, called Tandorix.*
LUCORA, .	*The Obstinate Lady, her Daughter.*
CLEANTHE,	*Her Sister, called Anclethe.*
VANDONA, .	*A young rich Widow.*
ANTIPHILA,	*A fine young Lady.*
NENTIS, .	*Lucora's woman, Vandona's Sister.*

The Scene—

LONDON.

THE OBSTINATE LADY:

A COMEDY.

——◆——

ACT I.—SCENE I.

Enter CARIONIL *and* FALORUS.

Fal. She has outgone my belief by 't.
I did not think that project would have failed :
I cannot speak her !
   Car.   The Alpian snow is not more cold.
   Fal. Her disposition is most strange.
   Car.   'Twere easier far
To spurn the sultry Cyclops' anvil down,
And kick it thus int' atoms in the air,
Than to obtain her love :
It were, my dear Falorus !
   Fal. O think not so, Carionil !
   Car.   Have I not cause ?
   Fal. At last, after a constant and a brave pursuit,
She may be won.
   Car.   Could I but hope so much,
Did all the stars' malignant influences*
Threaten fate opposite to my happiness,
I would not deem them worthy my observance,
But persevere till I obtain'd, or fell.†
   Fal. Conjecture still the best.
   Car. 'Tis easier to advise than to perform.
Had you, Falorus, been so oft dismiss'd

   * " Did all the storms, malignant influences."—*1st ed.*
   † " Felt."—*Ibid.*

Comfortless, scornfully sent away
By her own lips—O heavens! you could not think
    it!
  Fal. I could and would.
  Car.   With hope, friend?
  Fal. Yes; with an assurance.
  Car. Upon what ground would you build it?
  Fal. Upon a woman's frequent dissimulation.
Can you believe, when envious clouds deprive
Your eyes from the sun's beams,* that it shines not?
In these times, young ladies for a while
Do mantle their affections in dislike!
Let not an ignorance of virgins' wiles
Disturb your noble breast with weak despair:
Carionil, assume a confidence!
Were you inferior unto her in blood,
Or any whit deform'd, after her nays
You might suspect the period, but seeing
'Tis known, as noble blood runs through† your
    veins,
And that nature compos'd you in a mould
As excellent as she was formed in, and
With substance of as beauteous a gloss,
You need not let doubts puzzle you.

Enter above LUCORA *and* NENTIS.

  Car. Stay and admire with me! Exalt your eyes
To happiness!
  Fal. Your mistress and her woman, my Carionil!
  Car. Lucora! She's a transcendent of epithets!
  Fal. I see a lute! Let us escape their sight,
And it is likely we shall hear her sing!
  Luc. Now give it me! Is it in tune?
  Nen.   Yes, madam!
  Car. Forbear awhile to play upon the spheres,
Ye servants to the deities! The gods
Will blame you, if your music keep the air
Of her all-ravishing harmony from their ears!

     * "Sunbeams."—*1st ed.*   † "In."—*Ibid.*

A SONG.

I.

Sweet Diana! virtuous queen!
  By heaven's edict guide of night,
That dost affect the meadows green,
  And dost in fresh-leaved woods delight!
    Like to thy nymphs, suffer me
    To consecrate myself to thee.

II.

Thou that for lust didst transform
  Rash Actæon to a hart!
Either most strongly maidens charm,
  That men may never them divert
    From purity, or else make
    Them other harts for virgins' sake!

Car. How!—A vot'ress to Diana?
The heavens forbid that injury to earth!
Had the deceitful Syrens such a voice,
And bodies of so rare a form, I would
Ne'er come on shipboard, for fear of being drawn
To drown myself by swimming after them.
  Nen. I do not like her, madam.
  Luc. Who ever spoke ill of Daphne? Fie!
Banish such impious censures from you!
  Nen. Troth, madam, I should have been glad to 'a *
been my Lady Apollo!
  Luc. Oh, relish more of purity, Nentis! Alas! 'tis
a frail comfort can come with a husband.
  Nen. I think otherwise indeed, madam.
  Luc. Be all such thoughts remote from my breast!
My resolution shall be never† to marry!   [*Exeunt.*
  Car. Now you have heard her thoughts, Falorus.
  Fal. That she disguises not her love, you mean?
  Car. True; and I am most miserable.
  Fal. My happy friend you will be.

      * " To h' been."—1*st ed.*
      † " Shall never stand to marry."—*Ibid.*

'Tis an ignorant, common custom among young ones
    to do so.

Car. But she's a fixed star, and cannot move.

Fal. Fixed in your heart, 'tis likely ;
But otherwise, I doubt, nor do you.

Car. Y'ave stirred a feeble belief within me, friend,
That the excellent Lucora may be won,
And I will nourish it unto some heighth.

Fal. A necessary that none must want which do
Desire fruition of those whom they woo !

Enter JAQUES.

Car. O, honest Jaques !

Jaq. My lady presents her service to your lordship.

Car. She is in health, I hope?

Jaq. Very well.   And I am glad to see your honour
so, though I say it.

Car. She is not towards another husband yet ?

Jaq. No, certainly.

Car. Methinks her fortunes should give her a various choice.   You are elsewhere employed, I perceive.
Remember my best respects unto your lady.

[*Exit* JAQUES.

Y'ave heard of my cousin Vandona, Falorus ?

Fal. But very little.

Car. She's the most fantastic piece of womankind I
e'er chang'd breath with ; but a young one, wealthy,
and truly not unhandsome.

Fal. Lorece does intend to make love to her.

Car. Your brother, my Falorus ?

Fal. Yes ; so he told me.

Car. May he obtain her if you wish'd ?

Fal. Her estate would make the match a good one.

Enter CLEANTHE.

Is this the boy you so commended to me ?

Car. 'Tis he ; and think you him worthy the praise
I gave him ?

Cle. He'll come and wait upon you at night, my
lord.

Car. 'Tis well, Anclethe !

Fal. You spoke him not unto his merits.

Car. You are beholden to my friend, Anclethe !

Enter a PAGE.*

Fal. Your lord's in health ?

Page. And desires to speak with your lordship.

Fal. Where may I find him ?

Page. He'll be at his lodgings these two hours.

Fal. I'll wait upon him presently.

I am his servant !   [*Exit* PAGE.

Carionil, I must take my leave !

  Car. The gods go with you ! He may be my father-
in-law, but will not if he can prevent it. Adieu,
friend !   [*Exit* FALORUS.

  O, my Anclethe ! thou canst not guess the world
of torments I nourish here. I cannot number them
myself; and, because I cannot, I fear the gods will not.

  Cle. What can you ail, my lord ?

  Car. Canst thou imagine me free from misery ?

  Cle. Indeed I did !

  Car. No, there's a lady—she's above all ladies,
And, were she pitiful, I would swear, a goddess—
That does deny me happiness !
As thou hast me, Idalian archer, so
On her use thy eternal stringed bow ;
Draw to the head thy shaft, and let it fly !
For love, but love, there is no remedy.

                     [*Exit* CARIONIL.

  Cle. Wretched Cleanthe ! to what a multitude
Of woeful sighs my destinies have drawn me !
Could all the tears that I abundantly have wept
But find that recompense I dare not look for,
O they were showers to be belov'd, like those
That deck the spring with bravery. Carionil,
For whom I languish in disguise, it seems
Hath settled his affections on a lady
Does not return his love. May she continue
Obstinate ever ! But I must blame her judgment :

* Called, in the first edition, Tandorix.

Who can behold a man, with all the art
Of nature, fram'd to curiosity,
And hear the world report his virtues equal
Unto his form, and not admire and love him ?

Enter LORECE.

Lor. Now, my young sweet face ! what pretty foolish
whimsies trouble thy pate that thou lookest so com-
posedly ?

Cle. Sir, I am as I use to be.

Lor. Then you use to be scurvy ? Use the tavern
once or twice a day. You must not be so maidenly !

Cle. It best becomes me.

Lor. Canst thou swear ?

Cle. The gods forbid !

Lor. Canst thou sing ?

Cle. Not worth your hearing, sir.

Lor. Say'st thou so ? Then I will some things worth
thine !

I.

Of six-shillings beer I care not to hear—
  A barrel's not worth a carrot.
I, as others, think that there is no drink
  Like unto sack, white wine, and claret!

II.

Diana's a fool, and me shall not rule
  To live a bachelor ever ;
For I mean not to tarry in her livery, but marry,
  And quickly, believe me, or never !

III.

And I and my wife will lead such a life,
  As she shall think well befell her ;
For throughout the year, we'll tipple March beer,
  And seldom be out of the cellar.

IV.

All Stoical prate and Diana I hate,
    With her maidenly scurvy advices !
Green sickness upon her—sweet Venus I honour,
    For wenches and wine are not vices !

V.

Would Bacchus, the knave, had met with this brave
    Diana, this whey-blooded lady !
For the credit o' th' grape, he had made a rape,
    And got a puissant baby !

Cle. Y' are not melancholy, sir; your brother is
more solemn.

Lor. I melancholy? I scorn it, boy ! And yet I'm
not so merry as I was wont. The young gunner, Mr.
Cupid, has somewhat tam'd me ; but I am good mettle
still, thank my jovial fates, and will sound melodiously,
my young Paris !

Enter JAQUES.

Welcome to Hercules, noble Theseus ! Good boy, go
wait on thy master !   *[Exit* CLEANTHE.
How dost thou, old magazine of precious knavery ?

Jaq. I am glad to see your worship well !

Lor. My noble milliner* of words! thou that dost
grind thy speeches with a merry pronunciation, wilt
be my bosom, my cabinet, my friend, Jaques ?

Jaq. I will obey your good worship.

Lor. Liberally spoken ! When I have opened me,
will you be privy ?

Jaq. Very secret and officious ! It is good manners
in me. Your command shall wedge my tongue, hedge
my heart, and tie a true-lover's-knot upon it with the
strings of it.

Lor. Thou art an honest clod of earth, Jaques ! 'Tis
great pity the malicious sunshine warm'd thee not into
a diamond !

---

* " Milner" in first edition, signifying a miller.

Jaq. Your worship speaks above my brains.

Lor. I am marvellously enamour'd on your lady, Jaques. Vandona is my mistress!

Jaq. Wonderful news! Is my lady your worship's sweetheart?

Lor. Yes! but ignorant of my affection yet.

Jaq. I would be drunk were you my master, sir!

Lor. I would have a wine-cellar o' th' purpose. My estate, Jaques, is but mean—it must be craft must get her. Knowest thou any possible way to win her?

Jaq. Sir, I am passing empty of invention, but wherein I can pleasure you, tell me at any time, and I will not fail you. But the gods bless your good worship! Sir, would you marry her?

Lor. Yes, my old trusty Pirithous! Why dost wonder at it?

Jaq. She does nothing all day but read little comedies, and every night spends two or three hours on a great tragedy of a merry fellow, Dametas, and a company of strange-named learned lovers. She's no more housewife than you or I, sir—on my own proper knowledge, I swear, vow, and protest!

Lor. Thou art too earnest, my old-faced Saturn! I think her not the worse woman. Housewifery is the superficies of a genteel female, and the parenthesis of a lady, which may well be left out.

Jaq. You are a scholar; your bookship shall direct me.

Enter PHYGINOIS.

Lor. Who's that? Knowest thou him, Jaques? He walks corantoly,* and looks big!

Jaq. And like your worship, this tide first brought him to my eyes.

Lor. Hé came not by water, did he, old boy?

Jaq. I meant Time, sir, the London word.

Phyg. When we this passion into us receive,
Our former pleasures we do loath and abandon :†

---

* Trippingly, as though dancing.
† Phyginois, in first edition, goes on with the text, which, down

Jaq. Leave, by your leave !

Phyg. If it were foolishness in us to take
Affection, why did heaven two sexes compose ?

Jaq. Make would make rhyme !

Phyg. Why period to the Phœnix doth fire give,
But because it doth against nature consist ?

Jaq. Live, he should say. This is some very small
poet.

Phyg. I'll on, and am resolved to prefer
My life to be a service unto her !

Lor. What an affected utterance has this fellow !

Jaq. He'll ne'er make good ballad, warrant him,
that will not rhyme when he may.

Lor. The catastrophe was in rhyme, though. He
would be lik'd for a stage poet.

Phyg. Noble heroes ! the gods extend your fortunes
to your thoughts !

Lor. An academical idiom ! Enquire his name,
Jaques ! He delivers his mind after the garb of a
signor.

Jaq. Have you a name, friend ?

Phyg. I answer to Dracumelion !

Jaq. Good sir, let's trudge hence ; this is some great
conjuror !

Lor. Are you a necromancer ?

Jaq. Mr. Lorece, I fear he is some Saracen ! he looks
so dismal !

Lor. Art thou a Paynim ? Speak !

Jaq. For all your great looks, Termegant is an idol !

Phyg. I am nor one nor other, but your honour's
vassal, and a poor Englishman. Wilt please you to
hear the music of Helicon ?

Jaq. Law you now, sir ; how one may be deceiv'd !
I believe this whorson is a fiddler ! Can you sing,
sirrah ? Answer me !

Phyg. I am no fiddler, but live by my tongue and

to "service unto her," is here put into dialogue ; and the text
runs thus : " If it were foolishness for us to take affection, why
did Heaven two sexes compose?—why period to the Phœnix doth
fire give?—but because it doth against nature consist. He one
and the same resolved to prefer my life to be a service unto her."

legs.   Will you hear me, noble sir, speak a Parnassian
oration, or see me measure the ground with a dance?

Lor. What sayest thou, Jaques?

Jaq. Why, now, sir, 'tis dinner-time with my lady,
and I dare not neglect her, neither will I my own
stomach; and therefore, for me, he may show us a fair
pair of heels, and be gone!

Lor. Well, then,—spend this for me.

Phyg. Y' are, sir, the best part of a moralist.   You
are most liberal!

Lor. Come, Jaques!

Jaq. I follow you, sir.   Farewell, good man, Pra-
culemen!   The gods bless me, there's a name!

[*Exeunt.*

Phyg. Proceed, Phyginois, and be fortunate!
This project will furnish me with money to clothe me
both fashionably and rich enough, and then
I dare assail my Nentis with some confidence—
Politic lovers seldom miss.
Smile, heaven, upon my plot, that there may be
A crowned period to my policy!   [*Exit.*

SCENE II.

Enter POLIDACRE *and* FALORUS.

Pol. How do you like Lucora?

Fal. She's a lady above my thoughts, much more
my tongue!

Pol. Could not you wish her yours?   I have a desire to make her so.

Fal. Ambrosia, Hebe's cates, are for the gods!
Princes she doth deserve to woo her love.
You undervalue her, my lord!

Pol. The best is not too good for him that gets her.
Your breeding has been worthy your descent;
I've known you from your infancy, and am
Desirous to make you mine.

Fal. He enforceth me to an acceptance — I must

temporize with him. Most worthy Polidacre, I cannot attain to a greater happiness on earth than to bear the name of your son-in-law.

Pol. I thank thee, my Falorus! I'll go presently and get my daughter's consent. As you shall not want beauty with her, so you shall not money! I'll take my leave.

Fal. I am your most humble servant!

[*Exit* POLIDACRE.

What envious star when I was born divin'd
This adverse Fate? Who, having such a beauty
Proffer'd him, would refuse it? The pin'd man,
Whom poets' fantasies have plac'd in hell
With fruit before him, had not such a cross!
The true regard I bear unto my friend,
The brave Carionil, must not be slighted.
The sacred truth of friendship ever should
By force enfeeble all rebellious blood!

Enter CARIONIL.

Well met, my dear Carionil!

Car. I am happy in your company. Y' are my heart's best treasury, Falorus!

Enter LUCORA *and* NENTIS.

But give me leave, my friend.

Fal. O! I see the cause—your mistress!

Car. Retire, ye clouds, and weep out showers of woe,
Because ye may no longer stand and gaze
On her for whom the heavens their circuits go,
That they may see and wonder at her face!
Dear Falorus, withdraw yourself awhile.

Fal. The gods assist your suit!

Car. Thanks, worthy friend!   [*He withdraws.*
Hail! nature's most perfect work, and the continual idea of my admiring soul, for whom, if 't be your will, I must die, and by whom, if it is your dear pleasure, I shall live,—live in an unspeakable felicity by enjoying you, die happily for wanting you; and cannot live in such a penury.

C

Nen. Would I had such a servant! I should not
serve him scurvily.

Car. Honour your poor adorer, lady, with a gracious
look of your beloved eyes, and my misery for you
both with commiseration and remedy!

Luc. My lord, if you presume upon a woman's
Feign'd carriage to her wooers, leave it now!
For, if you'll give me leave, I'll call to witness
Every particular deity we adore :
That I will never have a husband! And
For your saying you must die for me, I hold it
A common compliment of idle lovers,
And wish you so much happiness, that you
May live well without me!

Car. O, be not so unmerciful!
Let not that tongue err into virulent words,
Which could have call'd Eurydice from hell.
Had your most excellent mother, fairest lady,
Inexorable been, you had not been ;
Nor crimson roses ever spread upon
Your lovely cheeks, nor had the world discover'd
Two planets more. Hath nature liberally
Heaped the rarest perfections she could give
Mortality upon you to no end?
No, surely ; nor can I believe that she
Meant to enclose a mind infractible
Within a body so powerful to subdue.
As you, even your dear self, was daughter to
A beauteous mother, so you also should
Indebt the world unto you by your issue!
Be not so cruel therefore, dear Lucora ;
Let not your tongue degenerate from your form.

Luc. Sir, you have heard me speak what I intend.

Car. Be not a tigress, lady!

Luc.   Anything but a wife!
Sir, I must leave you, and leave you this humour ;
The Court hath many ladies, take your choice.—Nentis!

Nen. Madam!

Luc. Come! My lord, take my counsel.

Nen. I could use him kindlier.

Car. What say you, lady?

Nen. Nothing, my lord. [*Exeunt* LUCORA *and* NENTIS.

Car. Doth a fair face presage a cruel heart?
Is't not a mere* full contrary in nature
That the softest body should be hard'st to win?
Nature is grown decrepit, and all things
Sublunary err against the rule of order.
Stir not, then, thou glorious fabric of the heavens,
And periodize the music of the spheres!
Thou even yet fast fixed globe of earth,
Whirl round in a perpetual motion!
Ye stars and moon, that beautify the night,
Change rule with clear Hyperion, and so cast
Succeeding time into another mould!
Then, with thy powerful beams, Apollo, draw
The ocean into clouds, and drown the world;
So there a new creation may befal,
And this life be a life celestial.

Enter FALORUS.

O all my happiness on earth, my true Falorus!
Lucora's beauty triumphs in my breast,
And shortly will destroy me. There's no beast
That haunts the vast Arabian wilderness
Of such a merciless constitution.
She'll never marry man!

Fal. She will, Carionil. Her father would have
her, and she has not so much evil as to contradict his
will. Where, then, can she make such a choice as
you? That, in a duel, your grandfather did kill hers,
y've heard her oft protest she values not.

Car. Does he desire it, or does your love flatter me
into a little possibility of obtaining her? Alas! if she
could like me, her father would very difficultly consent. He loves not my family.

Fal. Polidacre could not hinder you, were she willing.
But, friend, her father means to marry her. His own
lips offer'd her to me.

Car. O ye just heavenly powers! then I am lost,

* This only.

Prevent him not, she will be his.   Sad fates!
You shall not have Lucora!
    Fal. You wrong our amity by this suspicion.
I swear I will not!
    Car.   How?
    Fal. Consider, dear Carionil.   I grieve
To see my friend so over-passionate;
It is a weakness in you to be a pitied one.
    Car. My love o'ersway'd my reason.   Pardon me,
My best Falorus!   I believe your virtue
Would not act such an injury against
Your own Carionil!
    Fal. Shall we walk, and I'll tell you all that passed
'Twixt me and Polidacre?
    Car. I am a thousand ways obliged yours.
    Fal. You are my Carionil.   I wish no more
From you than perpetuity of love,
And that our hearts may never be untied.
    Car. You are too worthy for my friendship.
                                            [*Exeunt.*

SCENE III.

Enter ANTIPHILA *sola, reading.*

    " Fair Antiphila hath hair
        Would grace the Paphian queen to wear;
      Fit to tune heaven's lute withal,
        When the gods for music call;
      Fit to make a veil to hide
        Aurora's blush each morning tide;
      Fit to compose a crafty gin
        To take the hearts of lookers in;
      Able to make the stubborn kind,
        And, who dislike it, t' be judged blind.
      Though it is soft and fine, it ties
        My heart that it in fetters lies."

    It is a neat I know not what—I have not poetry
enough in me to give it a name.   These lovers are the

prettiest fools, I think, in the world; and 'twere
not for them, I cannot tell what we women should
do. We desire nothing more than to be praised, and
their love to us will do it beyond our wishes. I gave
Phylander, upon his long importunity, a lock of hair
and see into what a vein it has put him! I'm sorry
he had it not a week sooner; I should then, perhaps,
ha' had a sonnet-book ere this. 'Tis pity wit should lie
obscurely within any, that a lock will give it vent. I
love him not; I should rather choose his father, who is
as earnest a suitor to me as he. Yet I know, because
of his age, very few ladies would be of my mind; but
as yet I care for neither of them.

Enter PHYLANDER.

Now I must expect an assault. 'Tis in's ear already.
He's very fine.

Phyl. My dear Antiphila, you have received——

Anti. Your verses, sir? I have.

Phyl. I am your true adorer for them, lady.
Would your white hand had done me the honour it
    did them!

Anti. In what, sir? You must explain.

Phyl. That a touch of your skin might have ravish'd
me into happiness.

Anti. The lock has alter'd your discourse. I would
it had shut your mouth.

Phyl. There's no need of that, excellent Antiphila.
I would rather deprive myself of my tongue than that
any word of mine should be offensive unto you.

Anti. You relish too much of the court.

Phyl. Polite words can never misbecome a speaker
who hath such a subject.

Anti. Am I your subject?—You have called me
mistress!

Phyl. You are my saint, lady, and I must pray to you.

Anti. Saints hear no prayers, some say.

Phyl. Pray you show otherwise, by granting mine.*

* In place of this, Phylander, in first edition, merely says, "I
am a petitioner."

Anti. Have you any more papers ?

Phyl. My mouth shall speak mine own errand.

Anti. You must pardon me now, sir ;* I must leave you.   [*Exit* ANTIPHILA.

Phyl. She yet is obstinate ; but I am free
From doubt she will continue in that way.
There is no cause of fears in † women's nays,
For none of that sex means the thing she says.

Enter ROSINDA.

Now, Tandorix, where's my father ?

Ros. Faith, I know not, sir.

Phyl. You are one of the melancholiest servants he keeps.

Ros. It pleases you to say so, sir.

Phyl. They all report so of you.

Ros. I cannot tell, sir.

Phyl. Y' are over lonely ; be merrier ! You should put yourself into more company ; you should, Tandorix. I respect you for my mother's sake, for whose last sad letter you were entertained here.

Ros. I thank you, sir, for your kindness.

Phil. Farewell, Tandorix !   [*Exit.*

Ros. My son perceives my sadness ; but the cause
Deserves it fully. 'Tis now above a year
Since I did write that I did drown myself,
And bare the paper to my husband when
I thought his memory was somewhat lost,
And I inur'd unto this habit, drawn
To 't by a fond desire to know if he
Would keep his promise to me, which with oaths
He oft hath made, that never, if he should
Survive me, he would take another wife ;
But he, as other men, esteems no more
Of perjury than common breath. 'Twere fit
That husbands' vows upon the sands were writ. [*Exit.*

---

* "He will not be kept from it else. You must pardon me, sir."—*1st ed.*

† "Fear for."—*Ibid.*

ACT II.—SCENE I.

Enter LORECE *and* JAQUES.

Lor. I am beholding to thee, Jaques !

Jaq. I will be dutiful to your worship.

Lor. I should be glad to cope with your lady, now methinks I am of a prompter expression than usual : lovers and the muses are cater-cousins.

Enter VANDONA.

My Vandona, Jaques !

Jaq. I must vanish like a mist.   [*Exit.*

Lor. Farewell, grave Titan !

I'll out with a poetical soliloquy in her hearing for
    my preludium.
The gaudy stars are not more full of glee
When golden Phœbus setteth in the west,
Nor do the cheerful birds with more delight
Rejoice at the new livery of the spring,
Than I to have this miracle of beauty
Enter within the knowledge of mine eyes !

Van. He speaks well : I would he meant earnest. The gentleman seems very deserving, but he is something wild.

Lor. She shall be stoutly accosted. Impudency is a very happy quality in a wooer.

Van. H' comes !

Lor. Lady, you are not a puny in the court of Cupid, and therefore, I hope, need not the tedious circumstances of an annual service. I am bold to tell you plainly I love you, and if I find occasion, I will maintain it boldly.

Van. I pray you, Mr. Lorece, desist.

Lor. Never, my sweet Vandona ! My descent, I know, you doubt not, and my affection you need not. Whilst I live I shall love you, and if you die, your memory.

Van. I shall be catch'd ! We widows are glass metal, soon broke.

Lor. I can do no more, lady, and I will do no less.

Van. Your habit, carriage, and discourse, sir, show you a traveller.

Lor. My boldness, she means. Sweetest Vandona, I have been one. The habits, conditions, and situations of many great kingdoms I have exactly gathered into my table-books ; and also my fortnight's observation of the Antipodes.

Van. Oh, strange ! have you been there ? I wonder how you came thither !

Lor. I will tell you, lady. When I was bound thither, I was in Asia, at Tlaxcallan ; there we took ship, and in a pair of oars sailed to Madrid, the Catholic King's court. From thence to Naples, in Savoy ; from Naples to Crema ; and thence to Alexandria, where, against a tree, we suffered shipwreck. Into a new phalake we therefore got us, which was rigg'd for Frankfort, where shortly after we arrived, victuall'd our gondola, and threw away our fresh water.

Van. 'Tis a great way thither.

Lor. Thence we went to Lisbon, and after to Mantua ; and the next morning we came to the Antipodes, at twilight i' th' afternoon.

Van. What sights saw you there, sir ?

Lor. So many sights, dear lady, that they almost made me blind.

Van. Relate a few !

Lor. First, lady, the King is no man.

Van. I believe you, sir, for it never could enter my mind that any man inhabited there.

Lor. There they have no houses but the Emperor's palace, where Sir Francis Drake was entertain'd after he had shot the Pyrenæan Gulf, upon the Mediterranean Mount, in Russia.

Van. Where, then, lies all the court, I wonder ?

Lor. In the court, mistress.

Van. I guess, hem ! but cold lodgings.

Lor. Your ladyship is mistook—they are never a cold ; for the sun, being never above an hundred degrees above Saturn, makes that climate as hot as

Norway. They at the Antipodes hear with their noses, smell with their ears, see by feeling, but taste with all their senses,—for they are the most insatiable gluttons under the cope,—and feel not anything, for they cannot be hurt.

Van. This is wonderful; and I cannot imagine how their senses can be so contrary to ours.

Lor. No! Did you never hear, excellent Vandona, that they are opposite to us?

Van. O yes! I have indeed.

Lor. I will now tell you, madam, somewhat of the South Indies.

Van. Has not the Mogul of Persia his bread thence?

Lor. The King of Spain hath his gold there, of which the Hollanders took a great prize when they won the silver fleet.

Van. How was I mistook!

Lor. I will give you the situation of the country. Some of the ancient geographers,—as Heliodorus, the knight of the sun, Amadis de Gaul, and Palmerin d' Oliva,—affirm it to lie a thousand Italian miles from Isthmos at Corinth; but some modern writers, —as Don Quixote, Parismus, Montelion, and Merlin, —say it is a peninsula in Arabia Felix, where the phœnix is. But learned Hollinshed affirms the South Indias are separated from Armenia by the Caledonian Forest, from Asia Minor by the Venetian Gulf, and from China by a great brick wall. There, instead of cherry-stones, children play with pearls; and for glass, the windows are of broad diamonds. Hunters there have no horns but the unicorn's; no water runs there but Aganippe, Hippocrene, Scamander, and Simois. There are no hills but Olympus, Ida, and Parnassus; no valley but Tempe [of Ascia and Margiana];* no men but of the offspring of Scipio African, Julius Cæsar, Alexander the Great, Hector, Hannibal, and Hercules!

Van. It is a pleasant country.†

---

* Not in first edition.
† "It is a pleasant country then, and nobly peopled."—*1st ed.*

Lor. I will now tell you of the conditions of our neighbour nations. The Spaniards are humble, the Italians chaste, the French peaceful, the Dutch sober, and the Irish cleanly. I came at last to Virginia, where I saw nothing more worthy mention than an honest woman who cast herself into the sea because nobody would lie with her. In conclusion, at James Town Port I took horse, and the next morning, after a long and tedious journey, arrived in Wales.

Van. And what did you there, Mr. Lorece?

Lor. As soon as I could, I went to Merlin's Cave, which is obscurely situated on the top of a beech, where all the night he lay on the ground.

Van. What was he, sir?

Lor. He was an intricate prognosticator of firmamental eclipses, and vaticinated future occurrents by the mysterious influences of the sublime stars and vagabondical planets; generated he was by the inhuman conjunction of an incubus; and was immur'd alive in a cave by the pre-eminent magic of the Lady of the Lake.

Van. You frequent plays, do you not?

Lor. They are most commonly my afternoon's employment.

Van. I like him the better for it.   [*Aside.*
And you have read many histories?

Lor. Many, lady! I am a worm in a book: I go through them.

Van. This pleases me too.   [*Aside.*
Farewell, sir!

Lor. Admired Philoclea, leave me not so!

Van. What would you have?

Lor. Your consent, lady.

Van. Expect that a month or two hence.

Lor. Dear Vandona! sweet mistress!

Van. Indeed you must.

Lor. Nay, sweet Oxiana!

Van. Y'are too importunate!

Lor. Excellent Claridiana, Polinarda, Laurana, Bradamant!   [*Exit* VANDONA.

It makes no matter, I am sure to have her. How
    some women are taken with strange tales!
Next time we meet I do not doubt to get her:
Hercules could not woo a lady better.

Enter JAQUES.

Now, my old Anchises! how dost, truepenny? Be
merry, Jaques!
  Jaq. Is she tender-hearted?
  Lor. Respectful and pliant.
  Jaq. Good truth, I am glad on't, sir. My lady,
though I say it, is of a very good nature; my mind
always gave me she would be coming on. I beseech
your worship to be a good * master to me.
  Lor. Thou shalt find me so.   *[Exeunt.*

SCENE II.

Enter CLEANTHE, *sola.*

  Cle. Imperious love, that hatest whom thou
    woundest,
And those thou lovest best dost let alone!
If my obsequious duty unto thee
Can move thee to commiseration,
Instruct me how to win him, and, when I
Disclose myself, assist a wretched woman,
For it is in thy power to work my bliss.
He dotes upon a lady that regards
None of those miseries he undergoes
By languishing for her. With one fair stroke
Thy ignominy redeem! thou art call'd blind
Because how thou dost shoot thou dost not mind.
But what avails it me thus to implore,
Or rather to reiterate those deep wishes?
Millions of hours can witness I have said,
And yet find no help! Ah! dear and ever
Most lov'd Carionil, would'st thou wert so

     * " Loving."—*1st ed.*

Strongly inflam'd as I, or didst conceive,
Truly didst know, what misery lies here !
I think, though thou hadst sucked a ravenous wolf,
It would overcome thy nature, and thereby
Transform my sorrow to felicity !

Enter CARIONIL.

Car. I cannot hope a letter I have writ
To my Lucora can find that acceptance
And bring so good success I wish it may.
Sure never man so passionately ador'd
A lady of so froward a disposition.
If I could know the cause she is unkind,
I would destroy it, or destroy myself.
Anclethe ! art thou there, my boy ? Alas !
Why dost thou weep ? *

Cle. To see the sorrow you are always in,
And not to know wherefore. Though I, sir, am
Both young and little, I both dare and would
Venture my life to do you any service
That may redeem your happy days again !

Car. Alas ! poor boy, it is past thy redress ;
Yet I do thank thee for thy love unto me.

Enter ROSINDA.

Cle. My lord, a servant of my Lord Polidacre's !

Car. Tandorix ! What news ?

Ros. The lady Lucora commanded me to deliver
this paper to you.

Car. 'Tis most welcome ; would my heart could
read it !

Ros. I wish he had my daughter, for he's a most
    noble gentleman. [*Aside.*

My lord ! command you me any service ?

Car. Only my dear respects unto the lady that sent
you.

Ros. Farewell, Anclethe ! [*Exit* ROSINDA.

---

* " What are those tears for
    Thou dost weep away ? "—1*st ed.*

THE LETTER.

Car. "SIR,—I am sorry that, against my use, I
cannot answer you more civilly ; but I am blameless,
the fault being in your foolish passion, and not my
desire.   If in fairer terms you should receive my
reply, I am sure you would think it some beginning
of love to you ; according to your desire I have none,
and I wish your love was such as mine, so we might
be friends.   Yet I love you as a gentleman of my
acquaintance ; but if any more you trouble me with
letters or courting, I will hate you.   So I end.—Her
own,   LUCORA."

"Her own Lucora !"   I cannot now conceive
This lady of a humane nature.   Sure,
A woman cannot have so harsh a mind.
"So I end !"   What ! will she end so always ?
Oh, then, that I might end even now ! that all
The sorrow that possesseth my whole body
In every member would mutiny against
My heart, that so I might die speedily !
Is it not miraculously strange that this
Poor microcosm, this little body, should
Contain all the sorrow this great world can
Inflict upon it, and not sink beneath
So huge a burthen ?   One hill does overcome
The struggling of Enceladus, a giant ;
And yet I stand, I live !   What ! am I of
Lucora's temper—impregnable ?   Oh—oh—oh !
      Cle. Alas, my master ! good my lord, collect
Your strength, and be not thus effeminate !
      Car. I'm manly, boy ! for women cannot tell
What thing affliction is, their stony hearts
Relent so little at it in their lovers.
Oh ! I shall never have her !   Now I give
Liberty to a just despair to rack me ;
And it must ever do so.   What a chaos
Of misery is an unfortunate lover !
      Cle. I pray you, sir, put off this vehemency of pas-
      sion.   She will relent !

Car. Never, whilst I live.

Cle. She will; indeed, I know she will!

Car. Would she would love me after I am dead for her!

It were some happiness to think that, Anclethe!

Cle. I doubt not but she will shortly be yours, my lord,

And weep for joy to hear me make relation

Of this same violent passion you are in now.

Car. Thou art a good boy; but this lady—O my heart!

Could sitting down in Cassiopeia's chair,

And kicking proud Arctophylax from the sky;

Could stopping the Septentrian sevenfold team,

And putting out the starry eagle's eyes;

Could swimming violently up those rocks

From which the Memphian Nilus tumbles down;

Could the compelling of rash Phaeton's sire

To change his course, and run from north to south;

Could the adventuring to undertake

A journey through Africa's dread'st wilderness

When the Æolians do loudest breathe,

And veil the sun with sandy mountains' height,

Enforce her to repent the tragedy—

By these attempts drawn on me she should find

What truth of love was in her servant's mind.

Cle. Keep back his hands, O heavens! from violent deeds;

Let him not offer injury against

His own dear life!

Car. I have prattled too much, but I ha' done.

No longer shall my happiness be delayed,

Nor the displeased destinies any more

Jeer the sad depth of wretchedness I live in.

Thus—— Here I fall her cruel sacrifice!

[Stabs himself.

Cle. Hold! for heaven's sake, hold!

Car. 'Tis too late to prevent.

Patience, Anclethe! Commend me to Lucora,

That angel beauty without angel pity!

Tell her my woeful story,—how, e'er since
Thou knew'st me, I have languished for her ;
That I have spent whole nights in tears and sighs,
Whole days in solitude, to think of her ;
That I did suffer her unkindness, while
I had a dram of patience left within me !
Tell her how her most cruel letter rais'd
A despair higher than my strength, and that
Under her strange unkindness I am fall'n.
Weep not, Anclethe !   I am faint—struck dumb !
Fly, passionate soul, into Elysium !   [*He faints.*

   Cle. Oh, my dear lord ! brave young Carionil !
I'll wash thy wound with tears, stop it with sighs !
Unkindest day that ever wore the sun !
Thou art accurs'd, for giving light unto
His hand to guide it to an act so much
Beneath manhood.   O me ! I am undone !
What now will my disguise avail me in,
Foolish sister Lucora ?   O ye heavens !
Where lies our difference ?   Are we not the same
By birth on both sides ?—of one sex ?   Sure, nature
Degenerates against itself, or this
Untimely——   O ye gods ! I dare not name it,
Nor will I believe it.   He is alive !
So suddenly the world cannot be ruin'd ;
Which is if he be lost.   All virtue gone—
All valour, piety, and everything
Mortality can boast of.   My lord ! noble
Carionil !   He doth not hear me.   Alas !
I am for ever most desolate of women.
Injurious heart-strings, break !   Why do you tie
Me to a life millions of degrees more loathsome
Than the forgetful sepulchre of death ?
Would, some commiserating benevolent star,
Which carries fate in 't, would, in pity to
My misery, take me from it !   For love he
Lies here this bemoaned spectacle, and shall
My passion be undervalued ?   Tears, nor sighs,
Nor dirges sung by me eternally
Can parallel our loves at full.   It must be

The same way, and it shall ; the same blade
Shall be the instrument, and I receive it
Tragediously here on my knees. Would some
Kind body would inter us in one tomb !
Be firm, my hand, and bold !.

 Fal. Anclethe !

Enter FALORUS.

 Cle. My lord Carionil calls ! Is 't you ? Then——
 Fal. But I must hold you, and bereave your hand.
 Cle. And you may also die : your friend is slain ;
My lord Carionil is dead,
The paper in his left hand yet that brought
His reason into such subjection
That he even franticly did stab himself.

 Fal. I will extend my life till I have read it.

        [He reads the letter.

This lady is a rough-blown sea, on which
His worthy life has foully suffer'd shipwreck !
I have her ! Not Mercury pleading in her defence,
With oratory able to stint Jove's wrath
When he has bespoke thunderbolts of the Cyclops
To wreak some injury, should ever win me
To her bed ! Polidacre, mew her up,
Like Danae, in a brazen fort, or else
Make her to answer with her life this murder
She's accessory to. Proud piece of vanity !
I do want words to give my thoughts expression,
So much I hate her ! Prithee, Anclethe ! pardon
My injury against thy rest, for holding
Thee in a life so loath'd as this is to thee.
I'll lead thee——

 Car. Oh—oh !
 Cle. Withhold awhile, my lord ; he groans !
 Car. Thou art the cause, Lucora, and I must not
  blame thee.
I struck not that blow right, but this shall do 't !
I'm fainter than I guess'd ! I have not enter'd !
What ! who has stole the stiletto from me ?
Boy ! Anclethe ! restore it, as thou lovest me !

       D

Fal. Carionil, I joy you are recovered.
Death is grown courteous, or by this you had
Been wand'ring in the Elysian groves.
    Car. My friend, Falorus?
    Fal. Your loyal friend. Give me your hand, and rise.
I'm glad to see
Your wound no worse. 'Twas care and willingness
To die bereft you of your senses. I will show you
How you may win your mistress. You hear me?
    Car. I like it well. It may prevail—I hope
It will.
    Fal. Anclethe had slain himself had I not come.
    Car. Good boy, thou wert too kind.
    Cle. Indeed, my lord! I never shall desire to survive
    you.
    Car. Divulge my death.
    Cle.   I will not fail.
    Fal. Why, my Carionil, would you engage
So much yourself to any of that sex,
As for a disrespondency to lay
Violent hands upon yourself?
In truth, my friend, I wonder at it! justly
You merit more than they can satisfy
With their endeavours all of them!
    Car. Proceed not, good Falorus, in this language.
    Fal. What good do women? Old Amphitrite's face
Is not so full of wrinkles as they are
Of vices.
    Car. No more, as you regard, what always yet
You have profess'd, our long-continued friendship.
    O women, most admired creatures! how
    Can the just heavens these speeches so allow?
    What good do women? I do say what ill,
    Who do perform what men can only will?
    Why have we ears, if not to hear the sound
    And sacred harmony their tongues compound?
    Why have we tears, if not to weep when we
    Do chance a woman's discontent to see?
    Why have we eyes, if not to look upon
    Their beauties—nature's high perfection?

Why have we tongues, if not to praise them when
They slander'd * are by railings of ill men?
Why have we reason all, if not to deem us
Happy because some women do esteem us?
Ful. You are their worthy champion. What I said
Was out of passion for Lucora's dealing.
I will report ye're dead!
    Car. I shall be obliged unto you by 't.   [*Exeunt.*

SCENE III.

Enter PHYGINOIS, *solus.*

Phy. My clothes are almost made, and everything
That does belong unto the habit of
A gentleman I have prepar'd me richly,
For in these garments I dare not accost her.
I had good fortune to come with Cleanthe,
Who hath been very bountiful unto me.

Enter POLIDACRE, ROSINDA, ANTIPHILA, LUCORA,
and NENTIS.

Pol. Lady! I take it very kindly you
Would do me such an honour as visit me.
It shall be my study to deserve it.
    Anti. My lord, this is too ceremonious!
Pray you, let us walk.
I much approve of this air;
I know no place so sweet about the city.
    Ros. How observant he is! He would fain make it
a match; and I think she is willing enough. But I
shall prevent them with amazement.
I will see further in it first.
    Phy. The heavens, worthy gallants! be screne as
long as you presume under the safety of them!
    Pol. Know you this fellow, Tandorix?
    Ros. His name is Draculemion.
    Pol. O! I have heard of him.

* " Scandal'd."—1st ed.

Nen. His behaviour, madam, is strange.

Luc. 'Tis some frantic.

Pol. What wind brought you hither?

Phy. That which, noble sir, shall blow me all over the universe to do you service.

Pol. I thank you for your compliment, for your captainly protestation.

Phy. Brave bevy of gallants! my purse being millions of degrees voider of money than my heart of courage, I desire to empty my mouth of words to fill up the vacuum of it, if you please to lend me your attention, and afterwards to commemorate with munificence the worth of my oration.

Pol. Sweet Antiphila, what say you?

Anti. He speaks so strangely, I would fain hear him.

Pol. Draculemion, you know what to do?

Phy. Hail, but fair weather! I that have been the favourite of inconstant fortune, and term'd worthily by the worshipful title of a gentleman, am now debas'd into an humble fugitive. Commiserate this wonderful change, most excellent auditors! and let your recompense be a help again to restore me, and a story to exalt me towards the *fastidium* of my pristine felicity, and, at your connivance, I will post afoot to Mexico, drink your healths till I'm sick, and kill any I hear speak irreverently of you. These, and more than these, will I accomplish, though to my perpetual ignominy, or dissolution of my life, conditionally you will bestow fluently upon your slave so undeserving a title. Dixi.

Pol. Here's for all the company!

Phy. Will you give me leave to be grateful?

Pol. Yes, surely.

Phy. Fie! I'll not desire the Muses to replete
My willing genius with poetic heat!
This subject doth transcend them. I'll desire
Apollo to this lay to touch his lyre.
Thou charioteer of heaven, that dost invest
Thy swift-hoof'd coursers in the dewy East,
With harness worked by Mulciber, to light
The world, and dissipate the clouds of night!

For Phaeton's sake, not unto me unlike,
Thy sweetest notes unto this ditty strike!

Pol. If the exordium be so long, 'twill be very
tedious before the conclusion.

Anti. Dismiss him, therefore !

Pol. Farewell, Draculemion !

Phy. Would I might kiss thee before Nentis! [*Aside.*
[*Exit* PHYGINOIS.

Pol. Madam, how do you like the lord Falorus ?

Anti. Very well, my lord.

Pol. Him I have often motion'd to Lucora,
And he hath consented to marry her. Would it not
Be good fortune for her, think you ?

Anti. Indeed, I think it would.

Pol. How say you now, Lucora ?

Anti. For he is a much applauded gentleman,
Of good conditions, and of sweet behaviour,
Whose company is everywhere acceptable.
He deserves a good match—such an one as your
    daughter is.

Pol. How say you, girl ? Was anything I told you
of Falorus a falsehood ? Come ! prithee, do thyself
a good turn, and take him. Do, Lucora !

Luc. Dear father, pardon me ! indeed I have not
Any desire yet to marry.

Pol. Sure you have ! Bethink you, and speak wiser.

Luc. Truly, I have not, sir.

Pol. Y' are a stubborn wench, and I am sorry
It was my hard fortune to be your father.
Your shrewdness shall not carry you through so
    freely
As you believe it will ; it shall not, maiden !

Anti. Do not chide her ! she will be ruled by
    you.

Luc. Indeed, madam, I had rather live as I do.

Pol. No, I believe not that. There is some one
Or other far inferior unto him
Whom she's in love withal; perhaps some vile
Scum of the town.

Luc. Dear sir, you conceive amiss of me ; for I

Love no man yet, and hope I never shall
Be of another mind.
 Pol. 'Tis false ! I cannot believe you.
 Luc. If ever I should, I'd hate myself to place
Affection on a man of base birth or
Unseemly qualities.
 Anti. Be not angry, sir.
 Nent. I pray you, marry, madam, for it is
A state wherein one may securely kiss.
 Luc. Leave thy foolery !
 Nent. O ! 'tis a fine thing to have a coach of one's
  own to go to a play when you will,
And be restrained from nothing you desire to do.
 Luc. Marriage is no such liberty as you make it.
 Ros. Alas, poor daughter ! thou art to be pitied.
 Pol. Think of my will : I give you time.
        [Exeunt all but ROSINDA.
 Ros. They have hard fortune, which the gods
  remove,
That, where they cannot, are compell'd to love !
I would she had Carionil : I esteem not the ancient
 enmity
Between the families.

Enter PHYGINOIS.

Now, Draculemion ! how do you ?
 Phy. At your beck, and in good health, brave
  spark of generosity !
 Ros. Faith ! I am sorry I must leave you.
I must needs follow my lord, otherwise
We would have had one pint together.
 Phy. Thou art a jovial lad. Farewell !
          [Exit ROSINDA.
O my Nentis ! thou art a worthy Andromache, and
dost deserve Hector, the courageous Trojan wag.

Enter PHILANDER.

 Phil. They are not here!
 Phy. I must try my trick again.
Divine Apollo, and ye Muses nine,

Can ye behold his ruin unto whom
Ye have vouchsafed sacred poesy?
Or see him sleep under a hedge i' th' field
Who hath so often on Parnassus lain?
Or seek the river for to quench his thirst
Who at Bœotian Hippocrene hath
Pledged Mnemosyne in full-fraught cups?
Or wander barelegg'd, who upon the stage
Hath acted oftentimes in socks and buskins?
Or see him tann'd for want of an old hat,
Whose temples, unto his immortal praise,
Ye have so richly view'd begirt with bays?

Phil. Draculemion! I am glad to find thee! I'll
have a speech.

Phy. Your worship shall.

Phil. Why, well said!

As yet the contentious night has not exterminated
Hyperion from the celestial globe, who daily useth
to hawk with the firmamental eagle, and to hunt Ursa
Major round about the forest of the sky; to go to
plough when he wants corn with Taurus, and, when he
is hungry, to eat Aries, and, at night, when he comes
i' th' West, to court the lady Virgo to be his bedfellow, whom, because he cannot obtain, he lashes on
his horses, and goes and reports her stubbornness to
his friends at the Antipodes. Nor as yet hath the
trumpeter Boreas blown stormy clouds into our
horizon, to deprive our eyes of the powerful radi-
ance of his orbicular and refulgent head. Nor as yet
am I weary to do you service, nor will be while I am
able.

Phil. Here's for you!
What a wordy nothing thou hast spoken!

Phy. You have given me current silver for it.
Y'are a bountiful gallant! [*Exit.*

Phil. My father is my rival, and I find
To him Antiphila is most inclin'd.
What the Fates will, we never can prevent,
And, till the end, we know not their intent. [*Exit.*

ACT III. — SCENE I.

Enter FALORUS, *solus.*

Fal. A potion he hath took, and is o'ercome
By the deceitful working of 't, and lies
As if he had no interest in this life.
Lucora I have sent for, that we may
See how she'll take it, for by her carriage now
We shall perceive if there be any hope.

Enter CLEANTHE.

What ! will the lady deign her presence here ?
   Cle. She will, my lord !
   Fal. 'Tis well !
   Cle. And is at hand of ent'ring.
   Fal. Prithee, Anclethe ! bid them bring out my
      friend.   [*Exit* CLEANTHE.
Though once Carionil did not believe
My protestations to him, to relinquish
All title to Lucora, yet I meant it.
Were she a lady far more excellent,
And richer in the ornaments of nature ;
Did she exceed the fairest of her sex
More than fine-featur'd Mars the ugliest Satyr ;
Were her tongue music, and her words enchanting,
And her conditions gentle, like a goddess,—
I'd rather carry Ætna in my breast,
Than be disloyal to my friend; far rather !

Enter CLEANTHE, *and* Servants *putting forth a bed
with* CARIONIL *upon it.*

Thou art most dutiful, Anclethe.
O art !* nature's most curious imitatress !
How like a body late depriv'd of life
Does he lie sleeping, without motion !

          * " O, Anclethe !"—1*st ed.*

Enter LUCORA *and* NENTIS.

Cle. My lord, the lady Lucora!
Fal.   Draw back !
But stay you here, Anclethe.   [*Exeunt* Servants.
I thank you, lady, for this favour to us :
Were Carionil alive, he would requite it.
He would, unto the utmost !
    Luc.   My lord !
I'm sorry that a gentleman, reputed ever
Most wise, and voiced by a general fame
To be complete and perfect in all goodness,—
The which Carionil was,—should thus destroy
The great opinion all the world had of him.
His depriving himself of his own life
For that foolish affection he bare me,—
I having often told him that he spent
His service barrenly, and that it would
Yield him no fruit,—was such a weakness in him,
That his life's honour his death's shame hath ruin'd.
Hither I came at his dying request,
Which, his boy told me, was to have me see
What my obdurateness hath urg'd him to ;
For so he term'd it. His desire is satisfied.
Were he alive again, I could not love him.
Sir, I should love him less for the poor weakness
This act accuses him of—I should, believe me !
And so, my lord, I take my leave.
    Nent. Had I been his mistress, he had liv'd.
                               [*Aside.*

    Fal. Stay, lady !
Show more respect, for truly he deserv'd it.
    Cle. But kiss his lips, if you will do no more.
    Luc. The boy and all ?
    Cle. Speaks reason.   [*Aside.*
    Luc. His will I have accomplish'd. Farewell, sir !
                 [*Exeunt* LUCORA *and* NENTIS.
    Fal. Hath she a heart ? or, if she have, what metal
or stone is it of ?
Dost not thou think, Anclethe, that man happy

Who's free from all the molestations
That are concomitants to affection,
And to the grievous bondage of a woman ?
 Cle. My lord ! contingently.
 Fal. Thy timeless inexperience doth deceive thee.
Believe me, boy, there does not live a woman
Who more than complimentally is my mistress.
 Cle. Sir, you do not fear to love one of them ?
 Fal. Yes ; and the gods keep me still in that fear !
Sure such another [as Lucora] * put out Cupid's eyes.
O women, women !
 Cle. Truly, my lord, I do believe all ladies
Are not cruel ; indeed I do !
 Fal. Thou art too young to be suspected, otherwise
I should think that some subtle false one had
Beguil'd thy youth. Nature has worked the potion
  out.
 Cle. My lord recovers strength.
 Car. How is 't ?
 Fal. How does my friend ?
 Car. Repeat my destiny.
 Fal. Receive it with as calm a quietness
As I deliver it. Your ear !   [*Privately.*
 Cle. Vouchsafe him patience, O ye gods !
 Car. When huge-wav'd rivers from the earth's high
  banks
Precipitate themselves into the ocean,
Will stillness follow ? Can you think, then—can you,
I may be quiet ? Was Jove so when the great
Brood of the earth, the giants, did assay
Olympus' conquest ? Can I, then, a poor,
Dejected man, be calm, when all the misery
The world can send it pours on me fully ? .
Æolus, run thy vent'rous sword again
Into the rocks, and give an issue to
The winds, that they may with their ireful blasts
Remove the world from off its stedfast hinge !
Or blow the pole-stars out, and so let fall
This globe we breathe on ! Or, by whirlwinds' force,

---

* Not in first edition.

Both sexes collect together, and carry them
Int' places opposite,—the one into
The Arctic, the other the southern regions;
And let them of themselves propagate the like:
So women's tyrannies could do no ill,
And men perform what one another will.

 Fal. This savours franticly!

 Cle. Deprive him not of reason, but exalt
Him to himself, O heavens! Ah, me!

 Car. 'Tis true, the sea is always full of water,—
The lands do relieve it,—and yet has no cause
For lamentation; but woeful man
Hath but a few, indeed a very few,
Salt tears to mollify the burthenous draught
Of misery which his malignant stars
Compel him to endure.
What! his mistress' venom, obstinacy, not possible?
'Tis insufferable—above our frail carriage.

 Fal. The word friend weighs all titles of honour
  down;
And therefore not by them, but that, I beseech you
Not to neglect yourself. I 've lately known
The time when death almost inevitable
Could not unfix your thoughts. This cause is weaker.

 Car. How?

 Fal. Believe me, friend.

 Car. Believe you? I would believe thee, friend,
Didst thou affirm absurdest contraries,—
That the sun was extinguished, and the bright
Moon was blown out, and all the stars were fall'n,
And nature, yet harmonious, disordered
Into another chaos—I would believe you;
For, rather than you should pronounce a falsehood,
Things that are not would be.

 Fal. Alas! you are distempered.
I grieve to see you so for so poor a cause.

 Car. It is a weighty one; and if the brave,
Fam'd offspring of Alcmena had endur'd it,
He had enlarg'd his labours to thirteen,
And been another wonder to the world.

But, noblest friend, you know the history,—
How he the knotty club did lay aside,
Put off the rough Nemæan skin, and donn'd
Maidens' apparel, for the love he bore
To ruin'd Picus' daughter, young Iole.
    Fal. But he ne'er offer'd violence to himself.
    Cle. He did not, sir. Be counsell'd by your friend ;
Do, my good lord !
    Car. He had not cause ; she did return him love.
And, except in this case, I would suffer
Beyond expression from another hand
Without a thought to use mine own. But you
May say I'm passionate : 'tis right ; I am so :
I know 't, and you cannot expect less from me.
Were I as free from love as you have known me,
You should not tax me with that fault, although
Unstable fortune made an Irus of me.
But, you may call this boasting ?
    Fal. Far be it from me ; 'tis a perfect truth.
    Cle. Ah, alas !
    Car. Leave sighing, boy, prithee !
    Fal. Come !
You shall be temperate again, my friend,
And have fair likelihood to obtain your lady.
    Car. Impossible !
    Fal. I've formed the plot already ; you must be——
Draw near.
    Car. How !—a negro—an Ethiopian !—'tis frivolous.
She is too obdurate—most obstinate.
    Fal. Hath she not refused many of the bravest and
       handsomest gentlemen of this kingdom ?
You cannot deny it ; be, therefore, counselled :
She that cannot love a man of a better complexion,
On one of them may settle her affection.
    Car. I have some hope again. Boy, you shall stay
       with my friend ; refuse it not, I prithee !
For many conveniences it is necessary. I every
       day shall see thee, and shortly will take thee
       again.
    Cle. My lord, I beseech you !

Cur. Nay, my Anclethe, let me not use words.
As thou dost love me, deny me not.

Cle. Sir, I am charm'd, and will obey you.

Fal. Come! let's walk, and I'll instruct you fully.

[*Exeunt omnes.*

SCENE II.

Enter JAQUES, *solus, drunk.*

This London wine is a parlous liquor: 'twill turn you a man's head so long round, that at last 'twill set you it where his heels should be. Another glass on't had prov'd me a reeler, a cotquean, which I was never brought up too. I learnt a song of my old gran'am —many a good ballad she would 'a sung me by the fireside o'er a black pot, but your city wine is a more stinging liquor. She left me a very fair cow, but a villainous thief stole me her, foul cheeve him for it! and escap'd I know not whither. But all's one; much good do him with it—my ladies' worship service is better than a team of oxen. But the song must not be forgot.

I.

All that about me sit
Laugh at my pleasant wit,
And neither cough nor spit,
        Till I have done—a.
For I will sing a song,
That fitly shall be long,
To a cow, and not wrong
        Mount * Helicona.

II.

Don Quixote's Rosinant,
And Sancho's ass errant,
And Banks his horse do want
        What she may brag of.

* "Clear."—*1st ed.*

They would one's breech much gall,
And give one many a fall,
Sufficient therewithal
　　　　To break one's crag off.

III.

That Jove did love a steed,
I yet did never read ;
But by all 'tis agreed,
　　　　Io he loved.
No beast upon the field
Doth man more profit yield,　　'
Whether alive or kill'd,
　　　　As may be proved.

Well, I'll to my chamber and sleep awhile ; otherwise I'st ha' a foul deal of do to keep me on my legs this afternoon.

Enter LORECE.

Jaques is now a very Barnaby !
　Lor. Jaques ! soho, my boy !　　　　[*Exit* JAQUES.
His match is extraordinary ; sure the rogue's dead, he's so very deaf.
　The report is, that Doctor Aristotle cast himself into the sea because he could not, with all his rambling philosophy, find out the natural cause of ebbing and flowing of it ; but had his good scholarship been troubled with my mistress, he might ha' jolted his brains out against a rock, for his dulness in inventing a method of wooing to win her ladyship withal.　I here will sit and muse.
　　　　　　　[*Sits in a private place.*

Enter VANDONA *and* JAQUES.

　Jaq. Indeed, madam, I will be very serviceable unto you, if now and then you will suffer me to be blythe and full of merry moods.
　Van. Jaques ! where ha' you been ?
　Jaq. At the spigot.　Is it not a very rainy, wet day ?

Van. Thou art well washed within.

Jaq. 'Tis a very dark day. The sun shines very clear, tho'!

Van. Th' ast a light head, Jaques.

Jaq. And yet I cannot bear 't steadfast on my shoulders; wine's monstrous strong!
Let me see, who am I?

Van. Th'art a fool.

Jaq. The play's the better for 't.

Van. Y'are a drunken coxcomb; go!

Jaq. Thou captive Greek, I am a Beglerbeg!

Van. Thou wilt be a beggar, and thou leav'st not thy drinking.

Jaq. Thou me Roxalana! am not I the great Sultan?

Van. A booby!

Jaq. You show your breeding, to upbraid the majesty of the Grand Signor.

Van. Peace! no more fooling.

Jaq. You are drunk with north-country balderdash; you keep no wine, water your kittens * with beer. Nothing but wine shall be drank in my court.

Van. I shall be troubled with him else. Ambassadors wait your return at your palace.

Jaq. We will withdraw! Send the bashaws after me; they shall present me wine. [*Exit.*

LORECE discloseth himself.

Van. Is he here?
I shall be courted, certainly, and perhaps shall yield.

Lor. Most welcome, happiest genius of my life!
Dearest Vandona, let your lily hand
Enrich my lips!

Van. Y'are very complimental, servant.

Lor. Mistress! 'i faith, I love you, as for millions of causes,
So also for a natural demeanour:
It shows me you are no offspring of the city.

Van. You would marry none of them, servant?

<hr>

* "Kittlins."—1st ed.

Lor. No ; six thousand pounds cannot hide a squint eye, a crooked back, a red head, or a muddy face, though they may gild them.

Van. This is very satirical! [but there be beauties of all-coloured hair, eyes, and complexions.] *

Lor. I at any time will carry you to a play, either to the Black Friar's or Cockpit. And you shall go to the Exchange when you will, and have as much money as you please to lay out. You shall find me a very loving husband, in troth, dear lady.

Van. But, servant, you have been a very debaucht gentleman.

Lor. Forget what y'ave heard, and you shall hear no more on't. But we are extravagant ; come ! let's go to th' joiner.

Van. To whom, and for what, Mr. Lorece ?

Lor. To Hymen, in his saffron coat, to be married.

Van. Some other time ; a month hence will serve.

Lor. Then must I count another bout.

Van. What you please, sir.

Lor. O Cupid, the bowman !
I am not thy foe, man ;
For I love this woman
As well as I know man.
And therefore I pray thee
From mischief to stay me,
And quickly to lay me
In bed with this lady.

Van. What call you this, sir ?

Lor. 'Tis my imploration and ode.

Van. Y'are very fluent, sir.

Lor. And yet neglected. But I'll make Cornelius Gallus speak English, and he shall woo for me.

Van. What say you, servant ?

Lor. Be you attentive, and you shall hear.
My sweet Vandona, fine and comely lass,
Whose beauty milk and lilies doth surpass,
And the sweet roses, both the white and red,
Or Indian ivory new polished ;

* Not in first edition.

O spread ! O spread abroad thy yellow hair,
Like glorious gold, shining out as fair !
Thy purest alabaster neck, and show's
Which from between thy graceful shoulders grows !
Open thy starry eyes, and let us view
Their brows above them, of a sable hue !
And both thy roseal cheeks let us espy,
Beautified with a natural Tyrian die !
Put forth thy lips, their coral let us see,
And, dovelike, gentle kisses give to me !   [*Kisses her.*
Of amorous life thy breath did draw out part ;
Those kisses pierced me to the very heart.
Why didst thou suck my blood, O cruel she ?
Henceforth thy dugs, like apples, hide from me,
Which with ambrosial cream shall swell thy breast,
Discloseth cinnamon ; I yield, and best
Delights arise from thee !   Yet thy paps cover,
Whose growth and beauty do make me a lover.
For seest thou not that languishing I lie ?
A man half dead, how canst thou thus destroy ?

Van. This is mere flattery.

Lor. 'Tis but a spark, madam ! an almost invisible
atom of truth, which can scarce be discern'd in the
sunshine of your perfections !   Credit me, madam !

Van. They are most childish that will believe all
their servants say, my most poetical servant.

Lor. Most obdurate lady !

Van. Will you wrangle ?

Lor. Was ever widow so hard to win ?   Sure your
husband got not your maidenhead, you are so backward.

Van. Adieu, sir.

Lor. Not yet, I pray you, sweetest lady, if——

Van. Pray you, trouble me with no more speeches.

Lor. O cruel reply to a lover's suit !
If ever you have felt this passion's pain,
If ever you would pitied be yourself,
Or if you know that love hath power to kill,—
For all these, which you heretofore have been
Subject unto, commiserate a heart

E

So full of love for you that it will break
If you deny.
But if you will remain inexorable,
And frown on him who aye must fawn on you,
I wish my fortune may be yours, and that,
If ere you love, you may be served so.
  Van. I'm but a woman, and these words would
   move
A stupid rock to pity. Sir, I can
Resist no more ; your tongue has magic in 't.
You have o'ercome me ; and enjoy your conquest.
  Lor. My dear widow, let me kiss thee for this ! Thy
date of wearing black is almost out. O my joy ! me-
thinks I could outsing old Homer, the nine Muses,
and put their patron Apollo out of fame !

   Enter FALORUS, CLEANTHE, *and* PHYGINOIS *in*
    brave apparel.

My Vandona, yonder is my brother ! he will be joyful
to hear of my good fortune.
  Fal. Who's he ?
  Cle. A friend of mine, my lord.
  Fal. I shall be desirous, sir, both for your own and
for Anclethe's sake, to be better acquainted with you.
May I demand your name ?
  Phyg. Your servant is call'd Phyginois.
  Fal. How have you sped, brother ?
  Lor. She will be called your sister. Salute her ! go,
kiss her for 't.
  Fal. Lady, I hope my brother will deserve you,
[By proving an affectionate husband to you.] *
  Phyg. Madam, I am a stranger, but will endeavour
to make myself known unto you by any service I can
do you.
  Van. Thank you, sir !
  Phyg. My Nentis doth excel her sister.   [*Aside.*
  Lor. Come, brother ! will you go with us ?
  Fal. I'll wait upon your mistress.
    [*Exeunt* FALORUS, LORECE, *and* VANDONA.
     * Not in first edition.

Cle. My faithful friend, may all thy wishes prosper,
And a fair end crown them most happily.

Phyg. Sweetest of ladies !

Cle. Thou didst prefer goodness before the raising
of thy house.

Phyg. It griev'd me to think so noble a lady should
be so poorly dispos'd of ;
My brother's birth nor fortune could deserve you.

Cle. I was ignorant, and might have undone myself.

Phyg. But I did pity you.

Cle. And ever have obliged me to you for 't.

Phyg. If your sister's woman, Mistress Nentis, be
obstinate, and you prosper,
Hereafter you may do me a multitude of favours.

Cle. I ne'er will fail to do the best I can. Now, let
us follow them.
Love is a passion not to be withstood,
And, until hearts be mutual, never good.   [*Exeunt.*

Scene III.

Enter CARIONIL, *solus, like a negro, in strange apparel.*

Car. A lover's life is like the various year,
Which hardly bears one form a fortnight's space.
He, sure, deserves respect, that to obtain
His mistress thinks all trouble a content.
These two years have not had as many quarters
As I disguises,—scarce as many days
As I devices, and yet to no purpose.
What I may do in this I cannot guess,
But for my own purpose must hope the best.
My late long residence i' th' Spanish court, when I lay
there lieger ambassador,
Hath made me speak the Castilian language per-
fectly ;
Which will be my great furtherance, because
Polidacre affects that tongue exceedingly,

And I know will gladly give me a free access
Unto his house at all times.

Estoy yo, como deve, muy lobrego ;
Porque de mi, Lucora haze un negro.

Enter POLIDACRE, LUCORA, *and* NENTIS.

They shall not see me yet.

Luc. Sir, your daily importunacies have so moved
me, that I must yield unwillingly; only, I request to
have our marriage deferr'd a month. Dear sir, do not
deny me this !

Pol. I thank thee, girl !

Enter FALORUS.

Welcome, Falorus ! My daughter's yours after four
weeks be past.

Fal. Worthy sir, y'are too bountiful. Most excellent Lucora, you will make my fortune envied. I
must dissemble yet, for I will not wrong Carionil.

Nen. I like this well.

Luc. But I will rather die than have him. [*Aside.*

Car. I do not doubt my friend.

Pol. I have laboured much for you.

Car. Now I'll disclose myself, and counterfeit the
negro as well as I can.

Araucana.

Y pues en todos tiempos, y occasiones
Por la causo commun sin cargo alguno,
En battalas formadas, y esquadrones
Puede usar delas armas cada uno :
Por las mismas legitimas razones
Es licito el combate de uno a uno,
A pie, a cavallo, armado, disarmado,
Ora se a campo abierto, ora estocado.

Don Carionil, would I could hear of thee !

Luc. He is the brav'st proportion'd African I ever
saw. [*Aside.*

Pol. I will speak to him.

Habla, voste, yngles ?

Car. Yes, sir ! I learned your language at Bruxels.

Pol. I shall be most glad, sir, to be acquainted with you.

Car. Grave Nelides' years be doubled, most honourable hero, upon you ! Your courtesy has won one of the chiefest Ethiopian lords to become your servant.

Luc. What an unequall'd carriage he is of ! [*Aside.*

Car. You look, sir, like a noble gentleman. I salute you !

Fal. Well, Don Carionil, may'st thou prosper. Your mistress has consented a month hence to marry me ; but doubt me not, my friend !

Car. According to the Ethiopian custom,
Great lady, I adore your pantofle !

Luc. You are a worthy and a noble Moor.

Car. This is your shadow ; you shall command me, fair one.

Nen. Thank you, sir.

Pol. I heard you mention Carionil ?

Car. 'Tis true, I did so.
When we were in the Spanish court together,—
I being commanded thither an ambassador
From th' Emperor of both the Ethiopias
And of the mighty kingdoms and vast countries
Of Goa, Caffares, Fatigar, Angola,
Barne, Balignoza, Adea, Vagne, and Goyame,—
He wrong'd me ; and I am come hither to seek him,
And with my sword to punish his rude language.
If you will tell me, sir, where I may find him,
You shall eternally oblige me to you.

Pol. He is lately dead, sir.

Car. You do but jest !

Fal. I was with him when he died.

Car. Then he had not so honourable an end as was intended him.

Pol. If I should not seem too inquisitive, I would desire to know your quarrel.

Luc. I am much taken with this object. [*Aside.*

Car. You may command me anything.
We, meeting in the presence one afternoon,
'Mongst many things, did happen to discourse
Of ladies. He said that none of all the world
Were so beautiful as the Spanish.
I, that had read in many histories
The English have the best and loveliest faces,
Did tell him so, yet could not change his mind.
After long altercations, he grew hot,
Gave me the lie reproachfully, which forced me to tell
him, that though I owed so much honour to both the
majesties of our great masters as not for private
wrongs to disturb our embassies, I meant, before I
died, to visit his country, and call him there unto a
strict account.

Pol. I thank you for your free relation.
While you intend to stay in England, use
My house at your pleasure; I pray you, do.
Your company will be always welcome to me;
And I love the Castilian language, which
You speak both readily and purely.
May I demand your name?

Car. 'Tis Tucapelo, and I'm subject to
Great Prester John, whose powerful sceptre awes
Sixty-two kings; and in Garama live,
Magnificent for silken palaces.

Fal. His behaviour is without suspicion.   [*Aside.*

Pol. 'Tis dinner-time, or nigh; pray you be my
      guest!
You shall be very welcome, [sir, both now and at all
      times.] *

Car. I'll wait upon you.

Pol. Falorus, let me entreat your stay!

Fal. You shall command me.
          [*Exeunt* POLIDACRE, CARIONIL, *and* FALORUS.

Luc. Injurious tyrant, love! Nentis!

Nen. Madam!

Luc.   Stay a little.
How frail is any woman's resolution!

---

* Not in first edition.

I, that so seriously have often thought
Never to change my name, am now become
A slave unto a Moor! I feel the mighty
Fabric of all my maiden virtue totter.
What can befal me worse? But I may as well
Withstand a volley of shot, and as easily,
As resist these new desires. 'Tis very strange
That I, who have denied the earnest suit
Of so complete a gentleman as was
Carionil, and neglected his friend,—
For I will rather steal away, and do
Mean services to my inferiors
Than be his wife,—should doat upon a person
Some ladies scarce dare look upon,—a Moor,
A sunburnt Moor I'm utter stranger to!
What would my father say if he should know
My thoughts? Banish me ever from his sight,
And never more think of Lucora's name.
But love is not confin'd to the opinion
Of others. Oh, this is a revenge for my
Slighting of brave Carionil; yet, if
He were alive again, I could not love him.
Alas, I am undone! O that my fates
Had been so kind as to have wrought my heart
Fit and propense to have requited him!
Nentis, will you be silent of my love?
Be so good, Nentis.

Nen. Why, madam, will you have this blackamoor?
Methinks my lord Falorus is a handsomer man by
much. Alas! he will take you beyond the sea.

Luc. Nothing is strong enough to divert me.

Nen. Your secrets, madam, are as safe in my breast
as yours.

Luc. Befal what will, I am resolv'd.
Affection that doth tend
Not crookedly, but to a noble end,
Is worthy; and they stubbornly repine
At their creation who from it decline. [*Exeunt ambœ.*

ACT IV.—SCENE I.

Enter PHYLANDER *and* ANTIPHILA.

Phyl. Sweetest Antiphila!

Anti. I wonder, sir, in what I have so forfeited my
    faith
That I cannot be credited.

Phyl. Urge me not, lady, unto a belief
That will be my destruction.
Delay me rather with a little hope,
And save me from despair.

Anti. I can but say what I have said already;
You do not trust my tongue.   Pray take a parchment,
And there inscribe a sad and solemn oath,
And I'll subscribe that I will never have you.

Phyl. The fatal raven's hoarse crying
Is Thracian music unto your reply.
Would I had heard a thousand mandrakes groan,
So you had left me in silence!

Anti. I pity you; but did you know me truly, you
Would bless my denial, young Phylander.

Phyl. Bless it!   O lady,
Durst I but be so horribly profane
As to curse anything you please to do,
I would go study imprecations, and
Vent them in places that are haunted by
Wild walking devils; but my grand affection
Condemns that violence.*   Do not then suppose
That, though you were a Succubus, I durst
Utter such impious breath.   Be all the faults,
That either truth or poets' fictions
Have strewn on† women, in you, I will love you
With serious admiration.

Anti. Sir, I will release your affection.

Phyl.   Impossible!
Not the fairest creature, by diligent search pick'd out

---

* This line, "But my grand affection," etc., not in first edition.
† "Shewn in."—*1st ed.*

Of all the infinite myriads of beauties
Selected from the spacious kingdoms of
The earth, and I might choose her freely,
Should win upon my heart to dispossess you;
She should not, lady.

Anti. You will not hear me!

Phyl. Then may eternal deafness seize upon me!
Speak, lady; and though you do say the last
Word I shall ever hear, I will with joy
Be most attentive: the dark cave of sleep
Is not more quiet.

Anti. I am contracted.

Phyl. You are not, lady!

Anti. I am, sir.

Phyl. Unto my father?

Anti. No.

Phyl. Then sentence his sure death by naming him.

Anti. Will you destroy the man I love?

Phyl. And you him that loves you?

Anti. What is done cannot be undone.

Phyl. It shall!

Anti. You must not know his name therefore.

Phyl. If there be any manhood in his breast,
He shall disclose himself. I'll challenge him
By such sure circumstances, and set the papers
On public places by the play-bills, that if
He dares but use a sword he will be known.

Anti. So you will publish my disgrace.

Phyl. Too true. O lady, dear Antiphila,
Give me his name! I will not kill him foully;
We will meet fairly. I may die upon
His sword, and you thereby be freed from my
Unworthy suit.

Anti. Sir, promise me one thing, and I will tell you.

Phyl. Here is my hand; you shall charm me!

Anti. I must lie, and grossly, to be rid of his court-
    ship. [*Aside.*
It is Tandorix. You must not speak of it to any,
Or quarrel about it.

Phyl. 'Tis not! you mock me, sweet Antiphila.

Anti. Indeed, Phylander, I do not.
You will be secret for my sake, until
I do release you from your promise.

Phyl. Y'ave had my hand; silence must be my death.

Anti. I'll leave you, sir, and build upon your word,
For I perceive you are displeas'd.   [*Exit* ANTIPHILA.

Phyl. This 'tis to be a fool, which is the truest
And briefest definition of a lover.
What fury fascinated so my senses
As wilfully to make me become a slave
Unto the childish passions of a woman?
On this occasion would I understood
The saddest epithets of necromancy,
That I might join them to this sex.   O my heart!
I am o'ercome with rage, and will be rather
A perjur'd Mahommedan, and wade
Through streams of blood into her arms, than a
Soft-conscienc'd ass and let this villain have her.
Could envious hell suppose a body of
So delicate a composition could
Within it lodge a mind so poor and worthless?
This is a woman's weakness; no, 'tis a baseness
Cannot be match'd in all the faults of man.
But why am I so angry?   I will show
My fury not in idle breath, but deeds;

Enter ROSINDA.

And this shall be the time.   Thou base ambitious
Slave, before we part thou diest!

Ros. O good sir, why?   I ne'er offended you.
Heaven knows I love you best of all the world.

Phyl. Thou art the hinderance of all the bliss
I could expect or wish for upon earth.

Ros. Sir, let me hear the reason of your rage,
And, if you find that I have injur'd you,
I will not beg for life.

Phyl.   Find it!   I know it clearly,
And will not honour thee, vile man, so much
As t' let my tongue join such unequal names.

Ros. I understand you not.   Dear sir, be plain!

Phyl. Art thou prepar'd to die? If not, kneel here,
And pray thyself into a readiness.

Ros. Be not so violent!

Phyl.   Repent!

Ros. Let me understand my offence. The chrisom
    child *
Is not more innocent of wrongs to you
Than guiltless I.

Phyl.   The tears of crocodiles!

Ros. I humbly do upon my knees implore you
That you thus rashly will not take away
The life you never can restore, and will
Bewail for in an over-late repentance.

Phyl. To heaven, and not to me, make orisons.
I am resolved.

Ros. For your deceased mother's sake, at whose
Sad funeral letter I was entertain'd
Into your father's family, and for
Those tears and sighs and sorrows she did weep,
Groan, and express at her delivery of you,
Be merciful unto a faultless stranger.

Phyl. A tedious and an exquisite torture for
Thy death should not deter me from it. My mother,
Could she arise out of her wat'ry grave,
Appear in both our views, and be an eloquent
Suppliant unto me for thy life, should not
Prevail to win me to it.

Ros. Then nothing will satisfy. Keep in your sword;
I am your mother. Draw off this periwig,
And my face will establish your belief.

Phyl. It does indeed. Here, prostrate on my knees,
For my rude language I do crave remission.

Ros. And you obtain it, and my blessing too;
But you deserve blame for your violent fury.

Phyl. O let me kiss your gracious hand, and seal
My pardon on your happy lips!
Why did you grieve us for the sad report
Of your untimely end?

Ros. You shall know all anon. But yet conceal

---

* See Davenant's Works in this series, vol. i. p. 79.

My being, till your father's love be ripe,
And grown mature for a second marriage ;
I pray you, do.
  Phyl.   Mother, I will.
Now I've good hope Antiphila will be mine. [*Exeunt.*

SCENE II.

Enter CARIONIL, LUCORA, *and* NENTIS.

Car. And, my lady, you shall not wish anything,
If that an human power can obtain it,
But I will make it yours. I hope you do
Not wrong my love with a suspicion
That I cannot perform whate'er I promise ?

Luc. I do not, sir, distrust your affection ;
But give me leave to doubt I shall not live
According to my content in Æthiopia.

Car. Most noble lady, I, that have seen both places,
Dare promise you you will.

Luc. I cannot tell, sir ; I must believe you.

Car. For these few words, whose sweetness doth
  exceed
Vast and elaborate volumes of eloquence,
May all the joys that ever have made happy
The numerous Queens and Empresses that have
Been ornaments and glories to the world,
Meet unto their perfection in you.

Luc. My Tucapelo ! when I did see you first,
I fell in love as deep as lady could.

Car. And may I die when, in imperfect thoughts,
You do repent your choice. Mistress, I can
Make famous Gamara* as pleasing to you
As is your native country. You shall find
Delights above not equal to your mind.

Luc. Sir, your company shall be all things unto me.

 * *Qy.* "Amhara ?"—"Besides Aûxma, there are no cities in
Habessinia, and but few towns. They have neither castles nor
forts. The celebrated mountains of Amhara are their onely
citadels, where the King's children were formerly committed to
custody.—Lûdolphûs' *New History of Ethiopia.* Lond. 1682, *folio.*

Car. You shall not touch one drop of water but shall
Be of more virtue than the Thespian spring,
Where reverent poets of the former times
Quaff'd off huge bowls to great Apollo's health.
Young virgins, whose sweet voices do exceed
Mnemosyne's daughters, shall sing you asleep
Each night; and, when you grace the happy woods
With your rich presence, they shall make a concert
With the innocuous choristers of the spring,
To entertain the mistress of my life.

Nen. And I go thither, they shall teach me to sing.
[*Aside.*

Car. The jewel-tippets of your ears shall weigh
The curious points of precious icicles,
When Leo breathes hot vapours on the earth.
Your sedulous slaves, enrich'd by noble blood,
Shall bear your litter through the tedious streets
Of Gamara; while all the gallant youth
Within it runs to wonder at your beauty!

Luc. I do believe you love me so much, sir,
That you will show it all the ways you can;
And I do thank you for it, and love you,
And I will show it all the ways I can.

Car. O happiest speech my ears did ever hear!
Amphion's music made not such a sound;
Nor Orpheus' lute, that tam'd the stubborn spleen
Of Hell's inhuman dog, when he did play
For the redemption of his ravish'd spouse;
Nor Phœbus, when unto his gold-strung lyre
He for superiority did sing
His sweetest anthems and best madrigals
Against ambitious Pan, made harmony
To parallel the sweetness of your tongue.

Luc. If that all my endeavours can deserve
At this height your affection, by my fault
It never shall decrease.

Car. You over-act me much, but never shall
Have thoughts beyond me!

Luc. I pray you spare my company a while;
A while I would be private with my woman.

Car. Lady, I will do things unwillingly
At your command; but give me license, fairest,
To print my heart upon your heavenly lips
Ere my departure hence.—[*Kisses her.*]—The Ottoman
 Emperors,
In their immense seraglio never saw
Your matchless features in their numberless
Successive multitudes. I am so blest,
That my excessive joys cannot be guess'd.
 Luc. Nentis!   [*Exit* CARIONIL.
 Nen.   Madam.
 Luc. Unfold thy heart unto me. Let me know
What thoughts thou hast of me.
 Nen. I may offend.
 Luc. Indeed thou shalt not!
 Nen. Then I do wonder, madam, that you will
Bestow yourself, I think, unworthily.
 Luc.   How?
 Nen. This is unpleasing to you; I will be
Hereafter silent. I have offended you.
 Luc.   No; proceed!
 Nen. You are a lady until now unstain'd
With any blot, save obstinacy to
The brave deceas'd Carionil, and will you
Give the world reason, a good one,—pardon
My honest boldness, madam,—to tax your judgment,
And, which is worse, your virtue, for this choice?
Is not Falorus far more worthy of you?
Marry him, madam, and live still in England.
I'm sure my counsel would be seconded
By all the friends you have, did they but know
As much as I. But, madam, if you have
Settled your affection past recall, and are
Resolved, I will be most obedient
And secret unto all your purposes.
 Luc. And wilt thou go to Ethiopia with me?
 Nen. If I do get no servant before, and if
You will, if I dislike the country, give
Me liberty to return home.
 Luc. Most willingly.

Enter FALORUS, CLEANTHE, *and* PHYGINOIS.

Nen. My Lord Falorus !

Luc. Where ?

Phyg. If I can find the least opportunity,
I will try, Nentis, of what metal th' art made.

Fal. I hope, mistress, our company
Is not unwelcome to you.

Luc. By no means, sir.

Fal. How gently it pass'd her tongue !
.For that sweet word I kiss your hand, dear lady.

Luc. Where did you leave my father, my lord ?

Fal. Above, a-reading Guicciardin.

Nen. Sir, I can perceive when I am flatter'd.

Phyg. Earnest expressions of love deserve a better
name.

Nen. Why, sir, I cannot believe you love me.

Phyg. You need not doubt of that, mistress ; I do
With as much fervency as servant can.
I do beseech you, lady, to believe me.

Nen. They are of easy faiths that believe all their
servants say.*

Luc. What ail you, my lord ? you are not well.

Fal. Unwelcome guest, away ! I was thinking of——

Luc. Of what ?

Fal. I ha' forgot. Would they would all love me !
[*Aside.*

I am most strangely alter'd on the sudden ;
My friendship, I fear, will be too weak a tie
To make me silent.

Cle. My lord !

Fal. Thou hadst a master did deserve thee better.

Cle. But he is dead, and I am yours by his
Last legacy.

Fal. What would'st thou say ? [*Aside.*

Cle. I hope you're well !

Fal. He has found out an alteration in me ;
[*Privately.*

I must beware of public signs. I was

* This line not in first edition.

Full of Carionil; my thoughts were busy
Concerning him.
Madam, I pray you pardon my neglect
Of frequent visits; I have been too guilty.

Luc. You have not offended.

Fal. 'Tis your great goodness to say so.

Nen. This, sir, is too importunate.

Phyg. Too slack, dear mistress; but wink at my
    insufficiency.

Nen. You said you love no woman in the world
But me.

Phyg. And may you hate me if I do.

Nen. As I see you ready to give me full satisfaction
that you mean faithfully, so shall you find me willing
to requite you.

Phyg. No man can boast such happiness.

Nen. Sir, be moderate. You're not so sure of me
but, upon occasion, I can retire; neither would I have
the company take notice of us.

Phyg. You shall command me, mistress.

Fal. These passions are new to me; would I were
    private!
I never did observe her so well before.

Luc. My lord!

Fal.   What say you, madam?

Luc. You saw not my brother, Phylander, to-day?

Fal. No, truly, lady, I did not!

Luc. Your brother, Nentis says, shall shortly be
    married to
The rich widow, her sister.

Fal.   So he doth hope.

Enter TANDORIX.

Ros. Madam, dinner stays of you!

Luc.   You hear, my lord!

Fal. Nay, Anclethe, stay not for me; wait on the
    lady.
I'll follow immediately.

          [*Exeunt* LUCORA, NENTIS, PHYGINOIS, *and*
            CLEANTHE.

What ails me ?   Let me see !
What is the cause of such an alteration
I find within me ?   Doubtless it is love.
To whom ? to whom but to the worthiest
And sweet Lucora ?   Take heed, 'tis dangerous !
A sudden ruin so will seize my friendship,
And prove my former protestations
Feign'd untruths.   Cannot the noble name
Of young Carionil prevent me ?   No ;
Nor certainty of all the evil wills
Of all the friends I have.
Were both our better genius orators,
And here embraced fast my knees, and wept
Miraculous tears to quench the rising flames
Lucora's irresistible eyes have kindled
In me, or to drown this late impression love
Hath sealed upon my heart, I'd be as remorseless
As the most stern and unremoved Scythian,
And deafer than the people that inhabit
Near the Egyptian cataracts of Nile.
But I am base, base to infringe the knot
Of amity a long and serious knowledge
Of each other hath tied betwixt us.   'Twere safer
Sailing with drunken mariners between
Hard Scylla and Charybdis, than to suffer
My much divided thoughts, and forth of them
To work such a conclusion to my passions
As might hereafter confirm me noble in
The opinion of the world.   But I'm most ignorant,
And know not what to do.   Would I were so
Distraught that my own self I could not know !

[*Exit.*

SCENE III.

Enter LORECE *and* VANDONA.

Lor. Sweet mistress ! your bounty will become
An envy unto future times.
   Van. So let your love, sir.

F

Lor. But speak, my dear; what happy day shall give
A fair conclusion unto all my wishes?
Van. What haste, good servant?

Enter JAQUES.

Lor. Nay, be not angry, sweet!
Jaq. Madam, and please you, your own good servants
desire to show your worships some pretty pastime.
Van. It pleases us well; when begins it?
Jaq. E'en presently.   I'll go and tell them all what
  a woman you are.   [*Exit* JAQUES.
Lor. This is not usual with you.
Van. Indeed, servant, so seldom, that I remember
  not the like.
Sure 'tis for your entertainment.   They think I have
Been a niggard of it, and help'd to make it out.
Lor. You are too good!
Van. So you can never be.
Lor. And yet I will not fail to do my best.
Van. I pray you do not, dear Lorece, for 'tis a good
resolution.

Enter CLOWNISH MASKERS.

Lor. I see we shall have some odd thing.
Van. I wish, sir, it may prove worthy your laughter.
Lor. My fair Vandona, I believe you will have your
desire.
Van. Jaques is among them; he may move you.
Jaq. An' either of you ask what's here, 'tis a mask,
Which we actors do hope will content you;
If not, when it ends let us all part friends,
And of your attention go in and repent you.
I hope your worships will say I have pronounc'd this
  well enough?
Lor. To my content, honest Jaques.
Van. I'm glad you like it.
Jaq. Come, Hymen, thou fellow that always wear'st
  yellow,
Draw near in thy frock of saffron;
Once more, I say, appear before this gentleman here,

And this lady in the white apron.
If the boy thou dost bring has a voice fit to sing,
Let's have a merry new ballet.
Begin thou the song, and it will not be long,
We hope, before he will follow 't.

A Song.

Hymen. Say, boy, who are fit to be
    Join'd into a unity ?
  Boy. They that will permit their wives
    To live pleasant quiet lives,
    And will never entertain
    Thoughts of jealousy, if vain.
Hym. Now, boy, let this couple hear
    What should be the woman's care ?
  Boy. A wife should be secret, true,
    Most obedient, and no shrew ;
    Should obey her husband's will,
    While therein she finds no ill.
Omnes. Such a wife, and husband too,
    We do wish both him and you.

Lor. Prithee, sweet, let's be married this afternoon,
and this shall be our epithalamion.

Van. Stay my leisure, good servant ; 't will not be
long.

Jaq. Now, if you please to cast a glance hither, ye
shall see us dance.
Fiddlers, play, begin and strike ; what ye see do not
    dislike.   *[They dance.*

Lor. What a mad toy 'tis, mistress !

Van. Jaques ! this day use my wine cellar ; you and
    your company
May be as free in it as you will.

Hym. Her ladyship says well ! Good now ; ho ! let's
    go thither
Without more ado.

Jaq. Goodman Wedlock, where was your mind,
mar'le ?* Is there not a piece behind yet ? I'll not
budge a foot till I have discharg'd it.

            * I marvel.

Hym. Out with it, then!

Jaq. Mr. Marriage, put me not out with your grinning; for an' you do, all's spoil'd.

  Gentleman and madam, you have seen
  What our mask and performance hath been.
  If you like both, 'tis well; and if but one,
  Of the other would we had done none.
  For clapping your hands we care not two chips,
  We are satisfied if you join your lips.

Lor. I thank you all.

Van. And so do I.   You now may go.

Jaq. And so we must, for I ha' done.   All's done;
  this last what-do-you-call was the full end of it.

Hym. Why go we not?

Boy. I am very dry with singing and dancing.

Jaq. Follow me to the wine cellar!

          [*Exeunt* MASKERS.

Van. You must keep your promise; you are expected by this.

Lor. Lady, I kiss your hand: this is my *vale*.   As
  often as I come
I'll seal my welcome on your lips.   Farewell, widow!

Van. Remember my service to your brother.

Lor. Command me anything.   [*Exeunt ambo.*

SCENE IV.

Enter CARIONIL, *solus.*

Car. The tedious winter of my many griefs
Her calmer heavenly breath hath now blown over,
And all my tears and sighs are now converted
Into a happiness will soon be perfect.
The gallant courtier, Paris Alexander,
When he had stole the young Atrides' bride,
The sister of the two Tindarides,
And with great triumphs entered into Troy,
Was sad and melancholy unto me.
How wise the fates are!   Ere we can obtain

Perfect fruition of the thing we love,
We must break through great difficulties and tedious,
Unto the end that we may more esteem
And prize our happiness when we achieve it.
Thanks, excellent lady ! for your gracious promise ;
May every lover henceforth bless your tongue.
She hath prefix'd this hour to be the time
Wherein I shall outgrow all hope, and fix
Upon the proudest height of fortune's wheel.
Hail, happy hour !   This is her chamber window,
And this the door whereby she must escape.

Enter LUCORA *and* NENTIS, *above.*

Shine well, ye stars ! and let this project find
Your influences to a lover kind.

   Nen. See, madam, he is come ! my lord Tucapelo
     has not trespass'd on a minute.

   Luc. Then is our parting near ; your new servant
     hath prevented your journey.

   Car. Nentis !

   Luc. Most honoured Tucapelo, I am here
In presence, to give answer to my love.

   Car. Are you ready, worthiest lady ?

   Luc. I am, my love !

   Car. Neglect your jewels ; Gamara shall supply
     you..

   Luc. I care for nothing if I have but you.

   Car. Descend, my dear ! each minute is an age
Until I crown my joys with your possession.

   Luc. I come !   Nentis, farewell !   Report that my
Escape was unto thee unknown, and that
I stole away when thou wast fast asleep ;
I would not have thee blam'd for me.   Excuse
Me to my father all the ways I have
Instructed thee in.   *[Descendunt.*

   Car. Cynthia, triumph ! and let thy brother hear
His eyes did never witness such a stealth ;
Be proud in thy pale lustre, and make known
Apollo doth tell tales, but thou tell'st none.
Not yet ?   How tedious seems a moment !

Delays in love
Would raise impatience in Olympic Jove.

Enter LUCORA *and* NENTIS.

But she is entered ! Welcome, sweet Lucora !
Above expression welcome ! My crown of joy
I would not change for an imperial sceptre.
    Luc. I am most happy in your love, dear friend.
Thanks, good Nentis ! My woman cannot go
    with 's.
    Car. Then farewell, Nentis !
    Nen. May the propitious heavens
Crown both your heads with all fair fortune.
    Car. Our thanks go with you !   [*Exit* NENTIS.
    Luc. It is your promise, sir, that I shall live
Without contradiction in my religion,—
Enjoy my conscience freely : Your vow was solemn.
    Car. I do acknowledge it, and will perform it
True. Not to be denied? what a great frost chills
    my affection !
    Luc. Then I'll be confident.
    Car.   You may !
I am amaz'd and lost within a wonder.
Let me consider ; have I cause to love
A lady that hath so much neglected me
That she hath preferr'd a negro? and, 'tis likely,
When she knows me, will care as little for me
As e'er she did, and, if she meets with one
Of this complexion I feign, confer
Her perfect love upon the slave? 'Tis clear
I have no reason to do it ; neither will I,
For I am free, know liberty again :
This poor unworthiness in her hath loos'd me.
Would it not be a weakness in me—let me argue it—
To bestow myself upon a woman of
So obstinate a nature, that she lov'd me less
When she believ'd that for her sake I had
Done violence upon myself? It would be
A matchless one, beyond example, and which
Future times would admire but not parallel !.

Luc. Come, shall we hence? Delay is dangerous.
Car. No! be it what it will.
Luc. We must not stay here long.
Car. Nor will we.
Luc. Alas! what ails my noble Tuca-
pelo?
You had not wont to answer me so slightly.
Do you not love me still?
Car. No!
Luc. The heavens forbid! I am Lucora!
Car. I do confess you are, but must deny
I love you.
Luc. I could endure your sword with better ease.
Use 't, and revenge what ignorant ill I have
Committed against you. I had rather die
By your dear hand than to return from hence
With this strong poison in my breast.
Car. Kill you?
Lady, I would not do it to obtain
The sovereignty of the sea-parted earth.
Live many years in happiness; I wish it
With all my soul, else may I die unwept for.
But give me leave to leave you, and bestow
Laughter, not tears, for my inconstancy.
Think me unworthy of your worthy self,
For I cannot love you, nor will marry you.
Luc. Surely you will! Have you a cause to be
So merciless unto a passionate lady,
One that so truly wonders at your worths?
I pray you, sir, jest not so solemnly;
Thunder is music in my ears to this.
Car. I do not! Credit me, most fair Lucora,
I am in earnest, nor would I spend the time
In words. Shall I call Nentis?
Luc. Rather call basilisks to look me dead,
Than her to help me mourn your unkind parting!
O do not thus! wherein am I deform'd
So suddenly, that you so soon should leave me?
Car. This is a trouble to yourself; you cannot
Speak words enough to make me yours.

Luc. Can I not speak sufficiently ?   Then I
Will try if there be magic in my knees.
Look, sir, a lady kneels to you for love,   [*She kneels.*
To whom the noblest in the realm have sued.
  Car. All is in vain.
  Luc. Thou man, that art more lasting in thy fury
Than the Egyptian wonder through the storms
Of many bleak tempestuous winters ;
Say, worthless man, if it becomes thee well
To let a loving lady kneel to thee,
And thou be merciless and not raise her up ?
  Car. I pray you, rise !
  Luc. And will you then be reconcil'd unto me ?
  Car. No, I cannot.
  Luc.   Then will I turn a statue.
  Car. I pray you leave me, and forget me ever ;
Henceforth you shall not see me any more !
  Luc. Not see you any more ?
O faithless man, and full of perjuries !
Thy nature is transparent ; thou art false
As is the smooth-fac'd sea, which every wind
Disturbs,—a false barbarian, and born under
Deceitful Mercury.   A Briton would
Rather have died than thus have wronged me.
Thou art inhuman, and may'st boast thy conquest,
Tell your most savage countryman this act,—
If the just god of seas revenge me not,—
And number it 'mongst your proud cruelties.
  Car. Be pacified !   I pray you leave this rage.
  Luc. When I am dead I shall, and not before ;
And that shall not be long, for thou shalt see me.
Merciless man, thou shalt, and add that to
Thy bloody conquests, boast how a slighted lady
For thy unkindness made herself away.
This hand, wherewith I would have given myself
To thee, shall take me from my misery.
                          [*Offers to kill herself.*
  Car. Hold !   I am Carionil !
  Luc.   How ! say that again !
  Car. I am Carionil !

Luc.   That breath hath rais'd me and
made me myself.

Car. I counterfeited the negro to obtain you,
The wished period of my griefs; and might,
But will not love that woman that shall scorn
All my endeavours, and entertain a stranger,
An Ethiopian, and prefer him—no.
Judge, fair Lucora, if I have not cause.

Luc. Yes, yes, you have; but now you do not need
More of your rhetoric to dissuade me from you.
There are not in the world temptations
Can make me yours. I cannot give a reason;
'Tis in my nature, and a secret one.

Car. I am glad it is so.

Luc.   This is the happiest hour
My life did ever pass, and quickly chang'd.

Car. I rejoice at the alteration. Madam, you shall
Command me to do anything but marry you.

Luc. Then I command you never move me more.

Car. I will obey you.

Luc.   Now you may call Nentis.
She is not yet in bed; I see a light yet.

Car. Most willingly. Nentis!

Enter NENTIS, *above.*

Nen. What's the matter, marle ? *

Luc.   Come down !

Nen. I wonder much. I come, madam ! [*Descendit.*

Luc. You will be secret, sir, of what hath past ?

Car. You may be confident I will.

Luc. I else shall suffer much in my honour.
Women ! take heed; the men whom you deny
May win you to be theirs by policy.
They Proteus-like will vary shapes, until
Beyond their wishes they have plac'd their will.

Enter NENTIS.

Car. Your woman's come; good night !
Luc. Good night, sir !   [*Exit* CARIONIL.

---

* Besides " I marvel," this word also signifies " a gossip."

Nentis, I now will never pass the seas ;
Tucapelo is become Carionil.

Nen. Amazement seizeth me !

Luc.   Anon thou shalt know all.

Nen. I hope that now you will be ruled by your
friends, and take the lord Falorus to your husband.

Luc. Hang husbands !

Nen.   The gods bless them all, I say,
and send me a good one.

Luc. Let's to bed ! lock the door after you.

                              [*Exeunt ambo.*

SCENE V.

Enter CLEANTHE, *sola.*

Cle. How joyfully the birds salute the morn,
Warbling a welcome from their gentle throats !
But I am of another mind, poor maid !
Aurora doth no sooner blush upon
The world, but I make my complaints afresh.
I am in love, and for my wretched state
Can blame nobody, but sinister fate.

Enter CARIONIL.

Car. Well met, Anclethe ! I will hide no longer
Myself in this disguise. Again thou shalt
Be my Anclethe. Wilt thou be my boy,
And sing me songs as thou hadst wont to do ?

Cle. You have obtain'd your mistress, I see, my
        lord ?

Car. I have not, boy, nor will I seek her more ;
Some other time thou shalt receive the story.

Cle. My hour is come ; dear Cupid be my aid !
And will you never have another, sir ?

Car. I do not know, Anclethe ; but if I have,
She must not be so obstinate as this.*

Cle. But say a lady of a noble house—

---

*   —— " so obstinate as this.
    I soon should leave her if I found her such."—*1st ed.*

One that is not unhandsome—were in love
With you, did love you violently, my lord,
Would you not pity her, but be unkind ?
   Car. Boy, I do know what 'tis to love in vain
So well, and what a misery is in it,
That if she were but reasonably well,
She should not grieve for me ; indeed she should not.
   Cle. You are most noble ! old philosophy
Never defin'd a virtue which you want.
There is a lady, sir, and not ill-favour'd,
Born of an ancient honoured family,
So much in love with you, that if you do
Refuse her, my lord, you do deny her life.
   Car. What is she called, Anclethe ?
   Cle. My lord, my commission doth not reach so far;
She'd have her name conceal'd until y'ave seen her.
To-morrow morning you may meet her here.
She with a gentleman, a friend of hers,
Will here expect you about ten o'clock.
   Car. Well, I will see her, boy ! and if I find
Her answer thy report, I will be kind.
He that neglects a loving lady for
Weak causes, may the gods that man abhor !
                    [Exeunt ambo.

ACT V.—SCENE I.

A Banquet set forth ; then enter POLIDACRE, ANTI-
PHILA, SERVANTS, *and* MUSICIANS.

   Pol. You will pardon a sudden entertainment ?
   Ant. I hope we need not compliment.
   Pol. Do you instruct me.
Sit down, my sweet Antiphila, and taste. Fill wine !
All health and happiness to you, dear mistress !
   Ant. A true return of loyal thanks.
   Pol. Play a more merry tune ! I do abhor

Whatever relisheth of melancholy.
Sing "The spheres are dull;"
Apply it to yourself that best deserve it.

> The spheres are dull, and do not make
> Such music as my ears will take;
> The slighted birds may cease to sing,
> Their chirpings do not grace the spring;
> The nightingale is sad in vain,
> I care not to hear her complain;
> While I have ears and you a tongue,
> I shall think all things else go wrong.

> The poets feign'd that Orpheus could
> Make stones to follow where he would.
> They feign'd indeed; but had they known
> Your voice, a truth they might have shown.
> All instruments most sadly go,
> Because your tongue excels them so.
> While I have ears and you a tongue,
> I shall think all things else go wrong.

Ant. 'Tis pretty!
Pol. Reiterate again your yielding, lady,
And once more let your breath perfume those words.
Ant. Sir, I am yours!
Pol. And I my fair Antiphila's! your tongue
Hath made me happy.
Ant. May your joy last long!   [*Exeunt omnes.*

SCENE II.

Enter PHYLANDER *and* ROSINDA *in woman's apparel.*

Phyl. How glad I am to see you like yourself!
Dear mother, pardon an excess of joy.
Ros. Such signs of true affection need no pardon.

Enter a SERVANT.

Ser. Sir, here's a letter for you.
Phyl. For me! from whom? The hand resolves me.

Present my service to the lady that sent it:
Tell her, ere long I will come kiss her hands.

Ser. I will, sir!   [*Exit* SERVANT.

Phyl. Mother, I writ unto Antiphila,
And did desire her, for guerdon of my love,
To hold me second in her thoughts, and, if
She married not my father, to have me.

Ros. She may perform
What she believed would never come to pass.

Phyl.   THE LETTER.

"Sir,—I confess I am not contracted, and that
I told you so to make you desist. I should be exceeding ungrateful to deny you so small a request.
There is nothing hinders me from being yours but
your father; and I solemnly vow unto you, that if I
have not him, you shall have me. But let not this
beget any hope in you, for, if I be not his, it shall be
his refusal. Let it only manifest so much, that, had
I never seen him, I could have lov'd you most truly.
I pray you, let this suffice, and use me so. Choose
another mistress, and let me be her second; you will
love me well enough if you love another better.
Farewell!

Your father's

ANTIPHILA."

Ros. What writ you to her, son, concerning her
Professing a contract betwixt us two?

Phyl. That in my rage I met with Tandorix,
And offered to bereave him of his life;
Who thereupon did vow he was a woman,
And for a gentleman call'd Perimont,
Who often had denied to marry her,
That habit did assume, thereby to learn
More easily what did prevent her joy,
And whether he affected any other.
Thus I your being kept unknown.

Ros. I'm glad you did so!

Phi. You do well, mother, to wear a mask; you
shall

Thereby be sure to be concealed until
You find the fittest opportunity
Yourself unto my father to reveal.   [*Exeunt ambo.*

SCENE III.

Enter FALORUS, *solus.*

Fal. What will become of me, unfortunate man,
Who needs must live in fire or live in shame?
I know not what to speak, nor what to do,
Both fear and grief do so confound my senses.
I fear to wrong Carionil so much
As to be traitorous against our friendship;
And griefs unsufferable endure for the
Fairest of ladies, incomparable Lucora.
I would she had been kind unto my friend;
Unto him, then, I never had prov'd false.
Nor will I.   I will rather search out frozen
Climates, and lie whole nights on hills of ice,
Or rather will take powerful potions, and sleep
Out these unpleasant hours I have to live;
But then I shall not see that beauty.   Who
But senseless frantics would have thoughts so poor?
My reason forsakes the government of this
Weak frame, and I am fall'n into disorder.
Oh, I could sigh my body into air,
And weep 't into a lake, if merciless nature
Had made it of a substance suitable
Unto my wish now!   Methinks, I could level
A promontory into a province, and tread
The centre through to read the destinies
Of southern stars, and bless their fortunes that
Are born under their light, for I am confident
Their influences are more mild than ours.
There is no other fate can fall on me
Shall awe me now; I will be proud and daring,
As the ambitious waves, when wrathful blasts
Of northern winds do hoist them violently
Against the highest clouds, and rather will
Destroy myself than wrong Carionil.   [*Exit* FALORUS.

Scene IV.

Enter CLEANTHE, *in woman's apparel, and* PHYGINOIS.

Cle. And serv'd my sister well to leave her so.
Phyg. How much, dear madam, have you im-
poverished
Men's eyes by hiding your perfections
In their apparel ! Indeed, I flatter not ;
I do not know the lady owns such beauty.
   Cle. If my Carionil will like me, then
I shall attain the end of my desires.
May I appear but lovely in his eye,
And what I seem in others I will slight !
But, good Phyginois, I prithee, tell me,
In your affection what success you have ;
Is Nentis won, or do you hope she will ?
   Phyg. She's mine ! we are contracted.
   Cle. Joy wait on you,
And make your lives of many years pass pleasant !
Is it not ten ? Are all the clocks grown envious
Against my bliss, and will not let me know
How nigh his coming is ? for I esteem
Myself most happy in his company.

Enter CARIONIL, *like himself.*

   Car. This is the place Anclethe nam'd.
   Phyg. Madam, he's here !
   Cle. Befriend me, my good stars !
   Car. Here is a lady, and a matchless one !
Would two years since I had beheld this beauty,
When first I came from Spain and had my heart free ;
Then many a sad day had been merry unto me,
For unto her Lucora should have yielded.
Sweet lady, you that are the fairest creature
Nature did ever form, vouchsafe so much
Of happiness unto me as to give
Me liberty to touch your lips.—[*Kisses her.*]—Do you
Know me ? and have your ears ere heard

So poor a name as is Carionil?
But I am much mistook; you are not she
Whom here I was to meet. I needs must doubt
The fates did not intend me such a joy.

    Cle. I am!

    Car. Deceiv'd Pythagoras! hadst thou but dreamt
The sweetness of this voice, the music of
The spheres thou never hadst recorded! Speak,
Fairest and best of ladies; let me hear
If you have so unmatch'd a pity in you
As to look on me with a friendly eye.
Can you love me?

    Cle. Most noble sir, I do, most violently.

    Car. If that to live with you detained me not,
I should be griev'd that my joy for so great
A fortune did not stupify my senses,
And cast me into an eternal sleep.
Where is Anclethe? He is much to blame
In not attending you.

    Cle. Whom speak you of, dear sir?

    Car. My boy.

    Cle. I do not know a boy of that name, truly;
Nor, I think, is there.

    Car. You do amaze me!

    Cle. You may believe me, sir, for I am he.

    Car. Wonders in riddles!

    Cle. I am your page Anclethe, and sister to
Lucora, who for love attended you
Disguis'd, because I found, for the great enmity
Between our families, my father never
Would give me where I would bestow myself.

    Car. Your nurse did steal you when you was a
      child?

    Cle. Most true. This gentleman, her son, my
      friend,
Occasioned my escape, by giving me
A knowledge of my birth. His true relation
Can vindicate me from suspicion.

    Car. I need it not.
Were you not she, as I believe you are,

And mean of birth, I should account myself
A gainer by you. Sir, you have done that
Hath placed you in my heart among those friends
For whose sakes I my life will sacrifice.

Phyg. My lord, you do indebt me to your service.
In your acquaintance I shall be most honour'd.

Cle. Sir, if you please, he will relate my story.

Car. By no means ; keep it for your father, when
You do disclose yourself. But can you pardon
Those incivilities I did commit
When you was Anclethe ?

Cle. Wrong not yourself ; you did make more of me
Than I deserv'd, or could.

Car. But why, my sweet Cleanthe, would you not
Let me know who you was before ?

Cle. Dear sir, I saw how violent you was
In your affection to my careless sister,
And had no hope you would leave her for me.
And, if you did obtain her, meant to do
What my disastrous fate should prompt me to.

Car. Sweetest of all your sex !

Cle. But, if you never got her and o'ercame
Her obstinacy, to declare myself ;
If not, but love had triumphed in your fall,
I'd not have liv'd to see your funeral.

Car. The gods requite this goodness, and make me
  worthy
Of you, my dear Cleanthe. I contract
Myself upon your lips, which we will perfect
Ere you own publicly your father, for
The enmity will make him charge you otherwise.

Cle. I pray you, let us.

Car. A thousand thanks. Come ! shall we walk,
  fair mistress ?

Cle. Conclusions fair the fates to them do give,
Who constant in their loves and faithful live.

Enter FALORUS.

Car. Stay, dear Cleanthe, here is my friend ; he shall
Partake my joy. Well met, my best Falorus !

G

Fal. It seems you are not Tucapelo now.
Where is Lucora ? have you married her ?
   Car. No, I have not, friend !
   Fal.   Refrain !
I am your enemy; embrace me not !
Receive my sword, and pierce this heart, Carionil !
                                   [*Gives his sword.*
   Car. He hath not yet descried you.
Withdraw a little, dear mistress.   Sir, I pray you
To bear her company, for who can tell
What in this frenzy he may do ?
   Cle. Hereabouts we will await your leisure.
                [*Exeunt* CLEANTHE *and* PHYGINOIS.
   Car. What ails my friend ?   Let me but know the
     man
Is cause of this disorder in you, and
He shall not see the grey-eyed morning break .
From th' oriental mountains any more.
Let me partake of that unwieldy grief
Hath bow'd my friend so much beneath himself.
   Fal. Leave compliments, Carionil, and make
A passage for my soul, that it may leave
So vile a habitation as this body;
And, when I'm dead, rip out my heart, and in 't
Survey my fault, for I want words, and have
Not impudence enough to tell it you.
   Car. O, what might be the cause this matchless
     frame,
And worthiest cabinet that ever man
Inclos'd his secrets in, is so disturbed ?
Noble Falorus, think to whom you speak !
It is Carionil, whose life you do
Make burdenous to him by the suspicion
Of wronging him whom you have ever lov'd.
   Fal. You do deceive yourself; I lately have
Transgress'd against our league of amity.
If you desire to be a happy man,
And to enjoy what most you seek, be kind
Unto yourself, and run my body through.
   Car. Can I be happy and Falorus dead ?

No ; I should live a desolater life
Than e'er the strictest anchorite hath done,
And wear my body to an anatomy,
For real sorrow at such a dire mishap.
Live, then, my friend ! and may you number days,
Until arithmetic grow faint and leave you !
   Fal. You know not how much hurt you wish your-
     self.
Would you torment me twice ? If not, forget
Falorus utterly, and let me die.
   Car. I understand you not.
   Fal. Would you have me blast my own fame by
     speaking
My fault, and have me executioner
Unto myself ?
   Car. Release your soul of all her griefs, and say
From whence your sorrows have original.
Have you not oft told me of my impatiency ?
Give me now leave to be as plain with you.
The angry winds never enrag'd the seas
So much as some small grief hath done my friend.
I do conjure you by our former loves,—
For sure not long since we were friends indeed,—
To let me know why you are thus distemper'd.
I do not fear but I shall free you from
This passion, so precipitate and dangerous.
   Fal. You are most good, and get yourself, Carionil,
A name above the ablest character ;
None like it can decipher you.   And would
I always had continued Falorus,
Then I had yet remain'd your friend !   But, if
You needs must know the reason of my fury,
Draw out the sword, that, when you have receiv'd it,
Your hand and not your words may strike me dead.
   Car. Be not importun'd longer !   Ease your heart !
For, credit me, I grieve to see you thus.
   Fal. I am in love ; suppose the rest, and kill me.
   Car. With Lucora ?
   Fal. Too true.   Now curse me into dust, and with
Your breath disperse me in the air ; but spare me !

Chide me not for my falsehood, and inflict
But one punishment on me, and be that the sword.
Yet hear me speak one word or two before.
I have not woo'd her, nor have sought performance
Of that free promise that her father made me,
But faithfully have temporized with him.
Nor did I willingly consent unto
This passion; it did seize me violently.
  Car. Be you more calm. Take her, Falorus! you have
A liberty for me. I speak in earnest.
  Fal. Then all is well. Return my sword, dear friend.
Carionil, I will not hinder thee; [*Gives him his sword.*
My name shall not be blasted in thy sighs.
Fall, worthless man, 'tis pity I should live !
           [*Offers to kill himself.*
  Car. What mean you, my Falorus ? For heaven's sake leave,
And your own light rashly extinguish not !
I for Lucora do not care, and have
All my affection unto her recall'd,
And am engag'd unto another lady.
I stole her from her chamber in my disguise,
And then, bethinking me how she had us'd me,
I told her that I would not have a lady
Who would prefer a Moor before me. Her
Slighting of me made me leave her so.
  Fal. Is this not policy to delay my death ?
  Car. If e'er you found me false, believe me not.
  Fal. It then is true ?
  Car. Most true, Falorus !
  Fal. License me, friend, now to embrace you. Well met,
Carionil ! and welcomer indeed
Than ever yet man was unto me. I
Will live and owe my life unto you, and when
You please I for your sake will lay it down.
Freely I may Lucora now adore ;
And, rather than to lose her, I will try
All ways that are contained in policy.

Car. But say she never will consent ?
Fal.   I am
Most confident she will, to please her father ;
But, if she should not, I could suffer it.
'Twas not my love made me thus passionate ;
It was because in it I wronged you.
    Car. Did you not mark, when you did see me first,
A joy unusual sit upon my brow ?
    Fal. I had so much of sorrow in my heart,
That with it all my senses were possess'd.
    Car. But you perceiv'd I had left my disguise ?
What out of it did you collect ?
    Fal. I thought
Lucora had descried you, and you had
A peremptory denial to your suit.

Enter CLEANTHE *and* PHYGINOIS.

    Cle. Sir ! seeing you had made a fair conclusion,
And measuring each minute for an hour
Until I were with you, I rudely come
Uncall'd for to you.
    Car. Ever most welcome, my Cleanthe ! Friend,
This is the lady I did mention to you.
She was Anclethe, but is sister to
The mistress of your thoughts, and called Cleanthe,
Whom long since all her friends believed lost,
And have these many years left mourning for.
    Fal. A strange discovery, and admirable ! *
    Car. Some other time command the history ;
This mutually among ourselves we'll spend.
    Fal. Lady, account me servant to your virtues ;
And you, sir, may command Falorus always.
    Phyg. Your love will honour me, most noble lord.
    Cle. Sir ! I for you will intercession make
Unto my sister, and do hope shall prosper.
I will make known how much you are her servant,
And what affection my ears have witnessed ;
For I, unseen to you, did hear what pass'd.
    Fal. You will oblige me everlastingly.

         * "*Fal.* I am amaz'd."—*1st ed.*

Car. Now, let us walk!

Fal. Whosoever loyal friendship doth regard,
With fair events the gods will him reward.

[Exeunt omnes.

SCENE V.

Enter JAQUES, *solus.*

Jaq. I have a licence for my master and the brave
gallant Mistress Lorece; but it cost too much, a-
conscience. I would a writ five times as much for
half I gave for it; but 'tis the fashion among great
ones, so they have their wills they care not at how
dear a rate they buy them. This marriage is like
Christmas, when it comes it brings good cheer with 't;
we have fat venison—hold, belly, hold! and wine. I
am sure we shall want none, for the vintner had
twenty pounds on me this morning. I ha' bespoke
a merry company of fiddlers; oh, they are boon fellows!
And there will be old dancing, for I mean to sweat my
doublet quite through ere I leave.

Enter LORECE *and* VANDONA.

Madam, here's the licence your worships sent me for.
The parson and this will make all sure.

Lor. 'Tis well done, Jaques! for this, be thou the
Neptune of the cellar, raise a tempest and drown who-
ever doth go down the stairs; like old Silenus behave
thyself!

Van. When we have din'd, let's go to my lord
Polidacre's, and invite that house.

Lor. We will, my dear widow.

Jaq. 'Twill be a merry time, I see.   [*Exeunt omnes.*

Scene VI.

Enter Polidacre, Lucora, Antiphila, *and* Nentis.

Ant. I wonder we have not seen the Ethiopian
    lord to-day.
Pol. He'll not be long absent.
Lucora, thou hast my heart for thy consent;
Falorus is a worthy gentleman,
And one of an approved fashion—
He doth deserve a Princess. My Lucora,
I know his nature is most noble, else
I would not move thee for him, and although
The time is not expir'd, will you steal
So much from age and be his wife? I long
To see thee well bestow'd.
Luc. Whate'er you please t' command, I will per-
form.

Enter Falorus.

Pol. Here is Falorus! Welcome, my lord, I shall
Shortly say my son; my daughter I have won,
And, when I please, unto you she will give
Away herself.
Fal.   You are most noble!
But can you, fairest lady, look so low
As is Falorus? Can there be such a virtue
Of rare humility within you that
You thus confer affection upon me?
Luc. My lord, my father desires to make me yours,
And I have learn'd so much obedience
As willingly to do what he commands.*
Fal. I wish I could, most excellent Lucora,
Thank you in all the languages are worth
Your dear attention, you have made me so
Exceeding happy; I envy not his wealth
That owns the inexhaustible mines of fam'd Peru.
Luc. I thank you for this love, and have a hope,

* "Enjoins me."—1st ed.

If it within my power lyes, I shall
Requite you, sir.
 Fal.   My joy hath dull'd my senses.

 Enter LORECE, VANDONA, *and* JAQUES.

 Lor. Now, brother, have I not ended happily ?
Vandona is my own ; we only want
The ceremony ecclesiastical.
My lord, I am your servant !
 Fal. I have a mistress got, the richest beauty
Great Britain ever was renowned for.
 Lor. Much, very much, i' faith ; have you won her
For whom hopeful Carionil did die ?
 Fal. I won her not, Lorece ; her father's desire
Meeting with her consent hath made her mine
 Van. Sister, you have been a stranger to me ; I pray
 you be not so.
 Nen. You shall see me oftener.
 Lor. Thou may'st be Mercury, and I will glory
Thou art my brother.
 Van. Madam ! I'm very glad to meet you here.
 Ant. And I as joyful of your company.

 Enter CARIONIL, CLEANTHE, *and* PHYGINOIS.

 Lor. Wonders ! Carionil's alive again, and here !
 Pol. For some strange end he did give forth his
 death ;
But what young beauteous lady's that ?
 Luc. It is a face worthy of admiration. [*She kneels.*
 Pol. Rise, lady ; kneel not unto me.
 Cle. Then I were most unfit to be your child.
 Pol. How ! my daughter that was lost ?
 Cle. Yes, my lord ; and beg your blessing.
 Pol. May the good heavens make of thee, my
 daughter,
If you be she, an old and happy woman !
 Luc. I am a sister to you ; spare some time
For me to show how much I do rejoice
At this unlook'd for good. None of your kin,
Fair sister, are more glad than I to see you,

Whom we had never hoped to see.   I am
Most proud to be so near allied unto
So excellent a creature as you are.

   Cle. I am most joyful of your love.

   Ant. We are most glad to see you safe.

   Van. As if you were our sister.

   Cle. My thanks, sweet ladies.

   Pol. Dearest Cleanthe! confirm thy father in
His joy; relate thy life, that out of it
I may grow confident thou art my daughter.

   Phyg. Lady, leave that to me.   My lord, and if
You with her silence can so long dispense,
I would do that.

   Cle.   He is my nurse's son, to whom, my lord,
I owe all thanks for my escape.

   Pol. Sir, when you please you may begin.

   Nen. What! not a gentleman?   I am undone,
But must be secret in 't.   [*Aside.*

   Phyg.   My lord!
This lady's nurse, my mother, had a son
Older than the lady Cleanthe is by seven years;
Whom she did love so extraordinarily,
That for his sake she foully err'd from virtue.
She thought it was an easy thing for her,
If that their lives attained to those years,
To make your daughter wife unto her son,
Which is the cause she privily escap'd.

   Pol. Most strange!

   Phyg. By chance I heard this of my brother, who
Told me, against my mother's strict command,
What a great marriage he should have, and that
Cleanthe was the daughter of a lord,
Your honour's child,
Whom all we thought but of a mean descent;
For she had won the country to believe
That she did find her in the open field.
I, pitying her hard chance, did tell her all,
And promis'd her I would attend upon her
Until she had her parents happy made
With knowledge of her safety.

Cle. The rest I must relate.
Dear sir, be kind! and if I have done aught
You shall dislike, pardon my first offence.
I was no sooner come to town, but saw
This noble gentleman, with whom so violently
I fell in love, that for his sake, pray pardon me,
My own apparel I did lay away,
And did become his page. And when I did
Disclose myself, he kindly did requite me;
In brief, we are contracted.
I did not well without you to do thus,
But your forgiveness, sir, I cannot doubt.
He told me that there was a difference
Between our families, and therefore you,
If your consent was ask'd, would never yield.
 Jaq. Would I were i' the cellar! I care not for
  these dry and tedious tales.
 Pol. Whether I should or no I cannot tell,
But I am glad that it hath chanced thus;
This match an ancient discord will conclude,
And may the gods be favourable to it!
 Car. Most worthy lord, my faithful thanks!
 Phyg. Here also is a ring which by
Your father, my Lord Falorus, was given her,
When at the font he for her answer'd:
She wor't about her neck when she was stolen.
 Pol. I know it well, and now am confident
Thou art my lost Cleanthe; be his wife,
And may the heavens make up the match most for-
  tunate.
Carionil, I now am glad I have
A man so honour'd to my son-in-law.
 Car. My lord, if that I can perform my will,
You never shall repent your daughter's choice.
 Pol. I do not doubt I shall. Now, I would know
Why your death was reported?
 Car. I was in love long with your eldest daughter,
The fair Lucora, but could never win her.
Brought almost to despair, I did assume
The habit and colour of a negro.

Pol. Then you was Tucapelo?
Car. I was indeed!
Knowing she had refus'd the greatest marriages,
And many of the handsomest of the kingdom,
I fully did believe she never would
Like any man of this complexion,
And therefore feign'd myself an Ethiopian;
But first gave out my death, and that unto
Myself I had done violence for her.

Luc. Surely he will not do so unworthily
As to make mention of my fond affection.   [*Aside.*

Car. But all could not prevail.

Luc. I am glad he ends so.   [*Aside.*

Car. And therefore I desisted wholly; which, when
Anclethe saw, my sweet Cleanthe now,
She did disclose herself.

Pol. I do perceive the heavens intended you
Should reconcile our families.

Jaq. Here's love and love again! I would somebody would love me.

Luc. My dear sister, you must not think me rude
Because I do express my love so fully.

Pol. Be my Carionil!
All that are mine respect this lady, for
I do intend to make her mine.

Car. We are her servants, and most joyfully
Shall kneel unto a lady of her virtues!

Enter PHYLANDER *and* ROSINDA.

Fal. What lady's that?

Car. She's masked, and I cannot guess.

Pol. Phylander, this lady is thy sister, the lost
Cleanthe.

Phyl. Grow not too weak, my body, to contain
My soul within thee at these joys!
Fair sister, I am glad that I can name
So beauteous a lady as you are so;
For you the heavens be thanked.

Pol. Carionil's alive, and must be styl'd your brother;
Cleanthe him hath chose.

Perfect thy joys, Phylander, when thou wilt,
And hear their histories.
This lady you must call mother.
    Phyl. But I must not.
    Pol. How?
    Phyl. This here I will.
Dear mother, now confirm my words.   [*Unmasks.*
    Pol. Welcome to life, Rosinda; thy face and beauty
I do remember well.   But wherefore did you
Raise the report of your untimely death?
    Ros. That at a fitter time; this give me leave
To spend in joy.
My dear Cleanthe, for I do believe,
Because thy father doth acknowledge thee,
Thou art Cleanthe, my so long lost daughter.
Never was mother's heart so light; I cannot
Utter my joys, my tears must witness them.
To Time I am indebted that he hath
Spared my life until I see thee safe.
    Cle. I want expression; but my life shall be
A comment on my heart, wherein you shall
Perceive what your Cleanthe is.
    Phyl. Now you are mine, fair Antiphila!
    Ant. I will perform my promise.
    Phyl. Both your consents I beg.
    Pol. How's this?
    Ant. I did engage myself,
That, if I were not yours, I would be his.
    Pol. Then may the knot prove happy, and continue
A firm one while the gods do lend you breath!
    Phyl. It is my wish.
    Pol. Was you her servant, too? Wife, chide in
      secret; I was foresworn.
    Ros. We all are frail; mortality may boast
Of strength, but many conclusions deny it.
    Nen. Away! I will have none of you; I will not beg.
    Pol. You shall not need. I, for his love and care
Unto my daughter, will give him means befitting
A gentleman, which shall descend unto
His posterity; poverty shall not spoil his fortune.

Van. 'Tis nobly said! If you do like him, take him,
sister.

Nen. Now, I'm content!

Phyg. My joy is great! My thanks, sweet mistress! My Lord Polidacre, I am your grateful,
though unworthiest servant. Now, mistress, you
shall know the policy I won your affection with : my
affections being settled so high, and I poor, I made
myself Draculemion ; but your promise, worthiest
lord, hath now enriched me.

Jaq. O me! was you that merry fellow? You have
a parlous wit.

Phyg. One thing I must crave of you.

Pol. You shall obtain, sir !

Phyg. That you will pardon my mother.

Pol. I do, for your sake.

Luc. Since I perceive you in the bounteous way
Of granting boons, sir, I assume the boldness
To become a petitioner to you.

Pol. My dear Lucora, freely ask, for I
Doubtlessly shall consent to thy demand.

Luc. Seeing the gracious heavens have blessed our
house
With the recovery of my long lost sister ;
And since the powers divine have link'd her heart
To the affections of a noble gentleman,
A marriage like to grace your honour'd age
With hopeful nephews ; I humbly crave your licence
To enjoy the freedom of a single life,
For I've no inclination to become
A subject unto Hymen's glorious bondage.

Pol. Remember, my Lucora, all your promises,
And suffer not your obstinacy to cloud
The happiness of this evening.

Fal. My excellent mistress! you have rais'd me near
The zenith of all happiness, and will you
Now leave me on that mighty precipice,
To fall into a sad abyss of misery ?

Cle. My dear sweet sister! give me leave to trouble you
With a few words aside.

I saw the Lord Falorus for your sake,
Between a great affection and firm friendship,
In as high a passion as you can imagine
A noble and a faithful lover unto you.
He in his soul adores you, I am confident ;
And I'm obliged by promise to become
His intercessor for your kind affection !
I do beseech you, therefore, grace your sister,
Though bold, being younger, to importune you thus,
T' honour the Lord Falorus with your love !

Luc. I dare not, my fair sister, be so cruel
As to deny you in your first request ;
I'll entertain his flame and be his bride.
I will be plain with you ; had you been silent,
In a ship bound for Spain I had gone to-night,
With some ladies of our near kindred, towards Lisbon,
And so avoided the courtship of Falorus,
And all my father's continual importunities.
To make this escape more unexpected, and
The better to provide me for this journey,
I had consented when my father pleas'd
To marry him ; but your entreaties have
Prevailed above all my resolutions.

Fal. Dear madam ! let me beseech your assistance.

Ros. My lord, I will desire her, and am confident
I shall obtain. I pray thee, my Lucora,
Submit to the entreaties of thy friends,
And let not thy refusal of Falorus
Beget a sad look on this happy evening.

Luc. Madam ! you and my sister shall overcome ;
And though, my Lord Falorus, you may tax me
For an obstinate disposition, you shall find me,
Throughout my future days, to make amends,
And prove a very loving wife unto you.

Fal. Now you have fixed me in a fortunate
And glorious life.

Pol. I thank thee, Lucora.

Jaq. Everybody has his sweetheart but I. One or
other take pity on me, and let me not be a cypher
and stand here for nothing ! I see the fault is in my

years, otherwise serving-men are not so slighted by
ladies.   *[To the spectator ladies.*

   Pol. Let us withdraw ! you all
Shall sup with me to-night, and we'll design
The happy day that shall each couple join.

   Car. You that have mistresses, do not despair
To get them, be they ne'er so proud and fair.
One way or other, you have seen it done ;
The obstinatest lady may be won.   *[Exeunt omnes.*

THE EPILOGUE.

Lucora. The obstinate lady yet is obstinate,
And, careless either of your love or hate,
She dares continue so. Nor will I beg
Some friend within to come with his low leg,
And 's hat in 's hand, to woo your praise : It is
So poor that I had rather hear you hiss.
Our Poet bade 's be bold, for 's play was good,
And that 'twould take, if it was understood.
And so we are ; for what's our fate we must
And will endure, be 't lawful or unjust.
Unto your justice we appeal, which lies
Within your hands. Do what you please, and rise.
  Cleanthe. O sister ! this is likely to spoil all.
Gentle spectators, also give me leave.
Ladies and gentlemen, if we have said
Aught that hath pleas'd your ears, or pastime made,
Our time we have spent well : but if that we
Have tedious been, and you did sit and see
With weariness, our Poet will repent
That you this comedy we did present.
Y'ave paid the actors well; we thank you, and know it,
And wish that you would gratify our Poet.
He wants no money as the case now stands,
Yet prays you to be liberal of your hands.

TRAPPOLIN CREDUTO PRINCIPE:

OR,

TRAPPOLIN SUPPOSED A PRINCE.

H

Trappolin Creduto Principe; or, Trappolin suppos'd a Prince: An Italian Tragi-Comedy. The Scene, part of Italy. Written by Sir Aston Cokain. London, Printed by William Godbid, 1658.

THE ACTORS' NAMES.

LAVINIO, ...	*The great Duke of Tuscany.*
SFORZA, ...	*The Duke of Milain.*
HORATIO, ...	*Son of the Duke of Savoy.*
BARBARINO, } MACHAVIL, } . . .	*Two noble Florentines.*
MATTEMORES, ...	*A Spanish Captain.*
TRAPPOLIN, ...	*Suppos'd a Prince.*
MAGO, ...	*A Conjuror.*
PUCANNELLO, ...	*A Jailor.*
BULFLESH, ...	*A Butcher.*
CALFSHEAD, ...	*A Puritan.*
BARNE, ...	*A Farmer.*
TILER, ...	*A poor Workman.*
WHIP, ...	*A Coachman.*

A Notary.   A Guard.   Officers.   Attendants.

EO, MEO, and AREO, . *Devils.*

HYMEN, LUNA, MARS,
   MERCURY, JUPITER, } *Maskers.*
   VENUS, SATURN, SOL,

ISABELLA, ...	*Wife to Lavinio.*
HORTENTIA, ...	*Wife to Sforza.*
PRUDENTIA, ...	*Horatio's Mistress.*
HIPOLITA, ...	*The Captain's Mistress.*
FLAMETTA, ...	*Trappolin's Sweetheart.*
MRS. FINE, ...	*A Plaintiff.*

THE PROLOGUE.

GALLANTS, be 't known ! as yet we cannot say
To whom we are beholding for this play ;
But this our poet hath licens'd us to tell,
Ingenious Italy hath liked it well.
Yet it is no translation ; for he ne'er
But twice in Venice did it ever hear.
There it did take, and he doth hope, if you
Have your old humours, it will please here too.
He swears he hath not spoil'd it, and protest
We think it good, though he doth none o' th' best.
You often have heard worse i' th' house before,
And had we made the Prologue we'd say more.
That labour he hath sav'd us, 'cause he would
No partial friend should cry it up for good.
An excellent new comedy, as you say
When you have seen 't, he so will judge his play.
He is not peremptory, like to some
Who think that all is best from them doth come.
Ladies and gentlemen, you that do know
To censure rightly, as you think, so do ;
Our poet scorns to beg your hands, yet faith,
That at the end if he the favour hath,
This shall not be his last ; that he'll endeavour
To gratify you shortly with another.
Howe'er it takes, he for your presence sends
His thanks by me, and hopes we shall part friends.

SIR ASTON COKAIN, in the prologue to this play, advances the plea that, although he founded the design upon a piece he saw twice during his stay at Venice, it is not a translation. The original plot, however, in so far as it relates to Trappolin in his judicial character, is borrowed from a story in the *Contes de Duville*. The play appears to have been produced prior to the Restoration, and was revived after that event, with a new prologue written by Duffet. It was subsequently altered by Nahum Tate, and acted as a new piece at the Theatre in Dorset Garden, 1685, under the title of *A Duke, and no Duke*. This "farce" was printed in the same year in 4to, "with the several new songs set to music, with thorow basses for the theorbo or basse viol." These songs are three in number, but there is no marking in the text as to where they were intended to be introduced.

The play, so altered, was frequently performed throughout the last century, and was exceedingly popular. Nevertheless, the editors of the *Biographia Dramatica* say respecting it : "Probability, and even possibility, is broken through, and very little wit or humour to compensate for such irregularity. Yet, as its absurdities are of a kind adapted to excite the laughter of the vulgar, it has been revived at several times with little alteration and by different titles, and is even now [1812] sometimes acted at both theatres, tho' in a very curtailed and mangled manner, under the title of *Duke, and no Duke*." Robert Drury, who writes three other dramatic pieces, converted Cokain's play into "a farcical ballad opera," which was produced at Drury Lane in 1732 with much success, with the title of *The Devil of a Duke, or Trappolin's Vagaries*. The alterations differed from those of Tate, while twenty-one entirely new songs were interspersed throughout.

A combined version of the two altered editions was printed at Edinburgh in 12mo in 1733, "and sold by Allan Ramsay." The title is the same as that of Drury, but "as acted at the theatres of London and Edinburgh." In this all Drury's songs are retained, with exception of the finale, which, from having been a duet between Trappolin and Flametta, to the air of *The Yorkshire Tale*, is superseded by a duet between Lavinio and Trappolin, to the tune of *Nancy's to the Greenwood gane*. In addition, there are other fifteen songs, all to Scotch airs, from which it may be concluded that the publisher—the distinguished author of *The Gentle Shepherd*—was the adapter of

the piece, and that these songs emanated from his own pen.
The cast of characters at the Edinburgh Theatre was : —

Lavinio, Duke of Florence, . .	Mr. Paterson.
Brunetto, Prince of Savoy, . .	Mr. Ware.
Barbarino, } Lords, . . .	Mr. Miller.
Alberto, }	Mr. Fraser.
Mago, a Conjuror, ...	Mr. Bulkelley.
Trappolin, a Buffoon—False Duke, .	Mr. Wescomb.
Quaker, ...	Mr. Price.
Captain, ...	Mr. Mayfield.
Isabella, Duchess, ...	Mrs. Ware.
Prudentia, Duke's Sister, . .	Mrs. Woodland.
Flametta, Trappolin's Sweetheart, .	Mrs. Miller.
1st Woman, ...	Mrs. Bulkelley.
2d Woman, ...	Mrs. Ayres.

In July 1818 a comic melodramatic burletta, called *The
Duke and the Devil*, was produced at Covent Garden, and ran
for several nights. A magazine notice of the time says it is
"founded on an ancient tragi-comedy taken from the Italian,
and titled, *Trappolin Creduto Principe; or, Trappolin supposed a Prince*, written by Sir Aston Cokain, and first printed
in 1658. It possesses an infinite deal of humour. Fitz-William
played *Trappolin*, and in his extravagant and ludicrous per-
sonation of the *Duke* reminded us of Munden's *Sam Dabs*,
and in his drunken scene of Charles Kemble's *Cassio*, kept the
house in a continual roar of laughter; and Miss Beaumont
sang a sweet song very prettily." This is the latest account
we have of this piece, which, with fresh and judicious alteration
to suit the taste of the present day, might even now be revived
with profit to some enterprising theatrical manager.

TRAPPOLIN CREDUTO PRINCIPE:

Or, TRAPPOLIN SUPPOSED A PRINCE.

———◆———

ACT I.—SCENE I.

Enter TRAPPOLIN, *solus.*

MY wench Flametta is a dear rogue; the pretty fool dotes on me. My Lord Barbarino can do nothing with her; his pistolles and jewels she cares not for. And 'tis a handsome thing; no pomatum e'er touch'd her lips, or paint her cheeks, yet are they cherries and roses. I am most happy to be what I am, and to have the love of such a one as she.

Enter FLAMETTA.

Fla. Good morrow, Trappolin! how does my love?
Tra. First let us kiss, and after I will tell.
For ever thine, Flametta!
Fla. Oh, thanks, my dear!

Enter BARBARINO.

Bar. The villain Trappolin has a handsome wench, and, which angers me, an honest one. I have spent many weeks about her, but never could do any good; she will not, neither for love or money. And see where they are a-talking together.
Tra. Yonder is my Lord Barbarino! My dear Flametta,—I am your honour's servant,—this free promise of thine I can never enough thank thee for. —At your lordship's command.—How happily shall

we live together in marriage, both loving so well and truly!—Your honour's humble slave.—Let us kiss again!—Your poor vassal, my lord.—Thus will we spend our days in these delights; so will we kiss, Flametta!—I beseech your honour to pardon me.— We ne'er will be aweary of ourselves; if thou dost sigh, thy Trappolin will weep.—Your honour shall command me always.—And when thou sing'st, thy Trappolin will dance!

Fla. And I am thine, my honest Trappolin,
And ever will be constant unto thee.

Tra. I'll attend your honour presently.

Fla. There's no man alive shall make me prove
Unfaithful unto thee, so much I love.

Tra. Your lordship must pardon me a little;
I am something busy.

Fla. My Trappolin shall not bestow a kiss
But I will pay it him with usury.
It is impossible for thee to be
More thy Flametta's than Flametta's thine!

Tra. I will come to your honour presently.

Fla. Pardon, sweetheart! that now I must be
     gone;
My stay another time shall make amends.
A kiss, my dear, my lovely Trappolin;
With such I shall be never satisfied.   [*Exit.*

Tra. Farewell, my dear rogue! My lord, I come.
Your honour must pardon me—you saw how I was employ'd; I could not leave the poor fool. Your lordship sees she loves me, and protest her labour is not lost. Now, if your honour hath anything to command me, I am ready,—Trappolino, your poor servant!

Bar. You are a saucy, peremptory villain,
And I have well perceiv'd your base demeanour;
Although I see the wench is yours, you shall
Repent the freedom of your evil language—
Be sure you shall.   [*Exit.*

Tra. Good morrow, my lord!
Let him do his worst, I care not a rush for him. He would ha' my wench, and I am glad I abus'd him. I

ha' made his honour something choleric; let him
digest it how he will. [*Exit.*

Enter LAVINIO, *the Great Duke,* PRUDENTIA,
BARBARINO, MACHAVIL, *and others.*

Lav. The Tuscan glory have we yet upheld,
And from the fierce assaults of enemies
Rescued our cities, set them in a peace
As happy as the gods did e'er vouchsafe.
Sforza, the Duke of Milain, our old friend,
Who hath in all our wars still sent us aid,
Hath promised me the matchless Isabella,
His sister, for my wife; and, seeing now
We have no more to do with enemies,
I will to Milan go, and marry her,
And quickly unto Florence will return,
Where I will celebrate our nuptial
With that magnificence becomes our state.
You, whom I ever have found faithful to me,
Lord Barbarino and Lord Machavil,
To you I do commit the government
Of Tuscany until I return,   .
And full commission to do what you shall
See necessary for the good of Florence.
My dear Prudentia, the only joy
Of our deceased father, the last duke,
Live happy, and enjoy your own desires,
Which I do know are virtuous all.
  Pru. Most noble sir, it is impossible
That I should happy be and you not present;
But I am unworthy to beseech your stay.
Go! and be fortunate in a worthy choice,
While I to Heaven pray for your safe return.
  Lav. Dear, sweet Prudentia, and also lords,
Look well unto my prisoner Brunetto;
Yet let him want nothing but a free release,
For sure he is more than he seems to be.
I have been long about this journey; now
All things are ready.   My Prudentia,
Farewell; and, sister, be not melancholy,

For in few weeks I will return, and bring
A sister home to keep thee company,—
The beauteous Milainese.
   Pru.   And may she prove
According to your wishes, noble sir!
   Bar. And be a joy unto the Florentines!
   Mac. And be a happy mother, that there may
Not want an heir unto your highness!
   Lav.   Our thanks.
Onward! 'tis time I were upon my way.   [*Exeunt.*
   Bar. Now will I be reveng'd of Trappolin,
Who hath so boldly to my face abus'd me;
I have authority to do't withal.
I'll make him to repent his sauciness.

Enter TRAPPOLIN.

He's here! but I will do 't as if by justice.
   Tra. I can think of nothing but my pretty villain
Flametta! O 'tis a dear rogue! and she says she loves
me, and I know she does. When I have married her
I will betake me to the country, where we will live as
jovial as the day is long.

Enter MATTEMORES, *the Spanish Captain.*

   Mat. I'll fight for Florence while I have a vein
To hold my heart from falling unto death;
Nor shall the Longobardy Mantuans
E'er win a flag while I am in the field.
I'd make the Tuscan duke to know the man
Whom he hath trusted to conduct his troops,
Durst but Gonzaga ever stir again.
Methinks there is no nobler thing on earth
Than to see hills of bodies, lakes of blood—
No braver music than the martial drum,
Nor diapasons sweeter to the ear
Than unto it the warlike trumpets make.
When I but hear this harmony, I could,
Full of delight, venture my single person
Against an armed troop. Away with peace!
It is the canker and the bane of minds;

'Tis that which makes us to forget ourselves,
And spend our lives in sensuality.
Then glorious war, advance thy armed arm,
That soldiers may have ways to show themselves!
Would Goths and Vandals once again would come
Int' Italy, or Moors into our Spain,
That Mattemores might wear out his sword
With hewing bones and cleaving armed men!
Each thing doth to his centre fall, and I
Would unto mine, which is to fight or die!
Who art thou?

Tra. I?

Mat. Ay, you! What! are you too good to be asked?

Tra. I am Trappolin!

Mat. By that I know not. Art thou a man of war?
Is Trappolin in any captain's roll?
Is 't writ?

Tra. Yes, Seignior Captain, in the parson's book,
The day thereof my baptism is set down.

Mat. And in that honour oft hast thou e'er fought
With infidels, and slain a score or two?

Tra. Not I, heavens be prais'd! A score or two, said
you, Captain? Then should I sure never escape, for,
I promise you, many an one is hang'd for killing of
one.

Mat. Fie! what an ignorance is this! Hast thou a
mind to become now a soldier?

Tra. Indeed, Seignior Captain, I cannot resolve you
as yet. I am about a wife; I'll ask her if she will turn
soldier too, and then, if I like it, there's an end. But
I pray you, Captain, what is a soldier?

Mat. A soldier, Trappolin, is he that does
Venture his life a hundred times a day—
Would in his country's and his prince's cause
Stand cannon shot, and wood of steeled pikes—
Would, when his body's full of wounds, all night
Lie in the field, and sleep upon his helm.

Tra. Good Captain, pardon me! neither I nor Flametta will be soldiers. Heavens defend! Venture
my life so many times a day? there is more safety and

gain in turning thief! I love my country and prince
well, but myself better. 'Tis good sleeping in a whole
skin; 'tis better lying with Flametta in a warm bed!
Marry, I had thought a soldier had not been such a
fool! How many of them might there be in Florence,
sir Captain?

Mat. Thou coward, many hundreds.

Tra. The gods send them more wit, that's e'en all
that I can say. But I pray you, sir Captain, now I
think on 't, persuade my father and mother, sisters,
and uncles, and aunts, and all the kin I have, to turn
soldiers, that they may be kill'd quickly, and I be
their heir. I swear, Captain, you should lose nothing
by 't; I would give you a good present for 't.

Mat. Base coward!

Tra. Good Captain, what is the meaning of coward?
I have often heard that word, and would fain know
the true meaning of it.

Mat. A coward is a fellow base as thou,—
One that doth spend his precious time in sloth—
Cares not what alterations kingdoms have,
So he at home may welter in his pleasures;
A fellow that had rather sit all day
Drinking tobacco, and carousing cups,
Than dye his sword in blood of enemies.

Tra. Why then, Captain, in faith I am a very
coward; 'tis better by half than a soldier. I know
there is far more pleasure in a glass of good wine and
a pipe of true Varines than in bullets whizzing about
one's ears, and pikes or halberts, or what you will,
a-beating out one's teeth.

Mat. Thou dunghill wretch!

Tra. Seignior Captain, be not angry, for I vow I
mean earnest. I should never digest the soldiery life,
nor, am I sure, would Flametta; and the gods help
them that do!

Mat. Thou earthen-minded slave, 'tis pity thou
shouldst eat or drink that hast no better thoughts!

Tra. Not as long as I pay for 't. What the devil
have I to do with your soldiery, sir Captain? Give

me leave to be of my own mind, and a coward, for I'm sure no wise man but would say as I do; let those follow your wars that are aweary of their lives.

Mat. Thou art as dunghill a minded rascal as e'er I heard in my life. I would not for anything thou wast a Spaniard; thou wouldst be a slander to the whole nation. And, villain, I tell thee if thou wert one I would kill thee; Mattemores would do it, and so I leave it. [*Exit.*

Tra. Farewell, my Sir Don; go hang yourself! What have I to do with your wars, trow? For nothing would I venture to fight but Flametta, and for her I durst not exceed about it fisty cuffs, or a bout with a little pair of cudgels at the most. I should never endure to shoot off a gun, not I; the very noise of it would make me endanger my breeches.

Enter HORATIO.

Brunetto, honest Brunetto! how dost do? Be merry, man; this time will have an end, man, and till it come be as jovial as thou canst. Thou wouldst e'en 'a bless'd thyself to have seen how I vex'd the patience of my Lord Barbarin.

Hora. You have not, sure?

Tra. Marry but I have, and to the purpose too!

Hora. Then you are undone, Trappolin.

Tra. Why, man?

Hora. The Duke has left him and the Lord Machavil governors till his return.

Tra. The devil he has!

Hora. 'Tis very true.

Tra. Troth, then, I am but little better, I fear.

Enter OFFICERS.

1 *Off.* That's he!

2 *Off.* Lay hold on him!

Tra. Brunetto, I am undone! thy Trappolin must to the jail. Pray you, my small friends, give me leave to speak but one word; remember me to my sugar-candy, Flametta.

3 *Off.* Away with him !
4 *.Off.* To prison with the saucy rogue !   [*Exeunt.*
Hora. I came to Mantua to aid the Duke,
My uncle, 'gainst his foes the Florentines ;
Where, hearing every man to praise the beauty
Of sweet Prudentia, the report did win me.
Being taken in the wars, I was not sad,
Because I was to go where she did live.
But seeing so many Princes all desirous
To marry her, I knew the great Duke never
Would bestow her on Savoye's second son ;
And therefore yet I have concealed myself.
Nor doth she know I am Horatio :
For want of opportunity, I yet
Could ne'er so much as sigh within her hearing.

Enter PRUDENTIA *and* HIPOLITA.

Hip. The Lady Isabella, by her picture,
May be supposed to be a matchless fair one ;
Each feature of her face is wondrous good,
And her fine head of hair 's a curious colour.
Pru. In her we shall be happy all, for she,
The world reports, hath, equal to her form,
A noble and a virtuous mind. Who's that ?
Hip. He is your brother's prisoner, called Brunetto,
That in the wars of Mantua was took.
Pru. 'Tis a handsome man !
Hip. And thought of all the court a gentleman
Of good descent ; but he hath not disclosed
His parentage to any.
Pru. Why doth he not ?
Hip. That no man knows yet besides himself.
Pru. How melancholy he doth seem !
Hip. He hath good cause for it, madam ;
Who can be merry in captivity ?
Pru. 'Tis true.
A gentleman of good descent suppos'd ?
I never saw a man of braver carriage,
Nor one that pleas'd me better than he doth.
Aha !

Hip. Why sigh you, madam?
Pru. To think of fortune.   Perhaps this prisoner
Is of a house as good as the Medicis—
He hath lived before the wars of Mantua
In all the happiness you could desire;
And now we see him thus!
   Hip. Methinks I hear him sigh.
   Pru. And so do I.
   Hip. He's gone!   [*Exit* HORATIO.
   Pru. But with how sad a gait!
Methinks I am not as I was before.
Hipolita!
   Hip. Madam?
   Pru. Prithee go tune my lute, I have a mind
To sing a little; I shall forget to play
If I so seldom use it.
   Hip. I go, madam!   [*Exit* HIPOLITA.
   Pru. I have sent her hence that I might search
      my heart,
For sure it is not as it lately was;
It is so full of thoughts, I cannot find
The free access into it I had wont.
What should the reason be? what have I done
To breed this alteration?   Nothing I.
Ere I came here I felt myself as free
From this strange—what it is I cannot tell.
The place is not bewitched sure, nor have
I seen aught but this hapless prisoner.
Alas! poor gentleman,—for in his looks
And in his carriage I can guess him such,—
How little to the fates art thou beholden
To let thee live a prisoner thus!   How now?
What is 't I say?—talk of Brunetto?   Oh!
I am in love, the gods will have it so!   [*Exit.*

SCENE II.

Enter BARBARINO, MACHAVIL, MATTEMORES, *and*
OFFICERS, *leading* TRAPPOLIN *after them.*

Bar. This man, Lord Machavil, is one of those
That doth in Florence nourish vice: he is
A pander,—one that, if he sees a stranger,
Straight makes acquaintance with him, for what end
Yourself may guess.   So he may gain thereby,
He would betray our daughters, lead our sons
To brothels, vicious and full of rottenness.
   Tra. I wonder how the devil he came to know any-
     thing that I did.
   Bar. This writing yesternight was presented to me.
Here you may see what enormities he is guilty of.
   Tra. His lordship would show himself a great hater
of bawdry.
   Mac. 'Tis good we did examine him.
   Mat. And there is not such a coward in Tuscany—
He's able to corrupt an army.
   Tra. Seignior Captain, never fear it, for I ne'er
mean to come into one.
   Bar. Bring him before us !
   Tra. Ah, that I durst tell my lord's excellence why
he deals thus with me !   'Tis for a wench, and yet how
eager he is against bawdry !
   Off. Forward, Trappolin !   go before their excel-
lencies.
   Bar. Sirrah !   this paper doth not only show
You are a rogue, your looks declare you one;
Thou hast as ill a face as e'er I saw.
   Tra. And yet Flametta think'st as good as his ;
I did not lie and if I said a better.
   Mac. Ere we come to this panderism, I'll examine
him about other matters.   Sir, do you never use to
carry pistols about you ?
   Tra. Sometimes, and please your excellence, I do.
   Bar. Write down that, notary.

Tra. What does your lordship mean? I did not steal them.

Mac. I know well enough what I do. Sirrah! you want to shoot somebody!

Tra. Beseech your honour to take me along with you; I mean money.

Mac. That's vain! then, notary, tear it out.

Bar. Do you ne'er carry other arms neither?

Tra. Many times, my lord.

Bar. Notary, down with it! he shall be talk'd with for that.

Tra. Your honour is deceiv'd again; I meant only arms upon seals, or scutcheons from the heralds.

Mac. This is nothing, notary; tear it out!

Bar. A pimp I'm sure he is.

Mac. Do you never carry no love-letters, as from a gentleman to a lady, or a gentlewoman to a cavalier, or so?

Tra. Oh, very oft, my lord.

Bar. Do you so, indeed? Notary, write it down!

Tra. Your honour must understand me; letters of love, of friendship,—as when a lady writes unto her brother at Sienna, a wife to her husband at Pisa, a son to his mother at such a place, a father to his daughter married at such a town. I am often hired, and carry them to the post.

Mac. Notary, you must tear out this too!

Bar. But, sirrah! to come nearer to the matter,
Do you not keep intelligence with whores?
Have you ne'er played the ruffian? By your means
Hath no man been provided of a lodging?

Tra. This I have no excuse for; the whole city
    knows me a pimp,   [*Aside.*
And that it is very nigh my living.

Mac. What say you, sirrah?

Tra. My lords! I am but a poor fellow, and must live

Bar. By bawdry?

Tra. 'Tis but a friend's part.

Mac. A wicked one's. Notary, down with this at large!

I

Tra. Alas, my lord, what hurt is it? If I help a gentleman to a sound wench, where is there any fault? Good your honours, consider me; think not I am a man alone in this business—that many others live by it as well as I.

Bar. What an impudency is this!
Not only to do ill, but to defend it,
Is a transgression exceeds forgiveness.

Tra. Good my lord, take pity on me! Well-a-day, what should I do? I have not only done a favour in it for myself, but also a courtesy for many a gentleman.

Mac. Do not tear out that, notary.

Tra. Beseech your honours, let him tear't out!

Bar. What shall we do with this villain?

Mac. Why, let's hang him! and there's an end of him.

Tra. That's true, i'faith. Consider, my lords, that never man was put to death for such a matter, but rather that they have been beloved, and well paid by noble men and cavaliers.

Mac. Had we not best to condemn him to the galleys? or let's banish him!

Bar. Ay, that's the best!

Tra. Beseech your honours, pity me!

Mac. After to-morrow, Trappolin, if thou be'st seen in Florence thou shalt die—be hang'd! we banish thee for term of life! therefore prepare against to-morrow to be gone.

Tra. Pray your honours!

Bar. Notary, write down he's banish'd!

Mac. You rogue, it is irrevocable, and therefore make you ready.

Tra. I think I am the first man that ever was banish'd for such a matter. Were all of my profession in the city served so, I think we should make an army royal of us.

Bar. This matter is concluded, Trappolin;
Go, seek your fortune! My Lord Machavil,
We may depart.   *[Exeunt.*

Mat. Thou man of dirt, hadst thou a soldier been,
This banishment had never been pronounc'd.

Tra. But, sir Captain! I fear I should have been
kill'd, which is worse.

Mat. If for thy country, 't had been a noble death.

Tra. I had rather live, Captain, than die nobly.

Mat. Thou man compos'd of sand, in vain I spend
My breath to talk with such a slave as thou;
Go and be hang'd! for so thou dost deserve,
And might I judge thee, it should be thy end. [*Exit.*

Tra. Thou brazen-headed coxcomb, mayst thou go
to the devil with a drum before thee! I had as lief
be banish'd out of my country, and walk in peace, as
be out on 't in the wars.

Enter HORATIO.

Brunetto! O Brunetto! I must leave thee! I must
begone, man, to-morrow. Farewell, Florence!

Hora. Why, what's the matter, Trappolin?

Tra. Why, I have banish'd the Lord Barberino,
and the Lord Machavil.

Hora. How? you banish'd them?

Tra. They have banish'd me, or I them—'tis all
one; ordered away, and the devil a bit a money I
have. Hast thou a mind to a wench, Brunetto? Or
if thou hast no mind to one, knowest thou anybody
that has? I'd fain be earning a little money.

Hora. I wish thee well. Live honest, Trappolin,
And so thou shalt be sure to prosper better.
This ring I give thee; sell it, and the money
Spend to maintain thee.

Tra. Honest Brunetto! faith,
An' ere I can I will requite thee fully.
Farewell! I must also take my leave
Of my Flametta! We shall cry together,
Like unto schoolboys that are to be whipt. [*Exit.*

Hora. Alas, poor simple Trappolin! I pity
Thy fortune, yet 'tis better far than mine!
Of all mankind I am most miserable,
And lead a life would make a soul prove mortal;

Yet do I not repine. Most dear Prudentia !
I never can endure enough for thee,
So that at last I may attain my wishes.
There 's not a grief mankind did ever suffer,
Nor pain, I would not pass to make thee mine !
Thou art the centre of my wishes ;—all
Horatio's thoughts upon thy beauty fall !

Enter PRUDENTIA.

Pru. O heavens, be merciful ! and if I tell
Him I am his, let him say he is mine !
I have a fire within my breast must out—
Longer I cannot hide it ! If he now
Does not woo me, I shall solicit him.
How sad a pace he walks ! how melancholy
Does he look ! Love compels us unto things
In others we would scorn. I'll speak unto him,
Because I fear he dares not unto me.
Brunetto !
Hora. Divinest lady !
Pru. I thought a gentleman, for so I guess you,
Could have endured affliction better far,
That in the wars durst venture so his person.
Hora. Most excellent Princess, many thousand men
Can suffer well the dangers of a battle ;
But there are few, or none at all, that can
Bear out the passions of a mind afflicted.
Pru. Then you are discontent. Alas ! you long for
Your liberty ; and, truth, I cannot blame you.
Hora. Then should I hate myself, being a slave to
     one
Whom I desire evermore to serve.
Ye that command the destinies of men,
Now let me die, and if I shall not prosper !
Know, noblest lady ! that the prisoner
That speaks unto you is a Prince by birth.
I am Horatio, second son unto
The Duke of Savoy, and the Piedmont Prince.
At Mantua the fame of your perfections
Captiv'd my soul ; and when that I was took

I did account myself a happy man,
Being to go where you did live.   I know,
Most dearest Princess, that I am unworthy
So great a'happiness as is your love ;
Yet if you deny me—witness Heaven !—
I never will return to Turin,
But here die languishing for your refusal.
The Duke, my father, soon would pay my ransom ;
But thraldom, for your sake, I have esteemed
Above liberty and pleasures of a court !

    Pru. My thanks, most gracious heavens ! Bru-
      netto is
A Prince ! Most worthy, brave Horatio,
I scorn to dally with my happiness,
Like some that love to counterfeit their joys !
Know I do love thee dear as my own soul,
And that, if thou hadst now been silent, I
My heart unto thee had disclosed. Live happy !
And, if it in my power lies, thou shalt !

    Hora. Doubt, fear, despair, begone ! I am a man
That envy not the blessed lives of Kings !
Now she hath deign'd to say these happy words,
I care not though all mankind threaten me.
Most excellent and mercifullest lady,
Y 'ave raised me to a joy beyond my thoughts !
May all the gods requite you for this goodness,
And I wear out my life to do you service !

    Pru. My dear Horatio, enough ! I doubt not
Thy affection 's equal unto mine. We will
Love while we live ; and may we die forgotten
When we do cease to love ! Say I not well ?

    Hora. Admired Princess, you outspeak me much,
But never shall outlove me !

    Pru. Heavens be kind !
And make us in two bodies have one mind. [*Exeunt.*

Act ii.—Scene i.

Enter Trappolin, *solus.*

Tra. This banish'd life is very doleful! I walk I know not whither, and every step I go Flametta comes into my mind. I think how she cried when we parted, and swore that she would go too; and certainly so she would, if I had not told her she was not banish'd, and might not. Farewell, my true Flametta! and the devil take the two scurvy lords Barbarino and Machavil; for Captain Mattemores, he is a prattling ass. But, by my conscience, he could ne'er ha' turn'd me loose for such a matter. Farewell, my draughts of Montefiascone, and Bologna sausages! Methinks this is a very melancholy place—I have not seen a living body these two hours but they had wings or four legs. Let me bethink me whither to betake myself, for in Tuscany stay I must not. I'd to Rome and turn friar if I had any Latin in me. There is nothing of Milain or Naples, without I mean to turn soldier for one dinner a day. Farewell, all my good suppers I was wont to have! the wenches I help'd gentlemen to! Venice—ay, that's the likeliest place of all; and there I'll follow my own trade— I love to be fing'ring of Mons and Polax ryals. Well, then, I'll to Venice, and turn pimp; it is a good, gainful life in Italy, full of ease and pleasure— especially if the flesh be young and handsome. Methinks I hear a bustling in yon trees: I hope it be not a thief, for then I shall lose the ring Brunetto gave me, and may go hang myself. Yon's an old man; and he be one I care not, for sure I shall be good enough for him.

Enter Mago, *a conjuror.*

Mago. Son, you are banish'd; I know all the matter.
Tra. 'Tis true, old friend; I am indeed! But how the devil came you to know it?

Mago. Why, the devil told me!

Tra. Alas, that e'er I was born! I pray you, father conjuror, do not hurt me!

Mago. Son Trappolin, I am so far from hurting thee, that thee I do intend to make a Prince.

Tra. I pray you, pardon me, father conjuror; I have no mind to domineer or swagger in hell.

Mago. You understand me not: thou shalt return to Florence.

Tra. And be hanged there for my labour.

Mago. Be honoured there, and be suppos'd the Duke, who now in Milain is about his wife.

Tra. Faith, if you can bring this about, father conjuror, I should laugh indeed. But suppose it could be done, when his Highness comes woe be to my neck!

Mago. No fear at all. Leave all to me, and but remember what I say, and thou art safe.

Tra. Faith, I know not what to think of this, but conjurors can do much.

Mago. I'll do it, never doubt. Come near to me! Within this circle go, and do not fear though thou seest devils skip about thee.

Tra. Father conjuror, farewell! I'd rather live in banishment than see the devil.

Mago. Thou silly fellow, do not fear! In this,
Myriads of fiends dare not, nor can they, hurt thee.
Here thou shalt stand as safe from any danger
As ever thou didst yet in any place.
Think'st thou I have so little power over spirits
As they dare disobey what I command?
Tell me thy wish, and, if thou hast it not,
Before thy face I'll sink away with fear.
Give me thy hand, and come!

Tra. Father conjuror, i' faith I wish nothing more than what you have promised me already. Could that be done, I need ne'er be a pander again.

Mago. Why do you stay?

Tra. Shall I be safe?

Mago. As free from peril as you can desire.

Tra. Why, then, I'll venture, being for such a matter.
But, honest father conjuror, if for fear I chance
To die, let not your devils take my body.

Mago. Come, do not fear at all! there is no need.

Tra. I will venture ; but I pray you let not the
devils come too near me.

Mago. You that below frequent the Stygian lake,
And in Cocytus' waves do bathe yourselves—
You that upon the strands of Phlegeton
Do use to walk, attend unto my charms—
Appear! I charge thee to appear, thou fiend!
Thou that over man's head power hast, appear!
Eo, thou spirit, come!

Tra. Good father conjuror,
Let not the devils be too ugly, lest
I play the sloven, and annoy your nose.

Mago. Fear not!

Tra. Honest master conjuror, yonder comes your
devil. Pray you circle me once more, for I'm afraid
he'll be too bold with me.

Mago. Not all the fiends that are in hell can do
The least annoyance to thee, Trappolin ;
Thou art safe, and so believe thou art. Come, Eo!
Give me that hat enchanted.

Eo. Here it is!
Command me aught else ?

Mago. No, vanish now!
Son Trap., observe me well. This hat
Keep always on thy head ; 'tis Eo call'd—
One of the things will make thee thought a Prince.

Tra. 'Tis none of the handsomest ; mine's of a
better block. I think some Naples devil made it,
'tis so high-crowned ; one that saw me in this would
rather think me a fool than a Duke.

Mago. Meo, thou spirit of magic glass, appear!
I charge thee in dread Pluto's name to come!

Tra. More devils yet! Is the circle sure, father
conjuror? and 't be not, I pray you take an order
with it ; I have no mind at all to venture myself
against the devil.

Mago. Have I not told thee thou art safe? Fear not!

Tra. Yonder's another devil; I think of Moran, for he brings a looking-glass with him.

Mago. Deliver it! Begone!

Tra. I thank you for it, besworn; for in good earnest, father conjuror, I would have as little the company of your devils as is possible.

Mago. But before I give you this mirror, son,
Receive this powder, by magic art compos'd
And secret spells! He upon whom thou flingest it,
It hath such hidden virtue in it, will
Be took by all for Trappolin.

Tra. For me?

Mago. Yes, certainly, for thee.

Tra. Say you so? Why then, i' faith, with all my heart give it me. I swear unto you, old father, the very best man in Tuscany shall be Trappolin.

Mago. Here, put it up and keep it safe.

Tra. And I do not, hang me!

Mago. Now, are you ready for the looking-glass?

Tra. I am very ready indeed.

Mago. Son Trappolin, this looking-glass was
    wrought
In the deep caverns of the dark abyss,
Compos'd of the mud of Phlegeton,
And with the blood of tortur'd miscreants!
It is a mirror I have studied long,
And now have brought unto perfection.
This upon thee I do bestow, a gift
Such as the crowns of Emperors could not buy.

Tra. And yet, father conjuror, I have seen half a dozen better sold for a pistole.

Mago. They were the work of mortals. When
    thou hast
A cloak I'll give thee too, but look in this,
And thou shalt see thyself the Duke; and if,
When he returns again, thou meetest him,—
But throw the powder on him first,—and he
Begins to rage, bid him look in't, and it
Will show him the reflection of thee.

Tra. Say you so ? Why, then, give me the glass !

Mago. Here ! stand still ! I will now raise up the
fiend

That hath the cloak which I have promised thee.

Tra. Father conjuror, as you love your son Trappolin, give me another

Circle or two, for I promise you I fear this almost
worn out.

Mago. Still thou dost fear ? Be bold and confident ;

Hell cannot hurt thee as thou stand'st.

Trap. Why, then, let him come !

Mago. In Proserpine's dread name, our sovereign
queen,

Areo, I do charge thee to appear !

Thus, by the waft of this enchanted wand,

I do command thee, fiend, unto this place !

Trap. No more, father conjuror ! hold ! here comes
the devil ! He's a tailor in hell fire, for he brings
a cloak.

Aréo. Thou against whom fierce Cerberus dares not
bark,

Here is the cloak, which, to obey thy will,

We, that thy servants are, have made.

Mago. 'Tis well !

Begone ! I license thy depart. This cloak,

Son Trappolin, doth perfect thee the Duke.

Trap. I know not, but, on my conscience, the
poorest of his Highness' servants ne'er wear a worse.
It seems to me to have been made of these miserable
thefts of a beggarly tailor, 'tis of so many colours ; and
for the fashion of it, by your leave, father conjuror,
'tis very clownish, and something inclining to the
fool's fashion.

Mago. Thy words, son Trappolin, are vain. Those
counts

And marquesses that swagger it in gold

Shall not appear so glorious to the eyes

Of men as thou in this.

Tra. Father conjuror, I'll be rul'd by you ; put
on !

Mago. Thou art the great Duke now in show; the wisest
Judgments will believe thee so.   Now take the glass
and see thyself in 't.

Trap. Beseech your Highness, pardon me !   I am
A poor subject of yours, for a small matter
Banish'd by envious lords.

Mago. Why, Trappolin, what folly is this ?

Tra. Besworn to you, father, I thought I saw his
Highness, and was a begging to be pardoned.

Mago. Away with ignorance ! 'twas thy reflexion.
As thou didst seem unto thyself, so thou
Shalt likewise to the world appear.   Now, mark me !
Not one of these can make thee like the Duke ;
They altogether do.   Ne'er leave them off
Without thou art secure ; for, one but missing,
Thou wilt appear thyself.   The hat is call'd
After the devil's name that brought it, Eo ;
The looking-glass, Meo ; the cloak, Areo ;
And there are fiends within them.

Tra. Father conjuror, I thank you for your kindness ; take all your ware again !   Carry so many devils about me ? so I shall be sure to be carried to the devil by 'em !

Mago. Suspect no hurt ; they can as well destroy
Their immortality as do thee harm.

Tra. Why, then, honest father conjuror, I'll venture myself among them.   But I swear unto you, if they begin to stir, I'll e'en fling them all away without more ado.

Mago. Farewell, son Trappolin ! return to Florence,
And flourish in the pleasures of the Court ;
Other affairs command me to be gone.
Give me thy hand !   Farewell, son Trappolin !

Tra. Be not so hasty, my dear old father !   one word before you go.   How shall I say that I bring not my Duchess with me, but come alone ?

Mago. Why, anything—what you will.

Tra. I'll make 'em believe, then, that I licensed her

to stay as long as she pleases, and that I came alone
to see how they governed in my absence.

Mago. 'Twill do! Now, have you done with me?

Tra. I have. I thank you for all your things here.
Fare you well, honest father conjuror! [*Exit* MAGO.

Tra. Now, Trappolin is no more Trappolin.
What I am in my glass I'll look again—
The great Duke! Ha! 'tis well—'tis very well!
This scurvy cloak doth seem his gallant one,
And this base hat his Highness' beaver; my face,
My body, legs, and all seem changed;—i' faith,
The conjuror is a wondrous learned fellow.
You scoundrel lords that banish'd me, I'll make
Sport with your scurvy honours, that I will!
Eo, Meo, and Areo, attend
Unto your offices well, and guard your friend!

SCENE II.

Enter SFORZA, *the Duke of Milain;* HORTENTIA, *the
Duchess;* ISABELLA, *his sister;* LAVINIO, *the Great
Duke; with* Attendants.

Sfor. Most noble brother,—for so the temple rites
Of Hymen done do license me to call you,—
Honour our entertainment one half hour
Longer, and we will leave you with your bride.

Lav. Great Prince! the glories you have done me
     here
I leave to future chronicles to tell;
And still you do increase them! Sure no man
In Milain ever did receive such honours.
You always shall command me.

Sfor. Sir, we deserve no compliments; we have
Our wishes if you but rest satisfied
Of our good meaning.

Lav. Most gracious madam! the Roman Emperors
Would have wondered at your Court had they but
     known it.

Which of them all would not have bless'd his fates
For the fruition of so rich a beauty
As is the matchless Lady Isabella?

Isa. Sir! of your own you may say what you
please,
But I am sure you overpraise me much.

Lav. Dearest of all the world! thou dost deserve
Princes and poets both to speak thy worth!
Bless'd be the powers divine, that me of all
Mankind did choose to make most fortunate
In giving me the glory of the earth!

Sfor. Sit down, most noble brother! from your
bride
We will not part you. Sister, this place is yours.
So let them now begin!

Enter HYMEN, LUNA, MARS, MERCURY, JUPITER,
·VENUS, SATURN, SOL, *after music.*

Hym. Hither we are descended from above,
To gratulate your nobly-grounded love,
That you, most worthy happy pair, should know
The gods themselves are pleased with what you do.
Me you have honoured, and to honour you
I have brought the deities along which do
Command and rule the days, that they may bless
You all the year with plenteous happiness!
May Tuscany's cities boast of Milain's spouse;
And future ages, when they would compose
One grac'd with all the virtues, her express
To be a lady like this Milainess.
And may the most ingenious Florentines,
Your citizens, great Duke, busy their minds
In writing and in singing marriage songs,
Delectable epithalamiums!
While you do live, love ever; and may you
Continually your generous heats renew.
Thus Hymen wishes, and it will go hard
If what a god says gods do not regard.

Thus I could spend the night, but that would prove
A wrong unto my rites and to your love!

Here they dance, and HYMEN *leads it.*

Luna. Cynthia I am, that with my borrowed light
Outshine the stars, and do command the night!
Many a time, when else I veil'd would ride,
I will appear to see you with your bride.
Lamps nor wax-lights you shall not need, for I
Instead of them will evermore be by;
And may you, in this life you have begun,
Equal in love me and Endymion.
    Mars. Though my aspect be fierce, and wars pre-
      sage,
To you they shall be such as lovers wage,—
Sweet kisses, soft embraces, and such things
As amorous Queens enjoy and amorous Kings.
You therefore, without pity, both may fight
Battles, not full of danger, but delight;
And may they last until I part you two,
Which I do promise I will never do!
    Mer. Hermes I am, Maja's wing'd son, and shine
Among the planets in a globe of mine;
And though 'tis true I favour thefts and sleights,
Yet will do none t' diminish your delights.
Love, therefore, laugh, and kiss, embrace, and be
Secure—nothing can hurt you without me;
And if I ever do, may I forego
My sphere, and live among the fiends below!
    Jup. Of all the gods and goddesses I am
The most supreme, and bear the chiefest name.
For love, what is it that I have not done,
To bring my wishes to conclusion?
I for myself have done no more than I
Will do for you to make you live in joy!
Therefore, most happy pair of lovers, fear
Nothing, since Jove himself doth hold you dear!
Live merrily, and let this be your mover,
That Jupiter himself was once a lover!

A Song.

Ven. Since in my orb I shined fair,
    And lovers did befriend,
  The morning and the evening star,
    I never could command,
  Heaven-blessed pair, none like to you,
  Whom time shall never make untrue!

  May Hesperus and Vesper lose
    Their lights, fair Venus fall,
  If all her power she doth not use
    To prosper you withal!
  May other deities grant you life,
  I'll make you loving man and wife!

Sat. Though I am old and rigid in aspect
And cold, and youthful sports do not affect—
And though my influences many ways
Adverse to others be, and cross their days—
For you, heaven-loved pair, myself I'll force,
And run a milder and a gentler course ;
His ancient custom Saturn will forget,
Rise for your pleasures, for your pleasures set.
Doubt me not, therefore, for my vow is strong,
That for your sakes again I wish me young.
  Sol. Phœbus I am, the glorious guide of day,
That all the planets lighten with my ray.
I am the brightsome, lightsome charioteer,
That heaven and earth adorn within my sphere ;
And know what 'tis to be in love, since I
Followed my Daphne, who from me did fly.
May I lose all my glory, all my beams
Fall like my Phaethon int' ocean streams,
If all my faculties I do not try
To make you live in joy, and love enjoy.
In summer time, when you int' arbours go,
I will not shine to trouble you below ;
Will only peep to see you kiss and smile,
To make me think, this I have done erewhile.
In winter season, when the frost doth stay,
And hinder rivers to go on their way—

When flakes of snow do cover earth's green face,
I for your sakes will thaw off both apace.
In pleasures evermore you shall accord ;
Apollo cannot falsify his word.

Here they dance another dance, which HYMEN *leads.*

Hym. The gracious planets, which command the days
    By powerful influences, you have heard,
To bless you both according to their ways,
    Vowing to be your keepers and your guard.
Them for your sakes with me I brought along,
    That they might prosper you as well as I ;
Because this marriage knot I'd tie so strong,
    That it there nothing ever should untie.
You whom the heavens will prosper all your
      life,
    You whom on earth there's nothing can
      offend—
Most happy pair, most happy man and wife,
    Your lives in love wear out, and in love end.
Nor shall a poet, hired for his gain,
    Upon your tomb a feigned verse engrave ;
Men's tongues and tears shall make you both
      remain
    Above the power of an epitaph.
But may you live till you aweary be,
    Not of youselves, but of these earthly sports ;
And the eternal joys above would see,
    Which ever are in Jove's immortal courts.
Thus unto you do gods their wishes give,
    And unto them may you according live !
                    [Exeunt MASKERS.

Sfor. I think, Hortentia, now the mask is done,
Our brother gladly would go to his rest.

Hort. And it is time. Most noble brother, when
You please, we will attend you to your chamber ;
And, sister, we will see you laid in bed.
Methinks it is a very pretty thing
To see a virgin bride look pale and blush.

Isa. 'Tis sport to others, to the maid 'tis none.

Lav. Most excellent Princess, when you please, let's
    go!
For now each minute is as tedious to me
As years have been, so much I do desire
The chaste embraces of my matchless spouse.
    Sfor. And, worthy friend, let us entreat your stay
As long in Milain as is possible;
You cannot be in Florence more beloved,
Nor by the better nor the meaner sort.
    Lav. What I can do you know you may command
Unto my utmost power.
    Hort. Lights!
    Lav. My fairest, dearest love, your hand! This part
Of happiness makes me suppose the rest.   [*Exeunt.*

SCENE III.

Enter MATTEMORES.

    Mat. Those lazy times that do degenerate minds,
And breed new thoughts in most heroic hearts,
By noble spirits are to be abhorr'd,
And loathed as the ruin of their souls.
Whilst I did follow the triumphant war
Through fire and blood, I was a happy man;
I thought no pleasure was a parallel
To the loud cry of mortal-wounded foes.
But now I am transformed from myself;
Hipolita hath charm'd me with a look.
May I but hear her speak, how I rejoice!
May I but hear her sing, I think me blest!
O, how my heart's ashamed of my tongue,
Which never until now effeminate thoughts
Could win upon! O, would to heaven this lady
Were but a man, and circled round with death,
That I might kill her and release myself!
Or were she like the warlike Amazon,
With whom renowned Theseus did contend,
That with my honour I might challenge her

K

For an enchanter and a witch! How fondly
And foolishly I rave! Strongest resolutions
A woman's powerful beauty doth destroy;
He that can conjure men, unpeople towns,
Cover the sea with fleets, drink rivers dry
With armed squadrons he conducts to fight,
Whom potent Monarchs fear, and Emperors wish
To make their friend, a lady's smile or eye
Subdues above resistance, and makes die.

Enter HORATIO *and* PRUDENTIA.

Hora. Most dearest, worthiest Princess, I am blest
Above the proudest of my former wishes!
Your love to me was like a thing desired,
But far from expectation; as men
Forlorn and wretched, being content to die,
And sure to suffer, wish to live, although
They fully do despair of life. Of late
Even so was it with me: I lov'd you
Above my life's expression, but did ever
Despair the blessedness of such an honour.

Pru. My dear Horatio, I cannot speak
So well as you, but I can love as truly.

Mat. A strange discovery! I will retire
More close, and hear the rest.

Pru. And, noble sir,
Because I know my brother, the great Duke,
Will not at all or scarce allow this match,
I will with you, whensoever you command,
Leave Florence, and what fortune it shall please
The gods to send us bear with cheerfulness.

Hora. Excellent, merciful Prudentia!
I must pray Heaven make you a full requital,
For I shall ever be unable.

Pru. I cannot stay longer with you now;
At our next meeting I'll cloy you with
My company. A kiss!
Farewell, my heart's best pleasure! [*Exit* PRUDENTIA.

Hora. Let others travel Italy all over,
To talk of such a city, such a place,—

Go to magnificent and holy Rome,
Once the sole empress of the conquered world ;
To Venice rich, commanding, politic ;
Unto sweet Naples, plenteous in ability ;
Unto great Milain ; unto fat Bologna ;
Civil Ferrara, Ariosto's town ;
Strong-walled Padua, which Antenor built,
The Trojan prince, and Titus Livius fames
For his nativity and sepulchre ;
To subtle Bergamo, most highly honoured
For near relation to Torquato Tasso ;
To proud and stately Genoa, renown'd
By her seafaring citizen Colombo ;
Worthy Verona, old Catullus' city ;
Bloody Peruggia, warlike Bessia ;
Glorious Mantua, Virgilius Maro's birth-place ;
Good Rimini, iron Pistoya ;
Fine-languag'd Sienna, and industrious Lucca ;
Odd-humour'd Forly, honest old Ravenna ;
Ill-aired Simegallia ; Capua,
Effeminate and amorous, wherein
The Carthaginian captain's soldiers were
Spoil'd and debauch'd with pleasures ; Pisa hang-
    ing ;
Pesaro, a garden of best fruits ; Ancona
Prais'd for the Port Loyal ; and true Urbino,
Round Ascoli, long Recanati, built
Upon a steep hill's ridge ; Foligno, full
Of sugry* streets, among the Apennine ;
Faro, for handsome women most extoll'd ;
And Modena, happiest of them all,—
From beauteous, comely Florence, when I part
Without Prudentia, thunder strike my heart ! [*Exit.*
    Mat. A gallant resolution ! For the man,
I cannot blame him ; but the Princess, she
To look so low and dote upon a slave,
Seems very strange and full of wonder to me.
Had Delphian oracles, ever ador'd
For uttering truth, spoke this, I should have doubted ;

* Soft clayey streets ?

She whom we thought a saint, a pattern for nuns,
Thus to forget herself! it doth amaze me.
O women, I could rage against the sex!
And, lov'd I not Hipolita, I would.
She cannot hear me, and I needs must speak
A word or two. They are all false, and fickle all,
The poison of men's happiness; within,
Though they are fair without, most full of sin.

Enter BARBARINO *and* MACHAVIL.

Bar. Good morrow, Captain Mattemores!
Mac. How do you, Captain?
Mat. Your honour's humble slave! I am well, but
    sad;
And so had all the court good cause to be,
Did they but know so much as I.
Bar. Why, Captain,
What's the matter?
Mat. I'll not be silent, for her honour's sake.
Prudentia, the Princess, is in love.
With whom do you suppose, my lords?
Mac. I think with none, for we all know she yet
Hath slighted Modena's and Parma's Duke,
And seem'd careless of mankind.
Mat. Alas!
She were most happy were it one of them;
It is Brunetto she's in love withal.
Bar. How?
Mac. Impossible!
Mat. It is a thing most true; my eyes and ears
Have seen and heard it while I stood unseen.
Mac. You amaze us!
Bar. It is a thing I never should have thought,
Though spent my life in fond imaginations.
Mat. As I have seen an amorous cloud receive
A stately hill into her lovely breast,
And of his lofty head our eyes bereave,
And seem to lull his senses unto rest—
So did the scornful lady deign to leave
All her majestic state; and, sore opprest

With inward flames, her eager arms she cast
About his neck, kiss'd and embrac'd him fast.

Bar. Wonders !

Mac. How the great Duke will rage !

Mat. And do you not, my lords, in time prevent
  them,
They'll steal away, I fear ; for so she vow'd,
When he but said the word, she would.

Mac. By his imprisonment we'll hinder that.

Enter HORATIO.

Bar. Here is the man we spake of !

Mac. For the Princess' honour let us keep it close
As possible we can. You of the guard !

Enter the GUARD.

Bar. Seize on Brunetto, carry him to prison !
Bid Puchannello keep him safe !
'Tis our pleasures.

Hora. What violence is this ? O, had I been suffered
to wear a sword, some of you should pay dearly for it !

Mac. Away with him !

　　　　　　　[*Exeunt the* GUARD *with* HORATIO.

Mat. My lords, you have done wisely to prevent
So great a dishonour as might have ensu'd—
Tainted the family of the Medicis,
And been a lasting sorrow to the Duke.

Enter TRAPPOLIN.

Bar. His Highness is returned.

Mac. Great sir ! upon our knees we welcome you.
You come unlook'd for ; we did not expect
This happy time so soon by fourteen days.
Where is our Duchess ?

Tra. Your Duchess will not come till the gods know
when, for I do not : I have given her leave to stay as
long as she will. But besworn, I fear you have
governed but scurvily in my absence ; I hear that
you have banished an honest poor man call'd Trappolin ; is it true ?

Mac. So please your Highness, he deserv'd no less.

Tra. Why, what hurt had he done? Had he knocked anybody on the head? What was his fault?

Bar. He was a pander, and corrupted youth.

Tra. You lie, sirrah! not panders but whores do that, and not they neither if they be sound. Banish one of my subjects for such a matter? Besides, were there no more in Florence but he?

Mac. Be not displeased, we humbly pray your Highness,
For we did think we did it for the best.

Mat. I wonder at our Duke in this.

Tra. Well, I am very weary. I left all my train behind with my wife, and rid as fast as I could drive, that I might come unlooked for, the better to see how you behaved yourselves; which you have done bad enough. When I was almost at Florence, a saucy varlet robbed me and stole my horse from me, so that I was beholding to my legs to bring me hither. Barberino and Machavil, come you hither both of you!

Mac. What is your Highness' pleasure?

Tra. Sirrah Barberino! hold by Mach.'s breeches, and stoop, for on thy back I will ride to my palace.

Bar. I'll go fetch a coach for your Highness.

Tra. The devil take your coaches! Stoop, I say, without more ado! Where is your obedience?

Mat. I think the Duke's run mad, or foxt soundly at the least. I know not what to think of this.

Tra. You, sirrah Don! run by my side; supply my lackey's office. Wonder not, but obey!

Mat. There is no remedy. Heaven be merciful! I think his Highness ran mad for fear when he was robbed.

Tra. Now on, and do not loiter!
Thus, like the Roman Emperors, will I ride
To triumph through Florence. Stumble not, you had best.
Chariots them carried, a Tuscan noble me: mine is the statelier and the braver way.
Eo, Meo, and Areo, thanks!

Mat. He jeers us, and miscalls us.
Tra. On apace !
That I may quickly be in my palace.   [*Exeunt omnes.*

ACT III.—SCENE I.

Enter HORATIO, *in prison.*

Hora. Unto the man enthrall'd, black and obscure
Is the clear beauty of the brightest day ;
Through iron grates he only sees the light,
And thereby doth increase his misery.
Those whom he doth perceive in joy to pass
Augment his wretchedness, by making him
To think that thus I lately was myself.
But, admirablest lady of the world,
Divine Prudentia ! may I die abhorred
By all mankind if I repine at all,
Seeing for thy sake I do suffer this !
The exquisitest tortures curious inventions make,
For thee I would think sports, and undergo :
May'st thou live happily and free from care,
And all my miseries of no moment are.   [*Exit.*

Enter TRAPPOLIN.

Tra. Eo, Meo, and Areo, faith you are all brave
devils all on you, and my father conjuror an excellent
fellow.   I love to see myself.   Meo, thou art not the
work of Moran; no, the Duke himself I seem.   I now
must learn to walk in state, and speak proudly.   I'll
play such tricks with my lord banishers shall make
me sport enough.   Banish a poor man for doing
courtesies ! it is against the law of friendship.   I am
supposed a Prince ; the Florentines acknowledge me
the great Duke.   Whatever I do, though never so
bad, passeth with approbation.   Poor Trappolin turned
Duke ! 'tis very strange, but very true.

Would the fates favour panders in this wise,
He were a fool, besworn, would not turn pimp.
Seeing panders Dukes become, he is an ass
That may hav't, will let the office pass.
O me, Brunetto! Alas for thee, man, how cam'st thou
there? I think in my heart, an there be a mischief
in the world, thou wilt be at one end or other on 't.
So ho! Pucannello, Pucannello!

Puc. Who calls?

Enter PUCANNELLO.

Tra. That do I, sirrah! let me Brunetto out presently, and bid him come to me.

Puc. Your Highness' pleasure shall be done. [*Exit.*

Tra. Alas, poor Brunetto! marl what he has done to be locked in such a place. I think in my conscience 'tis not for any lechery, for I could never get him to 't, and many a time I have offered him many a good bit. Brunetto to come into the jail! I cannot tell what to think of it; but be 't for what it will, out he goes. My good friend Brunetto, who gave me a ring, shall not lie there. Honest Brunetto!

Enter BRUNETTO.

Hora. Great Prince!

Tra. He makes a very low leg, but I will not be outgone in courtesy.
Dearest Brunetto!

Hora. Your Highness doth forget yourself exceedingly; I am your prisoner.

Tra. My best friend, good Brunetto!

Hora. Beseech your Highness to remember yourself.

Tra. So I do, but never must forget thee. I am glad to see thee in good health, dear Brunetto.

Hora. I shall fall to the ground even now in this salutation. Beseech your Highness, I am your prisoner, your slave.

Tra. I am thy servant, Brunetto!

Hora. Wonders! I am astonished! Upon my humble knees I do congratulate your safe and speedy return.

Tra. And upon my knees I do embrace thee, Brunetto. Thou art an honest man, my most sweet Brunetto!

Hora. I know not what to think, nor what to speak. Beseech your Highness, rise!

Tra. Not without thee. Up, Brunetto, honest Brunetto; up, I say!

Hora. Beseech your Highness, I am your humble slave!

Tra. I am thy servant, Brunetto; and as long as thou liest on the ground, so will I too. Up, therefore! let us rise and talk. Away with your compliments! I cannot abide them. Up, I say, let's rise! thou shalt not stay, I swear.

Hora. I am amazed! by force I must obey. Great sir, I know not what to think; you honour me above all expression.

Tra. Honour a fig! I love thee, Brunetto. Thou art a good honest fellow; I love thee with all my heart! Compliment with me, and I will be very angry. Without more ado, I tell thee I love thee! Pucannello, so ho! Sirrah Pucannello, bring two chairs hither presently!

Hora. Your Highness!

Tra. Away with Highness! I say away with it! Call me Lavin Duke, plain Medicis; I cannot abide your Highness, your Excellency, your Worship—I hate such idle flim-flams. Dear Brunetto, how I love thee! I' faith, I do, with all my heart; and if I lie unto thee, I would I might be hanged.

Hora. Sure I am awake; this is no dream!

Tra. We will live merrily together; i' faith we will. Brunetto, how glad I am to see thee in health! Come, sirrah! what a while ha' you been a bringing a couple of chairs! Set them here, sirrah, and begone!

[*Exit* PUCANNELLO.

Brunetto, sit thee down! sit down, my man, I say.

Hora. I will attend your Highness on my knees.

Tra. Why, I am not thy father, am I ? Leave fooling, and sit thee down, that we may talk together. Sit thee here ! I will have it so.

Hora. I am astonished; I humbly pray your Highness !

Tra. Pray me no praying, but sit thee down ; sit thee here, man ! Brunetto, be ruled !

Hora. On the right hand? I know not what to think.

Tra. I am something a-weary, Brunetto, and will not sit without thee; therefore, I pray thee, make me stand no longer. Obey me ! for I am the Duke.

Hora. Here, then, so please your Highness.

Tra. Why, an thou wilt have it there, there let it be ; but I am mistook that's on the left hand. What ! do you think me a clown and without breeding, that I have no more manners in me ? For shame of the world, sit thee down, Brunetto, sit thee down, and without more bidding, without thou wilt ha' me lie on the ground, for I am so weary I can scant stand.

Hora. There is no remedy! I must obey.

Tra. So, well done ! Sit still, man ! What art doing?—art afraid of me ?

Hora. What does your Highness mean ?

Tra. Marry, and thou draw'st back, I'll draw back too. Brunetto, sit thee still, and let us talk.

Hora. I will obey your Highness.

Tra. Highness me no more ! Highness, I cannot abide it. My name is Lavin—call me Lavin Duke ; and 'tis enough, a conscience.

Hora. Great sir, I am far unworthy of these
　　honours ;
The noblest Florentines would be most proud
To be thus graced by their Prince.

Tra. I like not these set speeches neither. Let us talk as we were companions in a tavern together, and not after the court fashion. I am as weary of it as a dog ; I am, Brunetto. Prithee, man, how cam'st thou into the gaol ?

Hora. O pardon me, dread Sovereign !

Tru. On thy knees, man ? What meanest thou by this ? dost take me for Mahomet ? As well as I can pardon thee, I do—anything, whate'er it be, though thou hast killed everybody. Rise, therefore, I say, Brunetto, and set thee in thy place again, or I'll kneel too.

Hora. Most merciful Prince, hear me before, lest you
Repent your kindness towards me afterward.

Tra. Up, I say, Brunetto ! up ! I pardon thee anything, upon condition thou wilt rise and sit thee down.

Hora. It is your Highness' will.

Tra. Now, good Brunetto, without any fear,—for I swear unto thee I do not care what thou hast done, and forgive thee, whatsoever it be,—tell me the cause!

Hora. Dread Sovereign, I was for love put in.

Tra. Who put thee in ?

Hora. Your Highness' governors, Lord Barberino and Lord Machavil.

Tra. They are a couple of coxcombs for their pains. Who art in love withal ?

Hora. O pardon me !

Tra. Sit still, or I will not; and if thou dost, I will.

Hora. Your Highness' excellent sister — O great Prince !

Tra. Sit still, Brunetto ! Wast thou laid up for that ? Alas for thee ! Hast thou married her ?

Hora. So please your Highness, no.

Tra. It doth neither please my highness nor lowness neither ; I would thou hadst, and that's all the hurt I wish thee. Couldst thou think I, that loved thee so, would be angry with thee for this ? Hast thou her consent ?

Hora. I have.

Tra. I am very glad of it, and I here give thee mine too. Prithee, Brunetto, do me the favour to go and bid Barberino or Machavil come to me. I'll

send for my sister presently, and if she says so to me,
I'll soon have you married.

Hora. Your Highness shall command me to my
    death ;
More willingly unto my life, for so
This business doth import.   The heavens be praised,
And ever be propitious unto you—bless you
According to your own and my desires !   [*Exit.*

Tra. This Brunetto is a good, honest fellow, and
hath always behaved himself very well; and whatsoever he be, I'll give him Prudentia for the ring he
gave me—I will not be ungrateful.   He said he was
in love with my sister; and if he had them all, I would
e'en say, much good do his heart with them.   But he
means the Princess ; and though I have little to do
with her, yet if I can give her him I will.   Brunetto's
ring I shall- never forget.

Enter MACHAVIL.

Mac. Your Highness' pleasure ?

Tra. My Highness' pleasure, sirrah lord, is, that
you go and tell my sister Prudentia I would speak
with her presently.   I will expect her here.   Begone !
                                                    [*Exit.*

The Duke's life is very pleasant ; I take great content in it ; and were it not for one thing, I were most
happy, which is, I dare not disclose myself to my dear
Flametta, for she is a woman, and full of tittle-tattle
as the rest are.   Nor, if I could win her without
making myself known, durst I lie with her, by reason
of putting off Eo, Meo, and Areo ; otherwise sure I
should get her, for sure she would not refuse a Duke.

Enter FLAMETTA.

Fla. Here is the Duke alone, whom I so long
Have sought for, to petition for the repeal
Of my dear Trappolin.   Great Prince, as low
As truest humility can make a suitor,
Before you I prostrate myself.   Most excellent
And merciful sir, pity a loving maid

Who is bereaved of her joys; I beg
Poor banished Trappolin might be recalled,
Whom, when your Highness was to Milain gone,
Was, by those cruel lords whom you did leave
Our governors, sent into banishment.
Great Duke, you that have noble thoughts, and sure
A heart full of commiseration,
Kill me not with a cruel hard denial.

Tra. Ah, Eo, Meo, and Areo, hinder me! I must
counterfeit with her. Fair maiden, rise!

Fla. O let me kneel, great sir, until you say
My Trappolin shall be repeal'd!

Tra. Rise, I say! and we will talk of it; I cannot
abide to see anybody kneel, unless they are in the
church, that have legs to stand on. How may I call
you, maiden?

Fla. So please your Highness, my name is Flametta.

Tra. Mrs. Flametta, I say, give me your hand; rise
without more ado—rise, without you mean to say your
beads over. Mrs. Flametta, be rul'd! good Mrs. Flametta, be rul'd! Would I were hanged if ever Trappolin
come home and you get not up; up, I say, therefore!

Fla. I must be most rude.

Tra. Why, that's well done, Mrs. Flametta!
Trappolin, for whom you are a petitioner, young
mistress, is banish'd, you say; for what, it matters not.
Tell me what you'll give for his repeal.

Fla. Even anything I have—all that I have.

Tra. Are you a virgin? tell me true. If you are
not, it is no wonder, besworn; it is more wonder by
the half if you are, for I think there be not two of
your age in the city that be.

Fla. May I not prosper in my wishes, sir, if I be
not a maid?

Tra. And will you give your maidenhead to have
him recalled from banishment?

Fla. To him when he comes home, and we are
married.

Tra. Well said, mistress! But tell me, now, what
will you give me for to have him come home?

Fla. Even anything I have.

Tra. I am a great man, and, like them, will not do favours for nothing. Will you give me your shoes?

Fla. My shoes! Your Highness jests.

Tra. I swear unto you, mistress, but I do not; and if you do not give me what I ask, how ridiculous soever it seems to you, Trappolin ne'er comes in Florence again.

Fla. I wonder at the Duke, but will obey him. Here are my shoes, dear Prince.

Tra. Well done, I say; but I must have your stockings too. Off with them, therefore, without any more arguing!

Fla. My stockings! with all my heart, to have my Trappolin.

Tra. Very well done, Mrs. Flametta, you do very well. Give me your gown too. Do not wonder; these will do nothing without it.

Fla. Then shall your Highness have it.

Tra. I see you love that fellow well; 'tis well done of you. I think he be an honest man, which makes me the willinger to yield to his repeal. I say I must have that petticoat too, else all this is not worth a rush, i' faith.

Fla. I think the Duke's mad! And will you give me, then, your Highness' word?

Tra. I will.

Fla. I cannot help it; here it is!

Tra. I swear unto thee, young wench, give me thy under petticoat and thy smock, and I will give thee my word, and send for him presently to-night. This wench makes me curse Eo, Meo, and Areo.

Fla. Most excellent sir! there is not in the world
The thing that in my power lyes I would
Deny to do for my dear Trappolin,
But modesty forbids me to do this.

Tra. I shall not have them, then?

Fla. I beseech your Highness, pardon me.

Tra. I am very sorry I could not see her naked.

but it cannot be helped. Well! how many kisses will
you give me, my young mistress?

Fla. Kisses?

Most gracious Prince, a thousand and a thousand
    times

I'll kiss your hand upon my humble knees.

Tra. I have no pleasure in that; how many kisses
upon lips will you give me?

Fla. For Trappolin's sake, I'll do anything that
modesty will give me leave. Do what you please, sir.

Tra. Ah, honey sweet Flametta, how I love thee!
Prithee, kiss better: dear lips! I could almost wish
Eo, Meo, and Areo i' th' fire. Again, again, again,
sweet Flametta.

Fla. Shall Trappolin come home?

Tra. Do but let us kiss, and thou shalt have any-
    thing.

O me! what a misery it is to be a great man! Again,
    again, Flametta; Trappolin shall come home.

Fla. I am aweary.

Tra. So shall I never be. Again, again!

Enter PRUDENTIA.

Fla. The Princess, your Highness' sister!
You have gi'n your word?

Tra. Young mistress, I have not leisure to answer
you now. Come to me some other time, and I'll talk
with you further. Now take up your things, and begone!

Fla. I am assur'd I shall prevail: heavens guard
your Highness.   [*Exit.*

Pru. Now I expect my brother's rage, for sure,
Though ne'er so secret kept, my love unto
My dearest Horatio by some uncouth means
Is known. Say what he will or can, I am
Resolved, and my affections settled.

Tra. Fair lady, come hither! You are my sister, are
you?

Pru. I am your sister and servant, sir.

Tra. Compliment with me no more than I compli-

ment with you.　Good madam sister, sit you down! I
would talk with you a little.

Pru. He talks as though he were distracted.　I
obey you, sir.

Tra. 'Tis well done, good lady sister!

Pru. I never saw my brother thus before.
Sir, I am exceeding glad to see you
Returned in safety out of Lombardy;
But should have been more joyful had you brought
Your Duchess with you.

Tra. She'll come soon enough, ne'er fear't; but, sister,
I must be something brief, for I am a-hungry.　As
soon as I came home, I saw Brunetto in the gaol, who,
after many circumstances and fears, told me 'twas for
love of you that he was put there.　Tell me, sister
Prudentia, do you love him?　I'll be sworn the man
is a good honest fellow.　If you have a mind to him,
I'll give you my consent with all my heart; I vow, as
I am an honest man and the Duke, I do not jest.

Pru. Most worthy brother, thanks! I do confess
I love Brunetto, and were very guilty
Of cruelty if I did not, for he
Loves me, I know, as his own happiness.
Nor, sir, have I placed my affections
Unworthy: Brunetto is a Prince,
His name is Horatio, and he's second son
Unto the Duke of Savoy; for my sake
He changed his name and lives a prisoner.

Tra. How's this?—Is Brunetto a Prince?　You love
him, lady sister, you say?

Pru. Most truly, sir, I do.

Tra. Are you content to marry him?

Pru. I do desire no greater bliss on earth,
So that your Highness will consent thereto.

Tra. Lady sister, here is my hand; I am content,
i' faith, without more words, I am.　I am an hungry
now, and would be brief, sister mine; I say marry
him when you will, beshrew my heart and I be not
content; I had rather you had him than any man in
the world.

Pru. I know not what to think; he's strangely chang'd!

Tra. Let this suffice, madam sister. I am very hungry, I say; have you any good store of meat in the house? I could eat soundly now, sister, of a dish of sausages. Come, lady sister, let's to dinner. Begone! I have a good stomach, as I am an honest man. [*Exeunt.*

SCENE II.

Enter MATTEMORES.

Mat. I, that have led a life until of late
In spite of death, pass'd through the dangers of it
Dreadless, without regard,—whom never men
Conducted by brave captains to the field
Did yet withstand, am won and vanquished:
Hipolita, heroic Amazon,
In love hath conquered me with amorous smiles.
Methinks it is a thing most full of wonder,
That what not massy pikes nor murtherous guns
Could ever do, a lady's smiling eyes,
The beauty of a timorous woman, should.
Her eyes have darted fire into my breast,
Which nothing but her kindness can extinguish;
And be she cruel, I shall soon be ashes!
Do I thus yield? Shall I forget the sound
Of martial drums, the warlike noise of trumpets,
To list to the lascivious harmony
Of instruments touched by Hipolita's hand?
Shall I forget the ordering of a camp,
To ride great horses, to besiege a city,
To undermine a castle, to raise bulwarks,—
All for the love of a fair, fearful woman?
It must be so! These legs, that wont to lead
Arm'd men to battle, I must use in dances!
This hair, that us'd to be covered with a helm,
Cloggy with sweat and blood, I now must powder!

L

These hands, that wont to wave a dreadful sword,
Instead of iron gauntlets now must wear
Perfum'd gloves! I, that had wont to be
Under the chirurgeon's hands to cure my wounds,
Must have a barber now to keep me neat!
O love, thou art divine, and canst transform
A man from what he was! It is in vain
To think to shun the thing thou dost constrain.

Enter HIPOLITA.

Hip. 'Tis idleness that is the cause
    We lose our liberties ;
The busy Cupid never draws
    To yield unto his vice.

Away with love! it is a thing
    I hope I ne'er shall know;
When many weep, so I shall sing,
    Have joy while they have woe.

The happiness of love is poor
    Compar'd to liberty ;
Blest lovers do hard things endure,
    Their pleasures to enjoy.

May I live ever as I do,
    Free from that foolish pain !
I wish that no man may me woo
    Until I love again!

Mat. O heavens, is thus her mind composed? If I
Can win this lady, it will be a conquest
Deserves a trophy far above my best
Of victories! I will go try her. Hail,
Glory of Italy! compar'd to whom
The fair Egyptian queen would yield. Sweet lady!
Most excellent Hipolita, vouchsafe
To hear me tell your conquest and my spoil :
Whom the great Duke's greatest foes could never
    vanquish,

Your powerful beauty hath. Know Mattemores,
Whose valour Spain not only doth report,
But Mantua hath prov'd, your matchless eyes,
Transcendants of the brightest, lightest stars,
Have wounded fatally unto the heart,
Unless you prove as kind as you are fair !

   Hip. Do you jest with me, Captain ?

   Mat. My heart's delight ! sweet centre of my
    thoughts !
I vow by your rich beauty, if my heart
Could speak it would agree full with my tongue ;
I would tell my love more than I can express !

   Hip. What ill fortune, good signor, you have
    had,
To fall in love with one deserves it not,
Nor doth not care for you ! And I do hope
I ne'er shall bear affection unto man.

   Mat. Patience assist me mightily ! Not all
The murderous cannon bullets I have heard
Fly buzzing by my ears, nor dismal cries
Of dying soldiers, nor the horrid noise
Of rough tempestuous seas, have ever moved me ;
Only your harsh, unkind reply hath struck
Unto my very soul !

   Hip.   I cannot help it.
Had you now, Captain, been abroad i' th' field,
This ne'er had happened to you ; and to cure you,
The field will be the best. Go to the wars,
Busy yourself in fights, and you will soon
Forget you ever saw Hipolita.

   Mat. Most cruel fair one, be assur'd that ere
I would forget you, which I know 's a thing
For me impossible to do, I would
Into oblivion cast my best of pleasures—
Even all my pleasures ! I would forget to use
My sword, and all the military science !
Witness, triumphant son of Jove, great Mars,
I vow, by all the honours of a soldier,
I love thee dear as mine own heart, but this
Admirable lady much above it !

Nor do I displease thee in 't. I know that thou
Prefer'st the embraces of the Cyprian queen
Above the glorious battles of the field!
Therefore, dear lady, be most confident,
While I have memory, above all things
Your beauty will be fixed in 't.
  Hip.   Good signor,
Trouble me not to answer you again.
Let this suffice—I wish you lik'd me not,
Because I neither would have you nor any
To love a woman will not return affection.
  Mat.   O heavens !
Will you continue thus obdurate ever?
  Hip. Always ; believe it, Captain.
  Mat. I have not patience to contain myself !
An angry cloud full fraught with thunderbolts,
Work'd by the Cyclops on Campagnia's stithy,
Now hanging o'er my head, menacing death,
Presaging speedy, sad destruction,
Could not compel my silence ! 'Tis decreed
By my adverse malignant stars that I
Shall die, destroy'd by a fair cruel woman ;
Which, ere I do, I will a little ease
My troubled heart of woe ! Hear, merciless woman,
Whom I do curse because I love so dearly,
Hear me, and afterwards go glory * that
Your wondrous beauty and your savage heart
Hath made a man distracted—kill'd a soldier !
  Hip. A captain, and be thus mov'd by a woman's
   refusal ?
  Mat. Sweetest Hipolita, be merciful, and save
His life that honours you above the world !
  Hip. Pray you, signor, be answered!
  Mat. You are resolv'd, then, to ruin me ?
Curs'd be those battles, all that I have fought
And conquer'd in ! 'T had been more honour for me
To have been slain by my incensed foes,
Which were brave soldiers, than to die in peace
By the unkindness of a fair, proud woman.

    * To glory—to revel with delight.

Hip. Beseech you, leave your rage, and leave me,
    Captain!
Mat. More cruel than Hyrcanian tigers, hear
Me take my leave before I go!
    Hip. Proceed!
    Mat. Thou god of love, an if thou art a god,
Revenge thyself and thy wrong'd deity
On this unmerciful lady! Make her fall
In love with the basest of all mankind,—
A man so full of ignorance, that he
In shape alone may differ from a beast,
Not know that she is fair, and slight her beauty,
And be himself the most deformed thing
That ever burthened our mother earth
With his unworthy steps! Cupid, attend,
And yield unto my just request! Make this
Lady run mad for such a monster, shed
A thousand thousand tears upon her knees,
While he stands laughing at her! May you die
Raging for love, Hipolita, as I!
    Hip. I do begin to pity him. Sure I never
Shall have a man to love me better; and though
I once intended always to live single,
His words have altered my resolution.
Nor, if I take him, shall I do a thing
Will misbecome me, for he is a man
High in the great Duke's favour. Noble Captain,
It is your happy fate to conquer always.
I vow unto you by my honour, I think
Most seriously no man upon the earth
Besides you could have won. I'm the last
Of all your victories—Theseus-like, you have
Overcome Hipolita!
    Mat. And will you love me, then?
    Hip. I do, and always will!
    Mat. Blest be the stars that shin'd at my nativity!
I want words to express my joys; but, dearest
    lady, .
My sweet Hipolita, my forward actions
Shall make you know my heart above my tongue!

I am a soldier, and was never wont
To speak amorously.
 Hip.   You have said enough.
Love is but thought by words, by deeds 'tis known;
Show me you love me, and let words alone!
 Mat. Worthiest of ladies, when I cease to do
All that I can, then may your love cease too!

            [Exeunt.

Act iv.—Scene i.

Enter Barbarino *and* Machavil.

 Bar. He cannot counterfeit so much.
 Mac.   I know not;
But if he do not, surely he is mad!
What wild, fantastic things he does! and talks
Of Eo, Meo, and Areo, names
Unheard 'i th' court before.
 Bar.   Some Milan counts,
I warrant you, he means by them.
 Mac. The strangest thing of all is the release
Of Brunetto, and his extraordinary love unto him,
Whom he hath caused richly to be clothed.
 Bar. And useth him as if he were his better.

Enter Horatio.

 Mac. Yonder's the man we talk of! What a change
We see!—a prisoner but lately lock'd up safe,
And now to be the wonder of the court!
 Hora. Next Eo, Meo, and Areo, the Duke
Doth swear he loveth me; but who those are,
I cannot tell nor learn. My lords, good day!
Saw you his Highness lately?
 Bar.   No, sir.
 Hora. You speak as tho' you were displeased.
 Mac. We are not well contented, sir.
 Hora. The Duke is noble; utter your grievances to
  him!
 Bar. So we will, sir.

Enter TRAPPOLIN.

Mac. And now, sir.
Know, worthy Prince, we are your loyal subjects,
And what we say is for your honour.
Tra. If it be for my honour, I'll hear you;
But be as brief as you will.
Mac. Your Highness hath lately released Brunetto?
Tra. 'Tis a thing very certain.
Mac. We doubt not but done out of clemency,
Not knowing why he lay there.
Tra. Well, why was he put there?
Mac. Even for your honour's sake, most gracious
sir. The Lady Prudentia, your sister, loves him.
Tra. Say you so? So ho! Pucannello! so ho!
Puc. Who calls? [*Within.*
Bar. His Highness! come hither presently.
Tra. Bid the guard enter.

Enter PUCANNELLO *and the* GUARD.

You say Brunetto was put in prison because my sister
lov'd him? You think it good and fitting he were
there again?
Bar. So please your Highness, yes.
Tra. Pucannello, take me these two coxcombly
lords into your custody; they are never well but
when they are banishing somebody, or doing some
mischief or other. Brunetto was laid in prison because my sister lov'd him, and lay me these there
because I love them.
Mac. Beseech your Highness not to deal so hardly
With us, whom you have known so faithful to you!
Tra. Pucannello, away with them, I say! You of
the guard, see them in!
Bar. Most worthy Prince, be merciful! If we
Have done amiss, 'twas out of ignorance.
Tra. Sirrah rogue, away with them, or I'll lay up
you too!
Puc. Your Honours must have patience, and walk.

Mac. There is no remedy.

Bar. The heavens be merciful to Florence!
What ill malignant star hath so deprived
Our wise and noble Duke of all his reason,
That he remembers not who are his friends?   [*Exit.*

Hora. The gods be ever most propitious,
Great sir, unto you, and continue long
Your life, chief honour of the Medicis!

Tra. Prince Horatio, I am your servant. I pray
you forgive me my calling of you by your nickname
of Brunetto; my sister hath told me you are the son
of the Duke of Savoy. Besworn unto you, I am very
sorry I have not used you as befitted you; but it was
your fault, that told me not who you were. I have
talked with Prudentia, and she loves you, she says;
which I am glad on, and I'll marry you as soon as you
will.

Hora. Sir, it is true I am Horatio,
Son of the Piedmont Prince; but, being his second,
I durst not think me worthy of such honours
As your Highness hath done me, and therefore told
None but your beauteous sister who I was.

Tra. Enough, my friend! And, Prince Horatio,
Could you suppose I would deny my sister,
Though she were made of gold and precious stones,
Unto your Highness, and to such a friend?
You do deserve a better wife than she.
She's not half good enough for you; and if
I had another sister, you should have them both.
My friend a Prince! I'm very glad, i' faith;
But sorry that I did not know you such,
That I might have done you right. Would I were
      hang'd
If you are not far a better man than I!

Hora. Great Prince, you do forget yourself.

Tra. Your Highness must pardon me; I do remember myself well enough, yet Eo, Meo, and Areo have
made me something proudish. But, howsoever, I am
your servant, Prince Horatio—i' faith I am your very
dutiful servant! How say you now?—the Duke of

Savoy's son! I' faith I am your poor servant, Lavin, the Duke of Florence.

Hora. I am amazed! he's mad! Beseech your Highness' leave—I pray you, sir——

Enter MATTEMORES, *the Spanish Captain, with* PETITIONERS.

Tra. What have we here now? Does the Captain bring us morris-dancers? What lobs are these two?

Mat. So please your Highness, being importun'd much, these I have brought before you, that you might do justice.

Tra. Captain Mattemores, justice I'll do with all my heart, but execution let do who will for me.

Calf. Great Duke of Tuscany, vouchsafe to hear me, For what I speak is out of conscience.
This fellow, Mr. Bulflesh, a butcher, I saw,
Verily with mine own eyes, even yesternight,
When he was drunk, to kill my man, which he
Swore was good beef, and he would sell it dear.

Bul. Sirrah Puritan, you are a base scoundrel. Was not I drunk in your company to make you merry?

Calf. But, Mr. Bulflesh, you do know, and that full well, that I prayed you on my knees for your own soul's sake to drink no more, and profess'd to you that it was a great abominable sin in you to fox yourself, or be foxed!

Bul. Goodman Calfshead, you are a base, scurvy companion. Do you not know that for your sake I killed your man? Yet I meant but only to beat him soundly, because he poured not the wine into your codpiece. Did not I do it out of friendship unto you? —did I not, you Puritan you? And you to complain! O the ingratitude of Puritans!

Tra. Peace, both of you. Master Puritan, hold your tongue, I say! Will not Calfshead be drunk, Bulflesh?

Bul. So please your Highness, no; he will let a man sooner hang him than make him drunk. Besides, he is a fellow of strange opinions, and hath sent his son to Geneva to hear Jack Calvin preach. He stole a surplice to make his amorosa a smock of; and hath writ a paltry book against the bishops, printed it at Amsterdam in *decimo sexto*. He will lie and steal without comparison, is both for boys as well as queans when he hath money, and, like a true Italian hypocrite, is for any sin or mischief but our drinking.

Tra. Then know I very well how to do justice. Mr. Calfshead, you say the butcher killed your man when he was fox'd? Be you fox'd when you will, and then kill him for't.

Calf. Heavens defend! I ne'er was drunk yet, and never will be.

Hora. There is mad justice; he doth increase my wonder.

Calf. Bless me, murder? I would not do it for the world!

Mat. This is strange justice; the butcher doth very well deserve to be sent into the galleys at Ligorn.

Tra. I have done with you, Mr. Puritan; you may begone to the tavern. And, Bulflesh, you may get you to the shambles as soon as you will, for I have no more to say to either of you.

[*Exeunt* CALFSHEAD *and* BULFLESH.

I am ready for the next; speak, therefore!

Barne. Most excellent Prince, pity a childless father!
As yesterday my only son did walk
Under an house, this fellow, Gaffer Tiler,
Who was a-working on it, did fall down
Upon my son, and killed him with his fall.

Til. Mr. Barne, be not so eager. You know I bore your son no malice, and that it was an hundred to one I broke not my own neck.

Tra. This is an easy matter to conclude.
Friend Barne, you say this Gaffer Tiler
Fell off a house, and so did kill your son?
I will be very upright in my justice:

Go you upon the house from whence he tumbled,
And he shall stand beneath, and fall on him.

Mat. An the Duke be not stark mad, I am, to think him so.

Barne. So I may break my own neck.

Hora. He strangely is distracted.

Tra. Neighbour Barne, get you about your business, for I have done with you.

Barne. I must have patience.

[*Exeunt* BARNE *and* TILER.

Tra. Now let me make an end with these, and I have done.

Mrs. Fine. Deign, noble Duke, to hear my just complaint.
I am a poor and an unfortunate widow;
This man, Dick Whip, as the other day he drove
His coach, ran over a little child of mine
That was playing in the street, and kill'd it.

Tra. Sirrah Whip, is this true?

Whip. So please your Highness, I confess it is.

Tra. It doth not please me nor displease me, for I neither did it, nor was the child mine.

Whip. It was against my will—a thing of chance. Mrs. Fine cannot deny it.

Tra. Mrs. Fine, you are a widow, you say?

Mrs. Fine. A poor unhappy one I am.

Tra. You say that Whip the coachman hath killed your child; and how he did it I have understood. This is my justice—I will do you right: Whip shall lie with you until he get you another.

Mat. Madder and madder!

Hora. I cannot choose but smile.

Whip. Most willingly, so please your Highness. I am well content to do her that satisfaction.

Mrs. Fine. You shall be hanged first, that you shall! Is thus my expectation failed?

Tra. Mrs. Fine, be ruled; I will have justice done. Whip shall lie with you — you may marry him an you will. He killed your child, and he shall get you another—I say but right. And, Sirrah Whip, look

unto't; an you play the bungler, and fail, you shall
to Ligorn and learn to row. Mrs. Fine, be contented.
An you do not like him, you might have held your
tongue, for I know nobody that sent for you, and so
get you both gone!

Whip. The heavens preserve your Highness!

[*Exeunt.*

Tra. My friend and Prince, Horatio, go unto
My sister. Bid her to prepare herself;
I'll have you married within this day or two.
I long to see you both in bed together!

Hora. Most willingly I will do such a message.
The gods preserve you happily!   [*Exit.*

Mat. A strange discovery, if true.

Tra. Seignior Captain, I say I have done very good
justice, and in a little time too. I am not like your
scarlet coats, that will do nothing without money; a
company of fellows they are whose beards and hearts
agree not together.

Mat. Your Highness doth despatch things very
soon.

Tra. Though I am the Duke, yet I love to do no
hurt, as other men in authority would. I hate to
banish men, as Machavil and Barbarino ha' done.
Alas! poor Trappolin! I hear they have banish'd an
honest man call'd Trappolin. What the devil, Seignior
Mattemores, came in their heads to send a poor fellow
away out of his country without any money? Though
men may sometimes gather a reasonable sallet abroad,
he shall get no oil to eat it withal.

Mat. Great Duke of Tuscany, our noble master,
That Trappolin of whom your Highness speaks
Had little fault in him, good faith, at all,
Saving he was a most notorious coward!

Tra. Why, you Don of guns or pikes, do you think
every man's mind is given to the wars? Trappolin
was addicted to the peace, a poor fellow full of courtesies—one that will never deny to do a favour for a
friend. I will have a little sport with my Don of the
wars. O me, sir Captain, look yonder! Eo, Meo, and

Areo, I will put you off for a while; I will try some
conclusions.

Mat. Your Highness—— Where's the Duke gone,
    I marl?
What, Trappolin, art thou come again?
Faith, many a wench in Florence will be glad.
Follow thy old trade ; be a pander still.

Tra. Seignior Captain, I am your humble slave, and
if I can do you any kindness at any time, i' faith, Don
Mattemores, you shall command me. And if you
have but a mind to any beauty in Florence, pay but
me well for my pains, and her well for hers, and I will
not fail you. And, Captain, I can give you a delicate
poison, to despatch any enemy with whom you dare
not fight.

Mat. I see thou art resolv'd to be a rogue ;
'Tis pity that his Highness did repeal thee.
Next time I see him, sirrah pimp, I will
Make suit to have you sent into Ligorn.

Tra. You Spanish coxcomb, go hang yourself! Do
your worst.

Mat. Wert thou a soldier, I would fight with thee ;
Being a rogue, thou dost deserve my foot.
Take this, you rascal!

Tra. I will presently be out of his debt.—Who's
yonder? It is the Duke, or I am deceiv'd.—Eo, Meo,
and Areo! on again my hat, my glass, and cloak ;
sit close !—How now, sirrah Captain, where are your
manners? What do you think of me ? Who am I,
too ? I am not your lieutenant, am I? Stoop, and
take up your hat, and let me see if it will not become
your hand as well as your head in my presence.

Mat. I did not see your Highness.

Tra. Will you lie, too? Take that, and learn to
speak truth.   [*Kicks him.*

Mat. Most noble Prince, and my most royal master,
Pardon the error which unwillingly
I have committed. In Tuscany there lives not
A man that freelier for your sake would lose
His life than I.

Tra.   Well, get you gone; I do
Forgive you.   My Don at arms, remember
The Duke's to be observ'd; he is the man
That doth maintain you.

Mat.   And, most worthy Prince,
Did but occasion show itself, I would
Venture and lose my life to do you service.   [*Exit.*

Tra. An my father conjuror would come into
Florence, I would make him the next man unto my
Highness. He is a good man, and it is great pity that
he should go to the devil, as they say conjurors and
witches do.   Well, I am a brave fellow; I love to see
myself in my glass.   I am the Duke, i' faith, the very
Duke—I see me!

Enter FLAMETTA.

Fla. I will go and petition him again.

Tra. My rogue Flametta! I could kiss her to pieces,
bite off her lips, and suck out her eyes, I love her so
well.

Fla. The great Duke of Tuscany, the gracious
         heavens
Prosper your Highness ever!   I am the same
That lately did entreat for the repeal
Of my beloved sweetheart Trappolin.
Most excellent sir, pity my earnest suit,
And let me have my Trappolin recall'd.

Tra. This is a very precious villain; how she loves
me!   An I ever marry while I am a Duke, by Eo,
Meo, and Areo's leave, I will have her.—Your name,
little maid, is Flametta, as I remember?

Fla. So please your Highness, yes.

Tra. You sue to have banish'd Trappolin come
home?

Fla. Most humbly, most excellent sir, I do.

Tra. Well, 'tis all as please Eo, Meo, and Areo—I
can do nothing without them; and, my young mistress, as long as they are in authority, I can do little
for you.

Fla. Then, by your Highness' leave, do I wish Eo, Meo, and Areo in the fire!

Tra. Methinks they should be enough in that already, for the devil made them all.—Now I think well on 't, sometime when I have good opportunity I will off with my things, and have a little sport with her.—Since, fair maid, you are so earnest for your sweetheart Trappolin, he shall come home very shortly—he shall, believe me; but upon condition I will do it.

Fla. On any condition except my honour, sir.

Tra. That he shall lie with you!

Fla. Were we but married, most willingly.

Tra. If he gives you his oath to have you, will not that suffice?

Fla. I had rather we had married before.

Tra. You need not fear. Should he swear unto you, and break his oath, I would hang him.—And yet, though I ne'er mean to break my word with her, i' faith, I should very hardly hang myself for anything; the rope is a very dismal thing.

Fla. Shall he come home? Say the word, noble Prince!

Tra. Well, on my word, he shall, as soon as possibly I can; but on that condition that you will accept of him without marriage, upon his oath to have you.

Fla. I see his Highness is mad, as everybody says, otherwise what should ail him to talk thus?—Most excellent Prince, he and I would not disagree.

Tra. Well, here is my hand! he shall come home shortly. Now I must have a kiss, and leave you. I am very hungry; I ha' been so long a doing justice that I am very hungry. Give me a buss, sweetheart!

[*Kisses her.*

Fla. Heaven bless your Highness!

[*Exeunt severally.*

Scene II.

Enter Lavinio, *the great Duke,* Isabella, *the Duchess, with* Attendants.

Lav. My heart's sweet solace, my dear Isabella,
You are most welcome unto Florence!
Live according to your wishes happily,
And may I perish if I do not strive
In everything to please you to my power.
I'm sorry at my coming home I find
Such strange and unexpected alterations,
That, for to quiet them, I must deprive
Myself some hours of your company.
   Isa. Most excellent sir, I do account myself
Most highly blest, that am not only married
Unto a Prince, but one that can
And doth vouchsafe his love unto me, being
Defective of those beauties should deserve it.
To your affairs betake you, worthy sir;
I will expect you till your leisure serves.
   Lav. You are good unto a miracle,
Sweet Isabella! Attend the Duchess in!
Adieu, my love; some few but tedious minutes
Pass'd over, I will come unto you.
   Isa. I will await your leisure.
                       [*Exeunt with* Isabella.
   Lav. What mad fantastic humours have possess'd
In general the heads of the Florentines?
They have amaz'd me—speak as if I
Had been with them before my Duchess came.

Barbarino *and* Machavil *appear in prison.*

   Bar. You great commander of the Tuscan cities,
Pity your subjects and your loyal servants!
In what we sued for we had no design,
Neither the least intent, for to offend.
   Mac. Be merciful, therefore, most gracious Prince!

Let not the noblest of the Florentines
Wear out their days and thraldom in a prison,
Being men not long ago high in your favour.

   Lav. I am lost within a labyrinth of wonders—
I know not what to think. The chiefest of
The Florentine nobility in prison,
And sue to me as if I had commanded
Them to this place? Sure some ill spirit hath
Possess'd men's minds while I was absent. Do you
Know me?

   Bar. Your highness is the Duke our master.

   Lav. Are you not called Barbarino, and you
Machavil, the lords unto whom I left
The government of Tuscany in my absence?

   Mac. We are your loyal subjects, though your prisoners, and were left your deputies when your Highness went to Milan.

   Lav. How came you there?

   Bar. Great sir, you know most well
At your command.

   Lav.   I must be satisfied in this.
Pucannello, so ho!

   Puc. Who calls? What's the matter, I wonder?
                              [*Within.*

   Lav. Release me the lords presently, and send them
    to me hither.
The more I think of these accidents,
The more I marvel how they come to pass.
The men whom I did leave here governors
Are prisoners, and, which increaseth more
Amazement in me, they say it was I
That made them so. Some unheard malady,
Unknown unto the world before, it seems
Hath infected all my subjects with a frenzy.

      Enter BARBARINO *and* MACHAVIL.

   Bar. He hath chang'd his humour, it seems.

   Mac. And may he continue in this, if it be a good
one.

M

Lav. I am astonished to see the things
I every minute do; especially
You two, to whom I left the weighty charge
Of rule, in prison. Resolve me, for Heaven's sake,
How you came there !

Bar. Sure he doth jest with us.

Mac. Your Highness is disposed to be merry.
You know, most excellent sir, full well, that none
Except yourself could do it.

Lav. I do it?

Bar. He doth things in his madness he remembers
not when he's in's right senses, it seems.

Lav. Florence I left a wise ingenious city,
But I have found it now, at my return,
Possess'd with a strange unheard-of madness.
Who put you in prison? Collect your wits int'
    order,
And answer wisely.

Mac. I vow, by the prosperity of Tuscany,
Your Highness !

Lav. Most strange ! Why did I so?

Bar. Because we did, most gracious sir, give notice
Unto you how the Princess Prudentia,
Your matchless, beauteous sister, lov'd Brunetto.

Lav. Whom? What Brunetto?

Mac. Your prisoner, taken in the Mantuan wars.

Lav. My sister to forget herself ! I am
Full of amazement. She, that had refused
The youthful Dukes of Modena and Parma,
Dote on a slave slighted by all the stars !
My sister also so to lose her senses—
She that was wise, and honoured for her virtues !
Sure also this same strange infection
Of madness would ha' seiz'd upon myself
If I had stayed at home. I will not now
So marvel at the common people, seeing
The most discreet of the nobility,
And my own sister, equally distracted.

Mac. I hope he comes to himself again ; he talks
something more wisely than of late.

Lav. It is a frequent thing to see a city
Miserably groan under a heavy sickness—
To have the plague, or fierce diseases full
Of danger, rage and even unpopulate places;
But such a general frenzy to possess
And to distract all Florence is a wonder—
A miracle unmatch'd in history!

Bar. How he talks as if we were all mad, and he
had done nothing!

Lav. Are you sure you are both in your right senses?

Mac. Did once your Highness know us so?

Lav. Yes.

Bar. We are as free from any distraction
As ever yet we were since we were born.

Lav. You must both of you, tho', give me leave to
think what I know.

Enter MATTEMORES.

I'll try an he be mad too.—Captain, these lords say I
put them in prison; how say you?

Mat. So your Highness did.—He's distracted another way.

Lav. Good gods be merciful!—Why?

Mat. Because they spoke against Brunetto's liberty.

Lav. He's in the same tale;
Though they are deprived of their senses,
They do not differ.
But why, good Captain,—answer me a little,—
Should I desire Brunetto's freedom, being
Beloved by my sister, as they say?
Would it not be a great dishonour, think you,
Unto the family of the Medicis,
That she should cast herself away upon one
We do neither know whom or whence he is?
I pray you, Captain, if that yet you have
Any small remnant of your wit remaining,
Reply according to it.

Mat. An he be grown wise again, heavens be
praised!
It is a certain truth your Highness speaks,

That if your sister should bestow herself,
Being a Princess meriting so much
For her unequall'd beauty and her virtues,
Upon a man such as you pleas'd to mention,
It would be a great weakness in her; but you
Yourself I heard, most excellent sir,
To call Brunetto Prince Horatio,
The second son unto the Duke of Savoy.

　Lav. How ? I call him so! Truth, Captain, you
Have heard these things which I did never say.

　　Bar. You never heard him call Brunetto so?

　　Mac. Never; this is the first time I ever heard
　　of it.

　　Lav. My wonder is so great, I do want words
Whereby to give it vent; I see that all
My subjects, being distracted, think me mad!

　　Mat. And more, so please your Highness, you did
　　send
Brunetto, whom you Prince Horatio called,
Unto your sister, to bid her prepare
Herself, for you within a day or two
Would see them married!

　　Lav.　　　　　　　　　Enough!
Captain, I swear unto you by my Dukedom
That rather I would send Brunetto, though
He were the Duke of Savoy's second son,
To have his head struck off than on that message
You say I did.

　　Mat. He doth remember nothing.

　　Bar. If the Duke be come to his right senses again,
I beseech the gods keep him so!

　　Mac. And I.

Enter HORATIO *and* PRUDENTIA.

　　Mac. Beseech your Highness, look! let your own
　　eyes
Be witness of their mutual affection!
Behold the Princess your sister and Brunetto!
Let us withdraw where we may stand unseen,
And you shall hear them talk what I have said.

Hora. Dear lady, you have raised me to a fortune
So high, that when I look upon myself
I am amaz'd, and wonder at your goodness.

Pru. Most noble Prince, let my unfeigned love
Excuse the weak expressions of my tongue!
I'm glad my brother bears so noble a mind
As to be willing to unite our bodies,
As we have done our hearts.

Hora. Not only willing, divine Prudentia,
But earnest for us ; he doth seem to grieve
That two such faithful lovers as we are
Should live so long asunder.

Pru. It is a worthy nature in him.

Lav. I can contain myself no longer ; though this
Be out of madness done, I will not suffer it.
Sister !

Pru. Live long, most worthy brother, happily!

Lav. So should I wish for you, bore you a mind
Deserv'd yourself !

Pru. What mean you, sir ?

Hora. Good heavens, be kind, and do not now undo
What you have almost brought unto perfection !
I fear his madness, that once favoured me,
Hath chang'd his mind to my undoing!

Lav. I will but spend few words. Are you a son
Of the Duke of Savoy's ?

Hora. Your Highness knows I am his second.

Lav.   Whether
You are or no, I care not ; and if you be,
My sister once deserv'd a better husband;
And she shall rather in a monastery
Spend all her future days than be your wife!
And be you what you will, sir, I will show you
That you have wronged me, and I do not fear
The Duke of Savoy, if he be your father.
Pucannello, Pucannello, come hither !

Mac. I like this.

Pru. He's wonderfully distracted! Most worthy
      brother,
Be not so much unmerciful!

Lav. Peace, Prudentia ! I never thought
You had so weak a reason.

Hora. He's mad to my undoing ! Gracious gods,
Soon make him leave this humour !

Bar. I hope he's come unto himself.

Enter PUCANNELLO.

Lav. Sirrah, convey Brunetto into prison !
Lock him up close !

Puc. Here's do and undo. Will our Duke ne'er be
in his
Right senses again?

Pru. My dear Horatio, love me still, for I
Unto thee will be constant, though I die !

Hora. Though I be tortured unto death, my dear !
[Exeunt with HORATIO.

Mat. I know not what to think of these alterations.

Lav. Thus, but the heavens assist, I hope to bring
Int' order from confusion everything. *[Exeunt omnes.*

ACT V.—SCENE I.

Enter TRAPPOLIN, *solus.*

Tra. The Duke is come home, and therefore my
hardest part is behind. Father conjuror, an you be
not my friend now, I am undone. Eo, Meo, and Areo,
sit you all close, and lose not a jot of your virtue.
Happen what will, as soon as I meet his Highness I
will try the virtue of my powder on him, let him take
it how he please.

Enter PRUDENTIA.

Pru. Here is my brother ! I will try him ; perhaps
He may have chang'd his sullen humour now,
And set the Prince Horatio at liberty.
Most excellent, noble sir !

Tra. My dear sister, how dost thou do? Why look
you so sad? Ha' you got the green sickness to-night
with lying alone? An you have, I will take an order

for your cure very shortly, and to your liking, too;
I'll have you married within these two days at the
furthest.

Pru. Married, sir! Unto whom?

Tra. Unto my friend, your lover, Prince Horatio.

Pru. I am glad of this. Alas, sir! why then have
 you
Made him a close unhappy prisoner?

Tra. I see the Duke hath met with him.—
You do deceive yourself, lady sister; indeed
You do! Put up my friend in prison? Heaven
 defend!

Pru. Sir,—pardon me for speaking truth,—I heard
When you commanded it.

Tra. Sister mine, if I did I was drunk, and now I
am sober I will let him out. Sirrah Pucannello! so ho!

Pru. May he continue always in this vein
Of kindness! Thus, his madness is not grievous!

Tra. Madam sister, I am very sorry I was such a
beast as in my drink to commit such a fault. I pray
you forgive me!

Enter PUCANNELLO.

Puc. What is your Highness' will?

Tra. It is that you set Prince Horatio at liberty,
and send him hither presently.

Puc. I wonder!—Most willingly!   [*Exit.*

Pru. You are a gracious prince, and the high gods
Will recompense your pity unto lovers!

Tra. What a swine was I to do such a thing! I
am ashamed as often as I think on 't; I shall be
ashamed to look on my friend. Sister, you must pray
him to forgive me!

Pru. Sir, trouble not yourself; and be assur'd,
Unless you part us, you can never do
Offence either unto the Prince or me!

Enter HORATIO.

Hora. It seems his mind is changed—the heavens
 be praised!

Tra. Prince Horatio, an you do not forgive me my locking of you in prison, I shall never be merry again. I did it when I was drunk, and my sister knows that as soon as she told me on't I sent for you. I pray you, therefore, forgive me, good Prince Horatio!

Hora. Most excellent sir, I was a man unworthy
Of this sweet lady's love did I not freely!

Tra. I thank you, i' faith, Prince Horatio, with all my heart, I swear unto you! Here! take you my sister—take her by the hand, lead her whither you will, and do what you will unto her with her consent; I am very sorry I parted you so long. I know lovers would be private though they do nothing but talk, therefore I will not hinder you. Fare you well, both my princely friend and lady sister!

Pru. The gods preserve you!

Hora. And reward your goodness!   [*Exeunt.*

Tra. Thus what the Duke doth I will undo; such excuses will serve my turn well enough.

Enter BARBARINO *and* MACHAVIL.

Here are my lord banishers. It seems the Duke hath set them at liberty; but in they go again, as sure as the cloaks on their backs!

Bar. May the good angels that attend upon
Princes on earth defend your Highness always
From every offensive thing!

Mac.   And may you live
A long and happy life, enlarge your state,
Excel in fame the first great Duke!

Tra. Your good wishes I like, but credit me, my lord banishers, neither of you. Who let you out of prison?

Bar. He's mad as e'er he was!—Your Highness, sir.

Tra. You lie, sir! Pucannello, come hither quickly!

Mac. Heavens be merciful! we must in again, I see!
He does and undoes, and remembers nothing.

Enter PUCANNELLO.

Tra. Sirrah rogue, why did you set these two at liberty?

Puc. Your Highness did command it.

Mac. If our Duke must be mad, the gods grant him
That which he had the last!

Tra. You ill-faced rascal, you lie!

Puc. Beseech your Highness, remember yourself; it was at your command!

Tra. It may be so, but I am sure I was drunk then, and now I am sober they shall in again; therefore take them with you. Begone, I say!

Bar. There is no remedy.

Mac. Good gods, pity Florence! [*Exeunt.*

Tra. Eo, Meo, and Areo, thanks! i' faith, yet I am supposed the Duke! Father conjuror, by thy art I am suppos'd a prince! Stick to me still, and be my friend!

Enter ISABELLA.

Here is the Duchess! Eo, Meo, and Areo, be true to me, and I'll have a kiss or two at the least.

Isa. Sir, you are fortunately met.

Tra. Who are you, lady madam?

Isa. Do you not know, sir?

Tra. I'd have you tell me.

Isa. I never knew him so before.—I am your wife!

Tra. I'm glad on't, I promise you; come and kiss me, then.

Isa. You are wondrous merrily disposed.

Tra. Madam Duchess, I am something jovial indeed; I have been a drinking Montefiascone very hard. Kiss me again, my dear lady wife!

Isa. He's drunk!

Tra. You are a handsome woman, I promise you. Prithee, tell me, my lady Duchess, am I a proper, handsome fellow?

Isa. Do not jest with me, sir; you know you are
Him whom above the world I do esteem!

Tra. Well said, my lady wife !

Isa. I ne'er saw him so distempered before.

Tra. Have you nothing yet in your belly ?

Isa. You know I am with child, sir.

Tra. Faith, but I do not, for your belly swells not.

Isa. I am full of wonder !

Tra. Lady wife, get you in, I am half drunk, and now am unfit for you ; but give me a kiss or two before.   Madam Duchess, fare you well !

Isa. I had thought he had not been addicted to
A vice so loathsome as drunkenness.   [*Exit.*

Tra. Yet all happens very well ! Protest the Duchess is a gallant woman—I almost like her as well as Flametta.   I could lie with her ; and I would, but I am half honest, and will not wrong the Duke nor Flametta.   Why, is not my wench as good as she? Wherein do they differ, but only in clothes ?   Flametta's a woman as right as she, and perhaps, naked, as handsome !   What good in the night do jewels and fine clothes to a woman when she hath them not on ? Besworn I am very merry !   Eo, Meo, and Areo are brave, tame devils, and my father conjuror an excellent learned fellow !

Vienca wine and Padua bread,
Trivigi tripes, and a Venice wench in bed !
                               [*Exit singing.*

SCENE II.

Enter LAVINIO.

Ye glorious planets, that do rightly guide
The giddy ships upon the ocean waves,
If some of your malignant influences
Have rais'd this madness in my subjects' heads,
Let some of your benign influences
Again restore them to their former senses !
Those Florentines, whom all their enemies
Could not impeach, could not withstand in arms,

Suffer not, you immortal powers divine,
Thus to be ruin'd by distraction !

    MACHAVIL *and* BARBARINO *appear in prison.*

I am astonished !   O heavens, I know not what to
    think !
Pucannello ! Pucannello ! let me out the two lords,
and send them to me presently ; I'll talk unto 'em
here at large.
    Bar. His ill fit 's off.
    Mac. The gods be praised !
    Lav. I do not think that since the infancy
And first creation of the world a madness
Pestiferous and equal unto this
Was ever known.   Good heavens reveal, and soon,
The cause, that I may do my best to help it !

    Enter BARBARINO, MACHAVIL, *and* PUCANNELLO.

    Mac. Long may this fit continue !
    Bar. If it hold always, sure he's in 's wits again.
    Lav. I wonder, lords, and justly, that you, whom I
have known to have the noblest judgments, should
thus become distracted.   You in your fits of frenzy
run to prison of yourselves, and think I sent you !
    Bar. Most royal sir, we grieve to see these days.
You did command us thither.
    Lav. I ?
    Mac. Your Highness' self.
    Lav. You are both deceiv'd.   To do such idle errors,
And lay the blame on me, doth more amaze me !
Pucannello, how came these in prison ?
    Puc. So please your Highness, you were angry with
    them,
And did commit them.
    Lav.   I commit them ?
That thou art mad is not so great a wonder.
I tell you both with sorrow, witness Heaven !
You are strangely bereaved of your reason !
Well, go ye in, and pray unto the gods

That they hereafter would be kind unto you,
And keep you from relapse!

   Mac. Heavens bless your Highness!

   Bar. And be unto you a perpetual guard! [*Exeunt.*

   Lav. Famine, plague, war,—the ruinous instruments
Wherewith the incensed deities do punish
Weak mankind for misdeeds,—had they all fallen
Upon this city, it had been a thing
To be lamented, but not wondered at.

Enter ISABELLA.

Oh, my dear Isabella, I have brought thee
From Milan, flourishing in all delights,
Into a city full of men distracted.

   Isa. He's not sober yet.—Go in and sleep, sir;
You do not well to betray your weakness
Unto the public view.

   Lav. My wife and all!   O heavens!

   Isa. What say you, sir?

   Lav. My Isabella, thou hast cause to curse me
For bringing thee unto a place infected!
The air is sure pestiferous, and I wonder
Now how I have escaped.

   Isa. Good sir, I pray you sleep.

   Lav. Wherefore, my Isabella?

   Isa. Why, you have drunk too much!

   Lav. Madness unmatch'd!
Dear Isabella, withdraw thyself into
Thy chamber; I will presently come to thee.
There we will pray unto the angry gods
That they would from 's remove this heavy ill.

   Isa. I will obey you, sir, to get you home.
Good gods, ne'er let him thus offend again!   [*Exit.*

   Lav. What have I done so much offensive to
The supreme powers, that they should punish me
Not only with the madness of my subjects,
But the distraction of my wife and sister?

Enter HORATIO *and* PRUDENTIA.

What do I see?   They do embrace and kiss!

My sister's madness will undo her!   How
He came at liberty I marvel much.
Whom I would have to lie in prison walk in freedom;
and whom I would have in freedom run of themselves
to prison.

Pru. Most noble brother!

Lav. Sister, I grieve to see thee thus.

Hora. Excellent Prince!

Lav. Sure the good angels, that had wont to guard
The Medicis in all their actions,
Have for the horrid sins of Florence left us,
And fled to heaven!

Hora. His mind again is altered.

Pru. Dear brother, do not frown and look so angry.

Lav. Peace, sister, I'm asham'd to hear you speak;
Each word you say is poison in my ears.
Pucannello!   Jailor!

Puc. I come.   [*Within.*

Pru. What mean you, sir?

Hora. I must again to prison.   Fickle fortune,
How soon a happy man thou makest wretched!

Enter PUCANNELLO.

Lav. Sirrah, why did you set this man Brunetto,
Or this Horatio—I know not what to call him—
At liberty?

Puc. Will he ne'er be wise?—Your Highness bade
    me.

Lav. I?   Bethink you, and answer truly!

Puc. Your Highness knows I durst not for my life
Ha' done 't without your licence.

Pru. Sweet brother!

Lav. Silence would become you better far.

Hora. Life of my heart, do not disturb yourself;
I am unworthy you should speak for me.

Lav. Sirrah, take him again, and look to him better
than you have.   Your madness shall not excuse you
if once more you serve me thus.

Hora. I must be patient.   Good heavens, soon alter

this sullen fit into his former kindness! Farewell, my
sweet Prudentia!   [*Exeunt with* HORATIO.

Pru. I wonder, brother, what pleasure you take
In crossing me after this sort!

Lav. It is vain to answer frantic people.

Pru. I?—I am mad? 'Tis your perverseness
makes me.   [*Exeunt.*

SCENE III.

Enter TRAPPOLIN, *solus.*

Tra. Yet I cannot meet with the Duke. I long to
see him look like me. I would fain powder his Highness. Eo, Meo, and Areo, I thank you, faith—my hat,
my glass, and cloak! Honest father conjuror, I will
love thee while I live!

Enter BARBARINO *and* MACHAVIL.

Hell's broke loose again! I do what the Duke undoes,
and he undoes what I do.

Mac. Long live your Highness!

Tra. Amen.

Bar. And happily!

Tra. Amen, I say. But how, my small friends,
came you hither? I thought you had been under lock
and key.

Mac. I fear he's ill as e'er he was.

Tra. Sirrah Pucannello! so ho! so ho! Come
hither, you rogue.

Bar. We must in again.

Mac. Good gods, will this frenzy never leave him?

Enter PUCANNELLO.

Tra. Goodman dirty-face, why did you not keep me
these in prison till I bid you let them out?

Puc. So please your Highness, so I did.

Tra. Dare you lie so boldly? You take me for a
doctor,—Gracian of Franckolin, I warrant you,—or a
fool in a play, you're so saucy with me!

Mac. Good gods !

Bar. Was ever heard the like ?

Puc. Beseech your Highness to remember yourself !

Tra. Now I bethink myself, perhaps I might do it when I was drunk. If I did bid you give them liberty, it was when I was foxed, and now I am sober lay them up again. Walk, my good lord banishers ; your honours know the way.

Puc. Will this humour never leave him ?

Bar. We must endure it.

Mac. There is no remedy.

Tra. My lord prisoners, get you gone; I am an hungry, and cannot stand to hear any suppli- cation.

Puc. You must obey, my lords.   [*Exeunt.*

Tra. Yet all goes well, all goes exceeding well—
My will's obeyed ; I am suppos'd the Duke ;
My hat, my glass, and cloak retain their force ;
And father conjuror does not forsake me.   [*Exit.*

SCENE IV.

Enter MATTEMORES, *the Spanish Captain, solus.*

Mat. Though, horrid war, thou bear'st a bloody sword,
And marchest o'er the world in dreadful arms !
Though fearful mankind, on their humble knees,
Beseech the gods to keep thee from their homes !
Yet art thou, when trick'd up in dismal robes,
Presaging death and ruin to a state,
More lovely to a valiant soldier's eyes
Than are the pleasures of a wanton court !
And sure, if our great Duke Lavinio
Had been i' th' field expecting of a foe,
He ne'er had been distracted as he is !
'Tis peace that doth bewitch us from ourselves,
Fills most heroic hearts with amorous toys,
And makes us to forget what honour is !
But, for Hipolita's sake, I must not speak

Anything ill of love.   Love, I must say,
Is good, but war leads the more noble way.

Enter LAVINIO.

Lav. How do you, Captain ?
Mat. I am your Highness' creature.
Lav. Saw you not lately Barbarino or Machavil ?
Mat. Yes.
Lav. Where are they ?
Mat. Your Highness knows, in prison.
Lav. O heavens, in prison again ! Good gods, when
will you remove this frenzy from the Florentines ?
Mat. I see there is little hope on him.
Lav. Why are they in prison ?
Mat. Because your Highness did command.
Lav. Never, Captain ; I never did command it ! Go
and bid Pucannello let them out.
Mat. Sir, he dares not at my bidding.
Lav. Here, take my ring, and do 't !
Mat. One humour in the morning, and another in
the afternoon ! Will it never be better ?   [*Exit.*
Lav. Would I did know what heinous sin it is
I have committed that is so offensive
Unto the gods to cause this punishment,
That I might sue unto them for forgiveness,
And they be reconciled and pity Florence !
I'm full and full of wonder.   Perhaps some fiend,
Permitted by the heavens, assumes my shape,
And what I do undoeth.   Was ever known
Such a distraction in the world before ?

Enter TRAPPOLIN.

Tra. At last I have found him.
Lav. This the impostor is that hath deceiv'd
The eyes of all ; it can be nothing else.
Tra. I vow and swear I am something afraid ; but I
will be bold.   Eo, Meo, and Areo, sit close ! Come
out, powder, come out ! Father conjuror, I rely on
your powder.
Take that for my sake !   [*Flings it on him.*

Lav. What rudeness is this?

Tra. I have done 't, i' faith. Trappolin, I have repealed thee for Flametta's sake.

Lav. How is this?
If thou art a fiend, the gracious heavens be kind,
And give a period to thy wild proceedings!
But if thou art a conjuror, I'll have thee
Burnt for thy magic, as thou dost deserve.

Tra. Trappolin, talk wisely.

Lav. Why dost thou call me so?

Tra. Aha! a man forget himself so! Art thou not he?

Lav. I am the Duke.

Tra. Beware of treason. Do you know your own face if you see it? Look here!—what say you now?

Lav. I am bewitch'd! Thou art a conjuror,
And hast transform'd me to a banish'd rogue.

Tra. For Flametta's sake I pardon thee this language, but learn to speak better, lest you walk again.
[Exit.

Lav. Heaven, earth, and hell have all agreed together
To load me with a plague unknown before
Unto the world! The heavens have given consent
Unto my misery! Hell hath plotted it!
And the deceived earth believes me mad,
And now will take me for a banish'd rogue!

Enter FLAMETTA.

Fla. Oh, joy above expression! Behold,
My Trappolin is come! Love, welcome home!
Thou art beholding unto me, my dear;
'Twas I that won the Duke for thy repeal.

Lav. I am amazed!

Fla. Give me a hundred kisses! Let us spend
An hour in kissing; afterwards we'll talk.

Lav. Away!

Fla. Have you forgotten me so soon? I am
Thy true Flametta, lovely Trappolin!

Lav. Begone, I say!

N

Fla. Dost thou reward me thus for all the pains
I've took to get thee home again?
   Lav.   Leave me,
Thou impudent whore, or I will kick thee hence!
   Fla. Oh, faithless men! Women, by me take
     heed
You give no trust unto this perjur'd sex!
Have I all thy long banishment been true?—
Refused Lord Barbarino with all his gifts?—
And am I slighted thus? I will complain
Unto his Highness of thee!

Enter MATTEMORES.

Lav. Have you done 't?
Mat. What?
Lav. Have you set the lords at liberty?
Mat. What's that to thee?
Lav. Give me my ring!
Mat. He has heard the Duke sent me with his
ring, and this impudent rogue dares think to get it.
Sirrah, is it not enough to be a coward and a pander,
but you would be a thief too?
Lav. I am bewitched!
Fla. I fear my Trappolin is turned madman.
Lav. Suffer not this, ye gods!

Enter TRAPPOLIN.

Mat. I have set the Lords Barbarino and Machavil
at liberty, according to your Highness' order, and
here is your ring again.
Tra. Better and better.—I marvel where the Prince
Horatio is?
Mat. He forgets everything.—He's in prison!
Tra. Sure he is not!
Lav. How this impostor devil acts me!
Mat. Your Highness did commit him.
Tra. Fie upon 't, what things do I do in my drink!
Here, take my ring; go and set him out, and come
hither with him presently.

Lav. I am the Duke, and will be obey'd !
Go not, upon your life !   He shall lie there.

Fla. Sure my Trappolin's run mad for grief in his
banishment.

Mat. Peace, frantic, peace ! do not disturb his Highness !

Tra. Regard not madmen.   Go !

Mat. I'm gone.   [*Exit.*

Lav. Thou traitor !

Fla. Dear Trappolin, be silent ; regard my tears !
Thou wilt undo thyself.

Tra. Maiden, an your sweetheart continue thus,
I'll have him sent abroad again.

Enter PRUDENTIA.

Fla. Sweet Trappolin, for my sake hold thy
  tongue !

Lav. I rage in vain—good heavens be merciful !

Pru. Dear brother, pity me ; regard my sorrow !
Release the Prince Horatio, and no longer
Separate their bodies whose hearts the gods have
  joined.

Tra. Sister, have patience a little, a very little ;
Prince Horatio will be here presently, and I'll make
an end with you.

Lav. Prudentia, art thou not ashamed ?

Pru. What sauciness is this ?
Most worthy noble brother, all my heart is full of
thanks for you ! Would I'd a tongue could utter them !

Enter MATTEMORES *and* HORATIO.

Mat. Your Highness' ring.

Tra. 'Tis well, Captain.   Sister, and Prince Horatio,
Here, take my signet ; by the warrant of it go
And get you married.

Hora. Our humble thanks !

Lav. I do want patience.

Hora. 'Tis best to do it whilst he's in good
  humour.
Are you content, sweet Princess ?

Pru. With all my soul I go. [*Exeunt.*

Lav. Sister! sister!

Mat. Peace, lest you be soundly punished, sirrah!

Fla. Good Trappolin, be quiet.

Lav. I am the Duke!—I am Lavinio!
This is a fiend of hell, or an impostor.

Mac. Will your Highness suffer this?

Tra. I pity him; he knows not what he says.

Lav. I am bewitched!

Mat. I am sure thou art distracted.

Tra. 'A done, you had best!

Lav. Thou enemy unto our happiness,
Know the gods will relent; in time be wise!

Tra. There is no remedy; he must go to Pucannello.
So ho! Pucannello! so ho!

Puc. I come! [*Within.*

Fla. There could come no better of it. Beseech your Highness, pardon him; he's distracted!

Lav. You are all distracted, all bewitched!

Enter PUCANNELLO.

Tra. Sirrah, take Trappolin, and lock him up safe.

Fla. You'd take no warning.

Lav. Oh, Florence, how I pity thy decay!

Tra. Away with him!

Mat. Pucannello, take him, and begone!

Tra. You of the guards, see him laid safely up.

Lav. I will not go!

Puc. We then might force you. [*Exeunt.*

Fla. Alas! poor Flametta! thy Trappolin cares not for thee. I beseech the gods to give him his right senses again!

Tra. Come, Captain!

Mat. I attend your Highness. [*Exeunt.*

Scene V.

Enter BARBARINO *and* MACHAVIL.

Mac. The strange distraction of our Duke will give
Sufficient matter unto chronicles
To make whole volumes of him.
Bar. Yet he believes himself right in his senses,
And we, out of our wits, think him mad !

LAVINIO *appears in prison.*

Lav. Would I had been born to a mean estate,
So in 't I might have lived happily !
The greater honours that men have, the greater
Their troubles are.   The beggar that hath nothing
Lives a more quiet life than monarchs do.
Lord Barbarino and Lord Machavil,
Get me releas'd !   I am the Duke Lavinio,
Bewitched, as you are, by an impostor.
Bar. Go, Trappolin, and sleep.   We have heard all—
Thou art run mad.
Mac. Go sleep, poor Trappolin !
Lav. Be kind ; good gods pity our miseries !
Bar. Leave talking, and go sleep.

Enter TRAPPOLIN.

Mac. His Highness.
Bar. How fares our noble master ?
Tra. I have not been sober a day together this good
while.   Eo, Meo, and Areo have made me foxed ; but
now I will leave it.
Mac. Who are they ?
Bar. I know not.
Tra. It's in vain to lay them up any more, I
having had sport enough with them.—Trappolin,
whom you banish'd, is come home stark mad.
Mac. Exceedingly.
Bar. And raves most strangely in prison.

Enter FLAMETTA.

Fla. Here is his Highness. I will not leave him till
He doth release from prison Trappolin.
Most excellent sir, perfect your noble kindness—
Give liberty unto poor Trappolin !

Tra. With all my heart I would, would he be quiet.

Fla. Alas ! he is distracted, and doth not know
What he says ; and therefore why should you regard
    him ?

Tra. Well, fair maid, for thy sake, that lovest him
so, he shall come out. Pucannello ! so ho ! Come
hither !

Bar. He will do anything, and undo anything.

Mac. Sure there was never such a duke i' th' world !

Enter HORATIO *and* PRUDENTIA.

Tra. Welcome, sister and brother, I hope I may
say ! Are you married ?—are you content ? Tell me
if anything remains that I can do for you. Speak it,
for I am ready ; the Duke, your servant.

Pru. Most worthy brother, you have perfected our
joys, for we are married !

Tra. I am very glad, lady sister, that you are so.

Hora. Here is your Highness' ring.

Enter PUCANNELLO.

Tra. You, sirrah of chains and keys, set me Trappolin at liberty presently, and send him hither !

Puc. Will he never be wise ? I would he would
make another jailor—I am weary of the place. I can
never be at quiet for putting in and setting out.

Fla. The heavens reward your goodness !
                            [*Exit* PUCANNELLO.

Tra. Brother and Prince Horatio, I am something
given to be drunk. Eo, Meo, and Areo are good fellows ; but, I pray you, pardon me.

Hora. Sir, you wrong yourself.

Tra. My friend and Prince Horatio, I'll ne'er
wrong myself, I warrant you. But you I have, and

my sister Prudentia; but it was when I was foxed, and I will never be so again.

Enter MATTEMORES *and* HIPOLITA.

Mac. I am glad he will once let us be quiet.

Bar. I should be very glad if he would continue it.

Tra. How now, Signor Captain! ha' you got a sweetheart?

Mat. A fair mistress, so please your Highness.

Tra. I see, my Don-at-arms, when you cannot follow the wars of the field, you will of the bed.

Enter LAVINIO.

Fla. Prithee, my Trappolin, now hold thy tongue! Be wise, my love.

Lav. Leave me, thou frantic fool!

Tra. For Flametta's sake I have given you your liberty; use it well.

Lav. O heavens! endure not this impostor thus With his enchantments to bewitch our eyes!

Mac. Will he suffer him?

Bar. Perhaps one madman will pity another.

Lav. Ye Florentines, I am Lavinio—
I am the Tuscan Duke; this an enchanter,
That by his magic art hath raised all
These strange chimeras in my court!

Mat. Your Highness is too patient; it were more fit he rav'd in prison.

Fla. Sweet Trappolin, be rul'd.

Tra. Hold your tongue, I say.

Hora. Poor Trappolin! art thou distracted too?

Lav. You lords of Florence, wise Machavil, and
You, Lord Barbarino, will you never come
Out of this frenzy? Valiant Mattemores,
I am the Duke! I am Lavinio!
This, whom you do suppose is me, is some
Hellish magician, that hath bewitched us all!

Tra. He will not be ruled. Pucannello, take him again!

Fla. Beseech your Highness!—Trappolin, come away.

Pru. Ah, my poor subjects, how I pity you,
That must obey the monstrous wickedness
Of one that works by necromantic means,
And is forsaken by the blessed gods!

Tra. Away with him!

Enter MAGO.

Mago. Stay!

Tra. Yon's father conjuror!

Bar. What new accident is this?

Tra. I hope he'll do no hurt.

Hora. What will the event be, marle?

Mat. What old long beard's this?

Mago. A word with you!
Will you, if I clear everything,
Pardon what's past?

Lav. Do you know me, then?

Mago. You are the Duke.

Tra. Father conjuror, do no hurt, and I'll give you
a hundred pistoles to buy you sallets and oil i' th'
wood.

Mago. I'll talk with you even now.
Will you promise me?

Lav. I swear by all the honours of my state,
By both my dukedoms, Florence and Sienna,
I will forgive whatever's past!

Mago. Him and all?

Lav. Him and all.

Tra. Good father conjuror, remember your son!

Mac. What will come of this?

Mago. Be not affrighted.

Mat. Never, not I!

Mago. Whate'er you see,
Fear not; nothing shall hurt you.

Pru. This is a conjuror.

Hip. Sweet Captain, stand close by me.

Bar. What strange events are these?

Mago. Eo, Meo, and Areo, appear!

Tra. I am undone, I fear. Father conjuror, remember your son. I'll give you two hundred pistoles!

Mago. Appear, I say!

Enter Eo, Meo, *and* Areo.

Pru. Alas!

Hora. Fear nothing.

Hip. O me!

Mat. Be bold; I am here, Hipolita!

Mago. Go, take the hat, the glass, and cloak from him.

Tra. Ah me! ah me! Here, here, here, here—come not too near me! Eo, Meo, and Areo, farewell, all on you! Father conjuror has undone me!

Bar. Trappolin?

Mac. Two Trappolins?

Fla. I know not which is mine!

Mago. Attend a while!
Thus, with the waste of this enchanted wand,
I do release your Highness.

Mat. The Duke?

Hora. Wonders!

Mago. You have engaged your word: y'ave pardoned all—me, who have done and undone everything, and him, and everybody!

Lav. I have.

Mac. The heavens be praised! Long live your Highness!

Omnes. Long live the Duke!

Hora. What will become of me?

Mago. I'll perfect everything.
Brave Prince Horatio, your elder brother,
Prince Filberto, is dead. Sir, you cannot
With reason dislike this match; they are
Married, and your consent doth perfect it.

Lav. Now I am assured he is a Turin prince,
Heir to the dukedom of Savoy, I am glad
They are espoused. Sister, I wish you joy!
Sir, I entreat forgiveness for what's past!

Hora. All's forgotten.

Pru. Thanks, gracious heavens !

Lav. I'll have your wedding solemnized with state.

Mac. I am glad this Gordian knot's untied.

Tra. I shall be hanged, father conjuror.

Mago. The Duke hath pardoned you and me all.

Tra. Then let Eo, Meo, and Areo go to the devil, from whence they came. Flametta, I am thine !

Fla. Ah, my dear Trappolin !

Tra. Here is your Highness' ring.

Mago. From henceforth I abjure my wicked art.

Hor. I for thy love to me will send thee into Piedmont, and give thee an earldom in Vercelli.

Tra. The heavens reward you ! You know I always made much of your Highness' majesty. Flametta, thou shalt be a countess !

Mago. Son Trappolin, I am thy natural father, twenty years since banished ten years from Florence. Through my misfortune I have served the Turk in his galleys.

Tra. By your leave, father, you have served the devil too, I'm sure, for you are one of the best conjurors in the world. Welcome unto the court, your son of honour, and to Flametta's earlship ! Will your honours forgive me too ?

Mac. Yes.

Enter ISABELLA.

Bar. For the princess' sake, I do.

Tra. I thank you both. Now all's well again. Henceforth I will live honestly, and be the devil's butcher no longer !

Lav. My Isabella, welcome ! Everything
That did molest our happiness in Florence
Is took away. Now we will spend our time
In courtly joys ; our famous Tuscan poets
Shall study amorous comedies and masks,
To entertain my beauteous Milaness.

I have a story full of ridiculous wonders,
Within to tell thee at our better leisure.
  Tra. The weaker side must yield unto the stronger,
And Trappolin's suppos'd a Prince no longer.

[Exeunt omnes.

THE EPILOGUE.

Ladies and gentlemen, you that now may
Approve, or, if you please, condemn our play,
We thank you first; for here it was not writ,
In sweet repose and fluencies of wit,
But far remote—at Rome begun, half made
At Naples, at Paris the conclusion had.
Yet the perfection is behind, which, if
You give's a plaudit, you in England give;
Our nation's courteous unto strangers, nor
Should you refrain unto this traveller.
I must not sue; there's nothing now remains
Saving the guerdon of our poet's pains:
He for himself is careless, only would
That for the actors' sakes you'd say 'tis good.
We are doubtful yet, your hands will set all right;
Do what you please, and, gentlemen, good-night!

THE TRAGEDY OF OVID.

The Tragedy of Ovid. Written by Sir Aston Cokain, Baronet. London, Printed for Phil. Stephens, jun., at the King's Arms, over against Middle Temple Gate, in Fleet Street. 1662.

The Tragedy of Ovid. Written by Sir Aston Cokain, Baronet. London, Printed for Francis Kirkman, and are to be sold at his shop, under St. Ethelborough's Church, in Bishopsgate Street. 1669. 16mo.

PUBLIUS OVIDIUS NASO, who gives the title to this tragedy, was born at Sulmo, on 20th March, about forty-three years before the Christian era. Intended by his father for the bar, he was sent early to Rome, thence, in his sixteenth year, to Athens; but although he excelled in the study of eloquence, the natural bent of his mind was poetry, and in despite of every remonstrance, and the proverbial poverty of poets, he still continued to follow in the wake of the Muse Erato. He soon gained admirers, and Virgil, Tibullus, Propertius, and Horace corresponded with him. Augustus himself patronized him most liberally; but having incurred that Emperor's displeasure, he was, in his fiftieth year, banished to Tomos, a town on the western shores of the Euxine Sea. The cause of this sudden exile is doubtful, but these lines from his pen would seem to indicate that it was in consequence of his having come to a knowledge of some great impropriety in the court or family of Augustus:

> " Cur aliquid vidi ? Cur noxia lumina feci ?
>   Cur imprudenti cognita culpa mihi est ?
> Nescius Actæon vidit sine veste Dianam,
>   Præda fuit canibus non minus ille suis."

Again :

> " Nescia quod crimen viderunt lumina plector,
>   Peccatumque oculos est habuisse meum."

And further :

> " Perdiderunt cum me duo crimina, carmen et error,
>   Alterius facti culpa silenda mihi est."

In his banishment, Ovid applied frequently to the Emperor, in lines of entreaty and adulation, for a remission of his sentence, but without effect; nor was Tiberius more yielding than his predecessor to Ovid's petitions, backed though they were by many ardent and influential friends at Rome. He did not live long after this. His death took place in the fifty-ninth year of his age, A.D. 17, and he was buried in the land of his exile.

The greater part of Ovid's poems are extant. His *Metamorphoses*, in fifteen books, are curious, on account of the mythological traditions which they record. His *Fasti* were divided into twelve books, six of which have been lost, which is much to be regretted, as, judging from the books which remain, much light would have been thrown upon the religious rites and ceremonies, festivals and sacrifices, of the ancient Romans. His *Tristia*, in five books, as well as his *Elegies*, exhibit much elegance and refinement of expression. The *Heroides* are, in poetic diction, excellent. His three books of *Amorum*, and the same number *De Arte Amandi*, with the *De Remedio Amoris*,

are equally redolent of fine poetic imagery, but their insidious
tendency is apt to corrupt the heart and engender immorality.
He wrote some other pieces, among which is a fragment of a
tragedy called *Medea*, no doubt influenced by the common belief
that it was at Tomos where Medea cut to pieces the body of her
brother Absyrtus. Ovid was thrice married. He had only
one daughter, but by which of his three wives is unknown; she
herself became the mother of two children by two husbands.

Of *Ovid's Tragedy*, Langbaine—*Art.* Cokain—says: "This
play was printed since the rest of his works, though 'tis frequently bound with them. I know not why the author gave
this play the title of *Ovid's Tragedy*, except that he lays the
scene in Tomos, and brings him to fall down dead with grief at
the news he received from Rome, in sight of the audience;
otherwise he has not much business on the stage, and the play
ought rather to have taken the name from Bassanes' jealousy
and the dismal effects thereof,—the murder of his new bride
Clorina, and his friend Pyrontus. But this is an error which
Beaumont and Fletcher have heretofore committed, as Mr.
Rymer has observed, in *A King and No King*, and therefore
more excusable in our author. The passage of Captain Hannibal's inviting the dead carcase of Helvidius to supper is
possibly borrowed from the Italian play called *Il Atheisto
Fulminato*, to which language our author was no stranger, and
on which foundation the catastrophe of *The Libertine* is built,"
i.e. Molière's *Don Juan, ou le festin de Pierre.* Some portions
of the plot and language, which in themselves are good, derive
their source from Ovid's *Elegies*. The situation of Alonzo,
Carlos, and Leonora, in Young's *Revenge*, is not unlike that of
Bassanes, Pyrontus, and Clorina in this tragedy.

Charles Cotton, to whom this play is dedicated, is best known
from having been the friend of Izaak Walton, and author of the
second part of the *Complete Angler*. He resided for a great
part of his life at Beresford, in the county of Stafford. He
had some reputation for lyric poetry, but was particularly famous
for burlesque poetry. He translated Corneille's *Horace*, printed
in 4to, 1671, with a dedication to his dear sister, Mrs. Stanhope
Hutchinson. Of his burlesque works, *Scarronides, or Virgil
Travestie*, which appeared in 1678, and has been frequently
reprinted, has been always regarded as exceeding not only the
French, but all those who made any attempts in that kind of
poetry, the incomparable author of *Hudibras* excepted. His
translation of Montaigne's *Essays*, in three volumes, is still
considered the best. Some of his minor poems, published
collectively in 1689, are of great excellence, and the volume has
commendatory verses by Colonel Lovelace, Sir Aston Cockain,
Robert Herrick, and Mr. Alexander Brome.

The date of his death is uncertain, but it has been conjec-
tured that it was some time after the Revolution.

TO MY MOST HIGHLY HONOURED COUSIN,

CHARLES COTTON, Esq.

NOBLE Cousin, as soon as I had finished this play of mine, called the *Tragedy of Ovid*, I sent it to wait upon you at your house in Beresford, where it found so courteous and generous an entertainment, that I should accuse myself of much ingratitude did I not dedicate it to you, and entreat your favour that it might visit the world under the secure patronage of your authentic name. I beseech you, therefore, to afford it so much grace, and to give it leave to lie in your parlour window, since you have been pleased to signalize it with two excellent epigrams. This is but a small testimony of my thankfulness to you for an abundancy of high and obliging favours that I have, upon all occasions, received from you. To which you will infinitely add by continuing in your good opinion,

Sir,

Your very affectionate kinsman,

And most humble servant,

ASTON COKAIN.

O

TO THE AUTHOR,

UPON HIS TRAGEDY OF OVID.

LONG live the poet and his lovely muse,
The stage with wit and learning to infuse !
Embalm him in immortal elegy,
My gentle Naso; for if he should die
Who makes thee live, thou 'lt be again pursu'd,
And banish'd heaven for ingratitude!
Transform again thy *Metamorphoses*
In one, and turn thy various shapes to his.
A twin-born muse in such embraces curl'd
As shall subject the scribblers of the world,
And, spite of time and envy, henceforth sit,
The ruling gemini of love and wit.
So two pure streams in one smooth channel glide,
In even motion, without ebb or tide,
As in your pens Tiber and Anchor meet,
And tread meanders with their silver feet.
  Both soft, both gentle, both transcending high,
Both skill'd alike in charming elegy ;
So equally admired, the laurel's due,
Without distinction, both to him and you.
  Naso was Rome's fam'd Ovid ; you alone
Must be the Ovid to our Albion,
In all things equal, saving in this case,
Our modern Ovid has the better grace.

CHARLES COTTON, *Philodramatos.*

TO THE AUTHOR, ON CAPTAIN HANNIBAL.

AN EPIGRAM.

YOUR Captain Hannibal does snort and puff,
Arm'd in his brazen face and greasy buff,
'Mongst Puncks and Panders, and can rant and roar
With Cacala the turd and his poor whore;
But I would wish his valour not mistake us,
All captains are not like his brother Dacus.
Advise him, then, be quiet, or I shall
Bring Captain Hough to baste your Hannibal.

CHARLES COTTON.

DRAMATIS PERSONÆ.

PYRONTUS, . . *A young Lord.*
PHYLOCLES, . . *His Friend.*
BASSANES, . . *A young Lord.*
MARULLUS, . . *His Friend.*
PHŒBIANUS, . . *Pyrontus' younger Brother,*
    called also CARALINDA.
HANNIBAL, . . *A banish'd Italian Captain.*
CACALA, . . . *A young Fellow, his man.*
PUBLIUS OVIDIUS NASO.
DACUS, . . . *A Getic Captain.*

CLORINA, . . . *Bassanes' Bride.*
ARMELINA, . . *Her Sister.*
CYPASSIS, . . *A Bawd.*
SPINELLA, . . *Her Daughter, a Courtezan of Tomos.*
FLORETTA, . . *A Roman Courtezan.*

MASKERS.   A SPECTRE.   SERVANTS.

The Scene :—

TOMOS, *a city in Pontus.*

THE PROLOGUE.

A MANY famous poets do not refuse
With prologues to usher in the tragic muse :
The reason, gallants, I presume to say
To Tomos you are welcome all to-day.
For fear, lest when y'ave seen 't, you should repent
[Of loss which then you cannot well prevent],
I tell you, though our play is new, 'tis writ
After an ill old mode, with little wit ;
For in it there is a devil and a fool—
Such sights as boys affect that go to school.
This said, you have our leave, without offence,
To take your money again, and to go hence.
Nothing of Ovid, then !   Enough, enough
Dancing and fighting, and much amorous stuff.
If any of these invite your stay, pray know
We hope to please you, whether you will or no.
But if you shall dislike it, gentlemen,
Revenge yourselves, and never see 't again !

THE TRAGEDY OF OVID.

Enter PYRONTUS *furiously, intending to fall upon his sword, and* PHYLOCLES *after him, who with his foot strikes it away.*

Pyr. Uncivil man, begone ! before my rage
Increases above my troubled patience,
And I for this untimely courtesy
Make thee to harbinger my soul in death !
    Phyl. Alas, my lord ! why will you take away
The noblest life that ever honour'd Pontus ?
I pray you, think upon 't.
    Pyr.   I am resolved ;
Nor will I live to see Clorina made
A wife to any man besides myself.
    Phyl. Ah! who would not run mad, and tear his
        hair,
And weep until his eyeballs did dissolve,
To see the bravest man of all this land
So passionate, and for a scornful lady ?
    Pyr. Kill me, Phylocles ! thou wilt do a deed
The gods will love thee for ; for I am one
Full of those things that virtuous souls abhor,
Else sure Clorina would not use me thus.
    Phyl. To my own death, to do you real service,
You may command me readily, my lord ;
But to entice me to advance my hand
Against your life—great Jove, and all the gods
Whom we do reverence and fear, forbid !

Pyr. Phylocles, dost thou love me ?

Phyl. You know, my lord, I do, above my life !
In our late wars, when we did aid our friends
The fortunate Romans, I attended you ;
And when your horse's fall left you a prey
Unto the barbarous cruelty of the Parthians,
I, careless of my life, ran to your aid,
And brought you off through many of their deaths.
Command me anything, so you except
Your noble life, and I will do it freely !

Pyr. As well except you will not stir a foot
To do your friend the greatest favour for him,
Which with an ease, so easy as is walking,
You may perform.

Phyl.   What would you have me do ?

Pyr. Begone, my Phylocles ! Is this a day
For me to honour with my life, wherein
Clorina, slighting all my years of service,
Which I have paid to her with as great fervour
As any of our priests adore the gods,
Will give away herself unto Bassanes ?
Away, my friend, and let me die !

Phyl. My lord, I will obey you, on condition
That I may find you as I leave you—safe,
And, till I see you next, untouched, and living !
I have some hope I may bring comfort with me—
Calm all these passions, and create a joy
That may occasion triumphs in your heart.

Pyr. Go then, my friend, and prosper ; but be sure
Thou dost not trifle with me.   Thou well knowest
The nature of Pyrontus is averse
To suffering of abuses.

Phyl.   I am gone,
With hope to bring you comfort speedily.   [*Exit.*

Pyr. False tyrant, love ! I would I had thee here !
With thy own bow I'd shoot such passions in thee
As should be overstrong for thee to bear.
Fond boy ! I'd make thee dote on chaste Diana,
And pluck thy golden feathers from thy wings,
To write with them repentance to the world.

Which of the fatal sisters did provoke
Thee, careless of man's happiness, to do
Those bloody deeds which thou art famous for ?
O, that I knew her ! and when I am dead
I'd pass the dreadful waves of Phlegethon
But I would find her, and destroy her too !
Upon Ixion's wheel I'd torture her,
Till with her baleful cries she did awake
The porter Cerberus from his drowsy den ;
Then would I give her body unto him,
And he should eat it, and she be forgot.
But, cruel love, hadst thou been kind to me,
And equal fire raged in Clorina's breast,
Not only in Tomos, but throughout all Pontus,
I would have raised altars to thy praise,
Where night and day, whilst time makes night and
    day,
I would have had such anthems caroll'd to thee
By happy lovers, that eternal Jove
Should have wish'd himself to have been the god of
    love !

     Enter OVID, PHYLOCLES, *and* ARMELINA.

   Phyl. My lord l the beauteous lady Armelina,
Attended by the poets' glory, Ovid,
By the entreaty of the excellent bride,
Are come to woo you to your life !
   Pyr. 'Tis a miraculous kindness that the fair
Clorina on this solemn day affords me.
Had she but pleased t' have been so merciful
In former times, I had not drooped thus
Now all the city Tomos lays aside
Neglected care, and puts on jollity.
Madam, what is the pleasure of my deity ?
And thou, full soul of poetry, sweet Ovid,
What unimagin'd harmony of comfort
Bring you unto me ?
   Arm.   My lord, if that my sister
Still doth retain the least of power over you,

By me she doth entreat you to continue
Among the living.　By all the love you have
Profess'd unto her, she conjures you t' bear
The chances of this day worthy your birth
And all the noble actions of your life.

 Ovid. It is an unbecoming weakness in you,
Degenerating from the former fulness
Of all your honours, all your immense knowledge
Of sage philosophy, and of yourself,
Thus to captive your reason, and become
Slave to the passions of an heart let loose
To the pursuit of barbarous appetites.

 Pyr. Sweet Armelina! you whose every word
Strikes music through my ears unto my soul—
You who in your soft language have apparell'd
The commands of my goddess, must have power
To make me die continually by living.

 Ovid. Assume a better courage, and contemn
These trifles which you rashly deem misfortunes.
My lord! you are the glory of this country,—
The basis upon which not only Tomos,
But the nobility of Pontus, build
Their glories on, instructed hitherto
By imitating you, their great example.
A little time may alter your opinion
Of beauty.　You may chance to see ere long
Another lady that may please you better;
And then this day you do account so miserable
You in your calendar will mark a festival.

 Pyr. Peace, gentle Ovid! this is blasphemy
Against the divinity of her fair soul,
And that rich heaven of happiness, her body.
Jove hath no beauty like her on Olympus:
She's nature's masterpiece, and glorifies
This angle of the world so, that I prize it
Above triumphant Rome, and all the splendours
The court of great Tiberius is renowned for.

 Ovid. You shall overcome me, so you will yourself:
Say anything, my lord, and I will hear you—

Do anything, and I will honour it,
So you forbear to trespass 'gainst your life !
 Arm. My sister doth expect, if you have ever
Borne real affection to her, that you should
Return her word by me that you will lose
This resolution of self-murder. She will
Love you as far as honour will give leave,
Entertain welcomely your company
And conversation, whilst you prove yourself
Delighted with her virtue. And she knows
The Lord Bassanes will most joyfully
Continue you within the catalogue
Of his friends most belov'd, while you exceed not
The limits of a candid amity,
Nor attempt treason to her nuptials.
 Phyl. I see a calmness in your looks, my friend.
Thanks, gracious madam, for your pains ; and may
Thy Roman gods reward this kindness, Ovid !
Yet he were savage that had ears so deaf,
And dull an intellect, as not to yield
To your great reason and most eloquent tongue.
 Ovid. Your partial love doth too much overvalue
My poor endeavours. Hark !   *[Music within.*
 Arm.   The music doth
Invite us in. Pray ! glorify this ceremony
With your fair presence.
 Phyl.   Hymen will, my lord,
Owe you a blessing for it.
 Ovid.   Light a more
Auspicious torch, and, for a courtesy
So timely given, drown your more happy head
With future bliss above your hopes. *[Exit* OVID.
 Pyr.   Lead in !
I'll but collect myself and follow you. Armelina !
 Arm. You will oblige us all.
 Pyr. My friend Phylocles !
 Phyl. I am here, my lord.
 Pyr. Oh, how a thousand passions combat here !
But which of them shall prove predominant ?
Commands, received from my fair, cruel mistress,

Already have determined what strange miracles,
Great deity of love, are in thy power!
Affection prompts me to advance my hand,
And turn the genial bed into an urn
By setting this Bassanes' soul at liberty.
But I must needs recall this infant thought,
Or an inglorious stain may fix upon
My reputation.   He was ever noble
In all his actions to me, and we
Have long ago contracted such a friendship
That it hath been look'd on as an example
Worthy an imitation.   Besides, he
Was never made acquainted with my love;
He, then, is innocent of any injury
Committed against me, and doth no more
Than I.   The bright Clorina he affects,
And so do I; and so must all the world
That are not blind, or senseless, when they see her.
His stars befriend him, and those eyes of heaven
Did look a squint at my nativity;
And he hath far more merit to deserve her.
Come, Phylocles!   She is my only goddess,
And I must quit me of profaneness, too;
What she commands, strike no forbidden blow.

> *[Exeunt.*

SCENE II.

Enter DACUS, CYPASSIS, *and* SPINELLA.

Spin. Mother! Captain Dacus promis'd me a new
gown against this masque, and hath not kept his
word with me.   I desire, therefore, I may be quit of
his company.

Dac. Pretty grumbling heart! my tenants are slow
in paying their rents; I else had not failed thee.   But
you are very fine as you are, Venus be thanked!

Spin. That's no cost of yours.   I am the more beholden to another friend.

Dac. To whom ? the bridegroom, I warrant you, Spinella.

Spin. 'Tis he indeed !

Cyp. The Lord Bassanes was ever her noble patron.

Dac. But I hope she will lose his bounty hereafter, Cypassis.

Spin. Your jealousy prompts you to talk thus.

Cyp. After honeymoon's past, he may return to her again.

Spin. You shall become more liberal, or I will shortly cashier you from my acquaintance. What ! do you think we venture reputation for nothing but oaths, flattering words, and a little foolish pleasure ?

Cyp. Indeed, son, a young gentlewoman must be maintained with other materials. If she goes not fine and cleanly, she is not fit for good company ; and if she keeps never so little a while ill, and it comes to be known, she may bid farewell for ever to all her holidays ; the honourable and worshipful will not care for her embraces.

Dac. Are you against me too, mother ? I had thought Madam Cypassis had had a great kindness for me than so.

Cyp. Captain Dacus ! you know I have much respected you from our first acquaintance ; but you must think of performing better with Spinella for the future. My poor girl else will not be able to live decently in the fashion, unless she should live more common than I could wish.

Spin. Mother ! you shall not need to fear that, for I can be married when I will, and this wedding of my dear old friend invites me much to take that course. Juno ! direct me to the best, for Venus, whom I have hitherto served, is but an ill tutress !

Dac. Prithee, sweet Spinella, leave this melancholy discourse ; it sounds too unkindly, especially on a marriage day. We should now talk of love, maidenheads, music, banquets, masques, and so forth.

Spin. Captain Dacus ! I must confess my genius is

towards mirth indeed ; but you must not, then, give
me cause of sorrow.

Cyp. The truth is, Captain, you must not be so
close-handed for the future.   The Lord Bassanes
being married, peradventure may turn foolishly uxo-
rious ; and then you must either get you better
tenants——

Spin. Or a new mistress.

Dac. Still in this key?

Cyp. What hath been done yet hath been kept
private, and so it concerned all our reputations ;
but, now I think better on it, it is your best way,
Spinella, to take a husband if he be worth having.

Spin. He can scarce be worse than this servant.

Dac. Pretty one! afford me better words, for I
dearly love thee ; and, though I never made use of
my credit yet in that kind, I will take up a new gown
for thee to-morrow.   On that condition I may take it
up as often as I will.

Spin. Then you shall have leave to do your best,
or worst.

Cyp. Agreed, agreed!
'Tis well y' are come.

Enter MARULLUS.

Spin. We thought Bassanes had forgotten us ; but
we meant, you see, to come unsent for.

Mar. You might have been welcome if you had ; I
should have got you good places.   But Bassanes is a
gentleman of his word, and hath sent me to conduct
you accordingly.

Spin. I thank his bridegroomship.

Mar. You are angry, I warrant you, that he's
married.

Spin. Not I, Venus bear me record!   Much good
do him with his fresh meat ; he will be weary of it, no
doubt, ere long, as he hath been with others.   So you
may tell him, Marullus.

Mar. And then you hope for him again?

Cyp. Juno and Diana defend ! I dare swear she hath no such thoughts.

Dac. So durst not I.

Mar. Nor I.

Spin. I care not what you say ; you are both minded to jest with me. But is not the young Phœbianus returned from Rome against these solemnities ?

Mar. Pyrontus wrote for him.

Cyp. 'Tis marvel Bassanes would not stay for his arrival.

Spin. No wonder at all ; all men are so mad of a new face when they can get it.

Cyp. Though often they leave a better for it.

Dac. Well said, mother ! thou speakest oracles, old Cypassis.

Mar. With some regret. This marriage is not yet digested by them in earnest. I must entreat you to beware of your behaviours. You are desir'd to pretend no acquaintance to the bridegroom. These slips of youth are fit to be conceal'd.

Spin. Or Clorina may grow jealous ?

Mar. 'Tis good preventing the worst. 'Tis time we walk.   [*Exeunt omnes.*

SCENE III.

Loud music, then enter PYRONTUS, BASSANES, PHY-
LOCLES, OVID, CLORINA, ARMELINA.

Bas. Welcome for ever to my hand, Clorina,
Who long hast been the regent of my heart !
This day hath made me owner of such riches,—
The mine of joys in my delicious bride,—
That I our mightiest Cæsar do not envy.
Why does my dearest blush ? because thy modesty
Doth see so many beauties here inferior
To thy supremest one ? But blush on, fairest,
Like to a setting sun, at the approach

Of this so longed-for night, that's to determine
Your virgin honour.

    Clor.   Now you make me blush
Indeed, my lord.

    Pyr. I wish you, madam, a life so circled in
With joy, that you may never breathe a sigh ;
And, when you shall grow weary of the earth,
Become Jove's dotage, and be Queen of heaven.

    Clor. My Lord Pyrontus, I return you thanks,
And hope th' immortal gods will recompense
This kindness with an happiness transcending
Whatever yet you could desire !

    Ovid.   May heaven
Propitiously smile on you with all those
Bright ties that do enlighten night and day !

    Arm. I did not think this city could have shown
A multitude so gallant of both sexes.

    Bas. They come, I thank them, to grace our
       nuptials.

    Phyl. They come, no doubt, to see and to be seen.

Enter MARULLUS, DACUS, CYPASSIS, SPINELLA.

    Mar. Hymen be praised, we are come in time !

    Cyp. Venus, bless mine eyes, what a fine show is
       here !

    Spin. Indeed, Captain Dacus, you have endeared
       me much ;
We are beholding to your lusty shoulders,
That made a pretty lane through all the crowd.

    Dac. My best of strength shall evermore attend
To do you service.

    Mar.   Here let us keep together ;
This is the best room that is left.   Pray tell me,
How do you like the bride ?   Do not her eyes
Dart subtle rays, such as may kindle fires
Within the breasts of all mankind ?

    Spin. I do not know how some may love heart-
       burning.

    Cyp. It is a pretty lady, but I have seen
Some faces that have seemed as well.

Mar. Oh! envy, Madam Cypassis! Where, beseech
you?

Dac. I hope Spinella would be loth enough
To change with her.

Spin. I am not yet a-weary
Of mine own.

Bas. It doth grow late, and time they did begin.

Ovid. They only waited your commands.

Mar. That's Publius Ovidius Naso, the chief poet
Not only of Rome, but all the mighty empire.

Cyp. I know him well enough, and was acquainted
Many years with him ere I saw this country.

Ovid. May music bring
Some deities from Olympus' top, to grace
This night's solemnities!

The Mask.

*The Masquers all attired according to the fancies of the
ancient poets.*

After a flourish of loud music, enter HYMEN, CUPID,
and VENUS, *singing.*

Ven. I smil'd with eyes that darted rays
Of sweet desire on either's face.

Cup. And I such shafts did put in ure*
As only they themselves could cure.

Hym. And I, love's best physician, quick found
Each other's hand, might heal each other's
wound.

Ven. May they dissolve in love, yet prove
No diminution by their love.

Cup. May they their fears and pain requite,
And spend, in such revenge, this night.

Hym. Whate'er they do, they may with ardent
zeal,
For they have licence under my great seal.

* Use.

P

Enter MERCURY.

Mer. Jove hath commanded me to let you know
You shall not want a grace that heaven can show ;
By virtue, therefore, of my sacred wand,
Juno and Pallas hither I command,
That they, with Venus, may again contest
To whom belongs the golden apple best.
And Paris, by my caduceus' power,
I charge to come from thy Elysium bower.
Now let thy doom meet the just will of Jove,
And thou shalt feast with deities above—
Forego thy solitary shades, and sit
A judge upon Olympus for thy wit.

Enter JUNO *and* PALLAS.

Pal. Wherefore are we thus summoned to appear
To human view and to these mortals here ?
Jun. I hope Jove now will not disturb our reign,
And fall in love with womankind again.
Pal. Surely long since, Queen of the deities,
He did abandon terrene vanities.
Jun. Daughter ! he swore, by Dis, to me himself,
He would for ever leave all amorous stealth ;
For Juno cannot but suspect the worse,
He once so long continued such a course.
Pal. Pallas hath often blush'd to hear Mars tell,
Following his father's steps he did but well;
My brother was to blame.
Jun.   Alas, my son
Gloried to imitate what Jove had done !
Your sister Venus was a handsome child.
Pal. And Mars, when he was young, was very
    wild.
Mer. Saturnia, needless I do know your fears ;
Had Jove meant so, he'd not have met you here.
Paris is slow in his approach ; sure some
Fine dreams have fix'd him in Elysium.
Again I must command him to appear.

Enter PARIS.

Par. You need not, Maia's son, for I am here.
I had not made such stay, but was in talk
With my fair Queen in a delicious walk,
Where Agamemnon and the Spartan king,
And all those many Princes they did bring
To fight for the revenge of that fam'd rape,
Did laugh at our discourse, not envy at.
Thrice happy are those shades, where none do hear
Those passions that so tyrannize it here.
The Grecian chieftains have a thousand times
Curs'd their own rage that cross'd us in our crimes ;
For when their wiser souls were loosened from
Their bodies, forced unto Elysium
By violent deaths, and clearly understood
Those follies they had sealed with their blood,
Amazement seiz'd upon them all.   Our Troy,
Which that so fatal quarrel did destroy,
Had flourished still in pomp—all they and we
Had liv'd in peace and in felicity,
And died in our own beds, had they been bless'd
T' have had those thoughts wherewith th' are now
    possess'd.
We are not jealous in those plains of bliss :
They for fruition care not, there, that kiss.
Helen of Greece and I, without despite
To Menelaus' self, take what delight
Pleaseth us there the most.   Every one there
Slights those things most they doted upon here.
Our bodies being compos'd of elements,
Incline mankind to seek to please the sense ;
But there our spirits, being unconfin'd,
Strive at the satisfaction of the mind.
Though souls embrace, they organs want and places
To raise a jealousy at their embraces ;
We at our old amours do often laugh.
  Mer. Then you was in discourse, which I broke off ?
  Par. No matter, Mercury, 'tis fit I pay
My duty unto Jove, and him obey.

What, therefore, is his will, that I may soon
Submit to his inevitable doom?
    Mer. You must again an umpire be, and tell,
In beauty, which of these doth most excel.
    Par. My judgment I have given once, and why
Should that again to my discussion lye?
    Mer. 'Tis Jove's decree, and he, if you refrain,
Will make you subject unto Pluto's reign,—
From the Elysium plains remove you quite,
And cast you into an eternal night;
Instead of Helen's voice, where evermore
You shall hear Cerberus' bark, Cocytus' roar;
And dreadful Phlegethon, with horrid noise,
Torment your ears as darkness shall your eyes.
    Par. I must submit.
    Mer.   Here, take this golden ball,
And give't to her that's handsom'st of them all.
    Par. I shall, in my opinion, doom aright,
But wish that Jove had chose some other wight.
But the last time these goddesses employed
Me in this kind, it was on sacred Ide;
Why therefore here, in so remote a town,
And countries so far distant from mine own?
    Mer. Cast but your eyes about this crowded place,
And you may judge it is to do a grace
To some in this fair company.
    Hym.   To-day,
That generous youthful pair became my prey.
    Cup. But they had never been your captives bound,
If I had not compelled them by a wound.
    Mer. Jupiter, to do honour to this night,
Hath summoned these t' appear to human sight,
And hath commanded you, before this throng,
To give that apple where 't doth most belong.
Be well advised, after exact survey,
How you dispose the golden fruit away.
    Par. Prime goddesses of the Olympic court,
That Paris grace again with your resort,
I on my knees beg leave, that what I do
For one may not offend the other two;

Because our poets have profess'd that we
Have been afflicted for my first decree,
For thence two of you did our foes become,
And hastened on the sack of Ilium.
I must obey imperious Jove's command.

   Ven. And we to thy arbitrament will stand.
   Juno. I do protest, by all my rule above,
I'll not be angry, howsoe'er it prove.
   Pal. And, Priam's son, I will be nothing stirr'd,
Or discontent, if others be preferr'd.
   Par. Having implor'd your mercies, now I fall
To look to whom belongs the golden ball.
Juno hath sweet black eyes, Pallas fine hair,
Venus is just proportion'd, wondrous fair.
As I have done before, again I must—
Venus, the ball's thine, and my judgment just.

                                [*Gives it to her.*
   Juno. To tax thy doom were but a needless shift.
   Pal. Nor do we envy her the pretty gift.
   Ven. To show there is no falling out, let's all
Fall in, and dance, before this pair, a ball.
   Juno. You and I, Trojan prince, will lead the sport
You have been famous for in Priam's court.
   Par. Supremest goddess, you a grace confer
Too high upon your humble honourer.
   Juno. Hymen, Cupid, and Maia's son, advance!
Let's show these mortals an Olympic dance.

            All the MASKERS *dance.*

After a flourish of solemn loud music, enter JUPITER.

   Mer. The king of gods and men! Hail, thund'ring
     Jove!
   Pal. Why hath my father left his throne above?
   Jup. Perceiving Venus and her wanton son,
To do some service, were by Hymen won,
From my star-paved court, and looking down
Upon the world, and, in it, on this town,
I soon espied the business; therefore, straight
Summon'd you both to meet, this nuptial night,

My daughter Venus, here that we might do
A grace divine unto these happy two.
How Paris hath bestowed the ball I've seen;
But give it me again, you amorous Queen
Of Cyprus, it hereafter must not be
A trophy to the Paphian deity.
    Ven. Great Jupiter, I yield to thy command.
    Jup. And I thus give it t' a more beauteous hand.
                         [*Gives it* CLORINA.
Here may you flourish long in bliss! and when
You weary grow of the abodes of men,
I'll fix you both, t' amaze all human eyes,
A glorious constellation in the skies.
Pallas and Venus do not take offence,
For she is a superior excellence.
And frown not, Juno; I no more will make
Converse with mortals for thy quiet's sake.
Hadst thou thus given the golden ball, I had
                        [*Speaks to* PARIS.
Made thee companion unto Ganymede.
Take hands, and dance, whilst our attentive ears
Do guide our feet to music of the spheres.

They dance the second dance.

A Song.

    Hym. Blest and best pair, make haste to bed,
           The bride still owes her maidenhead.
    Cup. There you can only find a balm,
           The fest'ring of my darts to calm.
    Ven. And youth and beauty may delight
           In all joys of a nuptial night.
    Chorus. There when you shall be left alone, and
           kiss,
           You need not envy to the gods their bliss.

    Jup. 'Tis time we leave these to a new delight,
And therefore Jove himself doth bid good-night.
                      [*Exeunt* MASKERS.

Bas. Let us to bed, my dear; I long to lose
Myself in thy embraces. Gentle Ovid,
The bright Clorina and myself shall owe
All power we have to serve you to the utmost;
And may propitious heaven incline great Cæsar
To look with gracious eyes on your misfortunes!

Ovid. You both vouchsafe too much of honour to
me
If you forgive the rudeness of my muse.

Pyr. I find myself extremely ill o' th' sudden,
And must not be so barbarous t' interrupt
With any sign of sickness the felicities
Of this bless'd company. Good-night to all!
Farewell, my lord! the happiest of mankind.
Clorina, too, good-night—you most unkind!
[*Exeunt* BASSANES, OVID, CLORINA, ARMELINA.

Mar. Captain, I do commit to your conduct ·
Madam Cypassis and her pretty daughter.
I must go help the groom to bed, and see
The bride to taste her last virginity-posset.
[*Exit* MARULLUS.

Dac. I shall be careful of my charge. Spinella,
I had rather have spent my time in bed with thee
Than have been at this masque.

Spin. So had not I with you.

Dac. I know you jest, my little rogue.

Cyp. Juno was of a demure look, and had a grave
behaviour.

Dac. Pallas had a smart cast with her eyes:
I warrant you she beat
Her husband, if she were ever married.

Spin. Venus, indeed, was the handsom'st of them
all.

Dac. But you are handsomer than she, my pretty
one.
[*Exeunt* DACUS, CYPASSIS, SPINELLA.

Phyl. 'Tis very late, and time to hasten home.
How is it with my noble Lord Pyrontus?

Pyr. I am undone, my Phylocles, for ever,
And have too tamely yielded to this match.

I should have challenged my friend Bassanes,
If he would not have given up his interest,
And by his fall rais'd up myself some hope,
Or lost her bravely with my life together.

   Phyl. My lord, for heaven's sake cast aside such
      thoughts,
And to your aid call generous patience!

   Pyr. The coward's virtue! O, the multitude
Of those grand joys Bassanes is possess'd of
By this conjugal knot! And O, the myriads
Of miseries my poor life is to wade through
By her severe command! Were I the mighty
Tiberius, and o'er the conquer'd world
Bore sovereignty, the Empire I should slight,
And give 't Bassanes for his room to-night.

                   [Exeunt ambo.

ACT II.—SCENE I.

Enter Captain HANNIBAL, CACALA, CARALINDA, *and*
FLORETTA.

   Han. From Ostia we have had a voyage hither
So fraught with storms and tempests, that I wonder
The sea-gods——

   Cac. The sea-monsters call them, rather.

   Han. Were not all tired with using so much rage
On us; and yet you, beauteous Caralinda,
Seemed fearless of the furies of the ocean,
Dreadless of thunder and lightning, whilst my man,
This rascal Cacala, did nothing but s——
And spew, and pray, when there was such a noise,
Betwixt the mariners' voices and the elements,
That Neptune could not hear the timorous villain.

   Cac. Sir, I did love you well—you have been
      bountiful
On all occasions to me, I else should never
Have left my native country, pleasant Italy,
T' have undergone a voluntary exile.

But had I ever dreamt on such a passage,
Such thunders, whirlwinds, and such horrible tem-
pests,
I would have taken leave to stay in Rome.

Han. Although Floretta sometimes wept for fear,
She did not bawl and whine like thee.

Cac. No matter ;
She does not know how precious a thing life is.

Flor. Surely I do ; but well enough imagin'd
That such ungovern'd outcries might disturb
The company, yet not incline the gods
The sooner to deliver us from drowning.

Car. In truth, Cacala, your fear was oftentimes
So full of noise the mariners could not hear
Their own voices to attend their necessaries ;
But you, perhaps, are valianter at land ?

Han. He's everywhere a coward, Caralinda!

Cac. I would confute you, sir, with all my heart,
If you and Mistress Floretta would consent to 't.
Were I in bed with her, I'd prove myself
As valiant as the proudest captain living !

Han. How, now, you saucy rogue ?

Flor. He talks most wickedly.

Cac. I had rather do.

Flor. You must go look a mate, then.

Car. Where do you mean to lie in Tomos, Captain ?
Good lodgings here, I think, are somewhat rare.

Han. As soon as we came to town I despatch'd
Cacala
T' inquire out one Madam Cypassis, a gentlewoman
Of my acquaintance in my very youth. She was
servant
Once unto the Princess Julia.

Car. You rather should say t' Ovid's fam'd Corinna.

Han. By your fair leave, I know I speak a truth ;
And were not Ovid timorous, he'd confess
He Julia veil'd under Corinna's name.
Cacala hath taken me lodgings at Cypassis',
Where you may hear of your humble servant, Han-
nibal.

Car. And does Floretta lie there also?

Han.   Yes, marry;
Venus defend else!

Car.   Then you do resolve,
It seems, to make a wedding on 't?

Han. By no means, madam; neither pretty
  Floretta
Nor I are yet such fools to slight our liberties.
Whilst we like one another we'll keep together,
And when we grow a-weary we may part;
The world hath other men and women enough,
And we are both of us yet ignorant
How soon we may affect variety.

Car. But fear ye not the gods? Are they well
  pleas'd,
Think you, with such a life?

Cac.   My captain ne'er
Feared anything. And for Mistress Floretta,
What man could do to her she never dreaded;
But how her courage stands towards the gods,
I cannot say.

Flor. You say too much, Cacala, and must learn
  manners,
Or I must pray the Captain to bestow
A cudgel on you.

Cac.   Sure his valour scorns
Such mean employment; he disdains to touch
A weapon that's beneath a sword or poniard.
My noble captain ever was accustom'd
To give me leave to jest.

Han.   But you must know
Your distance to Floretta.

Cac.   I know it but too well,
And always am more distant than I would be.

Car. But, Captain, I'd advise you both to marry;
It is a life that is more honourable.

Cac. You are deceived, Madam Caralinda;
Our Roman captains think there is more honour
In keeping wenches than in marriage.

Han. Out upon wedlock! I had rather hear

Alarms at midnight than the multitude
To bawl Thalassis at a nuptials!

Car. Y' are a mad captain, Hannibal!

Han.   I acknowledge it,
And ne'er had else been banish'd into Pontus.
But whereabouts in this town, Caralinda,
Do you intend to make abode?

Car. At Publius Ovidius Naso's.
I wrote to him from Rome t' entreat that courtesy,
And he returned me thither word by letter
I should be welcome. I have sent my servants
Thither to prepare for me, and to beg
His company here, that he may be guide
Unto his house.

Han.   Were Ovid in his youth,
He would be glad of such a purchase, lady;
Y' are of a tempting beauty. He had fam'd you
Equal unto his so renowned Corinna,
Had he been then acquainted with your excellences.

Car. You shame me, Captain Hannibal. I am
So conscious of my own deformities,
That I shall, all I may, shun public view.
Besides, I know the noble poet hath
Subdued his passions, and is now become
As rigid in his behaviour as the gravest
Of all the ancient philosophers.

Cac. These women such discourse affect, as if
They were pure vestal nuns; but they that do
Give credit to them are of a belief
That is not in my creed.

Car.   You must have leave
To talk. Know likewise, Captain!
Enjoy'd the generous Ovid his prime youth,
And flourish'd again in his own house
Adjoining unto our triumphant capital,
I should choose to live with him. I do prize him
As the supreme wit of the Empire,
Whose conversation ever was admired.
Besides, I dare presume on my own temper,
I fear not the temptations of all mankind;

And such averseness have to all that sex,
That here, in presence of the immortal gods,
I vow, in that kind, never man shall touch me !

 Cac. For all your confidence in your own chastity,—
I speak it with a reverence to your merit,—
Beware of the old game, and of the consequence,
Known commonly by the name of a great belly.

 Car. My life, through all my actions, shall vindicate
My reputation spotless !

 Han. Your beauties and unequall'd qualities are
Too potent charms for frail mankind to know,
And not be conquer'd by so many wonders.

 Cac. Besides, her clothes would set one's teeth on
  edge.

 Flor. On shipboard she went in an homelier habit.

 Car. The meanest clothes will serve at sea for
  women.
Captains in Tyrian-dy'd habiliments,
And with their divers-coloured plumes should flourish,
At all times, in all places, to beget
Awe and respect from those they do converse with.

 Han. Fair Caralinda, you speak oracles !
The hearts of all the Getes* here must do homage
To your unparallel'd perfection !
They will not only own you for most beautiful,
But the chief female gallant of the province!

Enter OVID.

 Car. Your praises so transcend, they make me
  blush.

 Ovid. Welcome, my sweetest cousin Caralinda !
May all the gods of seas and winds be prais'd
For your arrival in this country safely !

 Car. Thanks, generous Ovid ; I rejoice to see
The wonder of the Roman Empire living !

 Ovid. Oh, spare to overvalue so your servant,
A serious adorer of your virtues !

---

 * Getes, *sing.;* Getæ, *plu.* A people on the banks of the
Euxine Sea, described by Ovid as a savage and warlike nation.
—*Ovid de Ponto Tristia,* 5, c. l. 7 ; v. iii. c. l. 12 v. 10.

Admire only you have found me breathing,
After so many years here in exilement.

Han. Madam, because we see you in that company
We know you have an honour for, and who will
Conduct you to your lodgings, we will press
No further on your privacies, but take
Our leave for this time. May both gods and men
Bear hatred to Tiberius until he
Repeal the gentle Ovid! When we next
Do meet we will converse at large. May Jove,
Juno, Pallas, and the whole court of deities,
Be evermore auspicious to you both!

Cac. Also to me, master, and to Floretta,
Whate'er we do, I'd have the gods be merciful!

              [*Exeunt* HANNIBAL, FLORETTA, CACALA.

Car. I need not hope I shall be safe, but be secure
I shall be so, while I continue in
Your house.

Ovid. You, madam, to yourself shall promise
All privacy you can desire; you are
As secret as you were not in the world.
Although your native city you inhabit,
Your name shall not escape my lips. But why,
If without an offence I may demand it,
Affect you such concealment now, especially
When all your friends would be so proud to see you,
And in this time of public joy?

Car.   Hereafter,
At better leisure, I'll acquaint you with
My very soul in all particulars.

Ovid. I will await your time. But when you left
The world's great head, happy and flourishing Rome,
How was Tiberius moved by the entreaties
Of my dear wife, and some few real friends
That my repeal solicited?

Car. Your virtuous wife and many constant friends
Have not evaded any opportunity
In your behalf; and, though they have not yet
Effected their desires in that concern,
They do not despair of prosperous success.

Ovid. I have two powerful enemies, I believe,
And such who block up, with their imputations,
All ways of mercy; and yet they are men
I cannot accuse myself for ever injuring.
    Car. You always were too noble to do wrongs.
    Ovid. Even he that hath cruelty to heart
To tempt the wife of a poor banish'd man,
Amidst her sighs and tears for my misfortunes,
Makes use of all the mighty interest
He hath with Cæsar still to fix me here!
Pardon my passion, ye just gods, if I .
Do wish one day you will requite the mischiefs
Of Cornificius!*
    Car. Your wife could make good mirth with his
        affection,
Were not her heart so sad for your long banishment.
    Ovid. Some of my griefs I have flung on him, under
The counterfeit name of Ibis.
    Car. Those curses he richly deserves.   Our sacred
Empress, the sweet-conditioned Julia,
Hath from the island Trimerus,†—where she
Hath liv'd confin'd about these twenty years,—
Wrote to him oft in your behalf; but she,
Although she brought to him the world in dowry,
Could not prevail.
    Ovid.   She grac'd too much an exile!
    Car. But had much reason to solicit throughly,
She being believ'd to be the fair Corinna,
Whom in your poems you have celebrated.
    Ovid. I pray you, think not so; you wrong her
        virtues,
Of which I only was a true adorer!

---

* A poet and general of the Augustine age. His composit'ons
were much valued for their ease and eloquence, but nothing
remains of them except a few letters preserved amongst the
epistles of his friend Cicero. He had a sister Cornificia, who
is said to have been gifted with a poetical genius.

† On the coast of Campania, where Julia, daughter of Augustus,
notorious for her immorality, was starved to death by order of
Tiberius, *anno* 14.   The cause of Ovid's banishment has been
ascribed to his having come to the knowledge of the incestuous
intercouse between this lady and her father.

Car. Though you deny it ne'er so much, a many,
And of the nobler sort, believe it otherwise.
Droop not, best of poets, but courage!
    Ovid.   Alas!
My hopes sunk, with Augustus, to the grave,
And here my aged bones must find an urn!
Will you not see the bridal house, although
In this disguise, and sure to be unknown?
    Car. I all those inclinations must suppress;
It is the will of Heaven, and not mine own.
'Tis time we walk!
    Ovid.   I'm ready to attend you.   [*Exeunt.*

SCENE II.

Enter PYRONTUS, *solus.*

Pyr. This sweet and solitary grove, adjoining
To our city's walls, I have made choice to vent
My sorrows in:—this place, that many times
Clorina's smiling eyes have graced more
Than Phœbus with his beams could ever do.
Happy you trees, whose roots received vigour
From the life-giving virtue of her looks!
And you, sweet birds, that choose this shady place
To warble forth your various notes, were blest
To learn new airs from bright Clorina's voice!
And all those beasts are fortunate, that here
Enjoy the cool shades and the crystal springs,—
The waters and the grass receiving virtue,
From her rich presence, towards their ease and
    nourishment.
Even all the inhabitants of Tomos choose
This place to recreate their minds withal.
Pan, Faunus, Satyrs, and the Dryades
Have not afforded me so good success.
Wherefore, alas! thus do I vainly tax
The rural gods? Clorina is my foe,
Else I had been as happy as Bassanes,
Who is the most blest man of all the Empire,

And that unparallel'd beauty doth enjoy
Whose loss I must perpetually lament,—
Whose loss must sit so near unto my soul,
The world will want a cure to make me whole. [*Exit.*

Enter CYPASSIS.

Cyp. Thanks to these trees' auspicious shades,
    whereby
I, undiscover'd, have been made partaker
Of Lord Pyrontus' love unto the bride !
I will observe, with all the curious search
I may, what progress he intends to make,
And hope I shall raise motives to withdraw
Bassanes from the dotage on his wife,
And fix his heart again upon Spinella.

Enter PYRONTUS *and* PHYLOCLES.

Phyl. I have been searching for you long !
Cyp. 'Tis best I do retire, where, unperceiv'd,
I their discourse may overhear.   [*Aside.*
Phyl.   You should not
Give such a liberty to your melancholy,
Nor take delight in solitary walks.
My Lord Pyrontus, in your early youth
You were instructed by the ablest masters
That famous Athens or triumphant Rome
Could glory in, in all the principles
Of grave philosophy. Reflect upon them,
And raise yourself thence strength to conquer these
Unruly passions.
Pyr.   My dear Phylocles,
'Tis very easy for a man to give
That counsel to his friend he could not follow
Himself were he in his condition.
I want a power to perform 't. The world
Cannot afford me means. I must enjoy
Clorina, or I utterly am lost ;
And therefore, though Bassanes is my friend,
My amity cannot enjoin me silence :
I must pursue my suit, and will.

Phyl. Take heed ;
You then will run a course against all virtue—
Offend the sacred deities, whom we
Are bound, by strictest obligations,
To observe in all they have commanded us.

Pyr. But they are merciful, and will forgive.

Phyl. But 'tis inglorious to commit a crime
Out of a presumption of a pardon ; and
Your breach of friendship—all mankind will censure,
An act degenerating from true nobility.

Pyr. These morals, Phylocles, are cast away
On me, who am so overwhelm'd in love
I have not reason left to practise them.

Phyl. But you will have sufficient, if you would
Take up a resolution to withstand
This dangerous passion.

Pyr. 'Tis in vain to preach
These things to me. I must enjoy Clorina,
Or leave you, friend, for ever—I shall die !

Phyl. How this untoward love destroys your
sense !

Pyr. There is not oratory enough on earth
To win me from the pursuit of my love :
One way or other I must get Clorina,
And to invent a means to compass her
Shall be my only study ; and if I prove
So fortunate as to accomplish that,
I shall account myself a favourite
The most esteemed of by the gods !

Phyl. Fiends, rather !

Pyr. Then I shall find there is a fate attends
On lovers,—harsh beginnings, happy ends.

[*Exit* PYRONTUS.

Phyl. I will not give him over thus, but follow
him ;
And though I have small hopes I shall prevail,
Yet I, in friendship, am obliged to do
My best to stop him in this vicious course.
O brave Pyrontus ! how hath impious love
Abus'd thy reason with this mighty dotage !

Q

He that hath been the glory of this province
Will make himself, this way, the shame and scandal !
                                        [*Exit* PHYLOCLES.

CYPASSIS *discloseth herself.*

Cyp. Is he so hotly set that none beside
The bride can satisfy his luxury ?
This shall Bassanes know.   Now I will work,
With all the treacherous art I'm mistress of,
To raise a discord in their marriage.   She
Is made of flesh and blood, and may prove false !
Pyrontus is resolved to court her strongly,—
A gallant gentleman, handsome as any,
Perfect in amorous compliments, no doubt.
I wonder how he miss'd her if he ever
Made it his endeavour to obtain her favour.
I wish him good success.   May this Clorina
Fall into his embraces !   Then my girl
Spinella, it is likely, may arise
Into her former favour with Bassanes.
He's rich and bountiful, and such are welcome
Unto young women ; who will lose no time,
And love to live in flourish of the fashion.

Enter BASSANES.

Bas. I like this marriage well, for now I lead
My life in favour of our best of gods !
I have liv'd loosely long enough, and paid
My services to Venus and wild Priapus !
Juno will now befriend me, sure, and Hymen
Rain blessings on my head and family.
    Cyp. Good day, my Lord Bassanes !   What ! alone ?
Can you so soon deprive yourself of the
Fair sunshine of your bright Clorina's eyes ?—
Find in your heart to be out of her company ?
    Bas. I must not be a shadow to my wife,
Nor she to me.   We must not evermore
Follow each other ; so our loves might prove
Troublesome to ourselves.   But say, Cypassis,

What business brought you hither? Is 't for health's
    sake
That you are come to walk, and take the air?
Or out of hope to meet me here, to tell me
Fictitious stories of Spinella's love
To me?

    Cyp. I had not any such intention.
Affection to the groves, and a desire
To exercise myself a while in walking,
Did bring me hither. But I've lost my labour,
And, as you came, was a-returning home.

    Bas. This is a riddle. Who could hinder you from
    walking?

    Cyp. My own curiosity.
I have been list'ning to the saddest speech
That ever yet did pass a lover's lips.

    Bas. Prithee, Cypassis, who had the ill fortune
To vent his sorrows in thy hearing?

    Cyp.   A friend
Of yours, but 'tis no matter who; you are
In a condition of such happiness,
That it would be an incivility in me
To cause the least sad thoughts in you. Continue
In mirth and jollity; and so, farewell!

    Bas. I pray thee, stay awhile! I must confess
I have a curiosity to know
Who this is that you call a friend of mine,
Who can be sad now I am grown so happy!

    Cyp. My Lord Bassanes, I must crave your pardon.
Secrets of love, you know, should be conceal'd.

    Bas. I am no common prater.

    Cyp. For old acquaintance sake, I cannot choose
But tell you anything you shall request.

    Bas. I thank you. How doth fair Spinella? I
Should have inquired sooner of her health,
But your discourse drew me aside from it.

    Cyp. Oh! how you flatter me! I easily can
Believe you have forgotten her for ever.

    Bas. You wrong our friendship. Happiness I wish her,
As much as you and she can both desire.

Cyp. I'll tell her so; and so, again farewell!

Bas. Nay, tell me, ere you go, what friend of mine
Is grown so amorous and so passionate?

Cyp. Since you will have me, think!

Bas. I cannot guess.

Cyp.   It is Pyrontus.

Bas. It may be so; yet he
Never reveal'd to me he was in love.

Cyp. At that I make no wonder.

Bas.   Whom should he
Be so enamour'd of?

Cyp.   Clorina's eyes
Have beams enough a province to inflame.

Bas. My wife?

Cyp.   The very same.

Bas. He surely, then, will stifle
His passion generously, and not attempt
The wife of his approved friend?

Cyp. You guess amiss; he is resolv'd to try
Her to the utmost. He's a proper gentleman,
And, I believe, hath a prevailing language.
You may be civil to him, and be wary.

Bas. It is too likely. On our marriage night
He so abruptly did depart, he gave us
Not leisure enough to take our leaves,—a sign
He wanted patience to look on my joys.

Cyp. I thought he somewhat suddenly was gone;
But love's a passion not to be commanded!

Bas. What was 't he, in your hearing, said?

Cyp.   Alas!
Enough; too much. He doth deserve our pity.
Phylocles did surprise him, and did use
His best persuasions to divert him from
So vain and dangerous an affection.

Bas. Come to particulars, my good Cypassis;
Conceal not from me anything: the gods
Did guide thee hither t' overhear him. Why
Stand you in such suspense?

Cyp. Take heed, my Lord Bassanes! Oh, beware
Of jealousy! 'Tis an accursed fiend,

That otherwise your quiet will molest,
Involve you in a perpetuity
Of hideous chimeras. Fair Clorina
Is innocent, and of a spotless virtue;
She is not accessory to his fault,
If to be beautiful be not a crime.

 Bas. I am not jealous, neither will be ever.

 Cyp. A resolution worthy your great mind,
And worthy the respects you ought to owe
And pay unto the virtues of your lady.

 Bas. I know her excellent body is enrich'd
With so sublime a spirit, and so pure,
That vice dares not approach her thoughts. Be free,
Therefore, and tell me all thou know'st.

 Cyp. You may command me, and I will conceal
Nothing from you.

 Bas. Good old Cypassis! thanks.   [*Exeunt ambo.*

SCENE III.

Enter PYRONTUS *and* CLORINA.

 Clor. For shame, Pyrontus! Cease to prosecute
A suit so much beneath your honour, and
So prejudicial to my reputation!

 Pyr. What a misery,
To be condemned to an eternal penury,
And be forbidden to complain! Fair, cruel
Clorina, do not so insult! Although
I am most wretched, it's in your power to make me
Happy, when you shall please to be but kind.

 Clor. I am not of a savage nature, neither
Ever rejoic'd at anybody's grief;
I wish you all content, and ever did
A wife superior unto me in all things.
Sink not beneath this passion of your love;
You undervalued evermore your merits
To think of me in that way.

 Pyr.   You abuse

The truest affection amorous heart did ever
Pay to his mistress, if you think I can
Efface your image in my soul.   The centre
Of this vast globe we breathe on is not faster
Fix'd than your beauties here ; here, in my bosom,
They sit triumphant.   Etna in its torn entrails
Doth nourish lesser flames than burn me daily,
And yet you have no pity for my sufferings.
   Clor. Alas ! what would you have me make myself ?
A beast of such an horrid name, I tremble
But to think of it ?   All the gods forbid !
Would you have her whom you have cast away
Some kindness on become an whore ?   My heart
Trembles to think upon 't, and the swift lightning
Of blushes flies into my cheeks.   Methinks
My tongue doth burn like fire within my mouth
Since it did mention so abhorr'd a name.
   Pyr. Will you, then, never think me worth your
     mercy ?
Shall the vain terrors of an empty name
Condemn me to a languishing life for ever ?
   Clor. You gods are witnesses, that know my
     thoughts,
I would not, by the wreck of chastity,
And proving to my marriage false, redeem
Myself from the most cruel death that tyrant
Did ever invent for his most hated enemy !
   Pyr. More merciless than worst of all those tyrants,
Can you refuse a courtesy to me
Which my assiduous services may plead for ?
And such an one as can be never known,
Neither impoverish you in the least degree ?
Reflect upon my misery, sweet Clorina,
And imitate the gods in mercy.
   Clor. Rather the fiends, if I should be so wicked.
The Lord Pyrontus, whom I heretofore
Did look upon as a most noble person,
Accomplish'd with the virtues, hath declared
Or counterfeited himself an atheist, to
Allure Clorina from her purity.

The gods see everything; nature nor art
Can anything conceal from them. Thoughts which
Did never take the air in words, to them
Discovered lye ; and is it not far worse
To have the gods to see our crimes than men ?
Could I prove guilty of so foul a fault,
I should impoverish myself to nothing,—
A bankrupt be in honour ; which, who wants,
Is a companion fit for such wild people,
As never heard the name of virtue. Riches
Are fortune's trifles, neither altogether
To be despis'd or doted on ; but, well us'd,
Poor virtue is most rich. Virtue itself
Was, by the ancients, held the greatest wealth.

Pyr. In your discourse you are too much a stoic :
Young ladies' hearts should not so utterly
Be void of all compassion.

Clor. I must leave you.

Pyr. Not without hope of comfort, I beseech you ?
Let me but taste of those sweet delicacies
You cloy Bassanes with, if it be possible
He can be satiated with such delights !

Clor. I trespass on my modesty to hear you. [*Exit.*

Pyr. In a condition she so sad hath left me,
Joy is become an exile from my heart.
To love and not be lov'd is such a curse,
Jove, on his foes, cannot inflict a worse. [*Exit.*

ACT III.—SCENE I.

Enter OVID *and* CARALINDA.

Ovid. Trapullus is a great astrologer,
I' th' mathematics skilful to perfection.
For his profounder knowledge the Chaldæans
Submit all to him.

Car. Therefore I have reason
More strictly to observe th' advice he gave me,

And wait for the accomplishment of the fortune
Which he foretold me.
    Ovid.   But, fair Caralinda,
I would not have you either be too scrupulous
Or negligent.   The skill which they pretend to
Hath but foundation upon probabilities :
The glorious planets may incline, but force not.
We have a liberty within ourselves :
Our wills are free, nor slaves unto the stars.
    Car. Though I believe you, I am so superstitious
I shall expect the accomplishment of his prophecy.
Further discourse of it I shall forbear now,
And choose a worthier subject for our talk.
Tell me, dear Ovid, therefore, how the fair
Bride's fairer sister doth enjoy her health.
I left her, when I went to travel, like
Illustrious Phœbus rising in the spring,
Without a cloud about his temples, promising
A bright day to the world.   I left her in
Her early youth, but with so growing a beauty,
That surely now 'tis able to work wonders.
    Ovid. Indeed she is a miracle of perfection ;
Nature hath prodigally bestowed upon her
All her rich gifts.   She is so fine a virgin,
That I should wrong her to describe her farther.
Health dares not be so rude as to forsake her,
Nor sickness so uncivil to approach her.
    Car. You have delivered her to my amazement ;
But I did always look that she would prove
The glory of this province for her beauty.
    Ovid. But Armelina hath besides a soul,
Replenish'd so with goodness and all virtue,
That, were it lodged in any other body,
It would be lock'd up in a cabinet
Too mean for such a precious jewel !
    Car.   Ovid,
She is oblig'd to you for the rich character
You have bestow'd upon her !
    Ovid.   You mistake me;
I cannot speak her to her merit.   You

Will think, when you shall see her, I have injur'd her;
Her merits do so much exceed all language.
    Car. We two have from our childhood had a friend-
    ship,
And she will grace me to continue it,
If she be such an one as you have spoke her.
    Ovid. Ah, Caralinda! I am grown too old
To be a flatterer.

Enter ARMELINA.

                Here she comes, and I
Appeal to your own eyes to be my witness!
You grace me, Armelina, by this visit.
You seem a deity, and bring a comfort
To any place you honour with your presence.
    Arm. Duty obliges me to wait upon
A person so renowned as Ovid is,—
One banished from his friends and native country,
And in his age confined to our poor city.
    Ovid. You have a charity equal to your beauty.
This lady is my cousin, born at Sulmo,*
The place of my nativity. You will honour me
To favour her with your acquaintance, and,
As you hereafter shall approve of her,
With your fair friendship too.
    Arm.   The generous Ovid
New obligations lays upon me daily.
    Ovid. My kinswoman is your servant. Caralinda!
This lady is the excellent Armelina
We were discoursing of, and I commending,—
For who does otherwise that speaks of her
Doth sin against the greatest truth on earth,—
As she came in.
    Arm. Madam! I kiss your hand, and am ambitious
Of your acquaintance and affection.
So excellent a kinswoman of Ovid's
Must find my best respects and truest love.

---

   * Now Sulmona, an ancient town of the Peligni, ninety miles
distant from Rome, said to have been founded by Solymus, a
follower of Æneas.

Car. Admirable Armelina ! you are of
A goodness so immense, that you may cast
Away of it on others an abundance,
And not impoverish yourself at all !
    Arm.   I wish
Pontus had any person in it worthy
To be a suitor to you for your love,
That here you might be married, and fix.
We would not lose such grace as you are mistress of,
Now we have seen you once.   Ovid, methinks,
Should joy to have so great a comfort near him,
And settled past the fear of removal.
    Car. Madam, my stay may prove much longer than
You do imagine.   But let my occasions
Prove how they can, you, with your courtesy,
Have won so on me, that without your leave
I'll not return.
    Arm. You are too gracious, and have so engag'd me,
I know not what to speak or think.
    Ovid.   You saw,
I will believe, in Rome, one ·Phœbianus,
A gentleman of this country and this city ?
    Car. I saw him oft, and know him very well,
For he was pleas'd to afford his friendship to me.
    Ovid. When thinks he of returning ?   He stays
      long.
    Arm. I can imagine he is so discreet
That he had rather live in the metropolis
Of all the world, than in a solitude,
Retir'd, in a manner, from the world,
Upon the confines of the Empire here.
And to that purpose he hath mighty reason,
To choose himself, among the Roman ladies,
A wife whose matchless beauty shall have power
To fix him there for ever.
    Car.   By your fair leave,
Dear Armelina, I with confidence
Dare say he shortly will be here.
    Arm.   Why, pray you ?
Can he escape the Roman killing beauties,

And slight so much his own full happiness
As to return a bachelor to Tomos,
And here take up with an inferior woman
To be his wife ?   He hath too much discretion
To be found guilty of so great a weakness.

 Car. You are a stranger, it seems, to his affection—
For he hath left his heart here.   Divers times
He hath told me he hath such a mistress here,
That Rome and all the world doth want her equal—
That there is neither Cæsar, king, nor tetrarch
But would elect her rather for his wife
Than be an Emperor of the universe,
And have all mankind loyal subjects to him.

 Ovid. Who should that beauty be ?
 Arm.   This province, sure,
Hath none of so supreme an excellency
As he to you hath intimated.   Poets
Report that love is blind ; and if he choose
A wife in Pontus, after he hath seen
Those glorious ladies in Tiberius' court,
He will too late, by his experience, find
That he in his own choice was also blind.

 Ovid. Do you not know her name he so affects ?

 Arm. He is an handsome gentleman ; and if
He comes not back debauched with the luxuries
Of that proud city, nor infected with
The vices of it, he is a personage
Of eminent virtues.   Such he went from us ;
And I shall hope he will come back untainted,
And be an honour to his native country.

 Ovid. But still my curiosity is unsatisfied.
What might her name be he doth celebrate
With such encomiums ?

 Car. Perhaps it might offend him if I should
Reveal that secret.

 Ovid.   Do not think it !   I
Believe, if he were here, and I requir'd it,
He it from me would not conceal ; and I
Dare pass my word the Lady Armelina
Will be as private in 't as you can wish.

Car. Madam, I easily will believe that you
Care not at all to hear it.

Arm. I dare not, in modesty, be so inquisitive.
Ladies would have their loves conceal'd.

Ovid.   Sweet cousin !
Dear Caralinda ! tell us who it is !

Car. Sweet Armelina, I must needs obey !
'Tis you that he affects.

Arm. You jest with me, and he abuses me
To make me the subject of his mirth.

Car.   I'm sure
You are mistaken much ; he hath express'd
Too great a love for you to be in jest.

Arm. There may be other women of my name,
For aught I know, in Tomos or in Pontus.

Car. If you Clorina's sister are, 'tis you.

Arm. You make me blush. A better choice I wish
     him.

Car. Were all the beautiful ladies in the world
Together, and among them he might select
Freely which he should please, I know the vehemency
Of his passion such, he would take you.
And you are of an excellency so unparallel'd,
That he would wrong his judgment if he should
Err into any other choice.

Arm. You compliment too much ; you flatter me.

Ovid. You do an injury to your mighty merits ;
Deserve the praise of all the world.

Arm.   Pray let us
Discourse of something else.

Ovid. Since you will have it so,
Let us withdraw, and taste a glass
Of Cretan wine.

Car.   Dedicate one health
To Phœbianus, and his speedy return ! [*Exeunt omnes.*

SCENE II.

Enter DACUS, CYPASSIS, *and* SPINELLA.

Dac. Now we are friends again!
Cyp. All very good friends.
Dac. Spinella, too, will smile upon me?
Spin. Laugh at you also, when you deserve it.
Dac. My wonderful old mother! Dear Cypassis,
You are grown merrier of late, and it
Becomes you well—makes you grow fat, and hold
The relics of your beauty up together.
If there be any woman in the world
That doth remember the building of the Capitol,
I dare pronounce 'tis you. I wish I had ·
But as much money as you have spent in almanacs,
Reckoning but one for a year, since you could
Make use of them, and I should be as rich as
A governor of a province, and have gold
Enough to make daily high entertainments
Of the best sweetmeats and rich Grecian wines
For you and my Spinella, and maintain her
In clothes beseeming one of Cæsar's family.
Cyp. Well, well, Captain Dacus; for all you
Make a jest at my age, you would
Be very glad to live so long yourself.
Spin. I think there is small reason to imagine
He will arrive to such an antiquity;
His debaucheries will shorten his days. Besides,
He is so quarrelsome, that 'tis a wonder
That he hath liv'd till now.
Dac. Pretty Spinella, you steer another course;
Are tame enough, as gentle as a cade,*
And he that gives you money cannot injure you.

Enter HANNIBAL, CACALA, *and* FLORETTA.

Spin. You prate, you prate!
Han. Is the meat ready yet?

* Cade-lamb, a house-lamb; hence applied to a pet child.

Cac. Whether it be or no, my stomach's ready for it.

Cyp. It is; but we must stay for Lord Bassanes.

Han. Will he be here, Cypassis?

Cyp. Yes; and his friend Marullus.

Han. The more the merrier, my reverent mother!

Cac. But the fewer the better cheer, I say.

Dac. Jove save you, Captain Hannibal! and Venus,
Delicate Floretta, smile upon you always!

Han. Mars, Captain Dacus, be thy friend, and victory
Sit on thy sword's point when thou go'st to battle.

Cac. If victory be of any weight, he had better
Carry him behind him on horseback through the field.

Flor. You look, Spinella, very well to-day—are
    neatly attir'd.
You meet with wealthy servants, else you could
Not go so richly clad.

Spin. You wear as good clothes as I; which makes
    me conclude that
Captain Hannibal is of a wealthy fortune.

Flor. His sword hath been his money. 'Tis it that hath
Purchas'd him an estate sufficient
To live in nobler splendour than he doth;
But he's content without the noise of clients,
And a retinue of many servants : Cacala
Serves him for man, and me for maid.

Dac. I wish Bassanes would appear! 'Tis pity
Good meat, out of a compliment, should be spoil'd.

Spin. He is a person of his word.

Cyp.   And will
Be suddenly here, I dare assure it.

Cac. But how if he comes not this hour yet?

Cyp. We must stay for him.

Cac. I would, then, I were a lord, and the better of
the two; that we might go to our meat presently, and
he come at his own leisure, and sit down accordingly.

Enter BASSANES *and* MARULLUS.

Dac. Long look'd for comes at last!

Cyp. My Lord Bassanes, welcome! Friend Marullus,
Y' are welcome too!

Bas. You see I trouble you, Cypassis.   Why
Seems my Spinella discontent ?
   Spin.   Because
She is not yours.   You have forsaken me—
I have not seen you many a day.
   Bas. I shall not hereafter be such a stranger to you.
   Mar. These wenches strange temptations are ; yet
     sure,
Clorina's beauties and the sacred knot
Of Hymen will continue him in virtue.
   Bas. Your daughter looks exceeding well, Cypassis !
She's mistress of a beauty so supreme,
It is above the rage of time or sickness.
   Cyp. Venus be prais'd, she needs no art ! and never
Read Ovid's poem of the skill of painting.
She knows not what belongs unto a fucus*—
Her face doth ever wear its native colours.
   Spin. Mother ! the very thought of the ingredients
Of paint would powerfully deter me from it.
I should be sick to daub my face with ointments
Made of the spawn of snakes, spittle of Jews,
And mire of infants !
   Flor.   Many gentlewomen
Of good repute, and excellent features also,
Have not so nice a stomach.
   Cyp.   I credit it ;
And have known many, who use art themselves,
Rail at it with so fine an impudency,
As if they did intend to win belief
To paint they such aversion had, as they
Scorn'd with it to adulterate their faces.
   Mar. You women no dissemblers are !   He that
Can live without you is an happy man.
   Cac. In my opinion, you, Floretta, had
Better become my wife, than thus continue
A concubine to Captain Hannibal !

---

* Paint for the complexion, formerly much used by ladies, composed frequently of injurious mineral poisons :—
            "Fucuses for ladies !"
               —*Strode's Floating Island.*

Flor. I shall inform him of your sauciness
If you desist not from your suit.   Know, Cacala,
I scorn to be a wife to thee !
   Cac.   No more.
You have more cause to scorn to be a whore.   [*Aside.*
   Flor. What mutter you ?
   Cac. No matter of importance.   I conceit
Your conversations with the Captain hath
Inspir'd you with valour !
   Flor.   Prithee, wherefore ?
   Cac. Because you lead such an incontinent life,
I think you do not fear the gods !
   Flor.   Ha' done,
Or I will make you fear my Hannibal's anger !
   Cyp. Our meat stays on us.
   Bas.   Mother, lead the way !
Give me your hand, Spinella !
   Spin.   And my heart !
                                             [*Exeunt.*

   Dac. I fear Bassanes will renew his love.
Could I win her affection, I would marry her,
And take her to Rome out of his reach.   She is
Cypassis' only child, and they are rich.
She may turn honest after she's a wife ;
However, money makes an happy life.   [*Exit.*

SCENE III.

Enter ARMELINA, *sola.*

   Arm. Ovid's fair cousin, Caralinda, hath
Inspir'd a spirit of joy into me.   Those
Sweet words she told me of my Phœbianus
Sunk pleasantly into my heart, and thence
Disperse a comfort unto all my senses.
Before he travell'd, he would often whisper
Kind accents in my ears of his affection ;
But, though I wish'd him well, I durst not give
Too easy credit to his amorous tongue.

Yet from my childhood I have had a kindness
For him, as he profess'd he had for me.
His constancy my only comfort is,
And I will pay with my affection his.　　　　　*[Exit.*

SCENE IV.

Enter BASSANES *and* DACUS.

Bas. You should not be so angry ; he intended
You no affront.　He had been drinking ere
We came ; you saw he had as much as he
Could bear.　Come, therefore, in again ! shake hands,
And still continue friends.
Dac.　　　　　　　　It must not be.
Refuse my mistress' health ?　It is a crime
Which nothing but his death shall expiate.
His body goes to atoms for 't, and's soul
Whither it pleaseth surly Charon to waft it.
Have I been ever his continual friend—
Waited on all his worst extravagances
With my unwearied valour and my sword,
And am I slighted thus ?　I will rouse up
The dreadful furies from infernal shades,
To stigmatize him full of my revenge,—
The lasting stars of his ingratitude.

Enter MARULLUS, CYPASSIS, HANNIBAL, CACALA,
　　　FLORETTA, *and* SPINELLA.

Cyp. I'll have no quarrelling in my house !　You
　　shall be friends !
He shall drink Spinella's health, and have no more.
Cac. And you can hinder quarrels in a bawdy-house,
you have more power than a constable.　But if you
force him to drink her health, let him have something
more ;—have her too, though it be but to-night.
Spin. Leave pimping, Cacala ; I have no need
Of your assistance in this kind.　Bassanes,
Let me entreat that you would reconcile them !

R

Bas. Marullus, I conjure you by our friendship !
And, Captain Dacus, he shall have the bowl !
      [*Pointing to* MARULLUS.
 Mar. You shall command me.
 Spin. If you expect my favour, you must leave
These humours. Are you friends ?
 Dac.   I must obey you.
 Flor. Shake hands, and let us in again !
 Cyp. I need not of Clorina's health inquire ;
She cannot but be well whom you affect.
 Bas. Cypassis, this is a pretty compliment.
She's free from sickness, and I will be careful
To keep her clear from any vicious act.
 Cyp. Doubtless she's virtuous : trouble not your
 head
With jealousy.
 Bas. I will be wise, old mother !
 Han. Come, Captain !
We men of war are for the field, and there
Will be victorious. Let the woman here ! [*Exeunt.*

SCENE V.

Enter CLORINA *above, as in her chamber.*

 Clor. I am lock'd in, and at it am amaz'd,
But will conceal it from my servants while
I any excuse can find. It needs must be
My husband, for he last was with me here.
I did not hear him do 't, but in all likelihood
'Twas he, when's mind did run on something else.
I am so innocent, I should fear nothing ;
And yet so timorous that I am in dread.

   Enter PYRONTUS *and* PHYLOCLES *below.*

Pyrontus and his friend are come into
The garden. Gracious Heaven ! divert him from
The prosecution of his suit to me !
My troublesome thoughts have brought a drowsiness

Upon me : sleep shall entertain my time
Until Bassanes comes and opes the door.
I will not force the lock, because I am
A stranger to the reason I'm made prisoner.
Perhaps my husband knows some mortal danger
Design'd against me, and hath thus secur'd me
Till his return.   [*Withdraws.*

    Pyr.   My Phylocles, by all
The circumstances of our mighty friendship,
I pray thee vex me with no more dissuasions !
I cannot look upon my passion to
The fair Clorina as a crime.   If 'tis
Offence on her to be enamour'd, sure
All mankind that beholds her must be guilty.

    Phyl. You are so obstinate, my heart foretells me
You will draw mischiefs on your head !   For Heaven's
      sake,
Consider on your friendship to Bassanes !
Reflect upon the contumely you
Will bring upon you from the mouths of all
For your unbridled appetite to the wife
Of your approved friend, and for the breach
Of sacred amity by such a crime !

    Pyr. Your words you scatter in the wind to give
Counsel to me ; my friendship must submit
To my more powerful love !

    Phyl.   Noble Pyrontus,
'Tis not too late yet to consult with reason !
Pray, give me leave to wait upon you home,
Rouse your depressed virtue up, and let
Time, your own courage, and the gods' assistance
Clear your brave mind from all these vicious flames !

    Pyr. I will not leave the house till I have seen
And spoken with Clorina !

    Phyl.   You have heard
She is retir'd into her chamber, there
Hath locked herself up ; and you may believe
'Tis done to shun your courtship.   Will you go ?

    Pyr. I will not stir from hence till I have bless'd
My eyes with the most glorious beams of hers !

Phyl. I then must take my leave. If I can do
No good with my entreaties to my friend,
The world shall not inflict their curses on me,
As if that I conniv'd at his impieties !
I pray you come away !
    Pyr.   All-powerful love
Hath charmed me from obeying your commands !
    Phyl. Farewell, then ! but be wise, and follow me !
                             [*Exit* PHYLOCLES.
    Pyr. So let him go ! I, undisturb'd, may now
Enjoy my thoughts, and follow my own genius !
She is not sick, and yet she keeps her chamber,
And locks herself in, to my greater prejudice.
That is the window to 't. Oh for the power
Of Jove, t' fall on her in a golden shower !
Mercury ! thanks ! The gardener hath left
A ladder here. I'll rear it up, and venture
Thereby to get a sight of her, and, if
I elsewhere must not, there declare my grief !
                  [*Rears and climbs up the ladder.*
The window open !—everything foretells
Happy success ! She lies upon her bed—
Looks like Diana, toiled with rural sports !
Fortune hath thus far favoured me, and I
Will by her foretop hold, and venture in.
Degenerate minds are known by fear, and fate
Makes the audacious persons fortunate !
She sleeps ! Morpheus his heavy hand hath laid
On the fair lids of her bright eyes ! I'll kiss
Them open, till those suns appear,
And shall disperse those clouds !
    Clor.   My Lord Bassanes,
You to Clorina are most welcome ever !
Alas, I am deceiv'd ! What spectre 's this
That haunts me in Pyrontus' shape ?
    Pyr.   It is
No airy apparition, but the wretched
Pyrontus' self, who hath presum'd to steal
Upon your privacies !
    Clor. For Heaven's sake, go, and never see me more !

Yourself you too much trouble, and expose
Me, whether I will or no, to so much ignominy
By this intrusion, that, should it be known,
My reputation would be overthrown!
For Heaven's sake, hence! immediately retire,
Without a word!
   Pyr. Have you no pity yet?
   Clor.   Have you no goodness,
No care, and no respect for a poor woman—
A married one—and your friend's wife? You gods
Deliver me in safety from this monster!
Men have exil'd all piety from their hearts;
I must not hope for any succour from them!
Fie, fie, Pyrontus! if you have not made
A league with hell and mischief, vanish straight,
And purge your foul soul by sincere repentance!
   Pyr. Are you of so supreme a beauty that
It were profaneness to compare you to
The fairest of womankind? I think I may
Say Venus' self doth want of your perfections!
And can you harbour so severe a mind
Within so rich a body? Give a period
To your long cruelty, and mercy show!
   Clor. You blast me with your words, study my ruin!
   Pyr. Dearest Clorina, have a milder thought
Of my immense affection! In a body,
By nature's liberal hand fram'd to wonder,
Lodge not a soul for ever void of pity!
Slight not my knees, thus bow'd to move a tenderness
In your so long inexorable heart!
Neither despise my tears, which thus I pour
A sacrifice to your disdain. No longer
Attire your heart in robes of savageness—
Armour impenetrably cold. Oh, mollify it
With the remembrance of the assiduous service
That I have paid you upon all occasions!

      Enter BASSANES *and* MARULLUS *below.*

   Bas. Marullus, I have pass'd my word to make
This afternoon a visit to Spinella.

Mar. You will not so discourteous be, I know.
Your friend Pyrontus, as I heard within,
Is come to see you, and is in the garden.
It seems he has retir'd into some of
The solitary walks, being out of sight.

Bas. Faithful Marullus, I will not conceal
A thought from you that doth disturb my breast.
He's to our friendship false—loves my Clorina!
And, if he hath not yet, intends to tempt her
By his lewd courtship to incontinent life.
Because to-day I meant to go unto
Cypassis' house, I've lock'd her in her chamber,
To prevent him of his wild aims.

Mar.   I think
I hear his voice in the next alley to us.

Bas. My wife is with him; her tongue I'm well
    acquainted with.

Mar. It seems they are together.

Bas. Here stands a ladder at her chamber
    window!
How came it hither? Hark! O monstrous villany!
He by it is got into her chamber!
I am betrayed, Marullus!—basely injured!
Forsake me not, my friend, in my adversity!
Remove the ladder safely, without noise.
Watch here, Marullus, that he slides not down,
And so escapes, and this base treachery
By both of them be impudently denied!
So—so 'tis done without discovery:
Lay it down there, or anywhere. I now
Will go and make a third in her lewd lodging!

Mar. But, my best friend! noble Bassanes! let
    not
A rash impatience move you to say
Or to act anything unworthy you!

Bas. You need not fear me!   [*Exit.*

Mar. This is an accident so strange, I cannot
Consider it without astonishment.
If these the fruits of marriage be, high Heaven
Be prais'd that I have liv'd a bachelor!

Boast not henceforth, you women, of your wealths
Or beauties ; or if you make no better proof,
You bring an hell in dowry to your husbands.

BASSANES *unlocks the door above, and enters there.*

Clor. My husband's come ! Oh, you have ruin'd
    me !—
Work'd such a mischief that the gods will blush at it.
    Bas. Thou beast ! unworthy of the name of man—
Much more unworthy of the name of friend !
Thy crime so great is, that I need not lose
A minute in hearing lies for thy excuse ! [*Kills him.*
Die ! and go rinse in vain thy so polluted
Soul in the flaming streams of Phlegethon !
    Pyr. Let my last words, for they are perfect truth,
Find credit with you. Your Clorina's chaste !
I here surprised her when she was asleep !
    Bas. He's sunk to hell ! Now, my lewd huswife,
    come !
I'll find another room for your disports !
Thy unclean body shall no more infect
My nuptial bed !
    Clor. Protect, O gracious gods, my innocence !
    Bas. Walk in, Marullus ! I have suffer'd wrong,
And this adultress justice shall ere long !
                        [*Exeunt omnes.*

ACT IV.—SCENE I.

Enter DACUS *and* SPINELLA.

    Dac. I tell thee, sweet Spinella, I adore thee !—
Have for thee a more generous affection
Than the greatest lord in all this province hath.
    Spin. You mean Bassanes ? But, my doughty
    Captain,
He doth express his love in golden terms,
Which I more value than a soldier's oaths.

Dac. He loves you for himself, and not for you !
Mine is a virtuous flame.

    Spin.   Your dotage is
Forgetful grown of what is past !

    Dac.   I fain
Would marry you !

    Spin. Dacus, I am too young !

    Dac. Why jests my pretty wanton so ?

    Spin. Old women that love melancholy lives
Are the first creatures to make slavish wives !

    Dac. Have you so small esteem for holy marriage,
And can you think it such a bondage ?

    Spin.   Yes.
Are not such yoked together, and oftentimes,
Draw they not contrary ways, like dogs in couples ?
The tugging at an oar in any galley
Is as much liberty as your matrimony !

    Dac. Fie, pretty atheist ! Such profaneness quit,
And take a husband—take thy Captain Dacus !
A man whose sword shall reap the Parthian fields,
And bring thee in, by frequent victories,
A large revenue, equal to thy wishes.

    Spin. My glorious-talking Captain, I shall not
Be won with empty words !

    Dac.   Have you no care
Of future bliss or bare ?

    Spin. Plato and Virgil he hath read,—I smell him,—
And courts me with their trim philosophy.

    Dac. As you resolve to live, you do not mean
To serve the gods?

    Spin. There you come something near me !
But Venus is a goddess, and I shall
Serve her ! But, Dacus, to be plain with you,
I love a gaudy chariot and fine horses,
Servants of all sorts in rich liveries,
Delicious meats and wines, costly apparel,
And jewels of the highest value ! I must
Outglitter all the females of the province,
Or I shall want my will !

    Dac.   And all this bravery

Bassanes' wealth shall furnish you withal,
You hope, as I suppose ?   But, dear Spinella,
Think of his marriage !   He hath now a wife
Of great descent, who brought a fortune to him
So vast, I want arithmetic to name it !
And she may look to be maintain'd at th' height
Of all his means, and then your hopes will prove
Fleeting as shadows—vanish in the air !
 Spin. Twit me not with his wedlock, for our crime
Will now be greater, and he shall be brought
To buy his pleasure at a higher value.

Enter HANNIBAL, CACALA, *and* FLORETTA,—*the Roman
 Captain, his Mistress, and his Servant.*

 Dac. How fares it with my mighty man of war ?
Let us shake our victorious hands in peace,
And pray to Mars to set the world in uproar !
 Han. That timorous Princes may grow bountiful,
Court us to take employment on us, while
Their luxuries they may securely follow !
 Dac. Brave Captain Hannibal, such iron times
Would be a golden age to us !   Shall we
Together walk, and drink an health or two
To all the sons of battle ?
 Han. I am for you.
 Spin. Then I'll retire, and keep my mother company.
   [*Exeunt* HANNIBAL, DACUS, *and* SPINELLA.
 Cac. Gentle Floretta, stay !   Let me not lose
This opportunity to woo thy love !
 Flor. Where learnt your folly those fine words ?
 Cac. Your eyes have taught me to express my heart ;
They have infus'd a spirit of speech into me.
 Flor. You have been, certainly, with some pedagogue,
And hired him to pen this courtship for you.
 Cac. I love thee better than I love my captain.
 Flor. And I your captain much above you affect.
 Cac. What delicate eyes you have !   I'll kiss them
  out,
And wear them in my ears.
 Flor.   You shall be hanged first !

I'd rather scratch thy heart out with my nails,
And stuff a cushion with 't.

Cac. To sit and fart upon 't, and keep it warm?
Thou art a precious rogue, and I had rather
Have thee to be my wife than any damsel
That lives in the Suburra.   Give me a wench
In all the gamesome frailty of her youth—
Especially would she turn honest afterwards!

Flor. Thou talk'st at such a random, Cacala,
That th' art a pastime to me.   But why rather
Wouldst thou elect a beauty broken up
Than one that's sound?

Cac. To tell you the plain truth,
An honest woman is a bugbear to me;
I never took delight in their acquaintance.

> *Flor.* Run after your master; tell him I would
> speak with him!

> *Cac.* I'll pimp no more, but will henceforth grow
> honest.

Flor. I doubt me, Cacala, thou hast of late
Been troubled with some terrible dreams.   Hast seen
Pluto and his dark region in thy sleep?
What else should make thee talk of virtue?

Cac. The goodwill, Floretta, that I bear to you
Engages me to this discourse.   I pray thee
Take me unto thy husband, and we then
Will run away together, leave Captain Hannibal
To his new fortune, and resolve, both of us,
To lead our lives honestly for the future.

Flor. Out, thou villain!   Turn traitor to a master
So liberal to thee as my captain is?
But that I know he would frown thee to death,
I would acquaint him with this parley.   Amend,
Or neither he nor I will be thy friend! [*Exit* FLORETTA.

> *Cac.* I know not what to make of this wench, and
> yet I would fain

Make her my wife; but I think I am a fool for my
labour.
She'll hold her peace, I hope,—that's all my care,—
And then to get her I will not despair.   [*Exit.*

Scene II.

Enter Bassanes, Marullus, *and* Clorina, *with*
Servants.

Bas. So, place her in that chair, and to the sides
Tie fast her arms. Keep her hands open thus !
[*Here the* Servants *tie her fast, and fasten* Pyrontus'
heart in her hands.
Thus—that she may not close them or remove them ;
And put her paramour's heart into them—so.
Now, foul adultress ! thou may'st contemplate
Of the affection it did bear thee once—
Reflect upon the mountain of thy sins,
Which hath overwhelmed the false Pyrontus ! Look !
Thou most libidinous woman, what a ruin
Thy lust hath brought upon him and thyself !
Clor. I have at large, calling the gods to witness
That what I told swerv'd not a jot from truth,
Related to you all the particulars
Of his unruly love,—that he surprised me—
Came in at my window whilst I was asleep ;
With what an horror I was stricken at it
When I perceiv'd 'twas he ; how I rail'd at him,
Call'd him by the worst names that I could think
 on,
Bade him begone for ever from my sight ;
That I look'd on him as a basilisk,
The ruin of his honour and mine own ;
That I would tell you of him, my Bassanes—
Inform you what a devil's company
You kept i' th' likeness of a friend ! Just gods !
Protect my innocency, and by some means
Divine inspire these truths into his heart !
Bas. That wife who dares pollute the nuptial bed
Is prodigal enough of vows and tears,
To win belief from credulous persons she
Hath done no wrong, when she hath done all the
 wrong.

Clor. Thrice happy are those souls that from the
    cares
And slanders of this wicked age are free,
Walk up and down Elysium in their thin
And airy substances, and have them so
Transparent that their thoughts may all be seen!
Would mine were such!   O that the deities
Would lend their eyes a while to you, that you
Might search, Bassanes, every cranny of
My heart!   I do not know a thought I have
I would conceal from you.
    Bas.   Thou hast a soul
So ulcerous, Clorina, that the prayers
And vows of all the world can never cleanse it.
    Clor. Oh, the hard heart of unbelieving man!
Happy you virgins that do stop your ears
Against the charms of their bewitching tongues,
And evermore continue in your chastity!
I would to heaven I never had beheld
Hymen to light his pine!   Have I bestow'd
Myself on you to find such miseries
Under your roof?   I wish my parents had,
As soon as I was born, expos'd me to
The open fields, unto the cruelty
Of the most savage beasts; or, in a small
Unguided boat, left me unto the fury
Of an enraged sea.   Would any mischief
Had fallen upon me but this fatal marriage!
    Bas. Hearken, Marullus!   Are you not amaz'd
To hear her speak against our nuptials thus?
It is apparent that she doth repent her
Of taking me, and wish'd she had Pyrontus.
    Mar. I pray you, hear her out.
    Clor.   How you mistake
My meaning, my beloved and cruel husband!
I would it had been pleasing to the gods
I never had been a wife to any!
How fortunate a choice might you elsewhere
Have found, these dire mischances miss'd, and I
With my ill fate have no man else infected.

Mar. My heart is big with sorrow at her words,
And vents itself in this sad dew.

Bas. What are these tears for you do dry away?

Mar. I cannot choose but melt.

Bas. You are too tender.
Come! we will leave her to contemplate here
The horrid wickednesses she hath acted.
If that all sense of honour hath not left thee,
Clorina, die. It will be endless shame
For thee to live after thou thus hast brought
Perpetual ignominy on my poor family.

Mar. I pity her, Bassanes—much commiserate
Her so disastrous fate. She may be innocent!
I pray you think her so! I hope she is.

Bas. Her reputation's gone, for ever lost:
A sea of tears cannot wash off her guilt.
'Tis so infectious, I am tainted with it.
False woman, die! Lost honour never more,
By any means, admits of any cure.   [*Exeunt.*

SCENE III.

Enter OVID, *solus.*

Sure I was born when all the glorious stars
Were met in counsel to contrive a mischief.
Under pretence of my loose youthful studies
For the composing of my art of love,
In my declining years, when I expected
Ease and a quiet life, I was exil'd
From Rome, and here confined, to end my days
Among a people rude and almost barbarous,
Except a few of th' gentry and nobility—
In a cold country, where fierce Jether pays,
Through divers channels, a continual tribute
Of his vast streams into the Euxine sea.
And many have imagin'd Julia,
Daughter of great Augustus, was too gracious
And liberal of her amorous favours to me,
Which caus'd him to inflict this punishment.

But, ere that Emperor left the world, he was
Informed, for that particular, of my innocency,
And was acquainted that, if I were faulty,
It was an error in me, not a crime ;
For, if I e'er enjoy'd her, it was through
Her craft, I taking her to be another.
But he was too severe : that excellent princess
He showed as little mercy to as me.
Now about twenty years, in the small island
Of Trimerus, near the Apulian shores,
Confin'd by him, sh' hath led a tedious life.
I must confess she had a generous kindness
For me, and took delight to read my poems;
But, by her letters and authentic witness,
Clear'd me sufficiently from that reproach,
And won thereby so much upon her father,
That I had been repeal'd if he had liv'd.
Since his decease, by divers messengers,
Persons of noble rank and quality,
And by her eloquent epistles, she hath
For my return to Rome importun'd much
The great Tiberius, her too cruel husband;
But he that to a wife, who brought him all
The universe in portion, shows no mercy,
Will not redress my wrongs.   Here I must mourn
Out all my life, and find my funeral urn.   [*Exit.*

SCENE IV.

Enter HANNIBAL *and* CACALA.

Han. This Captain Dacus is a jovial blade;
Doubtless a very valiant gentleman,
And of an heart as liberal as the air.
Cacala ! how lik'st thou him ?
     Cac. But so, so; yet
I was well pleas'd to see him pay the reckoning.
You are far from home, and Mistress Floretta is
As chargeable as a stable of running horses.

Han. It is grown something late, and time to think
Of our return unto our lodgings.   Look !
What's that ?

> [*Espies a man hanging on a gibbet.*

Cac. Sir, I see nothing.

Han.   Cast thy eyes
That way.   How now ? what is 't hangs there ?

Cac. Alas ! 'tis a poor fellow that was executed
Two or three days ago.

Han.   He had ill fortune.
Had he not better have follow'd Mars, and fall'n
In glorious battle, and his soul expir'd
Through many wounds, than ignominiously
Thus sneak to death in noose of paltry halter ?

Cac. My Captain Hannibal talks evermore
Of mighty battles, or his little whore.

Han. What mutter you, sirrah ?

Cac. I, by your valour's leave, was saying, Captain,
Yon man hangs in a pitiful cold corner ;
The north wind shakes his legs as he were dancing.
Of wine and women, and of all good meats,
He hath for ever took his leave.

Han. I'm sorry for 's hard fate.   Some lying people
Report some of the dead have walk'd.   If thou
Canst such a piece of fine activity show,
Come sup with me to-night ; thou shalt be welcome.

> [*Speaks to the hanged man.*

Cac. He bows his head.

Han.   Hang his head !

Cac. He need not put himself to such unnecessary
    trouble ;
He that small favour hath received already
From some of 's smaller friends.

Han. If th'art a good dead fellow, come, I say !
And sup with me to-night.

Spec.   I'll come !

Cac. I think I heard him answer he would come.

Han. Thou art so timorous, the echo of
My voice deludes thee.
Follow me, thou fearful puppy !

Cac.   A dog
His captainship makes of me.   Sir, I shall
Even tread upon your heels : I dare not stay
Behind an inch.
    Han. Come, then, for I fear nothing.
    Cac. By your leave,
I dread the gallows mightily ; and a thief
That can talk after he's dead is a terrible bugbear.
                                        [*Exeunt.*

SCENE V.

Enter ARMELINA, BASSANES, *and* MARULLUS.

Arm. I'm come to wait upon you, brother, and
To see how my dear sister, your Clorina,
Enjoys her health.   I found among your servants
A general sorrow as I passed along,
And you, methinks, reflect distracted looks.
What is the reason of this alteration
Throughout your family ?
    Bas. I am something troubled,
And now not in condition for discourse.
    Arm. What is the matter, good Marullus ?
Though I may suppose some business that hath fallen
Athwart his expectation hath distemper'd
His thoughts at present, yet I guess he is not
Sick ; therefore my afflicted heart misgives me
That my poor sister is not well.   Resolve me.
Alas ! I see some malady hath taken her,
And he, like a good husband, suffers with her,
Grieves for her want of health.   Is it not so ?
    Bas. Sweet Armelina ! at this present leave me !
I at another time will fitter be
To give you th' entertainment you deserve,
According to the utmost of my power.
    Arm. The gods be with you !   My poor company
Shall be no longer to you troublesome.
I hope to find my sister in her chamber,
And will go sit with her.

Bas.   She is not there.

Arm. Where is she, then? for I resolve to see her.

Bas. She's not in case to give you entertainment,
Or to receive a visit.

Arm.   Alas! you strike me
Almost as dead as I suspect she is.
For Heaven's sake, teach me where to find her!

Bas. She is alive.
I pray you let that satisfy, and leave us.

Arm. Not for the world!   I will not leave the
    house
Till I have seen and spoken with Clorina!

Bas. My dear Marullus, since this lady is
So very importunate she'll not be diverted,
Guide her, I pray you, to her sister!

Mar. I must obey you, and, fair Armelina,
Shall wait upon you.

Arm. Lead, and I follow you!
                    [*Exeunt* MARULLUS *and* ARMELINA.

Bas. Now she will curse me, and traduce my name,
Though, the gods know, her sister's in the blame!
He that refrains, for fear of women's tongues,
To right himself, basely submits to wrongs.   [*Exit.*

SCENE VI.

After a small supper set forth, enter HANNIBAL *and*
    CACALA.

Han. What! is this all we're like to have?

Cac. So please your soldiership, renowned Captain,
This is even all; and it may serve the turn,
Although I have an appetite as sharp
As your victorious sword, great Captain Hannibal!

Han. Where is Floretta, Cacala? Go call her!
She will rail at this meal, and call me covetous!

Cac. I needs must say, her stomach never failed her;
Though she's but little, she's a tall woman at a
    trencher!

Han. Run and call her !
Tell her the meat will be cold, and then 'tis spoiled.
   Cac. I may save that labour ; Mistress Spinella hath
Invited her to supper.
They and Cypassis eat to-night together.
   Han. Will Captain Dacus be there ?
   Cac. I think not, sir.
I never knew Cypassis but an hungry ;
She's not so bountiful as to invite
Others to eat her meat up !
   Han. How comes it, then, Floretta is their guest ?
Sit down, and be not troublesome ! you know
I'd have it so.
   Cac. I thank your valour. I have some small suspicion
Bassanes hath a liking took to your
Dear Damigella ; and Cypassis must
Court her, and tempt her to his various lust !
   Han. May be so, Cacala ; let him take his chance.
If he so lead, I'll follow him the dance !
Then I will woo Spinella, and he shall
Father the spurious issue I shall get on her !
Hark ! somebody knocks ! Rise, and inform me who
Is at the door. How, now ? What ! art thou deaf,
And hearest me not ? or dumb, because thou speak'st
    not ?
An apoplexy, sure, hath seized upon thee !
Sit down again and drink a glass of wine,
It will recover thee. Well done ! Now eat thy meat.
Again there knocks somebody at the door :
Rise once more, sirrah, and conduct them in !
Begone, or I shall kick you to your duty !
               [He opens the door, turns back, and
                   falls down as in a swoon.
This idle rascal, sure, the falling sickness
Hath got of late ! I must be at the charge,
I fear, to send for a physician to him.
I wonder who it is, for somebody knocks
Again. It needs must be a stranger, else
He such long compliment would not have show'd.
Still he knocks on ! I will go bring him in !

Enter SPECTRE.

Your name, sir, and your pleasure ?

Spec. My name Helvidius is.

Han. You are a stranger
Unknown to me ; I pray what is your business?

Spec. I come to sup with you.

Han. Though clad so meanly,
You shall be welcome !

Spec. I am not so rude
To press upon you uninvited, Captain !

Han. Who should invite you?

Spec. Sir, yourself !

Han. 'Tis strange
I should forget it, then !

Spec. I come unlook'd for, noble Hannibal,
But you did bid me to supper to-night.

Han. My memory hath fail'd me. Where, Helvidius ?

Spec. At the gibbet, by the city walls,
Where I did hang in chains.

Han. This is a courtesy deserves a welcome.
You are most welcome, sir, and so believe it !

Spec. You are my generous patron, and I thank you !

Han. Sit down, I pray ; sit down. So, 'tis well done !
Cacala ! Where's Cacala ? Give me a glass of wine.
What ! on the floor still ? Rise, man !

Cac. I dare not stir nor breathe, sir.

Han. He will not hurt you !

Spec. I shall not be so rude, where I find welcome,
To do a mischief.

Han. Fill wine, sir ! Much good do you, and here's
to you,—
To your fair mistress' health, whether alive,
Or your companion i' th' Elysian groves !

Spec. You much endear me.

Han. Could I have thought you would have supp'd
with me,
You should have been much better treated.
Sit down and eat, thou silly Cacala !

Cac. I am very timorous.

Han. His promise and my valour do protect thee !

Cac. This napkin, thus dispos'd under my hat,
Shall keep my eyes off him. I'll eat like a lion,
Because I sit in fear ; and after will
Chew the cud, as some beasts do, to digest it.

Spec. Good fellow, I salute thee with this bowl.

Cac. I have no mind to drink yet ; my master
Is the better pledger of such fancies.

Han. You shall not refuse him. Off with it, Cacala!
I'll conclude it !

Spec. It has gone round.
Captain, your kindness hath so far oblig'd me,
That I presume to crave a favour of you.

Han. You shall command !

Spec. I pray you, dine with me to-morrow.

Han. You jest !

Spec. I am in earnest ! You shall be most welcome !

Han. Where ?

Spec. At the gibbet.

Han. I'll come.

Cac. Now my belly's full, I cannot forbear
To cast a sheep's eye at him.
Oh ! oh !—[*Cries aloud, falls backward, and, with his
legs under the table, overthrows it and all
the meat.*

Spec. I thank you, generous Captain, and good
night !

Han. Farewell, sir, and expect me as I promised!
[*Exit* SPECTRE.
Rise, thou unmannerly beast, and let's to bed !

Cac. Good master, and thrice valiant Captain Hannibal,
See me in bed first, and asleep, I beseech you!
And let me have Mistress Floretta, for I dare not lie
alone !

Han. Follow me, and undress me.

Cac. Sir, I beseech you have a little patience !
Say that I shall not lie alone to-night,
And you will comfort me ! I otherwise

Shall be so weak with fear, I shall not be
Able to pluck your stockings off!

 Han.   Get whom
Thou wilt to be thy bedfellow but Floretta,
For her I cannot spare.

 Cac.   Then, I entreat you,
Let me lie in the same bed with you both !

 Han. You must some other lodging find !

 Cac.   Is 't so ?
Then I must old Cypassis try ; perhaps
A bottle of strong water will prevail so far with her
That she may give me leave to lie with her.
And yet I had much rather
Lie with my old grandmother or grandfather !

 Han. 'Tis said she was a beauty in her youth.

 Cac. Sure no man can report it that hath seen it,
For I believe her birth was in the days
Of Lucius Brutus, who was Rome's first consul.

             [*Exeunt.*

Scene VII.

Enter Marullus *and* Armelina *to* Clorina, *fastened
in a chair, with the heart of* Pyrontus *in her hand.*

 Arm. Y'ave made me such a terrible relation
Of his strange jealousy and his foul murder,
And 's barbarous usage of your dear sweet self,
That, my Clorina, I'm deficient
Of language to express my admiration !
But, my dull eyes, can you so long refrain
From dissolution into showers of tears ?
My heart is sure of stone, or it would break
At these effects of 's impious proceedings.

 Clor. Have patience, my best sister ! 'Tis enough
For me to be so miserable—I would not
My sufferings should beget a grief in you !

 Arm. Then I more stupid were than savages—
Than any beast in any wilderness,
Or any fury in black hell itself !

Clor. Oh, Armelina, how am I beholding
Unto you for your pity of my wrongs !
And yet I needs must grieve to see you thus
Afflict yourself at the sad sense of them.
But I beseech you to assume a courage
Worthy our noble family, to o'ercome it.
I shall but a few minutes longer trouble you
With my unfortunate company ! I find
My heart too weak to make resistance longer
Against the impetuous storm of my vast injuries ;
I find death stealing sensibly upon me.

Arm. The heavens forbid !

Clor. Prayers come too late now to divert my fate.
I pray you, therefore, good Marullus, haste
To my dear husband, and your faithful friend,
Tell him I beg but so much favour from him
As I may breathe my soul out in his presence,
And see him once again, and I shall die
Contentedly, and pardon him my wrongs !

Mar. Madam, I do beseech you to have patience !
I will go for him, and have hope he will
Be very shortly reconcil'd unto you,
For, from my soul, I pity your misfortunes !

　　　　　　　　　　　　　[Exit MARULLUS.

Clor. Shed no more tears ! You have, my Armelina,
Spent too much of that precious dew already
On poor unworthy me.

Arm. You are, Clorina, my elder and
My only sister, and can I perceive
Your innocency persecuted thus
And seem an unconcerned spectator of it?
It is impossible ! Give me leave, therefore,
T' express all sorrow I am capable of,
As tribute of my cordial affection
To your so lovely, sweet, and injured person !

Enter BASSANES *and* MARULLUS.

Clor. Welcome, my too unkind though my dear
　　　husband!
To your Clorina; welcome, my Bassanes!

My eyes grow dim, and I my heartstrings feel
To crack. Your harsh suspicion of my loyalty,
And so severe an usage of me, have
Cut off my life in prime of all my youth.
Here, with my parting breath, in presence of
The gods, within the hearing of your friend Marullus
And of my sister, I declare I die
Free from all guilt, and never injured you.
And so, farewell for ever! Gods, I come!
Afford my innocency in heaven a room.   [*She dies.*

   Mar. She hath took leave of life!
   Arm.   I did not think
Her death had been so near.
Farewell for ever all content and pleasure !
Since she is gone, no thought of joy shall ever
Possess my heart hereafter ; she that was
My only happiness is banish'd from me.
Look, monster of mankind ! this is a sight
Only befits the eyes of such a villain.
Here thou hast murder'd the most virtuous wife
That ever Hymen knew, and one that was
In her affection over fond of thee.
   Bas. Your passion makes you speak you know not
      what.
Your sister injur'd me in such high nature,
That she hath justly brought upon herself
The end that's come upon her.
   Arm. Th' Anthropophagians, that devour man's
      flesh,
By thee may be instructed in worse cruelties.
What hellish wretch but thy more hellish self
Would thus have used a lady of her beauty ?
To fasten with strong wires, in a case of mail,
A man's heart in his wife's own hand, and lock her
With chains into a chair fast, is a mischief
None but Bassanes durst have done. What tyrant
In history did ever act so ill ?
Perillus was an innocent to thee !
The vengeance of high Jove hangs o'er thy head,
To strike thee with his forked thunder dead !

Bas. No husband but a wittol would have suffer'd
The prostitution of his wife.

Arm. You slander her—basely belie her virtues!
She to us all hath cleared herself. Marullus
And I heard her relate the story,—it was
The saddest that did ever fall from tongue,—
Which she before had told thee all at large.
She doted on thee to her death, and with
Her last expiring breath protested freely
Her innocency from thy imputed crime.

Bas. I care not what you say; she was as foul
In her base actions as her face was fair!

Arm. Thou dost traduce inhumanly her virtue,
And I believe forbad'st she should have meat.

Bas. I did not think of it, and therefore gave
Forth no such order.

Arm.   If the least humanity
Remains yet in thee, let her be releas'd
From these so barbarous bonds; this heart remov'd
Out of her hand; it, with Pyrontus' body,
Delivered to his friends for sepulchre;
And I will take care for the funeral rites
Of sweet Clorina, my poor murder'd sister.

Bas. 'Twill ease me of some trouble and a charge,
Therefore I will consent to that demand;
And the gods keep me from a second marriage!

Arm.   Thou need'st not fear that; thou canst not
     find a woman
So lost to virtue and to honour that
Dare be a wife to such a bloody butcher!
Sure there's no woman in the world so senseless
And wicked as to give herself to thee.
I'll tell thy story unto all I meet,
And thy reproach shall ring through every street!

Bas. Your 'larum may run on, whilst I'll declare
To all the world how false you women are.

                              [*Exeunt omnes.*

ACT V.—SCENE I.

Enter OVID, PHYLOCLES, *and* CARALINDA.

Ovid. I am amaz'd much, and afflicted more,
With the sad news you have imparted to us.
   Phyl. All my entreaties could not win him thence ;
And therefore, missing him too long from home,
And knowing upon what design he stayed,
I did inquire of Armelina, who
Made me the sad relation you have heard.
Oh, brave Pyrontus, I lament thy fate,
That hast in love prov'd so unfortunate !
   Car. It is so sad a story you have made us,
That it draws tears from my eyes !   Though I was
A stranger to their persons, my weak sex
Allows me liberty to weep.   A man
Would not be tax'd of softness, to relent
At so deplorable a history.
   Phyl. Madam, I am so far from blaming you
For gracing with your tears their cruel fates,
That my heart chides mine own eyes for not melting.
Hell never plotted a worse tragedy,
Nor ever did so great a lover find
So merciless a death as Lord Pyrontus ;
Neither did ever virtue and beauty meet
So hideous a treatment as Clorina.
   Ovid. Have you their bodies seen since they were
      dead ?
Oh, Phylocles, if you those woeful objects
Have look'd upon, you have beheld a sight
More sad than ever Tomos was accus'd for !
   Phyl. Alas ! I brought the heart and mangled
      body
Of my dear friend Pyrontus to his house,
And did attend the corpse of fair Clorina
To Armelina's palace; where, alas !
No April shower ever fell so sweetly
As she doth weep over her sister.

Car. A word with you, dear cousin Ovid. My eyes
Are big with tears, and my poor heart is loaden
With grief! A thousand showers cannot drain them;
And time wants years enough to wear away
The sense and memory of this woeful day.

 Ovid. I must beseech you to have patience.

 Car. I have too much, dear Ovid! much too
  much!
But I will all the fortitude collect
That my poor heart is capable of, and shall
Suppress all signs exterior of grief.
You know the fortune which Trafullus told me?
I find it now points at me, and will therefore
Go walk abroad. You are acquainted well
With Phylocles; I'll leave you with him.

 Ovid. I will attend upon you.

 Car.   By no means.
You are old and sickly, and I will not be
So troublesome.

 Ovid. You shall not go alone!
Good Phylocles, my cousin Caralinda
Is something indispos'd, and hath a mind
To take the air abroad; you will oblige me
To bear her company. She is a stranger,
Which is the cause I crave the trouble from you.

 Phyl. The noble Ovid may command me anything;
But you confer much grace on me to give
Me leave to wait upon a gallant lady
Of so surpassing excellencies.

 Car. You compliment, sir, with me.

 Ovid. Hereafter you may like better of her company
When you are more acquainted with her.
Beware, I pray you, what you do! Take heed
       [*Speaks to* CARALINDA *aside.*
You give not too much credit to predictions!
Take heed your vengeance be not rash! Beware
You bring not ruin on your flourishing youth!

 Car. I will not play the Amazon, believe it;
And so, best poet, for a while farewell!

 Phyl. Your servant, generous Ovid!

Ovid. Sir, I am yours !

                [*Exeunt* CARALINDA *and* PHYLOCLES.

O love and jealousy ! what 'mighty power
You mighty passions have o'er human hearts !
How you too often join within one breast,
And joys that would aspire keep low supprest.
To be enamoured on a beautiful object,
As natural to us is as t' eat and drink ;
But to suspect whom we affect 's a crime,
Declares a guiltiness within one's self—
A want of merit !   Then a wise man should
Make himself worthy of his mistress' love,
Or never prosecute his amorous suit.
A discreet lover, in a beauteous outside,
Expects a mind adorn'd with all the virtues,
And holds it an impiety to think
So rich a soul can ever stoop to vice.
Therefore the lover that is rightly bred
Admits no jealous thoughts into his head.
I wish Bassanes had prov'd such, then he
Might have enjoy'd a happy life on earth ;
Too passionate Pyrontus then had liv'd,
And in some time might have o'ercome himself ;
The admirable and innocent Clorina
Had been alive ; this tragedy had never
Been acted here, which will be famous ever.   [*Exit.*

SCENE II.

Enter BASSANES *and* MARULLUS.

Mar. If you would give me leave, as your known
    friend,
Whom you have long grac'd with your amity,
To tell you freely my opinion,
And no offence take it, I should tell you,
My Lord Bassanes, I conceive you have
Been much too rash in your proceedings.
   Bas.   How ?

If such a thought you harbour of my actions,
I needs must tell Marullus that he thinks me
Guilty of my wife's blood ! Do not imagine
Your friend aspers'd with such a crime. She was
A gallant palace, to do her beauty right,
Where all the devils of lust inhabited.

Mar. I cannot tell ; but if one might give credit
To her so often serious protestations,
And to her vows utter'd with her last breath,
She was an innocent !

Bas. They that dare play
So foul a game value not what they say.

Enter CARALINDA *and* PHYLOCLES.

What lady is that ?

Mar. I never saw her before.

Bas. She is a miracle of such handsomeness,
She can no other be but Venus' self.

Phyl. Yonder's the murderer of my Lord Pyrontus,
And the base user of the best of women !
My blood is all on fire at this encounter !
My hilt seems loadstone, and my hand of iron ;
I cannot keep it longer from my sword.
A sudden vengeance he deserves, which shall
Fall on him. At this present I'll revenge
The slaughter of my friend, and the sad death
Of his so barbarously abused Clorina !

Car. Dear Phylocles, forbear ! I do conjure
you,
By all the love you bore unto Pyrontus,
Suppress your anger for a while ; yet know,
I wish him but a short reprieve, and hate him
As much as you. He at a fitter time
May find his destiny. Let it not be said
He died i' the presence of a tender maid !

Phyl. I must obey you, madam.

Bas. She is an object so extremely ravishing,
I must speak to her.

Mar. I had thought you had
Done with that sex for ever ?

Bas.   I resolv'd so ;
But beauty such a potent charm is known,
Strongest resolutions it hath overthrown.
Hail, female goddess ! or, if of womankind,
Hail, rich epitome of all the beauty
That ever yet in several women nature
Revealed to human eyes !
Car.   Good Phylocles,
Draw back a little ! I would find to what
His fine words aim, and he will be more sparing,
If y'are too near us, to express himself.
Phyl. I will retire a little ; but beware
His flatteries win not on your heart !
Car. I warrant you.
Bas. My friend Marullus, I beseech you walk
     aside.
Mar. I shall, my lord, obey you.
Good day to Phylocles ! Pray, shun me not,
For I am much afflicted at the tragedies
Bassanes' rage and jealousy have acted.
I had no hand in them, and could I have
Prevented them, they had not been performed.
Car. You both provoke my wonder and my blushes.
Become enamour'd of a stranger ?—one
You never saw before ?
Phyl. Marullus, he hath done such horrid acts,
The gods can never punish him enough.
Bas. It doth become your beauty to work such
     wonders.
Madam, I am one of the chiefest persons
Of all this province, and have a heart to love you
Above the expressions of a thousand tongues !
Car. Your name, sir, I beseech you ?
Bas. 'Tis Bassanes !
Car. What ! he that through his jealousy and fury
Murder'd Pyrontus and his innocent wife ?
Bas. You have been misinform'd. He did deserve
The fate he found ; and her shame broke her heart !
I am the same Bassanes, but not guilty
Of any crime : they in their deaths found justice.

Car. I've heard too much of them already.
But how can you, so fresh a widower, so soon
Give entertainment to a second flame?

Bas. Your beauty, that can work such miracles,
Is a sufficient reason.

Car.   I may prove
The like sad destiny Clorina did,
Should I become your wife.

Bas.   It is impossible!
You are an heaven where all the virtues meet,
And therefore cannot be inconstant to
Your wedlock vows.

Car.   I merit not, Bassanes,
This favour at your hands. If I e'er wed,
It shall be unto one of my own country.

Bas. Within a body form'd to all perfection,
That ever liberal nature and the gods
Could, can, or ever shall make up, fair stranger,
Give not an entertainment to contempt
Of your enslav'd Bassanes ; neither in 't
Lodge thoughts disdainful, nor a heart of flint!

Car. 'Tis an astonishment in me to hear you
To make so passionate discourse to me,
Even one whose name you neither know, nor fortune ;
I may be poor and vicious.

Bas.   Nothing but virtue
Can in a body so beautiful inhabit.
Vice dares not so presumptuous be as t' enter
Under so fair a roof ; and y' are so rich
In beauty, that I with more joy should marry you
Than t' be saluted emperor of the world!

Car. You court me now, indeed. I have some
  business
Of such concern, that at this time no longer
I can stay with you.

Bas. But must you needs begone?

Car. I must, in truth.

Bas.   When shall I, then, receive
So great a blessing as t' enjoy a second time
Your coveted company?

Car. Within this half hour,
I'll meet you here again. ..
Bas. Y'ave raised me to
A joy as great as Jove himself can know.
Car. Come, generous Phylocles ; I will impart
Our parley free to you, and acquaint you
With the whole cause why I entreated you
To stifle your revenge, and to retard
His death : you shall know all my secret thoughts.
Phyl. Sweet Caralinda, you oblige me much ;
I shall attend you anywhere.

[*Exeunt* CARALINDA *and* PHYLOCLES.

Bas. Marullus,
Cupid hath pointed all his shafts with the
Fair beams of this bright lady's eyes. I am .
Become enamour'd on her to that height,
That I must marry her or I shall die !
Mar. The heavens forbid !
Bas. Nay, rather, friend, may all the gods vouch-
safe it !
Mar. You know not what she is ; she may be much
Unworthy of such nuptials.
Resist betimes ; physic too late is took,
When sickness, through delay, is fixed at th' root.
Bas. Surely she can
No other be but Ovid's kinswoman,
Who, we have heard, so lately came to Tomos.
I will presume her, then, of noble birth.
That excellent poet is my worthy friend,
And I may hope will easily be won
T' assist me to attain her to my wife.
Methinks he should be glad to have his cousin
Well matched here,—to be fix'd a constant comfort
Both to his age and grief for his exilement.
Mar. May the just powers divine turn all to the
best !
Bas. If I obtain her to become my wife,
A heaven on earth I shall enjoy this life ! [*Exeunt.*

SCENE III.

Enter HANNIBAL *and* CACALA.

Cac. Sir, I entreat you, my too valiant Captain,
To give me leave to return home ; I have
No mind to such a formidable dinner.
    Han. What should'st thou fear ? My keen vic-
        torious sword
Carries spells strong enough to conjure down
All the unruly fiends of Pluto's court ;
Therefore, for shame, take courage ! Thou hadst
    wont
To have a good stomach to thy meat ; and sure
This gallant ghost will treat us very nobly.
    Cac. I have an horror to such company,
And had a thousand times much rather be
With Mistress Floretta, and converse with her.
    Han. Thou talk'st so often of her, that I think
Thou art in love with her.
    Cac.   I must confess
I have some smackering that way ; but the awe
I stand in of your indignation
Deters me from professing my respects.
I wish your captainship would cast her off,
And give me leave to make her my honest wife.
    Han. Thou talk'st impossibilities, fool Cacala,
To think to make an whore an honest woman !
Such an one would indeed prove a strange wonder ;
And he that should to such an one be wed
Might raise a mighty portion to himself
By taking money for the sight of her.
    Cac. His tongue's no slander.   [*Aside.*
    Han. Walk on ! we're almost there.
    Cac. I'm monstrously afraid !
    Han. Fear nothing in my company but the marrying
Of an whore.
    Cac. I ever dreaded stories of hobgoblins,
But evermore abhorred the sight of them.

Beseech you, therefore, Captain Hannibal,
Give me leave to go back.

Han. Thou shalt not leave me.   I will make thee
valiant,
And neither to fear men nor devils.

Cac. Heaven bless me !

Han. We shall have a brave dinner, without doubt.

Cac. Instead of a calf's head and glorious bacon,
A skull half rotten of some malefactor,
Stolen from a neighbour gallows to his own ;
And in the place of a brave side of venison,
The salt haunch of some executed bawd ;
And in the room of Grecian wines, the moisture
That doth distil from their hang'd putrified bodies.
Sir, I will take my leave.

Han.   Thou shalt go with me,
And, when employment calls me forth again,
I'll make thee my lieutenant.   We're almost there.
Look you ! he is come down from off his gibbet !
'Tis the most courteous fellow that e'er died
By scurvy halter.   Would his judges were
Truss'd up in 's place, and all the villanous jury
That did condemn so brave a spark !

Enter SPECTRE.

Spec. Welcome, thou noblest son of Mars !
Give me thy hand, thou servant to great Hannibal !

Cac. I wish you would excuse me the compliment.

Spec. You need not fear me.

Han. Cacala, be courageous, and dread nothing !
My friend Helvidius will no hurt do to thee.
Should Cerberus bark but at thee, with my sword
I at one blow would cut off all his heads.

> [*A table set forth, covered with a black linen
> cloth ; all the napkins of the same colour ; the
> meat and dishes, bottles, wine, and all things
> also.*

Spec. You see your entertainment, and are both
Most heartily welcome.   Let us sit and eat !

> [*They all sit down and eat.*

T

Cac. I do not like the colour of this linen ;
The meat and wine and everything is black.
   Spec. 'Tis the sole colour us'd in Pluto's court.
   Cac. The meat tastes well, though.   Though I had
     rather be
At a piece of bread and cheese at Madam Cypassis',
I cannot choose but eat ; I think my fear
Hath added to my hunger.
   Spec.   Gallant Hannibal,
I dedicate this bowl to thy Floretta.
   Han. Off with it, then, thou only worthy of
The other world! Here, Cacala, thou shalt pledge me!
   Cac. I'll do my weak endeavour.
   Han. I thank you, sir, and in requital drink
To him or her you most affect.
   Spec.   Y'are noble.
Friend Cacala, here's to you! and you conclude it,
   Cac. I dare not do otherwise.
   Han. Would you excuse my curiosity, sir ?
I would inquire why you were executed ?
   Spec. I'll satisfy you. The lords and gentry of
This city Tomos gave order to a statuary
To make the image of the poet Ovid
In beaten massy gold, for the honour he
Had done them by writing an excellent poem
I' the Getick language in Tiberius' praise.
When it was ready to have been presented,
I got into the house and stole it thence,
Melted it privately, and put it off
By little parcels—spent it on wanton wenches
And among boon companions. In my cups,
Bragg'd on 't to two false brothers, who betrayed me.
   Han. I would they had been born both dumb and
     fools !
   Spec. I pray you give me leave to be as free
With you. Why were you banish'd and confin'd ?
   Han. A poor old woman, and a witch, a friend
Of mine, pretended an occasion to make use
Of a live infant, ripp'd out of the belly
Of 's mother ; and th' enchantment she was hammering

Was for my service. I stole into a cottage
That stood alone, where such a woman liv'd then ;
Found her alone, and had so laid my plot
That I might undisturbed proceed ; cut up
Her belly, took her infant thence, and sew'd
A cat up in the place. So she enjoin'd me.
This simple sorceress, being for other
Matters accused, and like to die, confess'd
This prank.

 Spec. How chanc'd it you escap'd with life ?
 Cac. My captain is the greatest villain that
I ever heard of ! I will leave his service,
Although I have oft been told of this before.
 Han. The favourite, all-powerful Sejanus,
Did bring me off with life : I helped him to
Floretta's maidenhead, for which good turn
I also had some bags crammed with sesterces.
 Spec. You had good fortune to escape so well.
 Han. Some business calls me home. I give you
  thanks
For this brave entertainment ; so, farewell !
 Spec. I pray you stay awhile ! you shall look on
A little masque I have provided for you.
 Han. You much oblige me, and are over liberal
Of your high favours to me.

Enter, after very solemn loud music, ÆACUS, RHADA-
MANTHUS, *and* MINOS, *the Judges of Hell;* ALECTO,
TISYPHONE, *and* MEGÆRA, *the Furies; and dance
all together to low music.*

 Spec. Æacus, Minos, and Rhadamanthus, the three
Judges in hell ! Tisyphone, Megæra, and Alecto,
The Furies there, of equal number to them,
Lead in a dance.
 Cac.   Can devils be so merry ?
But I had ever thought there had been rather
Three thousand judges there than three ; I wonder
Their number is so few. So of the Furies,
For oft on earth one woman hath more in her.
     [*The dance ended, this song follows.*

Most happy is the libertine,
   And of mankind the most ingenious,
Who from grave precepts doth decline,
   And doth indulge his jovial genius!
      Oh, the joys, the joys,
      They have that follow vice,
         Without any fear of the gods!
      Who freely waste their treasures
      To purchase them their pleasures,
         And are with the virtuous at odds!

The atheist is the greatest fool,
   Who only aims to please his senses,
Thinking in heaven no gods bear rule,
   And tipples, murders, swears, and wenches.
      Oh, the woes, the woes,
      That follow all those
         Who wear out their lives in vice!
      That swear, whore, kill, and drink,
      And never them bethink,
         Till they fall into hell in a trice!
    [After the song is ended, they all seize on him,
       and carry him away.

Han. Must I be then betrayed thus? False
   Helvidius!
And foolish Hannibal to trust to spectres!
                     [Exeunt with him.

Spec. Away with him! Down to the infernal shades
Of griefly Pluto's kingdom let him sink!
A fouler soul was never seen in hell,
Where's witchcrafts, rapes, murders, and vicious life
Will find a suitable endless punishment!
                  [The SPECTRE *vanishes.*

Cac. This was a terrible sight indeed! Heaven
   keep me
But in my wits till I can see Floretta,
And I shall tell her such a tale as will
Make her turn virtuous, if she hath not lost
All love to th' powers divine, and fears no vengeance.
                      [Exit.

SCENE IV.

Enter BASSANES, *solus.*

Bas. I find myself half raised to happiness
Already, after my so late affliction.
The stranger lady's beauties triumph here,
Within my heart.   My hopes are fair enough
That I shall win her to become my wife ;
Then all my future days I shall esteem
To be a lasting festival, and more
To be priz'd by me than are all the feasts
Observ'd the year through in our calendar.

Enter PHŒBIANUS *and* PHYLOCLES.

Phœb. I now have made you well acquainted with
My person and my history, and have to you
Reveal'd the reason why I did entreat
You to forbear Bassanes, when your rage
Would fain have flung you on him.   Now you know
The cause why I will meet him.   Give me, therefore,
Leave, noble Phylocles, to go alone !
I fear him not at all, and shall not have
Any need of your kind assistance.   'Tis
The will, sure, of the gods, that I should singly
Encounter him.   Therefore retire, my 'friend !
Near hereabouts you can conceal yourself.
You within call may stay ; I shall have quickly
Despatch'd with him, and shall not fail then to
Holla you back.   See there ! he is a-walking,
And waiting my approach !
   Phyl. You must command me.
The gods be with you !   [PHYLOCLES *withdraws.*
   Phœb. Well met, Bassanes !   Ovid's kinswoman,
The stranger Caralinda, hath employed me
To you, to make apology for her
Not meeting you according to her promise.
Why do you look so wistly on me ?   Do you
Know me ?

Bas. I certainly have seen your face
Before—some alteration that I find
Some years of absence might have made.   Resolve me,
I pray you, sir ; are you not Phœbianus,
Pyrontus' younger brother, that have spent
Three or four years abroad?   If y'are not he,
I never saw two faces so alike.
 Phœb. I Phœbianus am, and Caralinda,
Whom you so lately troubled with your courtship.
Through the providence of the almighty gods
I met with thee in that disguise, and parted
From thee but to divest me of those clothes,
And bring my sword to our next parley.   'Tis needless
To tell thee more, and I have too much time
Trifled away in this discourse.   Pray draw
Your sword, for one of us must die !
Thou traitorously and unawares didst murder
My brave and hopeful brother !   Though he lov'd
Clorina, he deserv'd her better far
Than thou—never attempted violence unto her,
And in a little time might have subdu'd
His too unruly passion.   Thou hast broke
Thy innocent lady's heart with usages
More horrid than a Scythian ever practis'd :
Therefore, unless you will die basely, draw !
 Bas. You are a glorious talker, fine young man,
But I shall presently allay your pride,
And the fond confidence you seem to have
In your own valour.
  Phœb.   Let us try your skill !
 Bas. Y' ave sought your ruin by provoking me.
            [*They fight.*

 Phœb. So !   Have you yet enough?
 Bas. Oh ! you have slain me !
I have received so home a thrust, I die
Without another word !   [BASSANES *dies.*

Enter MARULLUS.

 Phœb. Marullus, in an equal duel I
Have kill'd your friend.   The gods did guide my sword ;

Justice was on my side.   He slew my brother,
And I in Roman honour could do no less ;
And to preserve my reputation clear
Among the Getes, my countrymen, than to
Fight fairly with him.

Mar. My mind misgave me some disastrous **fate**
Would overtake him for so foul a murder.
Though I am grieved at his sad death, I'm glad
You are, my lord, returned so safely home.

Phœb. You'll see his body convey'd unto his house?

Mar. I shall not fail.

Phœb. The gods preserve you !

Mar. Farewell, brave Phœbianus !

Phœb. Friend Phylocles !   [*Calls aloud.*

Phyl. I'm at your service, here !

Phœb. Stay, and I'll come to you.   [*Exit.*

Mar. Draw near, you that his servants are, and bear
This sad load to his palace.   [*Exeunt.*

SCENE V.

Enter CAPTAIN DACUS, CACALA, CYPASSIS, FLORETTA,
and SPINELLA.

Cyp. It was a lamentable spectacle
We met withal as we came hither.

Dac. An usual one—a dead man !
We soldiers smile upon a thousand such.

Cyp. Bassanes was an extraordinary person.

Dac. Cæsars and lords must die.

Cac. You talk of trifles.   The story I related you
Of my master Captain Hannibal's being took away
    with devils
Deserves to be call'd terrible indeed !
Hell broke loose on him ; devils and devils' dams
Seiz'd both upon him !   He would fain have hung
An arse, but no resistance could prevail.
Away they hurried him, and left me in
So great a fear I know not how I came home.

Flor. Thou hast told us too much of this already,
And too often.

    Cac. 'Twill never out of my memory.

    Flor. Nor from thy tongue, I fear.

    Cac. Oh, fear the gods, Mistress Floretta! fear
      them!

Take heed the devils show you not such a trick!
Turn virtuous, pretty one, and marry me,
For I do love thee above womankind.
Show thyself, therefore, to me a kind woman.

    Flor. Though I am sorry my Hannibal is perish'd
      so,

I cannot call him back, and must some care
Take of myself; and therefore, Cacala,
I'll be thy wife.   All his remaining goods .
Are ours.

    Cac. And I have something, too, to trust
In my own country.

    Cyp. Here's a match soon made up!

    Flor. We will return to Rome.

    Cac. With all my heart!

    Dac. And will my fair Spinella prove as kind?

    Spin. Now Lord Bassanes is dead, I am content
To receive Captain Dacus for my husband.
Mother, I hope of your allowance to it.

    Cyp. And you shall have it.   The gods grant you
      joy!

    Dac. My mother Cypassis now indeed!

    Cyp. You knew her father.   He was your country-
      man,

And a fine gentleman when he in Rome
Did marry me; I else should never have been
Content t' have liv'd in so remote a province.
Though his good nature and many losses at sea
Melted away most of his land, we have
Silver and gold enough to make you live
In plenty.

    Dac. Mother, I kiss your reverend hand
In gratitude.   What my own means may prove
Deficient in, my valour shall supply.

Spin. We'll have no fighting nor any quarrelling ;
I am for peace. Love hates the noise of war.

Dac. You are too timorous. Grow as affectionate :
For thus I print my soul upon thy lips.

Cac. Let us go home, send for a priest of Hymen,
And presently each couple on 's be married !

Omnes. Agreed ! agreed !

Cac. I dare not lie alone to-night, for fear
My Captain or his friends should give me a visit.

Spin. Was Hannibal a gentleman by birth ?

Dac.   My pretty one,
Brave Hannibal, the famous Carthaginian,
Who march'd like Mars even to the walls of Rome,
And fought against that senate for the world's empire,
In one of 's winter quarters at Salapia
Obtained the affection of a beautiful lady
Called Isidora, and from them he was
Descended lineally, as he lately told me.

Spin.   And is now
Descended to the devil—we have heard how !

                         [*Exeunt omnes.*

SCENE VI.

Enter OVID, PHŒBIANUS, PHYLOCLES, ARMELINA,
and SERVANTS.

Phœb. My father, on his deathbed, did enjoin me,
For education's sake, to stay so long.
You grace me, excellent Armelina, much,
After so long a trial to receive me.

Arm. I nothing have worthy your acceptation
But my reciprocal return of love.

Phœb. I kiss your hand for so immense a bounty.
But why, my fairest, would you never honour
My many letters with one single answer ?

Arm. I durst not, fearing among the Roman ladies
You might have made a second choice, and then
Have left me, blasted in my reputation.

Phœb. I was too true, and you was too severe !

Arm. But wherefore come you so disguis'd? and
   why
From me would you conceal yourself?
   Phœb. 'Tis reasonable that I should satisfy you.
Just upon my departure out of Italy,
My curiosity led me to Trafullus,
One of the chief astrologers of these times,
And happy in foretelling future fortunes.
I made friends to him, and received these verses:

" Return disguis'd in woman's clothes, and you
   The murderer of your friend shall pay his due!
   Obtain your mistress to become your bride,
   And with her gain a world of wealth beside."

Ovid. Bassanes his death, and fair Clorina's wealth,
You being her heir, added to your great portion,
Confirm for truth the soothsayer's prediction.
   Arm. And I again must thank you for so bravely
Revenging on Bassanes his foul cruelties.
But why, my Phœbianus, would you not
Disclose yourself to me?
   Phœb. You are my countrywoman, and I fear'd
So doing I should have broken my injunctions.
But now, divinest lady, when shall I
Be made so happy by your gracious self
As to receive you for my bride?
   Arm.   As soon
As I can give some stint unto my tears;
After my sister's obsequies are past.
   Phyl. Pray, listen! What noise is that without?
I think I hear a horn, and 'tis some post.

Enter a POST.

Phœb. From whence, my friend, come you?
Post. From Rome.
Phyl. What news?
Post. I've letters for the famous poet Ovid.
Ovid. Deliver them; I am that unfortunate man!
       [OVID *breaks open his letters and reads.*

I am undone for ever!—No more hope
For my return must ever flatter me!
My wife writes to me, she hath us'd the utmost
Of her endeavour, assisted by the chiefest
Of both our friends, and of most power with Cæsar,
For my repeal, or but, at least, removal
To a more temperate clime, and that th' are both
Refus'd her, and she enjoin'd perpetual silence
In my behalf. Besides, my friend Græcinus,
A Roman of high note, hath writ me word
The gracious Princess Julia, our great empress,
And my best friend, is in Trimerus dead.
One of these news were much too much to strike
My poor and crazy body into my grave.
But, joining both their poisonous stings together,
I needs must to the world this truth impart,
That Ovid dies here of a broken heart!   [*Dies:*

   Phyl. It was too sad a truth his last breath did
Express, for he, alas, is dead indeed!
   Arm. Death is too prodigal of his tragedies
In this small city. I must spare from my
Clorina's fate one shower of tears, to shed
Upon his grave!
   Phyl. Not only we, but all the Getic nation
Were worse than barbarous, paid we not that duty
To excellent Ovid's infelicitous end.
   Arm. He was a most accomplished gentleman,
A person affable and sweet conditioned,
And of the Roman poets the most ingenious.
   Phyl. He was in Italy at Sulmo born,
A pleasant city within the territory
Of the Peligui, and descended of
The ancient family of the Nasones,
Who had preserv'd the dignity of Roman
Knights from the first original of that order.
I' th' Asiatic wars he under Varro
Had eminent command, and well discharged it,
Who now, alas! after seven years' exilement,
Hopeless of a repeal, hath breath'd his last!

Arm. Take up his noble body, and bear it gently
To his own house; we all will wait on it thither.

Phœb. I'll have a stately monument erected
Without our city walls, near the chief gate,
To his fair memory, to declare the gratitude
Of Tomos to him for the honour it
Receiv'd by his so long abode among us ;
Enclos'd in which, within a marble urn,
Curiously wrought, his ashes shall for ever
Remain in peace, an endless grace to Pontus !

Phyl. No poet ever did more glory contribute
Unto the Latin language than his pen.
The soul of poetry feels a convulsion
By his decease.   He no superior knew
In that sweet art, and was great Virgil's equal.
His works have an eternity stamp'd on them—
Do far exceed the Consul Cicero's verses
And all the lines sacred Augustus ever
Writ in a numerous strain—all the fine poems
The darling of the people, the facetious
And valiant Prince Cæsar Germanicus,
Hath published with applause—and all such things,
Though wrote by hands that were the spoil of kings.

       [OVID'S *body being removed, exeunt omnes.*

THE EPILOGUE.

Noble and generous spectators, stay !
A word at parting, and then go your way.
Our author is stol'n hence in mighty haste,
Because he thought the house was overcast
With clouds on every brow, and was in dread
A storm would else have fallen upon his head.
I am his friend, left purposely behind,
T' inform him how his fate proves—harsh or kind.
Beseech you, ladies, smile !   Their general frown
Portends the men will hiss our tragedy down.
Command them clap their hands, for it is strange
If men forbear when women bid them change.
I thank you, ladies ! thank you, gentlemen !
To-morrow you may be welcome here again !